"There are many dusthouses?"

He nodded, then flinched as the movement disturbed something inside his broken nose. His voice was strained and high as he whined, "You sign a contract. Don't talk, don't tell, don't say nothing."

"Is that what you have? A contract with the dusthouse?"

"Yes."

"What's the deal?"

"They ... supply you. Good rates, cheap rates, best-quality stuff. Shit, it's not like there's any competition!" He mopped at a trickle of blood down his chin. "Only, they'll fucking kill me."

"What stuff?"

He hesitated.

"Come on," I said. "We've gone this far."

He said, "Fairy dust."

There was a long silence while we digested this. I said, "I don't suppose we're talking Peter Pan, think your happy thought and fly, are we?"

"It is," he explained, one word at a time, "the Best Shit."

THE MINORITY
COUNCIL
KATE GRIFFIN

orbit

www.orbitbooks.net

ORBIT

First published in Great Britain in 2012 by Orbit

A CIP catalogue record for this book
is available from the British Library.

ISBN 978-0-356-50063-8

Typeset in Weiss by M Rules
Printed and bound in Great Britain by
Clays Ltd, St Ives plc

Papers used by Orbit are from well-managed forests
and other responsible sources.

MIX
Paper from
responsible sources
FSC® C104740

Orbit
An imprint of
Little, Brown Book Group
100 Victoria Embankment
London EC4Y 0DY

An Hachette UK Company
www.hachette.co.uk

www.orbitbooks.net

Is the dust a problem? Yes. Do we have a moral imperative to do something about it? Absolutely. If we act now, will it be of benefit to the majority in the future, greater than the harm it could do at this present time? Well, there's a question worth the asking.

— *Report from the Sub-Chairman of the Minority Council on the Economics of Fairy Dust*

Don't tell me there's something wrong with the kids. Because then you gotta tell me that the kids have been screwed up by the schools, and the schools are being screwed over by the parents. Then the parents – they got screwed over by their jobs, by an economy that doesn't function, and the economy, that got messed up by the politicians, and the politicians, they got messed up by the press, and the press got screwed over by the punters, who got picked on by the banks and, before you know it, the problem is everyone who ever took out a tenner when they should have put a fiver into their savings account and took out a loan instead of a pension and then – *then* it's humanity that's the problem. It's the nature of what we are; it's the messed-up thing that sometimes gets called the human soul. You really going to do a fix on that?

— *M. Swift, response to memo, Harlun & Phelps Closed Archive 8/BI009A, Section 3*

Prelude: You Can't Be Everything to Everyone...

In which there is a meeting on a boat . . .

I had been in Deptford, hunting vandals.

Not your nice vandals, not the kind who trashed a park bench or burnt out a car.

These were the vandals who painted, on the walls of the houses, signs that sent all who looked on them, quite, quite mad.

They said they did it to show us the truth, and the truth was we were all being tricked. We were all insane, all of us who thought that the world was safe, and ordered, and had a purpose. They knew, they had seen, they were trying to make us understand.

I said, pull the other one, it's got bells on, you're just going around screwing up people because you're screwed up in turn and besides, if the world really is as dark as you think it is, then I'll take the illusion any day, thank you.

They answered, and who the hell do you think you are, jimbo (or words to that effect), you come swaggering on in here in the middle of the night and you're all like, Stop being vandals or else – well we know people, you know, we can do you.

I made a few pithy comments, along the following lines:

My name is Matthew Swift. I'm a sorcerer, the only one in the city who survived Robert Bakker's purge. I was killed by my teacher's shadow and my body dissolved into telephone static and all they had left to bury was a bit of blood. Then we came back, and I am we and we are me, and we are the blue electric angels, creatures of the phones and the wires, the gods made from the surplus life you miserable excuse for mortals pour into all things electric. I am the Midnight Mayor, the protector of the city, the guardian of the night, the keeper of the gates, the watcher on the walls. We turned back the death of cities, we were there when Lady Neon died, we drove the creature called Blackout into the shadows at the end of the alleys, we are light, we are life, we are fire and, would you believe it, the word that best describes our condition right now is cranky.

Would you like to see what happens when you make us mad?

They seemed to understand.

When they were gone, I walked along the river, heading east with the turning of the tide. Sorcerers in the big city go mad too easily; their hearts race at rush hour, their heads ache when the music plays in the clubs below the city streets, they breathe a mixture of carbon monoxide and lead nitrate fumes, and fresh air, clean, country air, brings on wheezing. I have always been careful to avoid the madness, but the river, on a clean, cold night inclining to winter, was a draw and a power that couldn't be resisted.

So I walked. Over muddy quays drained down to the bed, past timber warehouses and cement factories, beneath the white bulbous lights of brand new apartment blocks and over crooked paths between cracked tarmac roads. Past shops with brown-eyed mannequins staring emptily out from reflective window-panes, through the smell of Chinese take-away guarded by a forever-saluting golden Nazi cat, across car parks to shopping estates where the average price of the average good was £14.99 and this month's material of choice was polyester or plywood, past little chapels wedged in between the building society and the sixth-form college where, If You Believed It, You Could Achieve It. (Classes rated 'Satisfactory' by the Schools Inspector.) I kept the river to my left, paused to watch a flight of twin-bladed military helicopters following the curve of the water into the centre of town, leant out over a balustrade to see the silver towers of Canary Wharf catching cloud in their reflective surfaces, watched the train rattle away beneath Greenwich Hill, felt the shock as we crossed the Prime Meridian. Ley lines exist but, like all of magic, they are formed where life is thickest, and where meaning is imposed by man. Life is magic; magic grows where there is most life.

Quite how I ended up at the pier, I don't know. But my feet were starting to tingle with a dry heat that might at some point become an ache, and even the curry houses and not-quite-Irish pubs were closing for the night. At the Millennium Dome, an exercise in civil engineering somewhere between a white pleasure palace and a blister in a wasteland, the gigs were ending, doors were opening, and people dressed to honour their chosen band were tumbling out towards Tube, bus and boat. Signs were going up at stations announcing the times of the first and last trains, as a warning to all who might linger too long. The footpath under the river to the Isle of Dogs was closed, a sign politely suggesting that travellers try alternative routes: access only between 8 a.m. and 10 p.m. Monday–Saturdays, please do not ride your bikes in the tunnel.

I hadn't realised I'd been waiting for the boat back to the centre of town, but when it came, I boarded it, a catamaran that offered a full 30 per cent off the price of its fare, already 130 per cent higher than I had expected to pay. I paid anyway, and boarded a vessel built for a hundred and fifty tourists, now holding a crew of three and a cargo of twelve. A group of friends at the front wore T-shirts announcing that Life Is Punk, sported haircuts that in previous times would have been used to indicate rank in warrior tribes and were now worn to cause distress to difficult mothers, and talked loudly and with sweeping gestures about the brilliance of this and the horror of that. They seemed to be of that age when things were either one or the other, with no middle ground.

Near the back of the boat, a man was embracing a woman to keep off the cold wind from the river as we churned towards the west, and said nothing, and didn't need to. In the middle section, two women, carrying guides to Londra, leant out of the window and gleefully claimed to identify the Tower of Westminster, Buckingham Palace, the London Eye and Hampstead Heath.

I stood alone on the deck and tasted salt and smelt the river and felt the engine beneath my feet and knew that tonight there wasn't much I couldn't do, though I didn't feel like doing much anyway.

Then she said, "Sometimes people come here to get clean."

At first I hadn't realised that the voice had been addressed to me, but when I felt an expectation next to me, I looked round, and there she stood, hands on the railing, hair flicking back and forward around her face, tangling in the wind, her eyes sliding over me like oil across silk. We stammered, "What?"

"Not physically clean," she added, with a shrug. "More ... clean inside. The river, washing away our sins." I had nothing to say, but this didn't seem to bother her. She held out one hand and added brightly, "Meera."

We shook her hand, fingers sticking out of the fingerless gloves that hide the scars on the palm of our own hand. "Matthew," I said. There was a tingle on our skin as they touched hers, an aching at the back of our teeth. Her eyes locked onto ours, and they were the colour of fresh chestnuts, flecked with yellow, and, for a moment, it could have gone any way.

Her fingers tightened, before releasing their grip, and she looked away, back at the river and the city rolling by. "I could tell," she explained, casually, as if announcing breakfast. "The street lights dim a little when you pass them."

"Is that why we're talking?"

She grinned, and shook her head. "No."

"Then why?"

"We're the only people at the back of this boat who are alone. I thought maybe we could be lonely together."

She said that she was a risk analyst, working in the Isle of Dogs. Most nights, the people in her office went out drinking together – champagne, clubs, music. Sometimes they had teamwork evenings – paintballing, rowing, learning to play the ukulele . . .

"The ukulele?"

"It's a very easy instrument. Put us all together and get us playing: teamwork and music. Paintballing didn't work so well. A lot of very aggressive men in my office."

Tonight her colleagues had decided to go to a stripper joint and, for the first time, they'd invited her.

"And?"

"It was loud and dull. It didn't interest me."

So did she just leave?

Yes. She'd made sure to be seen first, sat around with the boys, made the right sounds – even paid £50 to a Ukrainian for a dance – and once everyone was too drunk to notice or care, she'd snuck away, down to the river.

"It's where I'm me," she'd explained.

I said nothing; confessions of an innermost nature were never our strong point. We passed Rotherhithe, new brick apartments and converted wharves whose names – silver, guns, pepper – told their histories, along with the black cranes still bolted into their walls. She said,

"I've got an aunt who's a witch. Or a wise woman. Both, I think. She's from Chennai, practises there. I got into it through her."

"Do you do a lot?"

"She taught me petty glamours and enchantments. Beauties, cheap charms, precious dreams – nothing special. That used to be the extent of it. What about you? Why are your eyes so blue?"

I hesitated. "Complicated."

"I'm interested."

"Very complicated."

"Your shyness only makes the story grow in my imagination. How much stranger can the truth be from what I'm imagining?"

"Truth is stranger than fiction," I suggested.

"I'm seeing dragons," she retorted. "Dragons and volcanoes and adventures and demi-gods. Am I close?"

"Everything except the tectonic activity."

"And you're not shy," she added, the brightness never leaving her voice. "Sad, maybe? Or is it fear? But not shy."

We fell silent. Tower Bridge, all blue metal and pale yellow stone, was swinging into view round the bend of the river. To the north the lights in the windows of Wapping were out, apart from the occasional fluorescent kitchen and the blue-grey of a late-night movie.

Finally I said, "Used to?"

"Used to?" she echoed playfully.

"You said 'That used to be the extent of it.' As in, that's no longer just what you do, with your magics. What's changed?"

She made no answer. At length she said, "Give me your hand."

I hesitated, but there was a seriousness in her face that hadn't been there before, even though the smile remained in place. I put my hand in hers. Through her gloves I could feel her skin cold from the river wind. There was a colour in the whites of her eyes, a yellowish stain that didn't belong, but which I couldn't place. She took a deep breath, and when her lungs were full, breathed just a little deeper and I felt the change.

It started with a sound. First a fading, as the chugging of the boat receded, leaving only the lapping of the water against the boat's hull; then a growing, as new sounds slipped in to take their place, as if they'd always been there, but had been drowned out by the noise of the here and now. A creaking of masts, a rattling of cloth, a flapping of sail. I listened, and heard the sound of voices calling out from the waterside, calling in East End accents for the dockmaster to come quick to the wharf, for that bloody old fool to mind his feet, for the sailors and dolly girls to clear the way, for the ship docked from India to wait her turn because there's ten tons of meat what will spoil over here unless it's run quickly down to market. And looking towards the banks, in the converted warehouses that lined the docks lights were springing up behind the windows, flickering candlelight and lamplight, and the water around us teemed with a hundred craft, fishermen guided by a single burning point of light slung over the end of their boat, pilots and watermen with their little vessels stained sewage-sludge green, the silent cranes on the sides of the river now in full motion, wooden wharves running out into the water from a place where stone embankment should be. I opened my mouth to speak, but Meera's fingers closed tighter around mine in a command for silence and as we passed beneath Tower Bridge, a bare shadow overhead, I could see the craft swarming around the Tower of London and the sky above it was full of a thousand cawing ravens, spiralling like a tornado overhead, unseen by any but her and me, and I looked upriver and London Bridge was sagging under the weight of houses clinging to its sides, half-timbered houses and crooked clinging shacks.

I said, "Meera . . ." but my voice fell away into nothing, a fog was rising off the river, smothering the boat but somehow through it the sounds kept coming, wooden wheels on cobblestones, dogs barking in the night, the ringing of church bells announcing the hour, a watchman's rattle, a donkey's bray of distress, the roar from an inn on the south bank. "Meera!" I begged. "You've got to stop!"

She didn't hear me. Her face was lit up with delight, her eyes bright, flecked with yellow, her fingers so tight in mine they hurt. A glow to the north caught my eye and, as I watched, flames sprang up in the darkness behind a skyline of crooked cramped houses leaning against each other for support, and they spread, and overhead London Bridge was crammed with faceless dark shapes of people pressing against each other and children crying and women screaming and the sky was full of ashes and the stars were blacked out by smoke and I said, "Meera! You have to stop, you've gone too far, we'll . . ."

Then the boat jumped to one side, bumping against something below and there was a barge with a canopy and a pair of men pulling at the oars, and they wore doublets and stockings and shoes with buckles on and flat caps and looking up onto the bridge there were heads, four heads all in a row, stuck on spikes, tongues hanging loose, eyes rolled upwards, ragged zigzags around the still-dripping necks where the axe had struck a dozen times in an attempt to break the spine, traitors' heads stuck on spikes and the shallow banks were stained with fresh raw sewage and not so far off at all, the place where the city stopped; and there was a boy on the bridge, and I heard a shout.

And for a moment, just a moment, I looked up, and met a stranger's eyes. He couldn't have been more than nineteen years old, in a rough cap, his face smeared with dirt and sawdust, and, God help us, he wore a dagger in his belt and a pouch on his hip and iron buttons and as he leant out across London Bridge and looked down towards the river, he saw me, and I saw him.

I felt the deck beneath my feet grow cold, arctic cold. My breath was slow, too slow, condensing in the air, sensation was going out of my feet and fingertips, there was a weight on my back, a pressure pushing me down and the river below was wide and dark and black, ready to pull us in. We gritted our teeth and with all our strength, with every ounce of power in us, grabbed hold of Meera's wrist and pulled our fingers free. Her breath was steam on the air, her face was lit up in wonder and delight. I shook her by the shoulders and tried to shout, but my words were lost in the fog. I pushed her against the rail of the boat and, in that moment of confusion, forced her hands together with a sharp clap.

There was a noise too low to be heard, but I felt it. If whales wept, that would be the sound they made; if oceans talked, it would have been their language. It passed straight through our belly and out the other side, a ripple on the air that tore the fog around us to shreds, and for a moment it all ran backwards. The boy on the bridge darted away, the houses stretched out across the night, candles flickering in the windows, rats scurried away beneath horses' hooves, fires rose and blazed and fell, leaving a cloud of ash, chimneys grew, smoke stained the sky, stone embankments advanced along the muddy banks, searchlights briefly swept the air and, far off, bombs blasted onto the docks of the East End before even that illusion was shattered and, with an unclenching, a letting out of breath, time returned to its normal place. I staggered as the spell broke, bumping into Meera who in turn caught hold of the railing for support. She was breathless, her face shimmering with sweat, but she was grinning, and her shoulders shook with a barely suppressed laugh. Our catamaran was passing beneath Southwark Bridge, towards the silver spike of the footbridge between St Paul's and the Tate, engines slowing now as it moved in to dock, unperturbed by everything I'd witnessed.

And she was saying, "Did you see? Did you see did you did you see?"

"Meera!" I rasped. "You can't do that, you can't, you mustn't, how did you do that?"

She clapped her hands together like a child, almost bouncing on the spot. "It's here! It's all here it's all here if you just look the city built on layers and layers can you hear it? Can you hear it all the time it's always there can you see?"

The cold night felt warm in comparison to where we'd just been. My legs were shaking. "Not possible," I stammered. "No one should be able to do that, no one! How did you do that?"

"Don't be a misery," she retorted. "Wasn't it incredible?" She opened her arms wide and for a moment I thought she was going to do it again. I caught her fingers in mine and pulled them back close.

Somehow the action had put us not a breath apart, her hands in mine. We hesitated, a strange tugging in our belly. She paused too, looking straight into our eyes, unafraid. Very few look into our eyes and are not afraid. What I'd meant to say somehow didn't happen. Instead I heard myself say, "It was ... yes. You're right. It was. Incredible. Promise me – promise me you'll never, ever do it again."

"Why?"

"That kind of power – that sort of magic – isn't meant. You can't do it. You'll burn. You'll go too far and stay too long and you'll burn. Promise me you won't."

She took an instant too long before she answered playfully, "Aw. It's sweet that you care."

Perhaps we could have said something else.

But the moment passed.

"I can see it now," she said. "You're the kinda guy who stands up when a woman enters the room, and doesn't like to see ladies walk unescorted back to the bus stop. A regular knight in shiny armour."

Our fingers were still tangled together, and didn't show any sign of letting go. Her eyes crinkled as she smiled. "Did I scare you?" she asked softly, as the boat chugged round the bend towards the Oxo Tower. "Back then, were you scared?"

"Do I get points for lying?" I asked.

"You care *and* you want points? I'm beginning to think you have an ulterior motive."

"I didn't mean . . ."

"Wouldn't be talking to you if you did."

"Is this how you talk to every stranger you meet on the back of a boat?" I asked.

"Yes."

"See – that scares me."

"But you're the first one I ever did magic for," she added. "Were you impressed?"

"Honestly, yes. Never do it again."

"Were you scared?"

"Honestly, yes. And may I add, as we're standing here, never, *ever*, do it again."

Her eyes widened; she stepped half a pace back as if trying to get a better look at me. "Oh, my God!" she exclaimed. "You weren't scared for yourself, were you?"

"I'd be pretty thick if I wasn't."

"Yes, and unfortunately, being pretty thick, you're not quite smart enough to lie well."

"I study the art when I can."

She laughed, and her fingers tightened in mine. "We're nearly at the end of the line," she said. "You're sweet. Some guys try to be sweet because they think it'll make women go gooey inside. They think 'Well shit, I ain't got brains, I ain't got brawn, I ain't got nothing worth saying so I'll try being sweet.'"

"Most people don't think I'm 'sweet'," I said, struggling with the word.

"What do they think?"

"Most people don't get much past the job description."

"What's the job description?"

"Protector of the city," I answered with a shrug.

"See what I mean? That's so sweet you could spin it onto a stick and call it candy floss. Don't try too hard, though. You'll spoil the effect."

Our boat was slipping in sideways by the next dock. Above us, directly overhead, the London Eye, built as a temporary Ferris wheel to last forever, was lit up pale violet, its dark capsules turning at a glacier's crawl through the night. Across the river, the Houses of Parliament were brilliant sodium orange, with flecks of blue and green cast onto its towers. The river was rolling east, washing away the smells of the city, great ridges and swells beneath its surface, like invisible smooth backs of whales.

Meera asked where I was going.

I said I didn't know.

She said she didn't live far.

I said I had work to do.

She said, "Yeah, of course you do, work, at this hour."

I wanted to say, look, it's not like that, but there are a lot of really good reasons why I should head into town now and find a nice homeless hostel to spend the night in like I usually do, or a doorway out of the wind or something and it's been lovely meeting you, but seriously, careful with the magic because that's the kind of shit that you don't want to screw around with and while it was great, it was deadly, please don't do that again. So yeah. Bye. See you around, maybe. Perhaps. Sometime.

What I found myself saying was, "Yeah, well."

After such inspiring prose, she would have been well within her rights to walk away.

She didn't.

And neither did we.

Part 1: You Can't Save Those Who Don't Want To Be Saved

In which a social worker makes a complaint, a phone call leads to more than just contractual confusions, and a narcotic becomes a source of heated debate.

Some five and a half weeks after the night on the river, I was sneaking in the back way to the office of Harlun and Phelps, bankers, financiers, dabblers in the arcane mysteries of the stock market and, quite incidentally, daytime employer of a very large percentage of the Aldermen who guard the city at night, when I heard a voice say, "... you are such a Nazi!"

The voice was young, female, indignant. It belonged to a woman in a bright purple hijab, white knee-length plastic coat, black slipper-shoes with a bow on them, and a glare that could wither moon rock. Upon reflection, her being in the goods entrance to the office of the Aldermen was no more implausible than my presence there; but whereas I was using the back entrance in order to avoid being caught by the Aldermen themselves and subjected to enquiries about memos, meeting agendas and roaming monsters, she was attempting to break into the back entrance for what appeared to be far more nefarious purposes.

A pair of security men were hustling her out to a barrage of "I have rights! Fascists, I demand my rights, I demand – you *pigs!*"

This last as she was barrelled out beneath the metal shutter of the goods entrance onto a ramp that ran down towards an underground car park where the mixture of bankers, financiers, analysts, secretaries, marketing men and magi who inhabited the glass and steel tower that I reluctantly called my workplace parked their expensive and sometimes environmentally self-conscious vehicles. For a second I considered going after her, but the urge passed and I turned back towards the concrete staircase that led to the service elevator.

This was a mistake. Where, not ten seconds before, the staircase had been empty and blissfully secretive, now it was inhabited by five-foot-seven's-worth of Alderman, dressed all in black.

In the city of London there are two types of Alderman. The first, more pleasant, variety sits on local councils, shakes a lot of hands, attends a lot of parties, cuts a lot of ribbons and sometimes, on more enthusiastic days, lays a few foundation stones announcing that in this year of our lord, the worshipful Mayor/Councillor/Alderman for [Insert Borough Here] laid this glorious stone for our civic undertaking which will be of benefit for all. Thus, between the hours of 10 a.m. to 5 p.m., a small class of individuals moves around the city, not necessarily righting wrongs with their every deed, but hardly contributing to the overall mass of evil.

They are the first kind of Alderman.

The second kind of Alderman picks up the reins after a suitable dinner break, and works between 6 p.m. and 5 a.m. These are the Aldermen who track down rogue nightmares and put them back to sleep; the kind who watch the old boundaries of the city walls for monsters that may come knocking in the night; who seal up the gates that should not have been opened, and hardly ever, if at all, hold parties with nibbles on sticks. In theory they serve the Midnight Mayor, soldiers in his army; reality having met theory, however, it clearly decided that theory didn't have the horsepower to move in these kinds of circles and told it to get back to the car park. They were magical, they were dangerous, a lot of them were dabblers in high finance, and if all of this wasn't enough, they liked to wear black and talk in short sentences to let you know just how mean they were. They were the banes of my life and it was of only some small satisfaction to think that we were, in our own quaint way, the bane of theirs.

And there on the staircase was one stood in front of me.

Born a few inches shorter than me, she'd more than made up for it with a pair of knee-high black boots complete with heels that should have been internationally outlawed for crimes against flooring. Her Alderman's black jacket was buttoned up tight round her neck and pinched closed around the wrists; her shape inside it was only mildly distorted by the weight of concealed weaponry. Her hair was auburn, cut to a bob; her nose was button and her chin was sharp, her ears too small and her eyes a little too large; she looked like a woman for whom good breeding had reached its logical conclusion and then run a bit too far. In one hand she had a black briefcase with a black lock, in the other she held a half-eaten tuna sandwich.

"Mr Mayor!"

She was smiling, a sound of triumph in her voice at having found me. Doubt and suspicion bloomed in the murky corners of my mind. "Uh . . . yes?"

The tuna sandwich waved in the air, shedding pieces of lettuce. "I'm so glad to have bumped into you; I just happened to be passing this way and when I saw you I thought, 'What a perfect opportunity'!"

I looked round at our surroundings. Service corridors in big finan-cial institutions were not meant to be seen or understood by anyone earning more than a minimum wage. This one's only feature was a single fire extinguisher. "You just happened to be passing?" I echoed, moving towards the goods lift in the hope that her boots would pre-vent her keeping up.

Hope faded as with a snick-snack of pointed heels she easily matched my pace. "Yes! Isn't it fascinating down here? I often come down to say hello to the gentlemen who work security, or just to explore. Of course office blocks are all supposed to look the same these days but you know, if you're just willing to open a few doors you'll find that there's a whole microcosm waiting to be found."

"Will you?"

"Oh yes!" she exclaimed, my meek not-quite sarcasm rolling right off her. "And fancy meeting you here, Mr Mayor, such good luck. Now I've got a few forms . . . " The next words vanished into a wodge of tuna as she stuffed the sandwich in her mouth and with her freed-up hand attempted to open the briefcase. I jabbed forlornly at the lift's call button and watched the indicator above flash its way down from the sixteenth floor.

With the sandwich back in her hand and the briefcase on the floor, she flourished a bundle of documents stapled together on thin green paper. "Now has Ms Somchit talked to you about the liability insur-ance? We're covering everything from reasonable property damage through to unavoidable contamination with vampiric substances or lupine contagions . . . "

Some bastard had stopped the lift at the ninth floor and seemed to be holding it there.

" . . . and until you get it we cannot guarantee any extra medical costs or more than a budget funeral should you find yourself injured in the line of duty . . . "

"I'm sorry, but . . ."

"Then there are the diary requests. Would you be free next Thursday to address the Worshipful Company of Magi, Maguses and Mages at their annual fundraising dinner on the subject of thaumaturgy in the modern age? I believe they do an excellent meal – three courses, canapés, string quartet, wine – shall I say yes?"

"What? Yes. No! Wait, no! Um . . ."

"We've had a request from a coven in Thamesmead regarding a blockage in the sewage system. Apparently someone's been dumping their waste straight into the system and now they can't get any peace for the cockatrice matriarchs hunting at night . . ."

"I'm sorry, who are . . . ?" I tried again.

" . . . and we just need your final go-ahead on the payment to the enchanters to reactivate the deep wards in the building, against any further magical invasion . . ."

The lift went bing, and the doors swished open just as I said, "Who the hell are . . . ?"

There were five waiters in the lift. They had white sleeves, black waistcoats, white aprons and polished black shoes. They stood round a trolley slung over with a white cloth, on which rested a single plastic bottle. Inside the bottle was a thick yellow-red mixture, bubbles rising furiously to the top. Every face was serious as they hurried past us, muttering earnestly to each other. I slipped into the lift, hoping the woman would be too busy watching their retreating backs to have noticed, but then a voice said, "Are we going to the twentieth floor, Mr Mayor?" and there she was, already pressing the button.

The doors slid shut with a finalistic ping.

We started to rise.

"Look," I said, "I don't mean to seem rude, it just happens that way, but who the hell are you?"

She gave a little "Oh!" of surprise and dismay, and in a flurry tucked the papers under one arm and the briefcase between her knees, and wiped her right hand on her jacket before holding it out.

"I'm Kelly!" she explained, and waited for me to understand.

I raised my eyebrows.

"Kelly Shiring?" she added, with an uncertain hope in her voice. "Your new PA?"

The sun was setting over London.

The previous Midnight Mayor had had an office on the highest floor of the building. Before being torn to pieces and, in the moment of his demise, taking the monumentally stupid decision to lumber me with the job of being his successor, A. Nair Esq. had sat behind a great long desk topped with leather, in a great long room whose windows looked over great stretches of London to the south and west, across the silver River Thames, through the summits of Centre Point and the BT Tower, past the four chimneys of Battersea power station and the red-white blip of Crystal Palace, to the greyness where the green belt began and the city toyed with maybe ending. At this desk, from three in the afternoon until six in the morning – for Nair was nothing if not serious about his job – he would be brought salads and thick drinks of semi-congealed vegetables and tortured vitamins, along with files on witches and wizards stepping out of line, news of phone calls that he might one day feel like taking, and the morning newspapers still warm from the press. All these would be laid in their appointed place, behind the pot for the black biros, which stood no more than half an inch away, and at a ninety-degree angle, from the pot for the blue biros, which was itself lined up at a right angle above the single, treasured, red pen for writing words that merited being in red. (Beware.)

As Nair's successor, I was offered a range of equally god-like premises for the conducting of my mystic affairs, and at long last chose a small office tucked away between the photocopy room and the canteen. I had no interest in the photocopy room, but we liked the idea of never being more than ten yards from a fridge and a cup of coffee. Twenty-four hours after choosing this office, I arrived to find my presence announced by a nameplate on the door. Some two minutes and thirty seconds later, this plate was gone and I was finding a place to hide the screwdriver. Twenty-nine hours later it was back; eighty seconds after that it was gone, my skill with the screwdriver having improved. The message was eventually received, and after a while it was generally understood that my office served merely as an open-plan recycling unit where things were thrown which might come in handy but were unlikely to be read any time soon. A schedule replete with committee meetings, forums, management discussions and policy events was quickly trimmed down to the barest minimum of time

spent in the building. Only one Alderman had been able to win from
me anything bordering on management synthesis, but she had met her
end in a tower block in Sidcup. And I had stood, and watched, and
failed, and she had died for my mistakes. Since then, no one had tried
to raise the question of my attendance record at senior management
meetings.

The floor inside my door was covered with paper. In an electronic
age, a forest had died for me to walk upon it. I stepped over requisition
orders for summoning rituals, overtime forms for a project team of
scryers seeking out a rogue necromancer somewhere out in Northolt,
and pie charts dissecting various abuses of magic over the last twelve
months – illusions, curses, enchantments, invocations and abjurations
against persons or private property that were considered, by the
Aldermen, to be a greater threat against the well-being of the city as
a whole. Only a greater threat, mind. The Aldermen were tough on
crime, tough on the causes of crime, but didn't give a damn about the
criminal or the victim. Who had the time?

The window looked north, across a city of shadows in the setting
sun. Low clouds formed a dark patchwork on a fiery sky of crimson and
gold. In five minutes they would fade to cobalt blue, then bluish-grey,
then the stained orange-black of an urban night. I couldn't see the
centre of the sunset itself, but its reflection blazed from the windows
of the Barbican's three towers, and made the pinnacles of St Pancras
darken the streets below. Lights were coming on across the city, catching behind them the shapes of people still at work, framed like living
images.

I played stepping stones until I got to my chair, and looked down
at it. Anything absolutely, supremely important was usually left there;
tonight someone had pinned a note to the chair back, written in large
black letters:

THE BEGGAR KING WANTS TO TALK

It hadn't been signed, and where the Beggar King was concerned,
it didn't need to be. Certain forces there are in every city which you
learn, fairly early on, not to muck around with.

Another note caught my eye. A yellow post-it, noticeable only for
its smallness, was stuck on the corner of my desk. Someone had
written, freehand with a blue fountain pen:

You can't save those who don't want to be saved.

I considered this, then scrunched it up and threw it in the bin on my way out.

Getting out of the building without being accosted was always hard. Word had usually spread and today when I closed the door behind me there was a small crowd of men and women in matching black coats and matching black expressions. The default expression for an Alderman in my presence was unimpressed, and this group was not breaking new ground. There were seven of them and, to deal with their collective lack of initiative or willpower, they had appointed a leader. He stepped forward, a man of about twenty-eight going on twelve, with caramel hair combed into a ridge above his forehead and locked in place with a wall of grease. He looked at me, and his silence suggested I should understand from that glance all the fine details of what currently annoyed them.

I said, "Hi," and tried making my way back towards the elevator.

They moved together, and he dropped into step beside me like an angry mother marching a child away from after-school detention.

"Mr Mayor . . ."

"You're Bryce, aren't you?"

"Yes, Mr Mayor."

"You're a stockbroker, by day, right?"

"That's correct, Mr Mayor."

"And you're here to tell me to leave off, have I got it?"

A wittier man might have smiled. He was not witty. "Mr Mayor, if I may say, your pursuit of Burns and Stoke is becoming detrimental."

"Nope."

"If you will hear me out . . ."

"Nope."

The syllable bounced off him like a paper aeroplane off ebony. "Mr Mayor," he explained, all soothing tone and restrained gesture, "Burns and Stoke's quarterly pre-tax profit has increased and they have been very earnest in their development of community outreach on the wave of this . . ."

"Burns and Stoke," I replied, "are a money-making machine abusing magic to achieve their success, and while I'm the first guy who'd say 'Well, what the hell's the point of knowing a few spells if you don't use

them occasionally?' what Burns and Stoke do is not a little light
dabbling in enchantment. It's not hiring an affable seer to make a
decent stab at the projected loss on the gold market in the next three
days, it's not getting a scryer to have a peek into the nickel mines of
Kazakhstan just to make sure the investment is ticking over nicely, it's
not getting a corner witch to dress your CEO up in a pretty glamour
when they shake hands with their business partners from Tokyo. I
could overlook all that, all that would be completely fine.

"What Burns and Stoke are doing, Mr Bryce, is using power to beget
more power and beget more power and what do they do with that
power? Knock me down with a feather but they go and beget yet more
power until suddenly I've got tectonic plates rupturing in Eastcheap,
flooding in Hampstead and a lawyer standing in my office with a pair
of vampire fangs dripping virginal blood and an expression on his face
of 'wasn't me, guv'nor'."

"Mr Mayor, Harlun and Phelps has invested heavily in this company . . ."

"Then I suggest you get un-invested soon."

"The greater good . . ."

"Don't even try." I'd reached the elevator.

"The greater good . . ."

"You still seem to be trying, Mr Bryce."

"The greater good of the Aldermen and the city itself will be served
by a strong financial sector whose relationship with the magical community is such that a mutually beneficial and reasonably arranged
settlement can . . ."

The doors opened and I stepped inside, turning to cut Bryce off
mid-speech. "No," I said and, for a moment, our eyes met, and his
words ran dry. "You do not use the 'greater good' speech to try and
justify something that you cannot be bothered to fix. You tell the
board of Burns and Stoke that either they stop fucking around with
higher mystical powers and get back to screwing up the economy in
a mundane and sensible way, or I'll come in and do it for them.
Happy?"

The closing lift doors cut off his reply.

The sun was down by the time I left the building, leaving nothing
in the sky but a pale grey stain, framed between tall buildings. Behind

lit-up windows the city workers were visible, alone or in a group. There, a man with a loosened tie who'd locked his door but was caught perfectly in the light of his wall-sized window played mini golf on a roll-out green mat. Next door a man and a woman quarrelled, gesturing abruptly in what seemed more than just a professional dispute. Here, seven sat in a board meeting, coats slung on the back of their swivel chairs; there, a woman stood in front of a pie chart projected onto a screen, showing Opportunities and Challenges but absolutely not problems to be overcome. Three floors up, a man sat playing solitaire, and there another kissed his wife, who'd brought in their child, complete with red wellington boots, to collect Daddy from work. The magic in this place was old, rich and silver; it clattered on roads of tarmac laid on roads of stone laid on cobble laid on mud. It oozed up from the shadows between the street lights and steamed off the glowing silver towers. It was a heat haze that made our skin tingle.

Then a voice said, "You're not one of them, but they let you inside. Why?"

I glanced round.

It was the woman in the purple headscarf who only a few minutes before had been screaming "Nazi!" at the security men of Harlun and Phelps. She regarded me with a look of speculation.

"Sorry. Don't know what you mean."

"Yes, you do," she replied. "Don't give me that. Do you work there?" She indicated the building I'd just left.

"Not really."

"But they do know you. They let you inside, right?"

"It's not exactly a nine-to-five job."

"That's fine, I don't need to get in nine to five."

She was a pale, coffee ice cream colour, with long rounded nails. The scarf that hid her hair was bright purple, shot through with silver threads, and layered so thickly it looked like she was wearing an uneven sponge.

There was a something about her, a crispness to the air, that set our senses itching.

I said, "What's your beef anyway? What's so interesting about that place?"

"Nothing," she replied. "But I need to talk to someone inside it and no one will let me get a foot in the door. I have rights, you know."

I waited for an indication of irony in her voice, and when it didn't come I made what would be the first fatal mistake of the night. I said, "Who d'you need to see?"

"This guy called the Midnight Mayor."

It was ten minutes later. We were in a chain coffee shop, drinking mass-produced coffee on a mass-produced sofa beneath some mass-produced art in a mass-produced frame proclaiming that Originality Can't Be Bought. The girl was explaining, " . . . and I said, 'I've been to the local wizards, the local wizards don't know shit, they're only into the magic because they think it'll help them find a girl, as if' and they were like 'Look, darling' – can you believe they called me *darling*? I mean what the hell do they think this is, the Middle Ages? – 'look, darling,' they said, 'even if we knew this Midnight Mayor bloke, which we're not saying we do, yeah, but even if we did' – I think they may have put in another 'darling' at this point – 'even if we did, you really think he's going to be bothered with you and your like, little problem or whatever?' And here, which I realise was wrong," she added, throwing up her hands in what might have been contrition, "here I said some things which probably weren't my most polite but you know, they were such arseholes, I couldn't believe it, and since then they won't let me get even a foot in the building. It's been so fucking frustrating!"

She threw herself back against the sofa. Her fingernails were beating out a rhythm on the side of her coffee mug that wasn't far off the Ride of the Valkyries.

I put down my black coffee with its layer of scum and said, "Sooo . . . you want to see the Midnight Mayor?"

She gave me a look, then added, "Yeah, like, wasn't that the whole point of the story?"

"Does it have to be him?" I asked. "I mean, you're talking senior dude here, the protector of the city and all that. And the guy, I've gotta tell you, the guy is usually a pompous ass. You tell someone they're the protector of the city and, before you know it, you've got ego issues, you've got character defects, you've got nervous tics – I mean, I'm just speculating, but that's how it sounds."

"No!" she exclaimed. "This is important, this is protector of the city stuff! What use is a guy whose job is to watch out for the magical security of this place, if he doesn't ever get off his arse and do it?"

My mouth was open for a comeback that my brain couldn't deliver. She broke in with, "So, you going to help me or what?"

"Well, I . . . "

"I just need five minutes to talk to him, convince him that he needs to get involved. Those fuckers downstairs won't even let me leave him a note! What arsehole employs people like that? It's all like 'Wow I'm the Midnight Mayor, I'm like, cooler and more powerful than you little people, so you little people can fuck right off.' I mean, don't you hate that?"

I managed a nod.

She let out a sigh, and shrank back into her seat. She was younger, I realised, than I'd given her credit for, barely in her twenties.

"So," she said, "what do you . . . like . . . do?"

"Uh . . . things."

"What kind of things?"

"I'm, like, a . . . magical consultant."

She raised her eyebrows.

"Well, you know, if there's spells people don't understand or problems that people can't solve, you know, involving monsters or magics or stuff, then they call me, and I come down and clean it up."

"Does it pay well?"

"Not really."

"You have to declare to the taxman?"

"What? Well, no, I haven't for a while, but that's complicated . . . "

"I *hate* wizards who don't declare to the taxman," she said. "I mean, I get that you're all busy summoning imps and enchanting elves and all that stuff, but you're still going to use the NHS, aren't you? You still want your rubbish collected, you still want your kids to have a decent place to go to school? Or are you just going to magic a stable job market and decent A-level grades into being? I think not, oh-no."

"Actually there's more to it . . . "

"So do you, like, work for the Midnight Mayor?"

I hesitated. Truth shot a sly glance at expediency, expediency waggled its eyebrows significantly, truth made a little noise at the back of its throat, and expediency jumped straight on in there.

"I'm the guy who does all the stuff he can't be bothered with."

"Does that mean you can get me in to see him?"

"Maybe."

"Good. When?"

"Well, I . . ."

"Tomorrow at nine any good? I've got appointments all day from ten, but can maybe do a lunch meeting. He'll have to come to me, of course."

"Maybe we shouldn't get ahead of ourselves," I ventured.

A look shot across the table that could have snuffed out a stadium flood. "You *are* going to help me, aren't you?"

I leant forward, clasping my fingers between my knees. "I'm not sure you mentioned your name."

"Nabeela. Nabeela Hirj."

"I'm Matthew, nice to meet you. What do you do?"

"I work for the council."

"Which council?"

"Kensington and Chelsea."

"And you do magic?" I asked, dropping my voice.

She shifted uneasily. There it was, that taste of cold thin metal on the air. "I . . . I've got a condition," she mumbled. "It's nothing. I mean, it's fine. It's nothing. But it's, uh . . . you know, you have to get answers, don't you?"

"I get that."

"It's not like it's something I do for a living. It's just something that's like asthma, you know?"

"Sure."

"Anyway, when I was a kid my mum asked around, trying to get a few answers, and she met a few people who knew stuff, and then one guy said there was this bloke called the Midnight Mayor and he fixed things. Anyway," she added, "I'm not here about me."

"Then go on. What are you here for?"

She hesitated, then said, "You want to know what it's about? Really want to know?"

"I suppose, yes."

"Then you gotta come see for yourself."

I tried not to sigh. The sun was undeniably down now. I could feel the Underground rumbling below, the rush hour slipping away into that indoors time when the kettle boiled and oil hissed in the pan. The Beggar King wanted to see me, the Aldermen were pissed off, and the night was about to begin.

"Sure," I said. "Why the hell not?"

There are three kinds of living in London.

There's living above stuff. In council flats, great blocks eighteen storeys high with views across same old same old, you live above someone else's bedroom, you wear slippers, not shoes and lay carpet, not wood flooring. At night people navigate by your sitting room window, using your building as a marker through anonymous streets. Or you live above a shop, a pub, an off-licence, a hairdresser, in a little flat that smells of the trades carried on below.

Then there's living next to something. In the streets of what's termed the inner city, terraced Victorian houses look over little brick walls or restored iron railings from sashed bay windows and white-painted porches.

Finally, there's living beneath something. It can be noisy neighbours walking overhead, life in the shadow of a mobile phone mast or under a flight path into Heathrow. However you look at it, this is the worst place to be. And in Nabeela's part of town, there was one particular big thing you could find yourself beneath.

I said, "Oh. *This* part of Kensington and Chelsea."

Nabeela was buttoning up her coat against the rising night wind sweeping over Westbourne Park Underground station. Not that it was underground here, where Tube trains crawled in the tail-winds of expresses out of Paddington and regional behemoths heading into London from Reading and Bristol. Houses clung to the edge of the railway cutting like chalk cliffs waiting to crumble, while on the other side, looking away north, was the West Way. It showed as dark mottled concrete just high enough that from the pavement you saw only the tops of passing vans. But you could still hear the motorway, the A40 bypass raised up above West London to carry commuters quickly from the suburbs to the city, without having to muck around with the piddling places in between. Nothing could disguise the fact that this was a beneath corner of town. It was where the expensive wine bars of Kensington gave way with a shudder to the council blocks of the

Harrow Road; where municipal libraries stocking works by local authors were replaced by Wormwood Scrubs prison, and sports halls yielded to skater parks.

"What do you mean, *this* part?" We'd turned out of the station and were marching down the nearest street crammed in beneath the overpass.

"Well, you know, you say Kensington and I think ... big houses, posh cars, shops selling organic Fairtrade baby socks, Conservative central office ... you know, Kensington."

"Yes, because London's so homogeneous all the time, isn't it? I mean, let's not go jumping out of our little boxes any time soon, shall we?"

"You have lovely toes and I've stepped on them ... "

"You leave my toes out of it!"

"I'm sure there was a point in this relationship when you wanted my help ... "

"I'm still not convinced your help is worth much."

"Thank you."

"You're not even dressed right."

I stopped and looked down at myself. Charity-shop jeans going through at the knees and frayed round the bottom, a pair of worn-out trainers just thin enough to let me feel the ground beneath my feet, a T-shirt that once had invited people to Save Camley Park and was now only readable in very bright light, and a coat designed to endure all weathers and all flavours of curry sauce. I said, "What?"

"At least the arseholes in that office were dressed like proper protectors of the city."

"Are you saying I don't look much like the Mi ... I mean, much like much?"

Nabeela looked us up and down, contemplated a fluent reply, and settled for a burst of laughter. She turned, and kept on walking. We seethed; I scuttled after. A short way on lay impounds for the dubiously parked, MOT garages specialising in people carriers upwards, depots for holding concrete sacks, and the rusted funerals of unlaid train track. Beyond rose once-grand terraces with pillared porticoes and seven doorbells each. We passed a gym in a converted two-storey factory which was now making its industrial heritage a selling point, and a barber's shop with advertisements showing the same three male models whose faces adorned every such window from Harringay to Hounslow.

Nabeela was saying, "I did social policy at college, you know, and helped out at this youth group as a kid. It was all about getting kids involved in their local area instead of, like, knives. Anyway, I graduated into this, like, dire recession and got a job working part-time on youth projects for the council, which pays nothing, I should add, but you know, you meet people, you do things, it's a living, isn't it?"

"And this brings us into Midnight Mayor territory . . . how?"

She tutted something I didn't catch, and turned the corner into an estate of little red-brick houses. The street was very much of the area: old married couples who'd lived there all their life, taking care of their window-boxes and sweeping their little concrete patio; and families of unruly children and screaming parents who'd been dumped there with not much better to hope for. We came to a house whose one distinguishing feature was a wind chime of blue and green glass tinkling in the breeze. A buzzer by the door was taped over and inscribed in ancient blue pen with the words 'NOT WORKING'. Nabeela marched up to the door and banged the letter box a few times.

A light went on behind the blurry glass in the top of the door. A shadow obscured the peephole, a chain was drawn back, and the door opened. A voice said, "I thought you'd be back yesterday," and a blast of centrally heated air and yellow tungsten light spilt out.

The owner of the voice was a woman, who time had placed in her early thirties but wear had pushed into her fifties. She had peroxided hair pulled back in a ponytail, brown eyes sunk above purple bags, and a smell of cigarette smoke around her like a fallen angel's halo. Her accent carried the memory of Northern Ireland, but time in the city had dulled it into a rough grumble along the edge of her words. She let us in with a look of resigned wariness and, as Nabeela bent down and pulled off her shoes, she said, "Who's this, then?"

"Matthew's with the specialist services I was telling you about."

The woman eyed me up suspiciously, but offered me her hand and said, "Izzie."

Then a voice from the living room boomed out, "Who is it?"

It too had a Northern Irish accent, but harder and stronger, and carried along by a pair of powerful male lungs. Izzie shouted back, "It's the council! They're here about Callum."

There was a thump in reply, and the sound of footsteps. A door opened, bringing a stronger blast of cigarette smoke and the sound of TV. I heard a voice proclaiming, "and tonight's winner, taking home a grand prize of . . . " before the door slammed again. A man appeared, dressed in a duffel jacket and oversized jeans sporting a glimpse of tattooed ankles. He saw me and glared instinctively, saw Nabeela and glared habitually. "Have you got money?"

"For Christ's sake, they're here about Callum." Izzie's voice was naturally high, as if shouting had become the default mode between them.

"I'm asking for him," retorted the man, shoulders going back and chin up. "You think I don't fucking care, I'm asking for him, so we can look after him properly, yeah?"

"Well they're not here about the money, okay?"

"I didn't know that, how'd you expect me to know that, I'm not psychic, you didn't fucking say!"

"I was going to say but you had to come in here and be rude, I mean for fuck's sake it's not like you even waited, did you, you never wait . . . "

Nabeela said, "Actually, if we could just . . . "

"Is that what this is, is that what this is about? It's about your ego, you're the one who has to do everything, isn't it, a precious little martyr you are . . . "

"If we could just . . . " tried Nabeela again.

"Well maybe if you ever got your arse off that sofa you could actually help in this house, actually do something . . . "

"We just want to . . . " Nabeela offered, to no avail. I wondered if I wouldn't have been better off going to a council meeting. The row was, as most rows are, nothing if not dull, an endless reiteration of established opinions. It showed no sign of faltering, even after Nabeela murmured, "We'll just go say hello to Callum . . . " and grabbed me by the sleeve, and dragged me up the narrow stairs.

Three doors led off the landing. A smell of shaving foam from one announced the bathroom; the second was shut tight and the third had on it the teenage standard signs of 'KEEP OUT!' and 'BEWARE OF THE DOG' and 'PRIVATE – DO NOT DISTURB'. Nabeela knocked and, though no reply came, turned the handle and went inside.

It was indeed a teenager's room. Posters and pictures covered every surface including the ceiling, where pages from magazines had been stuck above the bed. There were pictures of men with almost more piercings than skin, striking poses of musical manliness by racks of electric guitars. Posters showed women baring a lot of skin, in poses that might have been erotic to a monk being force-fed aphrodisiacs. There were a lot of pictures of motorbikes. Somewhere in the mind of the teenager called Callum, the forces of Environmental Awareness and Being Cool had met and gone ten bouts in the ring, before Being Cool had whopped Environmentalism out of the ring.

Callum himself was sat on the bed. He was fifteen, with hair shaven to near-skinhead at the back and top, but left at the front in a curly quiff, created by a hairdresser who didn't believe in showing them the back. He was barefoot and wore jeans and a T-shirt with a faded logo showing a pair of open hands. As we entered he looked slowly round, turning only his head, and said without expression, "Hello. You are Ms Hirj of social services."

Nabeela smiled and said, "Good evening, Callum. How are you today?"

She pulled up a chair, carefully depositing a pile of biohazard clothing onto the floor, and sat down in front of him.

"Thank you, Ms Hirj," he intoned, his voice neither rising nor falling. "I am well."

Nabeela went on, "This is Matthew. He's a consultant."

"Hello, Matthew." Callum seemed to have grasped the necessary details of speech without tackling its full potential.

"Would you say you were a wanky little squirt?" asked Nabeela suddenly.

I raised my eyebrows, waiting for a torrent of abuse, but Callum only replied, "I will do better."

"How can you do better?" Nabeela's voice didn't rise, but had an edge to it that warned of anger. "You've only got one leg."

Callum's eyes didn't flicker, and both hands stayed in his lap, on his two functional legs with their perfectly functional feet. "You are here to help me," he said. "Thank you."

"Help you? I'm not here to help you. Why should I care about you? In fact, you've become such a pain in the backside that I've hired

Matthew here to kill you. That's what you're going to do, isn't it, Matthew?"

"Uh . . ." I began.

"He's going to strangle you with his bare hands. Come on Matthew, let's kill him."

"Sure," I mumbled, not shifting from where I stood. "Bare hands. Strangulation. Right up my street."

Callum still didn't move, didn't even blink. Nabeela slapped him, not particularly hard, and snapped, "Come on, Callum, you've got a view on that?"

His head drifted back to its former position, one cheek faintly red from the slap. "You are older and work for the government. You know best."

Nabeela straightened up, and shot me a look of pure 'what do you think of that, then?'

I edged closer, squatted down, and looked into Callum's vacant face. If this was an act, it was brilliant. His eyes drifted towards me and seemed to focus just behind the back of my nose. I said, "You heard of psychotic breaks?"

"You are a consultant," he replied. "You are an expert."

"It's not psychological," Nabeela murmured. "And no, it's not an act."

"How can you be sure?"

"Well," she sighed, the expert dealing patiently with the layman, "there were no psychological warning signs, no history of mental illness in either him or his family, no causes, no gradual break, none of the typical symptoms of depression, psychosis or schizophrenia, no drug abuse, no crisis moment; nothing you would expect."

"But sometimes . . ."

"And there're twelve other teenagers in the North-West London NHS trust area alone who are suffering the same symptoms."

Callum went on blinking with clockwork regularity, staring through me. "Okay," I said finally. "Why the Midnight Mayor? This could be . . . a disease, it could be food poisoning, it could be . . ."

"Are you really that thick?"

" . . . I'm just saying . . ."

"Callum," interrupted Nabeela. "Tell Matthew about what happened three weeks ago."

"Was there a fight?" asked Callum.

"Tell Matthew about the sound you heard."

Something glimmered behind Callum's eyes, and his head twisted as if looking around to seek a memory. Then he said, "I was out with my friends. We were not doing our best. We were wrong. I heard a sound. It gave pain. Some of us were afraid but I think it was a good fear. It made me better. Then it went. Did I remember well?"

"What did you see?" asked Nabeela gently.

"It hurt," he replied. "Hurt."

"I know it hurt," she said, leaning forward and resting her hands gently on Callum's own. "I know it is hard, but I need you to remember for Matthew here. What did you see, the night it hurt?"

"We were doing bad," he breathed. "We are better now."

"You and your friends weren't being good? What were you doing?"

"Drinking."

"You were drinking alcohol?"

"We were drinking . . . beer." He stumbled over the word, spitting it out like a loose tooth.

"And then what?"

"Sound."

"The high-pitched sound, and then what?"

"Hurt."

"What did you see?"

His tongue darted over his lips, the first sign of anything other than dead neutrality. "Callum," murmured Nabeela, fingers tightening over his, "this is so important. Tell me what you saw."

"A shadow. Fell. Fell on us. Sound and hurt and shadow."

"What else?"

"Don't want to."

"Callum!"

"Don't want to."

"You want to be good? You want to be better?"

He hesitated, then nodded dully.

"Then tell us."

"Shadow fell on us. Sound. High sound. Sound hurt." Callum scrunched up his eyes in a mimicry of pain. "Here." He bent over double. Then straightened up and added, "Shadow had claws."

Nabeela's hands stayed resting on his. She smiled. "Thank you, Callum."

"I did good?"

"Yes. Very good."

"You are good," he concluded, like one reaching the end of a long and difficult thought process. "I did good. I hope to do good. Thank you."

Nabeela stood up, glanced at me and said, "Any further questions?" I shook my head.

"Good. Maybe now you can get your boss into gear."

The parents were still arguing as we let ourselves out. We closed the front door to a scream of " . . . bills? You think this is about the fucking bills . . . ?"

Nabeela and I stood in the settling gloom of an early London night, breath steaming.

"Okay," I said. "So what's the deal?"

She started walking, and I fell into pace beside her. As she walked, she talked.

"Callum used to run with a bunch of kids from the local estate. There were five of them, aged fourteen to seventeen, used to hang out together. They did a bit of graffiti, smoked a bit of pot, drank a lot of beer, were loud at night. We sometimes got complaints from the neighbours – those kids were up at midnight drinking and shouting and I've got work tomorrow – those kids overturned a dumpster – those kids pissed on my front door – that kind of stuff. It's horrid – if you experience it, I mean. Rubbish, pee, noise, it all adds up, and so yeah, we had the odd word with them. But they weren't criminals, they weren't into knives or skunk or meth or any of that. They were just . . . you know . . . noisy pain-in-the-arse kids.

"So three weeks ago I get a call from the local coppers. One of Callum's mates has turned up dead. He's lying on his back on the local football cage where the boys like to hang out. He's seventeen years old, and there's blood in his ears, and running out of his nose, and he's just staring straight up at nothing and there's these marks all over him, like animal marks, claw marks, but – and get this – no animal they've ever seen. I mean when the cops tell you that, you start thinking okay, banshee, werewolf, let's get out the garlic and the ginger or whatever. But when the cops arrived, the other kids were just standing there. Four of them, just stood in the middle of the pitch, and they're not upset, or shouting, or defiant, or covered in blood, or nothing. The police psychologist does as a shrink will and diagnoses them all with post-traumatic stress, but seriously? Four boys all with the exact same symptoms, all at once, just stood next to the corpse of their best mate? And they all say the same thing. There was a sound, there was a pain, there were claws, and then they felt better. I mean, my God, next to a corpse and they felt better. That's not werewolves, and it's not just their brains. That's something else."

"Is it just them?" I asked.

"There's been a few odd things. You hear of kids from problem estates, you know, the ones doing the drugs and the knives and stuff, and then one day they just turn round and go, 'I shall be good' and everyone's like 'Wahey, they're better now, they're going to be model citizens' and it's kinda left at that. No one cares if a kid stops being trouble; it's just one less bit of paperwork. But this is the first time anyone's died."

"And none of the kids said anything."

"Not about the murder."

"The police are sure it *is* murder?"

Nabeela gave me the look of a domesticated homo sapiens starting to wonder if it was such a good idea to invite the Neanderthal cousins round for tea. "Nah," she said. "Because, like, the dead kid totally tore his own skin to bits and completely managed to commit suicide by repeatedly banging his own head against the floor?"

"Anyone hear sounds of struggle?"

"No one heard nothing. Just the kids – they heard a high-pitched sound and that's it."

"Any signs of struggle on the four boys?"

"Nothing."

"And you think it's going to happen again? I mean, that's where you're going with this, isn't it?"

"What do you think, consulting-man?"

I walked on before answering, taking my thoughts one word at a time. "I think there's something here worth looking at. I think you've got very little to go on at the moment. I think if you took this to the

Aldermen they'd tell you to get out, and in the grand scheme of things they'd be right."

"Just wait a . . . " she began, but I cut her off.

"I think there still might be something else at work. And if there isn't, then there's a serious problem. I think you should probably have hired a private investigator. I think that the grand scheme of things is a cruel place. I think . . . I think . . . "

"Yes?"

"I think I'll try to help you."

"Good. You going to call your boss now or later?"

Despite myself, we smiled. "The Midnight Mayor's not all he's cracked up to be."

"And you're Superman on speed?"

"Just don't want you to be disappointed."

"I'm a social worker," she retorted. "If something, anything good happens, it's a small miracle. If something big happens, it's Jesus walking on the water."

We were heading back towards the station. A small chapel, with a poster outside exhorting us to 'Save the Roof', housed a beggar in its doorway. He sat with his knees to his chin in a thick blue sleeping bag, nails cracked and hair grown white. A paper cup for any spare change stood beside him. I paused, and fumbled in my pocket for coins.

Nabeela was saying, "You know, when I said 'You going to call now or later?' what I kinda meant was, can you call now?"

"You're quite . . . forceful, aren't you?" I replied.

Her look could have stopped a runaway cement truck. "Call your boss. There's something out there with claws. And this is your lucky day – someone else gets to deal with it."

I'd found a small fistful of change, and put it into the beggar's cup. He looked up, his gummy eyes red around the lids. He said, "Domine dirige nos."

Lord lead us.

The words were half lost behind his almost toothless mouth, but they were still familiar enough to slurp out like a fart joke at a royal wedding. For a moment our eyes met, then he seemed to lose interest.

"You're welcome," I breathed. The ceremonial scars itched where they'd been carved in my hand. I glanced down the road, and thought I saw, under the glow of streetlight, another man – shaggy coat, tangled beard, crooked broken-brimmed hat – before he turned away and vanished.

"What'd he say?" asked Nabeela as we walked away.

"Nothing."

"Your boss . . ."

"Where was it?" I demanded. "The murder. Where'd it happen?"

She didn't answer, but turned off down a street of scruffy terraced houses. A few hundred yards on, and we came to a tarmacked area of open space surrounded by plane trees. A chain-link cage enclosed a small, five-a-side football pitch. Empty beer cans and a drift of crisp packets littered the edge of the cage. But only one small bunch of withered flowers with a note proclaiming 'For Kenny' suggested anything out of the ordinary had happened here.

The gate onto the pitch had a thick brass padlock around a heavy rusting chain. But the lock gave easily to persuasion and I let us in.

If there had been blood on the tarmac, it had been well washed off, leaving just the usual stains of spilt drinks and ancient trodden gum. A wall at the far end of the pitch bore a mixture of graffiti good and bad – at the top end of the spectrum, an urban fox in bright orange and black turned its head quizzically out of the bricks to glance at us as it trotted by. At the less arty end were the usual scrawls – BMN TEAM or MD4EVR or JESTER written in flares of blue and green across each other. I walked closer, letting the urban streetlight twist around me, the better to shine on the wall, looking for the tags and enchantments of the magicians who dabbled in paint. The White City Clan were the foremost graffiti artists, but other affiliations in the city – the Union, the Guild, the Tribe – as well as local hedge wizards and witches – used graffiti to mark their territory and spread their powers. I ran my fingers over the bricks, feeling the mortar scratch beneath my nails, and felt . . .

Nothing.

A thoroughly disappointing wall.

Nabeela said, "What you doing?"

"Nothing. Nothing there." I turned away and, as I did, my hand brushed over a bit of paint half scratched out below the picture of a mermaid wearing a sailor's hat. And there it was, that buzz beneath my fingertips, taste of metal on my tongue. I bent down to see closer.

It was an eye, drawn about the size of a human head, with a vast black pupil and a tiny iris of grey, set in a perfect white oval. There were no eyelids or lashes, no gender or any other colour; but it was still, unmistakably, an eye. And, looking at it, I could not shake the sensation that it was staring right back.

I pulled my fingers away, straightened up sharply and turned my back towards the wall.

"Something?" asked Nabeela.

"Maybe."

I walked back into the centre of the pitch, careful to keep my back still facing the wall, and squatted down to run my fingers over the tarmac. "The kid who died – how old was he?"

"Seventeen."

"Claws, you said?"

"Callum said," she replied. "I just reported."

"Body buried?"

"Cremated," she answered with a grimace. "Not so much use."

"Family's wishes?"

"I didn't ask. You born suspicious, or does it come with the turf?"

"I've got baggage. Issues with death, you know how it is."

From where I was, I could see most of the street around. The houses were all pretty much the same, but on the corner, right at the edge of my vision, a little green and white sign lit up the night. A shop, stuck into the corner of a building – and, more than that, a post office. I stood up quickly. "Come on, then."

Nabeela followed, with the look of one not sure whether to be hopeful or grumble.

The post office was one of those little local institutions that sold as many water pistols and 'get well soon' cards as it ever handled mail. Its longest queues were probably pensioners arriving weekly to get their weekly tuppence from the harried woman behind the counter; alone in the night, it already felt threatened. The shutters were down, but a small ATM peeked through a cut-out in the metal. Above the cash dispenser was a CCTV camera.

I needed something to stand on. From the nearest small front garden, I dragged a heavy black bin by its encrusted handles, and kicked it into position below the camera. Supporting myself against the metal shutter, I felt the lid buckle beneath my weight as I shuffled my feet to the very edges of the bin. In this precarious position, I found the CCTV camera was just about reachable.

Nabeela said, "This is going to be impressive, right?"

I shushed her irritably and, leaning gingerly forward, put myself on the same eye-line as the camera. Tightening my fingers around it, I let my eyes drift shut and

flicker in darkness behind eyes rods and cones rods and cones pattern of darkness falling

and then

flickering becomes dancing, dancing becomes darting, black and white static, static in front of the eyes and in the ears and then

and then

and then here it comes run back and back a step further and
street!

The image was bad, a black and white world seen through a bad hangover, but it was still recognisable. I could hear the little insides of the machine ticking over like a sleepless dream in the back of my mind, feel electricity running through me in the ridged patterns of current down a circuit board, my arms wired with silicon, my belly a microchip relaying data in and out of me in short sharp bursts, the snick-snack of information banging against the inside of my skull like metal blue-bottles in a jar. The football pitch was scarcely visible, the base of the fence's nearest corner just peeking into my field of view. I forced the camera to roll back, digging into its memory.

It wasn't on continuous feed, but took only a few images per minute. Cars jerked in and out of the street, captured for an instant and gone. Women with buggies talked to each other on the way to the nursery and then struggled home with shopping in the seat where babies had been. Boys in baggy trousers swanned into the post office and left with fizzy drinks in hand. The local drunk danced a lurid dance round the nearest lamppost for an hour or so of deluded circling. Cars parked, cars left. The rubbish truck obscured the image of the street for a long moment, then it and a thick pile of black bin bags were gone.

I pushed further back, searching for police cars and monsters. The image blurred, only the houses a constant, people running in and out of sight, bicycles being chained and unchained from railings. A queue of pensioners grew outside the post office, shrivelled, then grew back. The postmistress opened and shut the place, opened and shut, opened and shut. And suddenly, for just a second:

There!

I felt a lurch in my stomach as I forced it to stop, dragged the image back to that flicker of police cars. There it was, a single police car rolling up into the street, coppers around the chain fence, then another police car, then a police truck, tape across the road, people in dressing gowns and slippers coming out of the front door to see what the fuss was about. I pushed back further, to before the first police car arrived and there they were, five of them, all boys, just like Nabeela had said. They had plastic bags, a beer bottle peeking out of the top of one, another splitting under the square bulk of a six-pack. They were only there for a moment before they had vanished inside the football pitch, out of sight of the camera. Images surged by, growing grainier as darkness fell. A couple of kids kicked a ball together down the street. A man and a woman paused to check their A–Z, bickering under a street light about where to go. An old woman pushing a shopping bag on wheels shot a dirty glance towards the invisible pitch. And then nothing.

And a little more nothing.

A plastic bag blew against the edge of the railings, and flapped there.

A car drove by and moved on.

The postmistress closed and left.

There was a shadow across the camera.

Then the first police car arrived.

Wait.

I pushed back. Forced the film to go slow, one crawling image at a time. When it came, it was almost too brief to see; but there, just for a moment in a flare of static, something half unseen flitted past the camera. No, not past the camera; across the lights. I wasn't seeing it, whatever *it* was: just a distorted shadow, a thing thrown by the light. I froze the picture, tried to find some detail in its grainy shape. The overstretching shadow of a body, swollen and lumpen? A protrusion that might have been an arm, or a flailing leg? Or possibly, just believably, a claw?

And then it was gone.

I let go of the camera with a shudder and slipped down from the top of the bin. Nabeela too was trying to hide a look of concern. I hadn't realised how much time had passed. My fingers were turning white, my nose was heading for numb.

"You okay?" she asked.

I nodded, trying to catch my breath.

"See anything?"

"Snatches. Bits."

Just how big, and how bad, could have been the thing that threw that shadow? No answer satisfied me. Then my gaze drifted over to the wall of graffiti; and that single black and white eye stared right back.

"Wait here," I murmured. As I walked back towards it, I opened up my satchel. Inside it I had all the usual tools of the sorcerer – blank keys, travelcard, map, Swiss army knife – as a matter of principle, and I also made sure to carry the most useful enchantment tool of the age. The can of spray paint I had for this purpose held a cobalt blue, and had done me all sorts of service. I shook it as I advanced on the painted eye, stopped a foot away, hesitated, then carefully began to write, straight over it.

I wrote:

IT HAS CLAWS

And as the drips ran down, washing over the perfect white of the eye, I turned and walked away.

We were on our way back to the Tube. As we got close to the station a train was just pulling out, blue-white flashes lighting up the houses clinging to the sides of the track as it screeched off towards Hammersmith.

There was a pause in the traffic on the nearby motorway, rare enough to catch my ear. In that pause, as I happened to look towards Nabeela, in its place there was the sound of hissing, of static hissing, so low and quiet as to be almost unnoticeable except for the lull in other noises. For a moment it was as though it came from close at hand – from where she stood – and ...

Then a bus rattled by, and Nabeela was saying, " ... so you'll be okay with that, yeah?"

"What?"

"If I can get something more, you'll bring the Midnight Mayor down to *see* what's happening?"

"Uh . . . I guess so. And, Nabeela?"

"Yeah?"

"Don't do anything . . . you know . . . "

"Dangerous? Brave? Noble? Unexpected?"

"Let's say . . . in violation of local council health and safety procedures."

She laughed. "Hey – I totally did that when I went to you for help, right?" At the barrier, ticket in hand, she hesitated. "Hey, Matthew?"

"Yes?"

"I don't know if you'll turn out a complete jerk or a waste of time. But, for coming down here, I mean, taking a look and all that . . . "

"Yes?"

"Thanks."

"No worries."

And that was the start of that.

The Hammersmith and City Line crawled out west, past decaying stations held up with scaffold poles and optimism. I had no particular justification in going this way, but felt that if I followed my instinct long enough, it would duly lead me to trouble. After all I was Midnight Mayor.

At Shepherd's Bush, the low, jagged townscape was disrupted by the great white mausoleum of the Westfield shopping centre, encircled by traffic and moated by car parks. Turning south, the track ran above the street markets of Goldhawk Road, covered over for the night along their alleyways butted against the brick arches of the railway. The approach into Hammersmith was slow and jolting as we waited for a platform to clear.

I thought about the eye staring over the football pitch where, a few weeks ago, a kid had died; killed, seemingly, by a shadow that came and went in a breath. I thought about Callum, staring through me in his gloomy bedroom. I thought about the beggar in the chapel doorway to whom I'd given a few coins, and the note on my chair – *THE BEGGAR KING WANTS TO TALK* – and that other post-it, left on the corner of my desk where its innocuousness guaranteed it would be seen.

You can't save those who don't want to be saved.

Outside the station, and I'd forgotten how much I disliked this part of town. Another shopping centre, this one a faded baby-pink, sat on a huge roundabout fed by yet another main road, this one from Heathrow and packed solid most of the day and night. Oversized pubs spilt out crowds, boozing alongside the stalled traffic, while buses vied to crawl up into the local terminal like a great herd at a watering hole. Hammersmith was a place between worlds, where motorway dwindled into A-road, where grand terraced houses with well-groomed gardens met with flats of immigrants fed on baked beans and Marmite; where great corporate offices shared sandwich deliveries with struggling enterprises whose every month in the black was a triumph beyond compare. It was a place of all magics at once, where, like hot and cold air colliding, the mystical flavour of the city created an unpredictable storm.

I started walking at random, heading south and west past curry houses, pet shops and mobile phone retailers specialising in unlocking without asking. I could taste the river, close but just unseen, its smell sometimes sneaking through gaps between the buildings.

I was nearly at Putney when she rang.

It would be nice to say I knew who and what it was, before it happened. But sometimes the phone just rings.

The number didn't come up as hers, but when I answered I could hear her breath, hard and slow. Though her voice was distorted by the phone and something more, something worse, I recognised it at once.

"Matthew?" she said. "I'm . . . in trouble. I don't want to go."

"Meera?" I breathed, stopping dead in the street. Sometimes you don't need to ask more questions, there was enough in her voice to know. "Where are you?"

"Don't let them take me!" she gasped, and there was a jerkiness to her voice that suggested it was trying to break. "Don't let them!"

"Meera, tell me where you are."

"I'm . . ." she began, and the phone went dead.

I cursed and redialled.

Her phone rang for nearly a minute and she still didn't answer. I was already boarding at a bus stop, heading for Putney Bridge station.

I phoned again as I crossed the Thames, remembering the cold of that night we'd taken the boat together from Greenwich, feeling it deeper now in my bones than just memory could recreate. Still no answer. At Putney I got out and beeped my way through the gate onto the mainline platform, leaping down the steps two at a time. The next train was in four minutes.

I pressed the phone between my palms, half closing my eyes, and forced my breath to slow. I slowed my thoughts, slowed my heart, forced the tension out of my arms, and opened my hands again to hold the phone between them like a lotus flower in the palms of a priest. Her number was already on the screen; I thumbed it, let it dial, and as it dialled, turned slowly on the spot, turning the phone to point south, west, north, and finally east. As it reached east it began to ring, loudly, a high tinkling coming from the little speaker. I swung south-east and the ringing faded down, lower; swung north-east and it rang louder. It wasn't a perfect tracking system, but it would do.

I took the train, heading east towards Waterloo.

At Clapham Junction the phone still rang towards the north-east. I stuck on the train for Waterloo as we pulled out past commuters crowding onto the platforms, headed to such strange, surely promising places as Winnersh Triangle, Epsom Downs or Carshalton Beeches. If Clapham had the largest number of trains going through it of any station in Britain, it was merely where people changed, rather than a place prized for its own qualities. Waterloo, however, was a destination, teeming day and night with crowds impossible to navigate at any speed higher than the platform-hunter's waltz. A swelling sea of commuters ebbed and flowed, from south London and the Home Counties, with the relentless quality of tidal drift. I wove past shops selling sausage pies, silk ties, mobile phones and novels about shopping and love recommended by people from the TV, and still my phone was ringing towards the north-east.

I dared not go underground and lose the signal, so struck out for the buses across the river. I caught one on the bridge itself, opposite the brightly lit walls of the National Theatre, whose flat grey shapes only came alive at night, under great washes of colour. As my bus headed up Kingsway, between grand buildings made from 1930s pride and Portland stone, my phone started ringing towards the east; I changed at Holborn and headed towards Chancery Lane and St Paul's. It had been over half an hour since Meera had called. I spent a small surge of strength on turning any red traffic light green as we approached the old city boundary and, when we crossed into the Golden Mile, once encircled by the London Wall and whose symbol was still the dragon holding a shield of twin red crosses, I felt it like a jolt of pure caffeine straight into the heart. My scarred right hand buzzed: here, of anywhere in London, I was at home. My phone kept ringing towards the east, and I wondered how much further I would have to go: Bishopsgate? Aldgate? Shadwell?

On Cheapside the signal turned south. I jumped off the bus at a stop near the blank stone walls of the Bank of England, and the Merchant Exchange's temple-like pillars. Tarmac gave way to cobbled stone and a church left over from the age of dark stone walls and low grassy graves peeked out between the glass towers of the city. My signal swung suddenly round and I followed, the sound of ringing accompanying me down an almost empty street. A sushi bar on the right was full of men and women in suits, never less than four to a table, eating expertly with chopsticks; on the left a small dry-cleaner's offered a forty-minute service for the harried executive. I could feel all the shadows here, taste the power in the streets, deep and dark and waiting, feel it move beneath my feet, a well of time and magic that had no bottom, waiting to be tapped. The old stone city walls may have been mostly demolished centuries ago, but there were other barriers, unseen, wrapped around this part of the city, designed as much for keeping secrets in as enemies out. On street corners or embedded in coats of arms on grand municipal buildings, we could feel the watching mad eyes of the silver-skinned dragons of London.

Close, now. The slightest turn of my wrist changed the ring tone. A small street of older buildings: a tiny sandwich shop with sash windows and an empty lantern-holder of black iron; next to that, a wine bar and, incongruous in this cramped old street, a door of shiny mottled silver. A small red carpet had been rolled out in front, and a man, if men came in grizzly bear size, stood outside. A badge on his suit proclaimed him a licensed bouncer for a club calling itself Avalon. The closed door behind him, and the bolted look on his face, suggested that Avalon was not a universally welcoming establishment.

But it was in the direction of that door, and that door alone, that my phone kept ringing.

I hung up. My battery was nearly dead, and the silence felt shocking after all that trilling.

I walked up to the bouncer and said, "I'm looking for Meera."

"Sorry, sir," he said, not unfriendly, but in the tone of voice of a man hoping he didn't need to get that way.

I smiled. There are two kinds of bouncers in London: the decent ones, just doing it for a living, who hope you don't mind that they've got a job to do and if you're going to throw up it's probably time you went home – and the bastards. This man was not a bastard, and, upon reflection, didn't deserve what was going to happen to him if he got in our way.

I said, "If I ask you to let me in without a fuss, it'll be difficult, right?"

"Are you on the member's list, sir?"

"Amazingly, no."

"Then I'm afraid I can't let you in sir, unless a member will vouch for you."

"Meera."

"Meera . . . ?"

"I . . . don't know her last name."

He smiled ruefully. "Sorry, sir."

I sighed, ran my hands through my hair nervously, then stabbed at my chest with my thumb. "Me – Matthew," I explained. "These streets," I added, opening up my arms to encompass the quiet, dark little road, "my streets. This door," – I pointed, hoping he'd hear the polite determination in my voice that was already in his – "my destination. These pinkies," I twiddled my fingers squid-like at him, "mega-mystic-tastic pinkies."

Polite scepticism, inclining towards the thought that he would have to get physical.

"My friend," I added. "I think she's in trouble."

"This would be . . . Meera?"

"That's her. Hey – I'll stay here if you want, so we can send someone to check on her."

"Can't leave this door, sir."

"What about someone inside?"

"You want me to ask someone to go in and look for a Meera?"

"Yup."

"I'm sorry, sir, but I'm sure if your friend wasn't all right, the management would take good care of her."

I nodded in resignation. "Did I mention," I asked, taking half a step back to put some room between him and me, "these pinkies? Mega-mystical pinkies?"

"You did mention, sir, yes."

I raised my hand, commanding attention. "Watch *this*," I said, and spread my arms wide.

It took a moment to come and, when it did, at first it was hardly noticeable. From every lit-up window of every silent office, from every glowing street lamp, from every reflected puddle of light and glimpse of passing car headlamp, out of every passage into every subway and from the glimmer of every wing light of every plane passing overhead, it came. At first it was just a bending, a turning, a twisting. Then it was more, then it was a snaking: coils of silver-cool office light and sodium-orange street lamp curling out like a solid living thing, washing down through the air, writhing along the cobbled streets, tangling around my feet and then rising back up to bubble between my fingers. At first a glow, then a buzz, then a burning, and still the light slithered, cold and silent through the city night, flickering around my neck and hair, running tendrils of brightness down my spine, wrapping like lovers round my calves, until the bubble of light in the palm of my hands was a football of illumination, growing brighter, and brighter, and brighter until . . .

We saw the face of the bouncer, eyes wide, skin lit up to a glow by the reflection from our bubble of light. His mouth was hanging open, his body locked rigid, unable to comprehend what he saw.

"This is the cool bit," I explained, and closed my eyes, and slammed my fingers together.

The light didn't exactly explode. Explosion implies sound, and there wasn't any of that. There was just a silent whoosh-slam that went straight through the belly and sent ripples through the cushion of the brain. Behind my eyelids a flash sent yellow eddies round the surface of my eyes. I heard a wail from the bouncer and felt the light rush outwards, in a tide like lightning in the night.

I opened my eyes. The bouncer was bent double, hands pressed over his eyes; a grunting came from deep in his throat. I said, "It'll pass, don't worry." At the sound of my voice he swung his fists wildly, eyes still scrunched up. As his punches went far wide, he shouted, "Police, police!" I sidled past, pushed at the closed silver door, and let myself in.

It was called Avalon.

It was a nightclub.

There are nightclubs, and then there are nightclubs, and then, finally at the furthest end of the spectrum, there are nightclubs. Some are about the music, some about the dance; some are about the sofas where the various genders huddle in darkness with bottles of fake champagne or jugs of lurid fluorescent cocktails, hoping other genders will notice them and their empty glasses; some are about specialists' tastes – the music of only the 1980s, the lights of the disco period, men looking for men, women looking for women, men looking for women who are looking for women who are looking for men looking for men – and those who were looking for all of the above in various shades of ultraviolet paint. Some were tribal places, clubs for Goths dressed all in black, faces made up vampire-white and drinks with names like Virgin Blood or Fiery Nights all mixed on a theme of tomato juice, ethyl alcohol and not much else; or clubs for teenagers just discovering that there is a place known as *after* the pub, where the drinks come in goldfish bowls with five straws and a paper umbrella, and the music was acoustic guitar meets electric bass, and the waiters behind the bars juggled their bottles before going in for the serving kill.

In every club across the land, the atmosphere infects the magic, twisting the nature of the spells performed inside them. Here, it was like walking into a gunpowder factory flooded with paraffin and left under a hot sun and a giant lens. The taste of magic was palpable on the first step down from the silver door. As I ducked past the cloakroom before any questions were asked and through a second door into the pounding darkness of the interior, I smelt cantrips flaring and dying in the dark.

The music was, as music is in these circumstances, a pounding anonymity of bass beats and crunching guitar. The bar was lit up vivid blue inclining to purple; lights inside the glass counter revealed glasses of every shape and size, and bottles were hung upside down ready to be tapped for any combination of drink you could imagine. The waiters wore black, and bopped along to a beat that we could not detect in the cacophony of sound. There was a dance floor, distinguishable by the weight of bodies pressed together beneath a rack of speakers, and flashing strobes that gave the dancers a strange out-of-phase look. It was the dance of don't-you-wish-it-was-sex, hands overhead so that maximum attention could be focused on the midriff. House style for women was tiny dresses that clung to every curve like tin to sardines; men were in black trousers and rolled-up shirtsleeves from a day in the office. Some of the men, who worked on such things, had removed their shirts, revealing improbable pectoral muscles, and bellies which probably couldn't remember digesting for fun. Black leather sofas ringed the dance floor, with candles on tables where non-dancers weren't even pretending to talk over the noise.

I looked around for Meera. Pushing through the crowd, I tried dialling her phone again. As it rang, another phone started ringing, not five feet away. I couldn't hear it, but I saw the screen flashing in the dark and as I edged closer I recognised my own number.

The phone was new and smart, black cover and bright screen. It had been left on a low, glasses-strewn table where a group of men in suit jackets and half-unbuttoned shirts were lounging. An ice bucket sat in front of them, and three women in heavy lipstick and straightened hair were doing more than society required to make themselves amenable.

All ignored me as I approached, and one started clapping at some unheard joke. I stopped dead. As his hands met and parted, sparks flashed between his fingertips. His eyes were giddy and wide, his face flushed with drink and something more, but the ozone tang in the air was unmistakable. There was a sickly yellowness about his eyes, unnatural and bright in the dim light and, as he moved to refill his glass, I saw the condensation thicken on the silver ice bucket.

One of them noticed me. Still laughing at the joke, he said, "You got a problem, mate?"

Not taking my gaze from the man with the yellow eyes, I answered, "I'm looking for Meera."

They laughed again, a great roar of sound, and the one with the yellow eyes drained a slurp from his glass.

"Not here, mate!" chuckled one. "You just missed her."

"Where'd she go?" I asked. "It's important I find her."

"You her boyfriend or something?"

"Something," I replied. "Just tell me where she is and I'll be out of your hair."

A certain something darkened in the face of the man who'd first addressed me. He couldn't have been more than twenty-five, but his cufflinks were gold, glimmering with diamonds, and his black leather shoes were mirror-bright. "Why should we know where she's gone? Sorry, mate, but you're wasting your time."

I didn't move.

"That was goodbye," he added. "As in piss off, okay?"

"You must be her colleagues from work," I said. "You've got the look."

He stood up. "What's that supposed to mean?"

"Is that it?" I asked. "'What's that supposed to mean?' People only say that when they know exactly what it means, but don't have the wit to come up with an appropriate retort. It's a holding phrase, and a bad one at that. Well, go on then! Concentrate really hard and see if you can come up with something better."

He shoved me.

Probably he'd wanted to go straight for the punch, but didn't have the physical confidence. I staggered backwards, and rebounded off a dancer who didn't seem to care. As I lurched back towards him, I reached up, grabbed him by the lapels and pushed him backwards onto the table top. Glasses broke; the ice bucket went flying. I saw fear flash up in his eyes as they met ours and, before rage could replace it, we hissed, "You little worm-man. Little spark in a sea of fire, glint and die, little mortal with little mortal mind that thinks if it burns bright enough, it will be seen against the storm. She should be your friend and you don't even care. I barely know her and I give more of a damn. Where'd she go?"

The others were on their feet, but weren't rushing into anything.

"She, uh . . . she went with . . . the men."

"Which men?"

"They knew her . . ."

"Which men?" He looked for a moment as if he wouldn't answer. We tightened our grip, half drew him up ready to slam him back harder, and he gasped, "The dusthouse! She went to the dusthouse!"

"What dusthouse? Where?"

"I don't know – they just said they're from the dusthouse, and she went with them, that's all I know."

"Why'd she leave her phone?"

"I don't know! I swear, man, I don't know!"

A crowd was gathering; even some of the dancers had turned to watch. In a few minutes there'd be phones ringing and police knocking, and then I'd have to deal with Kelly's innate enthusiasm as she tidied up another political incident. My gaze met the yellow-stained eyes of the man at the back. He was sat bolt upright now, knuckles white around his champagne glass, all sign of laughter gone. And where others wore faces of doubt and fear, his body quivered with pure, deep, personal terror.

I let go. "Thanks," I muttered. "You've been great."

Then, before the sirens could start to wail, I pushed my way out, into the open air.

A police car did arrive. It came twenty minutes after I'd left, and the nonchalance of the coppers who got out suggested they weren't rushing into a serious incident. They talked to the bouncer for five minutes, then stayed inside the club for another twenty-five, before emerging to drive away.

I watched all this from an office across the street, having let myself in round the back. I sat on top of the photocopier, that being the only comfortable vantage point, eating peanuts and waiting.

We were not good at waiting.

We were not good at being still.

People came and went from Avalon, unaware or uncaring about the minor incident that had recently happened. Something in what the man in the club had said – the dusthouse – stuck in my mind, though I could not pin it to any explanation. Frustration met boredom and spun a few turns round the pit of my stomach. Hours had now gone by since Meera's call.

It wasn't until half past twelve that the group of tipsy men and eager girls who'd sat with Meera came staggering noisily out of the club. One of the men was unable to walk without the assistance of two others, whom he thanked at repetitive length. I let myself back out of the office, wiping salt and peanut fragments off my jeans, and fell in behind them at a thirty-yard distance. They were taxi-hunting, and soon lucky, flagging down a black cab and giving the address of a nearby hotel where no good happened at bad prices. The man with sickly yellow eyes was among them. Their drunkenness made them not just loud, but blind to observation; I heard the address, let them drive away, then hailed my own cab to take the same direction through the sleeping city.

It dropped me off at a hotel on St Katharine's Dock, a concrete monster surrounded by a maze of locks and quays, yachts and pubs, and apartments stacked high, with balconies of glass looking towards the water. I pulled my collar up, ruffled my hair, and reeled into the hotel lobby.

A single sleepy receptionist was on duty wearing a badge proclaiming that Emilia spoke both French and Italian.

I staggered up to the desk, overdoing the length of my walk, and burbled, "Hey hey hey hey!"

Emilia looked up blearily, and into her sleep-drenched mind I began to spin a little extra fog. The dozing mind is always easier to influence, and I could feel the gumminess of her eyes as if my own were sticking shut. "Hey hey hey," I repeated. "Yeah, my friends, yeah, they just came in, yeah, there were like, three of them, yeah, and we were like, you know, together but they, yeah, they went ahead of me uh . . . can you tell me which room they went to?"

She scarcely hesitated, saying wearily, "Were these the three gentlemen and three ladies?"

"Yeah yeah yeah yeah!" I exclaimed. "Well, actually it's really the three ladies, I know, you know, I mean, like, Sandra, yeah, she's like, you know . . ."

I let the thought trail off and smiled what I felt had to be my most winning smile. If she noticed, she wasn't wowed; nonetheless she looked down at a computer screen, checking for information.

"Your friends are in 512. Do you want me to call up, let them know you're here?"

"Hey hey hey hey that's like really nice of you you know but yeah I'll just go up and say hi I mean they'll know I mean of course they will yeah, you know?"

She nodded, her eyes half-drifting-shut, and turned her attention back to the screen. I let my mind linger in hers as I headed for the nearest elevator, and only when the doors were sliding shut did I let the spell go, the fog drifting clear from her thoughts too late.

I rode the elevator to the fifth floor, and walked along a corridor of endless samey doors until I got to 512. I could hear more heavy music and a man laughing the laugh of the alcoholically lost. The lock on the door was a key-card job. In my wallet I found a business card that had once advertised the services of Sexy Babe Nadine, natural blonde and exotically talented, until I'd purloined it from the phone box where it had been placed, and scrawled over it with blue-black enchantments. I slipped it into the lock, pushed with just a bit more than physical strength, concentrated, and heard the lock click. Very gently I pushed the handle down, and eased the door open.

Inside, the living room was in darkness, but I could still see the outlines of a sofa, a low table, a TV with its red standby light glowing and a minibar. The sounds of music and excitement were coming from the bedroom, through a half-open door which spilt yellow light. The bathroom was full of steam, its light still on, revealing discarded clothes and soggy towels. On the floor of the living room were more clothes. The door to the balcony was open, letting in a cold night breeze. I padded across the carpeted floor, then drew quickly back into the bathroom as a voice in the bedroom said, "Hold on . . . "

In the steam-dripping bathroom mirror, I saw a man enter the living room. He was wearing a blue dressing gown too small for him and a pair of black socks. He turned on the lights and started fumbling through the pile of clothes on the floor. Pulling a little silver box from the pocket of his trousers, he sat down on the sofa and reverentially opened it. He pinched something inside it, then held one nostril shut and drew in a deep, long sniff. His whole body rocked back, eyes closing with relish. At length he closed the box, leaving it on the table, and stood up.

His gaze roamed towards the bathroom and I recognised him: dark brown hair cut short, thick neck, eyes a sickly yellow stain. His eyes slid right over my reflection in the mirror, and his body seemed to start, as if his limbs recognised something there, but his brain couldn't quite catch up. As he turned back to the bedroom we marched up to him, grabbed him by the hair and dragged him onto the balcony before he could squeak; there, we pushed him backwards until his head was out over the five-storey drop and his feet barely touched the floor. With one hand over his mouth we leant in until all he could see was our face. "You," I hissed, "are going to tell us all about the dusthouse."

He made a little numb sound, and we said, "We know you know something. That thing coming off you now, it's not surprise, it's not uncertainty, it's not even hope of escape. It's pure, unrestricted terror. We saw it when the dusthouse was named, we see it in your yellow eyes. What are you so afraid of? Try not to scream."

I eased our hand away from his mouth, and he drew in a few raggedy breaths. Then he wheezed, "Man – you are totally going to die."

I felt it a second before it hit, a surge of power from the middle of his being. It slammed into us and threw us straight back into the room, knocking us against the arm of the sofa. From the bedroom I heard a voice raised in concern, before being hushed by someone having far too good a time to care about anything else. I picked myself quickly back up as the man in the dressing gown followed me into the room. His hair stood on end and sparks flashed around his hands. He thrust his palm towards us as I turned, with the sweep of my arm catching a wall of pressure that nearly knocked me down again, and hurling it back at him. He covered his head with his hands and the spell parted around him, shattering the balcony windows.

Now the people in the bedroom did get interested: a woman screamed, and someone shouted out, but the man in the dressing gown was shrugging off the spell like a loose towel. Opening his hands, he hurled a whirlwind of darkness at me, which condensed to tar smoke raging with internal fires. I ducked behind the sofa and deflected it overhead, then smelt fabric burning and felt smoke sting my eyes. With a flick of his wrist he batted the sofa aside, the entire thing lifting up and slamming into the wall above the minibar, hard enough to splinter wood. I threw up a cone of spinning warm air around me, smelling of ventilation ducts and kitchen steam, which caught and flung away the shards of glass he hurled at me next. The bedroom door opened, and now someone was embarked on full-scale screaming, a proper horror-movies wail. And where the hell was he getting his power from? I knew every sorcerer in the city, or both of them, and he was not a sorcerer. But this – this was more than simple wizardry.

He moved towards me again, already midway through another spell. This looked suspiciously like a transformation: his skin was beginning to mottle over with concrete, his veins started to ridge and shimmer with an internal line of steel. I grabbed a fistful of electricity out of the nearest mains, and threw it. Blue-white lightning danced through the air and slammed into him, twisting his body and briefly disrupting his spell. I hurled it again and took a step forward. He reeled back, bending in on the point of impact, his dressing gown charring, and smoke rising up from it. I was nearly close enough to touch him. I threw another blast of electricity and, as he staggered, I swung round so that my elbow slammed into the side of his face.

The concentration went out of him, body slumping back, hands to his face. I'd felt something crunch as I struck, and saw blood roll between his fingers from his nose. There was movement behind me but we ignored it, grabbed the bleeding, tottering man by his dressing gown, and snarled so loud and so hard that the lights across the floor hummed and dimmed with the force of it, "Where is Meera?!"

It's hard to throw spells with a broken nose. The pain runs straight up your face, curls into the hollows of your ears, makes it burn to blink. Only yogi masters concentrate through that.

I dragged the bleeding man by his dressing gown to the nearest elevator, and rode up to the top floor. I marched him down the corridor, knocked on a couple of doors until I found one where the light didn't come on in answer, opened it, pulled him in, and closed the door behind us. I guessed we had a maximum of fifteen minutes until the police, by now curious as to this trouble roaming around town, arrived to ask annoying questions. I sat the bleeding man down on the end of the crisply made double bed, went into the bathroom, grabbed a towel, ran it under cold water, and gave it to him to press against his streaming nose.

"Jesus you fucker!" he wailed through blood and cloth. "What the fuck you do that for?"

"In fairness," I said, "I asked you for information and you tried to kill me."

"You attacked me!"

"You were prone to deceit by silence, and we are not famed for our patience."

"I'm fucking doing you for assault!"

"Sure, because you're going to have fun explaining how you fought me off. Let's talk dusthouse."

"Fucker!"

"We could try snapping your nose the other way, see if the break runs in both directions," we suggested.

"I don't know what the fuck you want!"

"Yes, you do." I sat down next to him. "Tell me about the dusthouse." I felt his intake of breath, but he still didn't answer. Ten minutes to the police, if I was lucky.

"So you're scared. Figured that part. I just say the word dusthouse and you look like you're wearing a python for a jock-strap. But the thing is" – we shifted closer, dropped our voice to a murmur – "we will find Meera. Heaven and hell will not stop us; we will break every part of you until you help us, but we won't let you die. We will keep you alive, even if you have to be tied together, so you can even resemble a thing that was once a man."

His body was so stiff, if we'd struck him it would have pinged.

"I can protect you," I added. "You're frightened now; I can keep you safe."

Silence. But it was a silence waiting to be broken. Finally, he said, "The dusthouse took her."

"Who are the dusthouse?"

"I don't know which one . . ."

"There are many dusthouses?"

He nodded, then flinched as the movement disturbed something inside his broken nose. His voice was strained and high as he whined, "You sign a contract. Don't talk, don't tell, don't say nothing."

"Is that what you have? A contract with the dusthouse?"

"Yes."

"What's the deal?"

"They . . . supply you. Good rates, cheap rates, best-quality stuff. Shit, it's not like there's any competition!" He mopped at a trickle of blood down his chin. "Only, they'll fucking kill me."

"What stuff?"

He hesitated.

"Come on," I said. "We've gone this far."

He said, "Fairy dust."

There was a long silence while we digested this. I said, "I don't suppose we're talking Peter Pan, think your happy thought and fly, are we?"

"It is," he explained, one word at a time, "the Best Shit."

"Are we talking . . . like cocaine?"

A derisory grunt from behind the towel. "Yeah, if getting screwed out of your fucking brain by a sex goddess is like going five minutes with your grandma in the rain."

"But it is a narcotic?"

"Man," he flapped expansively with his spare arm, "it's the dust!"

"So why haven't I heard of it?"

"Limited supply," he replied. "Only for the guys who can afford it, appreciate it. Specialist market."

"How special?"

"Are you loaded?" he asked, giving me a look that suggested he knew the answer. "And are you magic?"

I let the information sink in deep. "There's a narcotic," I growled, forcing the words to stay under control, "that's for magicians only?"

"Fucking *loaded* magicians," he corrected.

Connections were clicking into place, cogs meeting with other cogs and discovering that, actually, they might like moving that lever together. "You're on the dust," I said carefully. "You're taking it. That stuff you were sniffing earlier – fairy dust?"

"Wish you had some, yeah?" he grunted.

"What else does it do?" I demanded. "I can tell you get a high, else you wouldn't have been stupid enough to attack me, but what else?"

He gave a 'what you on about?' shrug.

"You," I explained, "are some overpaid, chubby half-cooked wizard with just a few tricks up your sleeve. You shouldn't have caused us a moment of distraction, and yet . . . in the nightclub power was fizzing off you that shouldn't have been there. And Meera . . . is she on the dust?"

"You have no idea, have you? Fairy godmother is going to take you down, chop you up and serve you as sushi."

Below – a long way below – I heard police sirens, audible only because I was waiting for them. "Meera was taking fairy dust, yes?"

"Yeah, she was on it."

"How long?"

"Six, seven months, I dunno. She was this chick from the other office, it's not like she mattered or shit."

I forced our hands to stay at our side. "So why'd the dusthouse take her?"

There it was again, that fear, deep and true and unmistakable.

"Dunno," he lied.

"I'm really trying hard to be nice; don't make me regret it."

"There's ... sometimes there's ... sometimes people go to the dusthouse and ... there's ... "

"There's what? Group therapy sessions, free sweeties for all?"

"Sometimes they go to the dusthouse and ... people don't come back. It's not going to happen to me," he added quickly. "I mean, I'm totally in control. I'm like ... I'm like way out there, you know? But Meera? She'd been on it a while, and there's the contract ... gotta go to the dusthouse when the fairy godmother calls."

"Where is this dusthouse? Where are they likely to have taken her?"

"Dunno."

"Yes, you do."

"We don't go there, we don't, man, we don't. Only the handlers know where it is, only our dealers."

"Then you're going to give me the name of your dealer."

"Dude ... " he whined.

"You know you are, so let's not pretend like you aren't. Let's just take it as read that you've been all manly and macho and didn't crack until the very last moment, and that way I don't have to break you into any more pieces than you're already in. Tell me who your dealer is, where I can find him, and I'll leave you alone. Whatcha say?"

"They'll kill you," he muttered. "They'll rip you to shreds."

"Then it's a win-win for you, isn't it?"

Behind his blood-soaked towel he keened like a distressed animal. Then, in a rare act of good common sense, he told me.

It was time to go.

I took the fire escape down to the next floor, but voices below gave warning of coppers coming up. There were CCTV cameras in the stairwell and corridors; none resisted my command, each turning slowly to avoid catching me in their lens. I found the nearest fire alarm, mumbled an apology to those whose sleeps were about to be destroyed, and smashed it with my elbow.

Amid the deafening noise, in every corridor alarms leapt to spinning red life. I waited for the first hotel guests, in dressing gowns and slippers, to stagger bewildered into the corridor, then let myself into a vacated room, grabbed one of the bathroom's white dressing gowns, pulled off my socks and shoes, shoved the socks in my bag and tied my shoes by the laces around the strap, and joined the mass escape. There was no screaming, nor jostling, but rather the quick shuffle of zombie-eyed sleepers, not a man nor woman who considered themselves in real danger and many of whom were already considering their letter of complaint.

There were coppers guarding the fire exits, inspecting all who passed outside. I pulled my dressing gown around me to hide my working clothes; only the trousers, visible below the knee, gave any sign of nefarious intent. No one was inspecting knees downwards, and it didn't take much to blend in. I lingered a few moments in the crowd gathered beneath the wailing hotel building, eased my way outwards and, when I was sure no eyes were on me, pulled off the dressing gown, bundled it beneath my arm, and walked away.

Fairy dust.

How had I missed this?

How the hell had I missed this?

I threw my stolen dressing gown into a bin as I passed the Tower of London, its walls blue-white from floodlights in the grassy moat. I paused to put my shoes back on and all the time thought, fairy dust. Dusthouses and, but of course, the fairy godmother, dealing in a narcotic that turned its victims' eyes all the same sickly yellow I'd seen in Meera the night we'd taken the boat. It made petty wizards powerful enough to perform deadly spells. And like all such things, it came with a price. Fairy dust.

At least now I had a name to look for.

I was only fifteen minutes' walk from the Aldermen's office. So, in those night-time hours when the streets are empty of all but the swish of a distant lone vehicle, or the wail of a reversing dustcart, I headed in to work.

The offices of Harlun and Phelps were closed. Except that, like most offices in the financial district, they had a security guard on the door, who sat reading books and playing solitaire through the lonely hours of the night. He acknowledged me, and pushed a button to open the heavy glass door. I padded through the expanses of the entry hall, summoned the one working elevator and rode up in silence to the fourteenth floor.

The doors opened onto a white open-plan office under strip lighting. Desks with photos of grinning toddlers, unread mail, sleeping computers, highlighted reports and post-it notes warning of dire events. I headed for a door labelled 'Responses Unit' in white lettering on black, and was about to unlock it when it swung open. A voice, trying to make surprise sound like delight, exclaimed, "Mr Mayor! I'm so glad you're here!"

Kelly Shiring looked as fresh as if she'd sprung fully spruced from a good night's sleep. She was dressed in Alderman black and held a mobile phone. As I opened my mouth to speak, she said, "You wouldn't know anything about a pair of wizards having a duel in a hotel in St Katharine's Dock, would you?"

I smiled my best smile, peering past her into the computer-filled room that served as the main operation centre of the Aldermen's dead shift, and said, "Why on earth should I know about that?"

There were seven of them.

They were, so they informed me, the Aldermen's night-time support team. They too wore black and, for men and women meant to serve at the whim of the Midnight Mayor, they didn't look very pleased to see me.

I sat at the end of the table, threw my bag onto the floor, stretched my legs out until they clicked at the knees and said, "Quiet night?"

They gave me a look that has been passed down from lance-corporal to lance-corporal ever since the first general surveying a battle scene asked his troops if they were looking forward to getting stuck in for round two, chaps.

"We're so pleased you're here, Mr Mayor," Kelly said over the silence. "I do believe this is your first time visiting our little operational unit . . ."

"And fine and sterling work you're doing, I'm sure."

" . . . but is there something specific we can do for you?"

I smiled, and saw at least two pairs of eyes darken at the sight. "Funny you should mention that."

Kelly beamed. "Of course! What may we help you with?"

"Fairy dust."

Silence as the words settled. A man with salt-and-pepper grey hair adjusted a biro, lining it up perfectly with the edge of the table. A young woman caught our eye, and looked quickly away.

"Fairy . . . dust?" queried Kelly.

"What is it, where does it come from, who controls it, and why didn't I know? In whichever order excites most."

The polite sound of someone clearing their throat. I looked at the man with the salt-and-pepper hair. His eyes were grey-green, his haircut conservative, the face showed faint lines: age, heading for fifty.

"Mr Mayor," he said. His voice was roughed around the edge with time, and polished down the middle with experience. "Shall we check on the coffee?"

Magicians have sometimes studied the effect of certain physical locations upon the mental energies of their subjects. Bus stops, super-markets, airports, all can induce in even the most uninitiated minds a trance-like state often two mystic intonations short of a sleeper spell. Likewise, there are certain parts of a building – the water cooler, the photocopy machine, the corner where the smokers sneak off for their breaks – where the phrase 'the walls have ears' should be taken seriously.

The man I was with knew this, for he walked straight past the water cooler and the coffee machine, and into a small, anonymous office with a plaque on the door that read – Mr. R. Templeman, Sub-Chairman. Quite what Mr. R. Templeman was sub-chairman of, it didn't specify. He sat down behind a desk freighted with empty air, and gestured for me to take the chair opposite. I eased into it, and waited.

He eyed me, and I looked at him. We found in each other a worthy opponent.

"Templeman," he explained. "My name is Richard Templeman."

"Hi," I replied. "I guess you know me better than I know you."

Maybe he gave the beginning of a smile. "Indeed, Mr Mayor. On your appointment, I did read your file. You are, if you don't mind me saying so, a mess."

I scrutinised his office: walls where pictures should have been, empty desk, empty in-tray. The desk held only one object of note, a stainless-steel model seesaw that pivoted on its axis, perpetual motion from nowhere to nowhere.

"Learn anything else?"

"You charge into things without considering the implications of what you do."

"Is that a warning, Mr Templeman?"

"Of course." His voice rose a sparrow's peep in what might have been surprise. "But it is a warning when I say do not go outside without your laces done up, for you might trip; do not stand in front of heavy trucks rolling inexorably downhill. It is a truism of life, offered in good faith. Whether you choose to follow it is up to you."

"This is leading to something I won't like, isn't it?"

Now he did smile, eyes crinkling in what might have been genuine appreciation. "Yes, Mr Mayor, I rather fear it is. May I ask what your present interest is in fairy dust?"

"I'm looking for someone."

"Someone . . . ?"

"She was taken to the dusthouse."

"Ah." The syllable hung in the air. "May I take it that you plan on going after her?"

"As you said, what you choose to think is up to you."

"Are you . . . aware of the nature of the dusthouses?"

"I'm aware that I probably need to be more aware before I go charging into one. I've done a lot of charging into things tonight, and it's not done anything for my mood. You could say I'm having a rare moment of reflection before the next dash towards disaster."

He spun on his chair, barely moving side to side. Then, like one reaching a decision, he said, "The dusthouses are highly protected. Fairy dust . . . enhances the capacities of individuals prone to magical activities. The exact biological effect is, at the moment, not well understood; but let me assure you, any attempt to break into a dusthouse by force could end badly. Even for you."

"I'd started to figure that by myself. That's why I'm here."

"The Aldermen," he went on, raising a finger at me for patience, "cannot ... no ... not cannot ... but will not ... assist you in any action against the dusthouses at the present time."

"Because ... ?"

"At any one moment there is a great number of threats against this city. Our relationship with various institutions – the dusthouses among them – allows us to focus our attention on greater and more immediate threats. Engaging the dusthouses in any sort of open conflict could cause far greater damage to the city than it does any brief good."

"So ... you won't help, because it could get messy?"

"That is the present policy."

"I thought I had a say in present policy."

"In a way. As Midnight Mayor you possess a range of abilities that has been handed down over thousands of years. You are, if you will, the living embodiment of much of the city's mystical heritage. But that doesn't make you a politician, Mr Swift, nor an economist, nor a social worker, nor give you any quality that makes you suited to direct policy decisions, besides, that is, your exceptional skill for implementing them. So, while we will always respect your views ..."

"I doubt that."

"... the kind of radical change you want cannot be worked overnight."

"Is that what I'm sat here for? So you can tell me no?"

"What do you know about the dusthouses?" His eyes gleamed; his voice was low and dry.

I said, "Fairy dust makes people high, makes people powerful, probably has a few nasty side-effects; I mean, I'm just speculating here. People seem terrified at the name, so I'm reasoning there's some things that might merit a little more information. That said, I'm on a clock, so if this conversation is going anywhere, now'd be the time to let me know."

"The supply of fairy dust is not technically illegal."

"Technically?"

"The legislation hasn't caught up with it yet, put it like that."

"But I'm guessing it's still fulfilling a few clichés of the drug business."

"People ... vanish. It's surprisingly hard to monitor heavy users, since their hobby isn't advertised. The problem with magicians is, they're not renowned for their free and frank census replies."

"Define 'vanish'," I groaned, trying to rub some of the sleepiness out of my eyes.

"They go into the dusthouses."

"And don't come out?"

"Not as far as we know."

"See, that sounds suspiciously like the kind of thing that gets judges hollering 'illegal'."

"There are no bodies," added Templeman. "No sign of foul play. People just . . . go into the dusthouses and don't come back."

"In no way is anything you tell me making us less inclined to burn this institution to the ground. Where does it come from? The fairy dust, I mean? I assume we're not talking battery-farmed fairies."

He nodded, with what might have been a smile. If a feeling could be done by halves, Templeman did it by a quarter. "To be frank with you, the source of the dust is another mystery we aren't yet fully on top of. There are rumours. But that is in itself a factor in the decision not to intervene too precipitously: we just don't know enough."

"So what do you know?"

"That it would be a shame for our latest Midnight Mayor to die starting a war he cannot win. After all, you've only just started coming to the meetings."

I smiled, leant back in the chair and put my feet up on the desk. If this displeased him, it was but a twitch in the corner of his eye. "Anything that's going to stop me?"

"Have you heard of the fairy godmother?" he asked.

"Oh, Cinderella, don't be sad, for you shall go to the ball?"

"The supposed head of the dusthouses."

"Let's say no."

"You've heard of, say, Triads? The Mafia, Yakuza, naughty men who deal in naughty dealings?"

"I've watched the news."

"Imagine all of that," he said, plucking the words from just above my head, "– the savagery, the power, the connections – then give it the ability to curse you and all your kin, and you begin to understand why we Aldermen are being so cautious in our dealings with the dust-houses."

I imagined.

"Well," I said at length, getting to my feet, "thanks for the warning. It was scary, it was bad, it was succinct and it was, for an Alderman, surprisingly free and frank. So well done you, full marks. I'll send you the post-match report when I'm done."

"I take it then you're still determined to find your friend?"

"Yup."

"May I ask ... who it is that's so important to you?"

I hesitated, hand on the door. "It's Meera," I explained.

"Is Meera ... someone you've known long?"

"Nope. Met her on a boat. Seemed nice."

"You are close friends?"

I thought about it. "Barely know her. Met her once. Now, if you don't mind, I'm going to go and cause a major political incident."

Templeman caught my wrist, and eased the door back shut. He wore a thin, tense smile. "Mr Mayor," he said, "do you know why I asked you to come and talk to me privately?"

"To freak me out?" I hazarded.

"The others," he explained, "won't violate Alderman policy and risk conflict with the dusthouse. There will always be a Midnight Mayor; it just needn't be you. So why should they take any major risk?"

"I get that."

"I don't think you do, Mr Mayor. They will not move against the dusthouses. I will." He saw my surprise, and added, "I've just been waiting for someone with the courage to ask."

"Okay," I said. "You've got an idea?"

He had.

"But there's something about it you won't like."

"I wouldn't believe in it unless there was."

"It involves you wearing a suit."

"No bloody way!"

He smiled apologetically. "Would you like to hear the rest?"

I'd been given a name by the man I'd threatened in the hotel room.

He'd said: Morris Prince.

Morris Prince, dealer in fairy dust. He'd cropped up on the Aldermen's system two years ago in connection with the death of a mage in Richmond, inasmuch as a scorched outline on a wall was considered proof of extermination. But nothing had been proven and, as he seemed no threat to the city as a whole, Morris Prince was allowed to continue quietly in his deeds.

His employment records put him down as a minicab driver, but the car registered to his name had been taken off the road by the DVLA three years prior. He didn't claim benefits, and seemed to hold down no other registered employment; but for all this he managed to live in a mews near Holland Park, a two-storey apartment converted from what had once been a wealthy man's stable. His small-time magic was one of blood and bones, of physical transformation rather than air and fire, and had in recent years affected his biology. His neck now started at his shoulder, purple-black veins appeared from deep beneath his skin, and he'd suffered an almost complete loss of body hair, including but not limited to eyebrows, eyelashes and scalp. It was said he could crush a man's windpipe with his thumb, pop out an eye with the flick of his little finger and snap a spine with a twitch of his knee. That these things were reported with such medical precision led us to wonder if they might not be true. While any sensible wizard could easily win a fight by staying out of his way, if you entered combat within reach of his great arms the conflict would be over very quickly indeed.

We had already learnt our lesson. We could fight, and defeat, men like the one at the hotel. But not forever. And not without sooner or later paying a price.

At this hour of the night, when good men were sleeping, naughty men like Morris Prince were doing nothing of the kind.

I caught the night bus towards Holland Park.

For a man who dealt in nasty stuff, Morris Prince had few vices. He ate well, exercised regularly, and was reasonably loyal to his sexual partners, in the sense that he would always buy them an expensive pair of shoes when their three months were up. He even had a recycling bin outside his flat. I had a look inside: champagne bottles, juice cartons and unopened magazines advertising new bathrooms for amazing prices. The lights were out behind his expensive blinds, but a security alarm flashed a regular blue light above the front door, and there were other kinds of alarm too. I found the trigger for the first in the gaps between the cobbles, where someone with a low sense of humour and a reasonable grasp of warding had rubbed salt into the mortar between the stones. I expected there would be more, but had no intention of trying to disarm them all tonight.

Instead I walked up to the front door, and rang the bell.

I was wearing a suit.

Not much of one. The white shirt was several sizes too big, the black trousers were a little too short, the black jacket was a slightly different shade of black from the rest of the ensemble and we hadn't been able to find a pair of shoes that matched. I still had my satchel, and my fingerless gloves to hide the scar on my hand, but if you ignored these discordant notes, out of tune, the picture was almost complete.

It took nearly a minute for someone to answer. That someone was a maid, complete with frilly apron, and she opened the door on the chain only. Her accent was Eastern European, her age probably no more than nineteen, and her gun small enough to hide in the pocket of her black jacket.

"Hello?"

"My name's Sinclair," I lied. "I'm here to see Mr Prince."

"Is Mr Prince expecting you?"

"No. He will, however, want you to let me in, since if you keep me standing outside for more than a few more seconds, it will be considered evidence enough for the men presently watching this door to move into the house in an aggressive and unpleasant way."

"You . . ."

"I'll wait inside the hall. Scout's honour."

She hesitated, then closed the door enough to take the chain off, and let me in.

The hall was a mixture of old and new. A passage that had once let in muddy servants to below stairs in their master's mansion had been converted into a shiny entrance with new oak floorboards and cream-silk-covered walls, off which hung the kind of Impressionist painting that put the mind-altering powers of LSD to shame. They weren't there to be regarded, but rather noted out of the corner of your eye. The maid said, "Wait here, please." There was a chair for this purpose, and a coffee table laden with magazines about fast cars and holidays in Dubai. It felt like going to an expensive dentist.

When the maid returned, she wasn't alone. A man in a black leather jacket, with the look of someone who'd never owned anything that wasn't black leather, walked right up close, and looked down at me.

He said, "No one here knows you. So who are you?"

"What a great logical progression," I said. "Clearly your boss is a man for whom if the thing is not perceived and understood, it cannot be real. Unfortunate, considering your present situation."

He moved an inch closer, which was enough to block out what little light remained to me in the room.

"Who are you?" he repeated. His voice was a low rumble that had been a long way to get from belly to lips and hadn't enjoyed the journey.

"Sinclair," I replied. "Dudley Sinclair. I'm . . . how shall we say . . . I'm an interested party. Now, I'm on something of a schedule here so, if we could just hurry things up, I need to talk to Mr Prince."

"Mr Prince doesn't talk to you."

"Mr Prince would rather not talk to me," I replied, my smile locked in place. "He would prefer not to talk to me; he would, if he could choose, not wish to talk to me. Regrettably, though, he shall talk to me. As, if he does not talk to me, then in . . . " – I glanced at my watch, fifty pence from a lucky-dip machine and complete with Bugs Bunny ears for handles; should probably find something better – " . . . about twelve minutes the Midnight Mayor, protector of the city, defender of the walls, guardian of the lonely nights et cetera et cetera, is going to come in here and burn the building down. Which would be unfortunate for us all. Did I say twelve minutes? I meant eleven."

Suspicion met caution and fought for control of each face muscle. To everyone's relief, caution won out.

He said, "Stay here."

"Don't take your time," I sang out.

He went.

A couple of minutes after that, he came back. This time, there were two other men with him, also in black leather and, behind them, in a smart grey suit complete with lime green tie, the bulked-up hairless figure, stinking of internal transformative magics, that could only be Mr Morris Prince.

He said, "Search him."

I stood as they turned out my pockets – empty – and rummaged through my bag. My small collection of loose change, spray paint and blank keys were tossed out onto the floor. They didn't impress. Two of the lackeys held my arms as if expecting a bunch of flowers to suddenly spring up between my palms as Prince advanced closer, looked me up and down and told them, "Out."

"Your loss."

They had the door open, one gave a shove and I fell out into the street. Picking myself up, I turned and said, "Eight minutes, Mr Prince, and I'd say the buzzards are already circling."

He didn't raise his voice, but said, cold and quiet, "You come back here again, and I'll see you torn to pieces."

The door began to close. For a moment we wondered if they were too dumb to have noticed. Then someone did. I heard a voice raised in surprise; then the door eased back, the shape of a man blocking the light. I looked behind me and, yes, they were there, dozens of them swarming for cover beneath the bins and down the drainage pipes to the sewers. The smallest was no bigger than a Christmas orange, the largest had made it to the size of a young terrier. Their eyes reflected yellow in the night, their tails were mottled pink. They were only there for a second, but it was long enough. Morris Prince had seen the rats.

The door opened further. I was already heading at a swagger for the end of the mews and the lights of the main road when a voice called out, "You! Stop!"

I didn't.

"You! Hey, you!"

There were running footsteps; and when a hand seized my collar and an arm swung me with Newtonian inevitability into the nearest wall hard enough to wind me, I wasn't surprised. Less predictable was the flick-knife pressed against our throat. Prince still stood in the spill of light from the door; at a gesture I was dragged inside, and the door slammed shut. This time, Prince did his own work, whacking an arm across my throat and pushing me back until I couldn't see much beyond his hairless scalp and the ceiling.

"Who are you?"

"Sinclair," I wheezed. "And thanks, but no thanks, I'm going to go now . . ."

The pressure tightened, causing a wave of hot black spots to blossom and burst across my eyes. I gagged and scrabbled at his arm, and he eased off just enough to let me breathe. "The rats," he demanded. "Yours?"

"Midnight Mayor's," I replied. "He's a sorcerer. He uses the rats, the pigeons, the foxes; they all spy for him."

"Why here?"

"I told you, he's coming."

"Why should I believe you?"

"You know what, maybe you shouldn't. Maybe I should just go now. If the rats are already here, he's not far behind." His eyes were bright as they looked into mine; I could see every fleck of grey in the pattern of his iris. "I tried to warn you, give you time," I added, "but sorry, too late. If you're going to die, I don't see why I should get burnt with you, and so if you don't mind . . ."

He grabbed a handful of my hair and slammed my head back against the wall hard enough to set off a ringing in our ears. "Who are you?!" he roared.

"Dudley Sinclair! I have contacts with the Aldermen, they warned me to warn you. The Midnight Mayor is going to kill you," I wheezed. "He thinks you took someone he knows, he's going to destroy this house. The Aldermen say this will cause a war between them and the dusthouses, they don't want that to happen, so they sent me to get you out of his way, to prevent it. I'm just a messenger!" I wailed. "I was told, get to Morris Prince, get him out, and then hide! For Christ's sake, I don't want to deal with some fucking mad sorcerer!"

He hesitated, eyes darting all over our face. It wasn't hard to feign fear. "If you are lying, they will never find your grave."

"Sure, sure," I gasped. "Just let me go and I won't . . ."

"No. We go together."

He marched down the hall while I was dragged behind him. A door opened into a garage containing three equally tasteless cars, ranging from tasteless in size to tasteless in speed. He opened the back door to one of these, a silver Mercedes that would have blended into any landscape about as convincingly as Michael Jackson in Mogadishu, and I was pushed inside. One man got in next to me, and Prince sat next to the driver.

The car was gunned into life, the garage door slid back, and we sped off.

I was a rabbit in a car of hungry wolves.

The lights rushing by in the night-time streets spread their hypnotic patterns across the dark interior of the car. I huddled back in my seat, and wheedled.

"Hey, guys, seriously. I was just meant to give you the message . . ."

"Enough." Prince's eyes were fixed everywhere on the streets around us. "Tell me about the Midnight Mayor."

"You took someone he likes, that's all it is! Last I heard about it, he went mental in this club in the city and beat up these users . . ."

"Which club?"

"Some place called Avalon, why, does it matter?"

Prince already had his phone out. I heard the little beeps of dialling. He didn't have to wait long to be answered and, evidently, hear someone confirm what I'd just told him.

Hyde Park was passing by, locked away behind dark trees and pointed railings. Prince wore a frown of concentration as he said, "The Aldermen sent you?"

"Yeah. They don't want to piss off the dusthouse. I mean I know they work for the Midnight Mayor and stuff, but have you heard about him? We're talking about a serious wacko. He's like this undead sorcerer guy with this serious, like, demon thing attached and the Aldermen say he doesn't listen to a word they ever tell him."

"Who's this friend?" he asked quickly. "The one he's looking for."

"I don't know . . ."

"Tell me what you do know, or you're out of this fucking car right now, and don't think we'll slow for the corners."

"Okay, okay! Jesus! It's some chick named Meera or something."

"Meera what?"

"I don't know, I swear, I don't know. She's a witch or something and he must be really into her, I mean *really* into her."

Prince's associate was already dialling again, a bare flicker of eyebrow enough of a command from his master. "Yeah, me. Look, did we get some woman called Meera pulled tonight? . . . I don't fucking know, just check it, okay? . . ."

And at the same time, Prince was making another call to a different number. " . . . Yeah. Yeah, I know the time, do I sound like I care? Listen – I need some info. Your boss, where is he? . . . "

Something in my stomach clenched up tight.

We tasted petrol on our tongue, felt the hum of the engine beneath us. We were ready: at a single sound we would pop the engine of the car like a cork, burst the tyres, set the fuel on fire beneath our seats. One whisper out of place, and we'd turn Morris Prince and his men into kebab meat.

Prince hung up. He hadn't got his answer after all. "Fucking amateurs!" I forced out a slow breath, and let the power go. Let it seep back into the churning engine and the humming car, let the smell of petrol out of my nose and mouth, the heat of fire waiting to happen out of my veins. "Can he track us?" he demanded, turning to glare at me.

"He's the Midnight Mayor," I replied. "He can find us anywhere."

"All this for some woman?"

"He's not normal. He's got no sense of perspective, no grasp of politics or the greater good. He's a liability to himself and to others." I gave a weak smile. "I did try to warn you, so yeah, if you wouldn't mind throwing me out of the car at the nearest corner, that'd be lovely, thank you."

"You stay."

For men who showed no feelings, they were starting to look fidgety. We entered Soho: by day a place of art publishers, graphic designers, film executives and a perpetual smell of chilli, garlic and ginger on the air. At night, though, Soho turned on the red lights, threw beer cans into the streets, set the policemen patrolling with growling Alsatian dogs and let its hair down. A reveller looking for a good time could start in an Irish pub, swing next door for a chicken korma, stagger out across the street to holler away in a karaoke bar, fuelled by sushi and vodka, and then fall into the moderately priced arms of whichever gender took their choice, all within twenty yards of each other.

Even at this hour of the morning, especially at this hour of the morning, men and women wearing too little for the cold tottered down the middle of the street on each other's arms, arguing about which way was for the bus and which for the cab, and who lived where and with whom.

And there was something above us, too.

I didn't point it out. I figured they'd find out for themselves sooner or later. Credit to the anvil-faced man next to me who, craning upwards to peer out of the window, responded calmly to what he saw. "Guv?"

Prince turned to look at him, eyebrows raised, the annoyed employer wondering whether he's made the right human resources decisions, now the crisis has come.

"Above," said the anvil-faced man. So Prince lowered the window, on a little electric hiss, and stuck his head out, and saw them.

As animals go, a circling pigeon lacks the same effect on the human soul as, say, a circling vulture. Admittedly circling is not a pigeon's natural state; a continual flutter from rooftop to rooftop is more standard, as if, on arrival at a new destination, the pigeon can't quite remember why it went there to begin with, and has to go back to where it started to see if the recollection returns.

But this was several hundred pigeons, swooping from roof gutter to parapet, forming a shoal-like mass that inexorably followed the route of the car.

Without turning, Prince said to me, "That him?"

"Oh, yeah," I said. "That's him."

We turned into another street, cobbles peeking from beneath the worn-down tarmac. An iron water pump stood as testament to a past of public filth and plague; a bouncer was trying to turn out the night's last drunkards. A black and white eye had been spray-painted onto the wall by his club's door, its huge pupil watching the entrance to a brothel on the other side of the street. Now was not the time to see this eye again. Our driver turned into a gap between buildings, sometime warehouses now converted to design fashion studios and advertising offices. A metal gate slid open ahead, revealing a tiny courtyard adorned with one CCTV camera, one parked white truck, one black emergency staircase down from the roof above, and one grey metal door. There were no windows or other sign of life. As the gate closed behind us, my anvil-faced minder said, "Out."

The pigeons were still with us, forming a jagged battlement along the roofline. I felt the rats scurry in the pipes below and smelt angry fox rummaging in the nearby bins. The door opened for Morris as he advanced on it, and I felt wards warp and flex, almost saw the stretching of silver-grey magic in the air around its hinges. A dull light slipped out from the doorway as if embarrassed to make a fuss, and a group of three people – two men and a woman – appeared. They wore blue overalls and white masks, plus white plastic caps and latex gloves. I hadn't expected that Morris Prince's associates would look like the staff of a hospital or laboratory.

But as I looked closer, I saw that where the woman should have had nails, the beginnings of black claws were sprouting, and her eyes hinted at the madness of a shapeshifter who can't quite maintain a constant morphic form. One of the men stank of magic, with the same crackle of inhuman power, and in his eyes was the same sick yellow I'd seen in the addict at the hotel. The third carried a sub-machine gun, slung over his shoulder as casually as a handbag.

I was hustled to the entrance and pushed inside. The door closed behind me with a clang.

Once it had been a factory. A sweatshop where nimble-fingered women toiled behind ranks of sewing machines while the foreman fried his morning egg on top of the stove. Trunking in a ceiling of galvanised steel divided into extraction pipes; plastic sheeting and old stained blankets divided up the concrete floor into alcoves. There was a dry, prickling heat. The place was illuminated by bare bulbs hanging at irregular intervals. Within the falling light you could see a dance of slow-moving dust, dropping through the air like sleepy flies. There was a background hum, of fans churning, of an air-conditioning system with asthma, of coughing in a distant corner. Somewhere a man was making incoherent, begging sounds, before his voice dribbled away like the end of an old cassette.

I was made to change my clothes; without arguing, I zipped up a blue overall and pulled on a mask; Prince did the same. We felt dressed for a medically messy funeral, the air too hot behind the mask, whose top was biting into our nose. A woman wearing the same uniform came up to Prince and whispered; he nodded, then told me to follow.

I was led further through the building, seeing dust turn in a thin haze through the air, felt it tingle and itch against our skin, the little snap-pop of flaring magics blooming and dying as fast as they'd come, sparks in the dark all around. There were wards everywhere, clinging to the skin; they were scratched into the concrete walls, nailed into the old shuttered windows, pressed in tight around the doors: thick, suffocating blankets of protective magic designed to shield against flood, fire, tempest, blizzard and vengeful mage. It could take months to build up this kind of protection, and months to destroy it. Except . . .

Except.

We couldn't resist looking down at our feet as we went deeper into the gloom. Except that magicians were thick, they were so often thick, they raised spells against other magicians, against demons and monsters, but they never stopped to think like a proper security consultant or clever thief, their heads were so full of magic that common sense didn't really get a look-in; and if you were smart, and if you were flexible in your approach, and if you didn't mind getting your feet wet, there was a hole in the defences. A hole we could use.

I was taken down a corridor of plastic sheets and dirty fabrics strung along a single rope overhead, until we came to a long piece of blue plastic pressed in against the wall. The woman with Prince pulled it back, and he said, "This her?"

The crude cubicle contained within its plastic walls was just long enough for a child to lie stretched out inside. A second sheet of clear plastic had been stapled to the floor. In one corner was a pile of ragged, puke-stained clothes, in another a bucket whose smell penetrated straight through the mask and twisted in the stomach. Lying on the floor, wearing a white plastic overall but no mask, her eyes open and breathing shallow, was a woman who might once have been Meera. Her skin was a sickly yellow-brown, the colour of old worm-eaten pine wood; her eyes had a bright film and oozed yellowish goo which clung to her lashes and thickened into crystals. Her lips were cracked, her hair was thin and shedding, her nails cracked, blood clotted black in the gaps, and she lay on her side, as if dropped there and unable to move, shuddering with every shallow breath.

Prince must have seen the horror on our face because he snapped, "Is this the woman?"

I stammered, "Yes. This is her. This is Meera."

Squatting down, he clamped his hand around Meera's face and turned her head up towards his. She gave a sharp intake of breath and, as his fingers dug into her skin, I saw it break and crack, like fracturing burnt sugar. "Woman!" he barked, shaking her. "Tell me about the Midnight Mayor!"

Her eyes rolled in her head, straight over him and then up and away. He shook her again. "You! Midnight Mayor!"

Her breath came as a ragged wheeze. I whispered, "What in God's name has happened to her?"

Prince let her head drop with a hiss of disgust. It bounced on the plastic floor. Standing up he wiped his hands on his overall, leaving a trail of yellowish something. "She's a fucking fairy. Happens to them all, at the end."

I took a slow breath through the confines of my mask. "Is she dying?"

"What do you think this is, a health spa? They come to the dust-house for nothing else."

Meera's head had rolled to one side and now, as her eyes drifted upwards, for a moment, just a moment, they met mine, and her lips opened in surprise. I locked my gaze onto Prince's.

"Then we've got a problem," I said, taking it one heavy word at a time. "Because if she's dying and you haven't stopped it, the Midnight Mayor is going to tear this place to shreds."

"He'll be massacred if he comes in here. I don't care how tough he thinks he is, he won't dare."

"It's not whether he thinks he's tough, it's whether he's crazy enough to do it. Ask yourself this – is the kind of guy who came back from the dead really going to be open to reasonable and rational policy planning?"

Prince hesitated, then shrugged in exasperation. "Well, what the fuck do you expect us to do? The bitch is dying, nothing we can do about that; couple more hours and she'll have turned like all the rest of them and then what?"

"Is there no cure for fairy-dust poisoning?"

"What do you think I am, Mother Teresa?"

"Mr Prince," I replied, "I'm not here to judge you or your business. I'm not here to save this woman's life; I'm not here to piss the Mayor off. I'm not here, really, for anything other than my fee. So here's what you're going to do: you're going to call a private ambulance, you're going to put this woman in it, you're going to phone for a woman called Dr Seah; then I'm going to speak to the Aldermen, because that is the only way I can get the Midnight Mayor off your back."

For a moment, I thought he might take the bait. Then he shook his head. "No one leaves the dusthouse," he said. "Not once they're brought in."

"Why?"

Silence. A well-trained silence that wasn't about to break.

I sighed, rubbing my forehead with the back of my hand. The air was suffocating, thick and hot behind the mask, and heat too high in the room. "Fine," I said. "Fine, it's your funeral. If this is the attitude you're going to adopt then I'd politely ask you to let me go, as I have no desire to be standing here when the bombs start to fall. I tried my best and I just hope my employers will understand that."

I turned and pushed my way past the blue plastic sheet and started marching down the passage. He waited too long; for a moment I thought I'd played it too hard. Then there was a scurry of feet and he said, "Wait!"

I stopped, turned back, eyebrows raised. "Yes, Mr Prince?"

"I need to make a call," he said. "Stay here."

"Make it quick."

As he hurried away, I ducked back inside the blue plastic sheeting of Meera's cubicle, knelt down next to her, took her hand in mine. Her skin was shiny, slippery, dry. No; and another word too. Another word which had been hammering for attention since the moment we walked through these doors and would now not be denied. Dusty.

Her eyes rolled slowly up to mine, she tried to speak and all that came was a little rasp from the back of her throat.

"Hey, Meera," I whispered. She sort of smiled, but the expression was glancing, gone almost immediately in a flinch of pain. Her tongue was yellow-brown in her mouth, flecked with black. "You rang?" I added.

Her fingers pushed deeper into mine. The rasping in her throat became barely audible words that disintegrated even as they formed. "Took you . . . long . . . enough."

"Know when I told you I was busy being the protector of the city and all that? It's not like I've not got commitments."

"Didn't . . . even bring . . . flowers."

"Left them at the door."

She almost laughed, and the sound turned to a hacking cough, body shaking, muscles tensing and, as she coughed, yellow dust filled the air, bursting in thick clouds from inside her lungs. I wrapped my arms around her, sliding my knees beneath her head to form a crude cushion, held her tight. When her coughing had subsided and she could breathe again, I sighed, "This is a bloody awful bloody mess you're in now, isn't it?"

"Dust . . ." she began. "Fairy dust . . ."

"You don't have to explain."

She tried to shake her head, and even that induced another bout of coughing, her back arching, the plastic beneath her staining yellow as each breath expelled a fine dusty mist. When it was over she gripped my hand in her slippery fingers and gasped, "Tried to stop, tried to stop, tried . . ."

"It's okay," I lied. "You'll be okay."

"Listen! Matthew, listen!" She kicked feebly, trying in vain to raise herself up. "Dust to dust," she breathed. "Dust to dust."

"Meera, you . . ."

"No! Listen! The beggars are watching, they're watching, the dust-house takes the dust but there's someone else, there's someone else who takes, you have to, it's the dust, dust and dust and . . . and . . ."

I hushed her, held her close, murmuring the empty sounds you make when words won't do the job.

Then a voice at the plastic door exclaimed, "What the fuck is this?" Prince was back, radiating fury and surprise.

"Back off!" I snapped. Meera's fingers were twitching in mine, unable to get a grip.

I looked down into her eyes, sick with yellowness and gum and she gasped, "I . . . I . . . I . . ." and then the sound dissolved. It went from sound to noise, from noise to breath, from breath to air as her head rolled back and her eyes lolled upwards and her fingers in my hands started to crumble; they crumbled from the ends backwards, fingertips and finger joints and knuckles and palm and wrist, it all started to crumble away into dust and her eyes were still moving, unseeing in her sockets as her wrist crumbled to the elbow, elbow to the shoulders and her feet turned to dust and the overalls that held her started to deflate from inside as ankles gave way to knees and her hair rained fine yellow powder down onto the floor and she tried to speak but there was nothing inside her left to speak with and as the breath rolled out from her mouth and nose it was heavy with dust that billowed and fell silently to the plastic ground and her skin fell away in little pieces that dissolved in the air to drifting flakes and suddenly I was holding nothing, there was nothing there to hold, but dust was falling all around, great clouds of yellow dust, enough dust to have once been human and the woman called Meera was gone.

I sat in shock, before the gag reflex took over and we crawled on hands and knees away from that settling cloud, staggered out into the corridor, dust falling off our overall as we ran, made it only a few yards before dropping to our knees and shaking, the taste of bile in our throat, our stomach too dry to empty itself. Our hands were stained yellow, every crease filled with yellow dust, our hair released clouds of it. We shook ourself to try and get free of it, wiped our hands on our clothes, brushed down every inch of our overalls, until a small pile of dust had fallen at our feet. Our eyes burnt, every breath burnt, and there were footsteps behind us and I heard Prince say, "Don't waste any."

Then someone shoved us aside, and a man in overalls and a mask was on his hands and knees and, God help us, he was vacuuming the dust from the floor, sucking it up like so much lint off a dirty carpet, into a small clear plastic bag with a nozzle attached, businesslike and effective, and we grabbed him by the throat and screamed, "Don't touch her! Don't touch her don't touch her don't you fucking touch her!"

I heard a sharp click behind my head. It was the sound of the safety coming off a pistol. Our eyes were blazing, our vision tinged sapphire blue, we could hear our heart pounding in our ears. I forced our hands away from the man's throat, forced ourself to stand, fingers open at our side, forced ourself to turn and look Prince in the eye. The pistol he held was customised silver with an ivory handle, but that didn't mean it wouldn't fire like any regular weapon for any regular man. He said, "Who are you?"

I looked down at the floor. Dust was still drifting in the air around me. People in overalls were already getting to work in Meera's plastic cave; I could hear the sound of motors whirring, fans turning. Calmly, they were harvesting the dust.

We looked up and met Prince's eye; briefly, he flinched. I said, dull-voiced, "I would like to use your bathroom now."

"What?"

"I would like to wash my hands."

He hesitated. Then snapped at the technician whose throat was still marked red from our fingers, "Swab him."

The man edged forward. Prince moved round to keep the gun still level at our head. From inside his deep blue pockets, the man pulled out a small plastic envelope containing white, slightly damp tissues. He took our unresisting hands by the wrist and cleaned off every last speck of dust, from between our fingers and the creases in our palms, sealing up his stained swipes in little plastic bags.

When he was gone Prince said, "I asked you who you are."

"Sinclair," I murmured. "My name is Dudley Sinclair."

"No, it isn't."

"It is."

"I asked. I made a call. Sinclair is a ghost, a legend, a power behind the throne but you know what he is most of all? He's not the kind of man who gets involved. So who are you?"

"Friend of a friend."

"You knew the woman?" he asked, gesturing towards Meera's cell.

"No," I replied, keeping my eyes locked on some point far, far away. "But she called for help. She was dying."

"She was a fairy. Of course she was dying."

"Yes," I said, voice dead flat. "You next."

For answer, he moved the gun a few inches closer.

We didn't raise our voice, didn't shout or rage or scream. "When the Midnight Mayor finds out what has happened here he will hunt you down. You will try to run, of course you will, but it won't be enough. The stones will open up to consume you, the lights will darken as you pass, rats, foxes and all living things will shun the places where you walk, shadows will cringe back into the hidden places of the alley, the air that you breathe will turn to blackened soot and all the world will know that you are marked. There is nothing you can do to stop this. This is how it will be."

He was not a man who scared easily.

Then, this wasn't easy fear.

"I should kill you," he stammered.

"What's the point?" I asked. "Won't change what's coming."

"Get out," he hissed, gesturing towards the door. "Go back to the Aldermen. Tell them if your Midnight Mayor comes, I'll kill him. I don't fucking care, I'll kill him."

"No, Mr Prince. You won't even know he's there."

They threw us out, and locked the door behind us.

As if that would be enough.

Templeman was waiting.

He was leaning on the bonnet of a black hybrid car parked illegally in front of a shop offering Adult Entertainment and the latest in PVC fashion for the connoisseur. It was drizzling, the gentle, senseless London drizzle that soaked right through without announcing that you were getting wet. The pigeons still sat overhead, watching.

He asked me, "Did you find what you were looking for?"

We didn't answer, but paused by the car to scan the street around us. Eventually we found what we were looking for: a ridged metal panel set into the pavement. We knelt down and slipped our fingers into the metal holes at either end, feeling inside them until we detected each one's locked catch. We turned with more than just strength, and the covering jerked free in our hands. We eased it upwards, letting a smell of congealed kitchen fat and diluted faeces wash up to hit us in the face.

"Boots," we said. "We need boots, a mask, gloves and, when we're done, detergent and lots of lemons."

For a moment Templeman looked like he might argue. Then he said, "All right. I can do that. Anything else?"

"Yes. Salt-water, a strip of rusting steel – steel, mind you, not just iron – water-resistant matches, a can of petrol and a crowbar."

Another pause as he processed this information. Then, "How long will you need?"

"Ten minutes, once I go down. When I'm in there, call the police, tell them there's a bomb."

"To what purpose?" he asked.

"There are people in the dusthouse. Not all of them are going to die tonight."

"You can't help every stranger," warned Templeman. "There are always consequences."

"Are you going to help or not?" we asked.

For what it was worth, he was.

"I'll see what I can do."

It didn't take him long. The crowbar was already in the back of his car. Meanwhile we sat in a doorway, watching nothing, listening to nothing. It was the hour of absolute stillness, when even the hardest of the partyers had gone to bed, the doors had been closed, the lights snuffed out. Muggers and bandits, with no one left to prey on, turned in for the night; cat burglars had made their hauls and in the supermarkets tomorrow's milk was stacked up on the shelf. In the emergency ward at UCH the last of the night's alcohol-poisoning victims and men caught up in the wrong pub brawl were laid up to sleep on a cocktail of morphine and absent-adrenalin, and the only ambulances now skidded through empty dream-time roads towards the flats of old women whose hearts had missed a beat, and old men whose alarms had started to ring in the night. At this hour, even emergencies were losing their drum roll of intensity.

We sat alone, and wondered if that was the dust from Meera's death clogging up the space under our nails. Could we scrape her out, like mud?

We sat, and did not move.

When Templeman returned, he brought big yellow boots, big yellow gloves, a bright orange plastic pair of trousers complete with braces, a bright orange jacket with two zips up the middle, and a gas mask which stank of rubber and chewed peppermints. We didn't ask where he'd found them. He also carried a plastic bag and, as we changed, he produced from inside it a small plastic bottle into which he poured eight paper sachets of purloined restaurant salt; a pack of water-resistant matches with warning signs on the pack; a piece of rusting old metal with deadly sharp edges that looked like it had been snapped off the frame of a rotting bicycle; and a small, half-empty can of petrol.

My feet swam inside their yellow boots, my palms were sticky with instant sweat. I took the plastic bag of goods off him wordlessly, felt the weight of the petrol moving inside its container, said, "Call the police" and, without another word, we descended down the open manhole, into the darkness below.

People think the wrong things about sewers.

They think piss and shit, a sludge of brown.

That's not it. That's just the scum that skims along the surface, that's just the loathsome icing on the cake.

It's the cooking fats, the congealed remnants of washed-away meats, the scrubbed-down rotting husks of vegetables, and yesterday's mashed potatoes. It's sanitary towels flushed into a toilet prone to blockages, it's old tissue paper never quite disintegrating, and it's human hair that tangles like spider silk and doesn't break. It's detergent from the washing machine and soap from the dishwasher, it's baked-bean grease and uneaten leek soup that has grown mould on its surface from being left in a broken fridge. It's the fat they fast-fried the chips in, and the remains of old rotting onion. It's pregnancy tests that gave the wrong answer and the condom that split; it's used nappies and puke and the bleach they tried to use to take away the smell. It's everything you've ever not wanted it to be, running busily away downhill through brick-built tunnels, towards pits of rotating slime or the wide open sea.

The mask wasn't there to stop the smell; that would have been futile. It was just there to minimise the initial shock, so that you only gagged instead of passing out. Walking was at first a slippery nightmare, feet going out beneath you, hands scrambling at walls of slime bred into the brick. I called a flare of sodium light to my fingers and had it burn as dim as I dared, the churning currents of the absolutely-not-just-water bouncing and twisting around my feet. We could feel the rats watching, moving away from us. They, at least, knew what was coming. The pipes feeding into the sewer tunnel were blessedly quiet, the ceiling low, head-banger height. I followed the tunnel along, its downward slope almost imperceptible to our shuffling feet, until overhead I felt the tug of magic, the wards of the dusthouse above my head, the ozone snap of its flare-pop power.

We stopped beneath it.

Once upon a time, not as long ago as people thought, Soho had been the kingdom of cholera and all the diseases of faecal-drenched drink. When enough people throughout London had died, and enough MPs had been offended at the capital's stench of decay and death, the present sewerage system was built, by Victorian engineers who didn't just believe their works should be made to last, but were so attuned to the idea that they didn't even bother to consider it.

Then, the sewers of London were a technological triumph, a marvel whose inception changed the face of the city. But within a short space of time, as with all things flushed down the drain, they were forgotten.

And that was a mistake.

I opened up my plastic bag and unscrewed the bottle of water, splashing its contents along the walls and ceiling before pouring what was left into the rushing water of the sewer. Then I opened up the can of petrol, and repeated the same procedure, tossing it onto the walls and then draining the rest into the water, where it ran away gleaming fly-wing blue on the surface of the scummy rush. The rusted lump of had-been bicycle we scratched along the walls, leaving a fine red scar-line of dust, and then this too was thrown into the tide. Out came the matches, and when they were struck they flared up vivid orange, burning too bright and hard in the noxious mixture of vapours in this tight hot tunnel.

I caught the flame in my fist, dragging it free from the stick of the match before it could go out, and held it in the palm of my hand, letting it grow bigger and rounder on the foul air, before tossing it at the nearest smear of petrol-stained wall. Already mingling with fumes and slime and salt-water, it had an effect more like a smoky Christmas pudding gone horribly wrong than a triumphant whoomph of flame. But it caught and held, dribbling lines of fire down the walls where the petrol had run, and spilt as little puddles, on the surface of the water like oil in a pan.

I pulled out the crowbar, and hesitated.

Then our jaw tightened, we raised the crowbar overhead and, before I could change our mind, slammed it point-first into the floor beneath our feet.

Where the fire was clinging to the wall, it flared, a burst of red-tainted flame flashing up and spreading into the mortar between the bricks, tracing the pattern of their construction.

We lifted the bar and struck again, and the salt-water that had spilt onto the wall began to bubble and hiss, eating through the bricks like acid, and spilling out foul grey smoke to mix with the fumes from the fire.

We drew the crowbar up a third time and, a third time, drove it down against the floor, and where the rust had scratched its way into the surface of the bricks, now it began to eat and burrow, forming first a stripe, then a crack, then a network of cracks, a spider's web of destruction that raced outwards across the walls; and we raised the crowbar and slammed it down one last time and in response the whole tunnel seemed to jerk sideways. As if a great pair of bellows was blasting in from both ends at once, mortar dust and dirt rained down, while the cracks spread across the ceiling cavity and the fire crawled into them and began to eat deeper and the bricks crumbled and the sludge beneath our feet hissed and raged and churned, and we ran as, behind us, the tunnel beneath the dusthouse began to cave.

Even in this day and age, the Worshipful Company of Magi, Maguses and Mages teaches of certain things that still hold power. Earth, air, fire, water; salt, iron and petrol will do at a pinch. Blood. Blood will always hold its magic, even when everything else fades.

Later, survivors would say that there wasn't a warning: no rumble, no creak, no silence before the storm. There was simply the crack that one second wasn't, and the next second was: a tear in the ground beneath their feet, a centimetre wide, into which the whole building seemed to lean like stones on a sagging sheet of plastic. It ran in a straight line, tracking the direction of the sewer, for Victorian engineers didn't believe in wiggling. They say there was a moment before it broke, a second in which the whole warehouse seemed to hang there, the two lips of either side of the line pressing against each other, like the keystone in a bridge holding it apart. Then it snapped, simply, cleanly, briskly; the crack stretched out and the floor stretched in, the crack became a hole, a stream, a river, a chasm slashing through the valley-caved floor, and as the floor went the walls went and as the walls went the ceiling went and the weight of the ceiling crashing onto the floor made the floor go the faster and spread the effect out to the furthest corner of the wall and they say that the metal staircases screamed like living things as the bolts they were strapped to sheared away from tumbling brick and the weight of slate smashing into the thin black railings caused them to buckle into obscene dented grins and they say that the air was yellow and boiled so thick that you could swim on it, having no floor on which to stand instead.

That's what they say, the ones who lived.

This is what we found on the surface, crawling out from the manhole onto the damp pavement:

Sirens in the night, coming from all directions to the scene of what was now a major incident.

Rattle of a helicopter overhead, diverted from its night-time course to this new adventure.

Car alarms wailing, lights coming on, doors opening as the residents of Soho and those who worked the graveyard hours poked their heads outside to see what the commotion was about.

Fine white mortar dust in the air, tinged with something else.

Black smoke in the air too, and the sound of office alarms going off, the flash of blue and white lights on security systems all around.

Templeman had the engine running on the car and was sat in the driving seat, head tilted calmly back against the rest, one hand on the wheel, the other crooked into the curve of the window, elbow-first.

Pigeons spinning silently overhead.

Street lights snicker-snacking erratically, power not sure if it was coming or going.

Smell of an open sewer.

And where the dusthouse had been, not a hundred yards away, there were now a lot of police cars, a large number of people shouting, a not insignificant percentage of whom were wearing handcuffs, and a shattered hole in the earth.

Magicians are not security experts. They only ever bother to ward doors and windows, and tell themselves that will be enough.

I got into the passenger seat of Templeman's car and said, "Sorry about the smell."

We were pulling out and heading away even before the door had slammed shut with the heavy sound of reinforced metal.

"Don't worry about it," he replied. "It's a company car."

A police car screamed by the other way as we headed south, towards Shaftesbury Avenue and the freedom of wide empty streets. As we turned out onto Cambridge Circus, the bright lights of theatreland on one side, the dimmer lights of commerce on the other, he said, "Are you pleased with how it went?"

We considered the question.

"It's a start."

"I'm sorry about your friend," he said at length. "Were you close?"

"We barely knew her. But I . . . we . . . I didn't . . . no. No, we weren't close."

"The fairy godmother will know what you did," he added.

"We know."

"The other Aldermen will not approve."

"Wow, that's new."

"Do you . . . have a place to go? Someone you can stay with?"

"No."

"A friend . . . ?"

"No."

We drove on in silence. Somewhere the stationmasters of London were getting up, opening the barriers for the first early morning train. Night buses were returning to their depots and daytime buses were being fuelled for the morning run. Sunrise wouldn't happen for a while, but the city had long since stopped caring too much about the cycles of night and day.

Templeman asked, "What do you want to do now?"

We knew what to answer. "We're going to destroy the dusthouses," we replied. "All of them. Everywhere."

Part 2: You Can't Save Everyone

In which crime turns out to have consequences, and the thorny nature of civic responsibility gets a beating.

Templeman knew a hotel.

It was tucked into a new development of glass and yellow brick, near St Paul's Cathedral. The staff knew him, and his credit card, and they knew not to ask too many questions. They even avoided looking appalled at my smell, though the receptionist's eyes watered.

The theme of the hotel was purple leather inclining to black, with polished copper fittings and low orange lighting. In that nothing in it was made of plywood, it had class; but it made tiring work of being cool.

Templeman gave me the key to my room, and a plastic bag containing lemon shampoo and antibacterial soap.

He said, "Only you and I know you're here."

We said, "We won't hide."

I added, "Thank you," as he left.

Then we washed.

First we washed away the stench of the sewer, and rubbed antibacterial soap into every inch of our skin until it burnt with septic heat. Then we washed ourself in lemon soap, rubbing it into our hair, our eyebrows, the gaps between our toes and; when we'd done that, we scrubbed again and thought of dust, dust under our nails, and for the first time since we had left the dusthouse and slid through the sewers of Soho, we were sick.

There was nothing in our stomach to throw up anyway, so we slid onto our hands and knees in the shower and threw up clear white acid flecked with foam.

Then we sat on the shower floor and let the antibacterial heat burn through us. When we began to grow light-headed with heat and fatigue and weakness, we got out, brushed our teeth twice, staggered into the small, overheated bedroom, put a ward on the door and then, after a moment's consideration, another onto the floor, lay down on the bed with the light still burning, and failed to sleep.

It wasn't sleep, and it wasn't waking, but the dead time when the brain replays a loop to infinity.

When I finally bothered to turn my head, I saw a clock announcing it was 8.30 a.m. The light coming in through the layers of curtain was thin and grey.

I lay and contemplated our situation.

I had gone to war with the dusthouses.

Not twelve hours before, I hadn't heard of them, and yet with the tally standing where the tally stood, I was afraid of them. Perhaps in the same way, Prince had been afraid of the Midnight Mayor – blindly, without rationale, and with a certainty that was well founded, if poorly judged.

I wondered if Prince was dead.

I had called the police, though we had hesitated at the act, and perhaps that action had saved some of those inside the dusthouse. The collapse could not have been instant either, but rather we imagined Prince looking down and seeing his end as the cracks spread through the floor. Had he understood then what he had done? Had he understood what it was we had lost?

Maybe not.

At 8.40 there was a knock on my door.

I opened it on the chain.

Someone had left a breakfast tray, and a package of new clothes. There were even some shoes, and the size was right. When had Templeman found the time to check shoes? He'd also gone through my satchel, and stuffed an extra three hundred pounds down the pocket at the back. He was giving me options, should the moment come to run.

The clothes were a pair of charity-shop jeans, a long-sleeved shirt that smelt faintly of mothballs, and a woolly jumper stitched together by someone who knew what all grandmas loved for Christmas. At 9 a.m. on the dot there was a buzzing from my bag, which turned out to be my mobile phone. The number was unknown.

It was him.

"Good morning, Mr Mayor," he said. "Would you care to join me for a walk?"

The walk was in the Middle Temple.

Anyone with a little knowledge of the city might still be surprised when examining the map of central London to find three large, intricately shaped areas of green close by the tight winding streets of the golden Square Mile. Further exploration will determine that these are not public parks, nor residential squares, nor expensive estates. These are the Inns of Court, a spacious lost world of paved courtyards, wind-tossed antique fountains, and cobbled streets, and of wide enclosed grounds with wrought-iron benches, gravel walks and perfect lawns, open to the public only at exceptional times. No Victorian drama set in London is ever filmed without entering the Inns' bewildering byways; nor can every tourist enter on a first attempt, thwarted as they are by high gates and furtive entranceways, unannounced to all but the obstinately curious, the legally qualified and the criminally accused. This is barrister land, where every other sharp suit is complemented with a wig, a gown and parcels of papers tied with traditional red ribbon. Here, with a depressing energy for someone who probably hadn't slept, Templeman was walking his dog.

The dog in question was small and white, and looked as if it yapped a lot. Templeman was still wearing Alderman black, not a crease out of place.

We walked together around a private garden set back from the river. On three sides stood dignified buildings full of lawyers; on the fourth, beyond tall railings and huge plane trees, traffic scurried along the Embankment. The morning was bright and winter crisp; the air, biting.

"In fifteen minutes," he said, "you will get a call from your PA."

"God, I'd forgotten I had one of those."

"She is going to ask you a number of questions. Fourth on her list will be whether you were involved in the destruction of the Soho dusthouse last night. You will tell her you know nothing about it."

"We will?"

He smiled, apologetically, glancing towards his feet. "I mean to say ... it would be advisable if you did so."

"Why? Aren't the Aldermen supposed to be on my side?"

"There is no 'your side', Mr Mayor. There is the good of the city; and you, for all that you are an important player in this picture, are only a part of the city. There is no loyalty to little men when big pictures are at stake. When your PA suggests that you come into the office, you will decline in your usual manner. She will at some point advise you that the fairy godmother has got the wrong idea about your involvement, and has even now sent his personal guard to find you. She will suggest you leave the city for a while. I, on the other hand, do not suggest this."

"But you do suggest something else."

"You struck a blow against the dusthouses last night." We turned a corner, for another lap past a tulip tree and a mercilessly pruned wisteria. "Your achievement was not necessarily that you destroyed a dusthouse, but that you had the courage to do so. However, it was only one dusthouse."

"I'm still waiting for the suggestion."

Beyond the riverside traffic a tourist boat rode the high tide. A few chilly-looking passengers on the top deck were waving at passers-by.

"Do you know how Al Capone was brought to justice?" he asked.

"This is going to be important, right?"

"Tax evasion. For years the authorities tried to bring charges of profiteering, murder, extortion, prostitution, corruption – any and all – against him, and he always slipped their net. But they got him at last, on tax evasion."

"I hate to break it to you, but accountancy isn't my strong point."

"The trade in fairy dust is, like everything else, a business. It has supply and demand, PR and marketing, costs and liabilities. The only sure way of bringing down this business is to make the terms of trading so bad that no one in their right mind will sustain it. Do you know where the dust comes from?"

We turned another corner of the raked gravel path. I said, "No one would take the dust if they knew it meant death."

"The detail is not strongly advertised."

"People must know."

"It is a question of what is certain, and what is not. If you take dust you are certain from the very first taste that you will be euphoric, powerful, do things that most men couldn't dream of and feel things that most men do not have language to describe. That is known, and understood. The possibility that you may die from the addiction – that is unknown, unproven and, therefore, not understood. What did you see in the dusthouse?"

"I . . . we did not understand what we saw."

"You saw, perhaps, your friend die?"

"Yes."

"And not merely stop-death. Dust-death."

"Yes." A thought hit, like a tsunami that passes straight through the thing it strikes without slowing for obstructions. We breathed, "You knew."

"Knew?"

"Knew what happened in there."

"No, Mr Mayor. Suspected. That is all. The dusthouses keep tight secrecy for a reason, but in time you have to ask – where does it all come from? Where does the fairy dust come from and why does no one know? Suspected, that is all."

"They're killing people deliberately!" The sound of my voice bounced round the walls, was rolled up in the hum of traffic.

Templeman paused, then said, "Yes. They are. But we could not prove it." He added, "The science is poorly understood, if you can call it science. From what we do understand, the body metabolises fairy dust in two parts. The first, the quick hit, shall we say, can rush through the system in less than twenty-four hours, leaving a relatively harmless chemical trace that is removed from the body by its own natural defences.

"The second part, the part that kills, is never truly broken down by the body but builds up in the blood. It's responsible for the yellow you see in the eyes, and we believe the dusthouse dealers monitor all their clients for signs of degeneration, in order to ensure that they are ready for transportation to the dusthouse when the moment comes. A pinch of dust too far, a taste too many, and the body reaches saturation point, a level of dust in the blood which the human frame can no longer sustain and," he snapped his fingers, "conversion. Disintegration, we might say. No one really knows the exact chemical processes involved but, from dust to dust, the host becomes quite literally, what they sniffed."

"Murder," I said. "You'll talk to me about the greater good?"

He shrugged. "The addicts – fairies, if you will – are willing participants. They choose to take the dust, they choose to keep on taking the dust even as their bodies begin to show the first signs. It's no greater or lesser a crime than that perpetrated by the cigarette companies."

"The corpses of smokers aren't chopped down to make more cigarettes!" I snarled.

"So your problem is the processing, rather than the deed?"

"She's dead!" The traffic ate up some of the sound of our voice, but even the little yappy dog stopped and looked up, from behind its master's heels. Templeman stood, stared us in the eye, then kept on walking.

"Yes," he said at length. "I am sorry for your friend. But try to understand: any attempt by the Aldermen merely to shut down the dusthouses without consideration of the full picture simply escalates the situation. We take as our case study the metropolitan police: if it shuts down drug dealers who carry knives, they are replaced by those who carry guns. If they arrest the ones with guns, they are replaced by ones with guns and body armour, and so it deteriorates. While there is a demand, there will be a supply; the only guaranteed way to stop the production and distribution of fairy dust in the future is to remove one or the other."

"And how do you suggest I do that?"

"I don't know yet. Your intervention was, I admit, unexpected, if fortuitous. I have long been a minority voice among the Aldermen, advocating against the opposition of my peers. So when you arrived last night, full of rage and ready to strike, I'm afraid I acted with ... rather embarrassing alacrity. Now you may be in danger – for that, I apologise."

"Don't."

He smiled at some private thought. "For now, I suggest you keep your head down. I will talk with a few other sympathetic individuals and sound out the situation with the rest of the Aldermen. If the fairy godmother does move against you, a decision will have to be taken whether to follow the path you have set, or ... "

"Bugger off and let him use my bits for stir fry?"

"Words to that effect."

"We aren't good at staying still."

"I didn't think you would be. If, however, you must engage in acts of monumental power and destruction, may I please urge you to carry on your person an emergency contact number in a flame-proof container, just in case."

"You're taking the mick," I said.

His deadpan face was nothing if not remarkable. "I really do not see how you can think that." He smiled, an expression at odds with his pale features. "I don't yet have a solid plan for you, Mr Mayor – I apologise for that. The secret will be in thinking like a businessman, in analysing weakness of supply and demand. Hitting the dusthouses themselves merely attracts attention. But, as you perhaps learnt last night, even that can be an advantage. The name of the Midnight Mayor is intimidating, even if the reality is . . . " He just managed to stop himself.

"A little underwhelming?"

"More complicated."

We were nearing the gate back out onto a public area of cobblestones and the Temple's little shut-off streets. He held it open for me like a hotel porter, and closed it carefully behind us; the little dog waited obediently at his feet for the metal catch to clacker shut.

He said, "I will be in touch as soon as I have news to give you. In the meantime . . . "

"I know. Keep my head down, don't blow anything up, don't accept lifts from strangers, don't get caught by the godmother. On it."

As we were parting he hesitated. "Mr Mayor," he said, "I regret that we haven't had a chance to cooperate until now."

"Well . . . thanks."

"Good luck," he added, and walked away.

As I headed back to the hotel, I reached for my phone.

She said, "Yo! Matthew! What's up, dude?"

I said, "Penny, you know how I promised I'd be open and honest with you, and never ask you to do something stupid without explaining it properly?"

She said, "Oh man, you are totally in the shit, aren't you?"

My apprentice talked like this. We'd learnt to tune it out. "Penny," I said, "I want you to be calm and mature about this, and not shout or anything, but I may have accidentally destroyed a dusthouse last night, and it could just be that a mafia boss who trades in narcotic substances for the magically inclined is going to try and kill me and everyone I've ever loved. Happily, everyone I've ever loved is either dead or absent at the moment, but, when he realises that, he may just go after everyone else in a fit of pique, and that, Penny, includes you."

Silence.

My Penny Ngwenya, sorceress, ex-traffic warden, presently muddling along by doing shifts at a temp agency while looking for 'the dream kick-ass job for a dream kick-ass girl', rarely fell silent, and when she did, it was an ear-shattering din.

Finally she said, "You total tit."

"Hey, I'm just letting you know . . ."

"I've got *plans*," she exclaimed. "I've got things a girl's gotta do. I've got . . ." her voice dropped to ear-withering scorn, ". . . I've got a *date* tonight. With a guy called Femi. And he's really nice. I mean, he's stable, and reliable, and really nice, and we're going to have tapas and you know I've got a thing for tapas, and he said it wasn't just physical, although of course he thinks I'm beautiful and, like, awesome in every way, but he likes me for my mind, you know, it's this whole deep fucking soul-to-soul shit I'm talking about here. How the fuck am I meant to explain to him that I've gotta skip out on the date tonight because my magic teacher has gone and pissed off a mafia boss?"

"Washing your hair?" I suggested meekly.

"Piss off!"

"Sorry."

"Couldn't you just go say sorry or something?"

"I'm not sure he's that kinda gangster."

"Matthew . . ."

"Penny, I'm just letting you know, in an affectionate, responsible way. How you choose to deal with this information is up to you, but may I suggest that the one thing which would really blow your date with this Femi guy would be having the tapas restaurant raided by a pack of angry mobsters just as he's about to order another round of garlic sausage."

Penny had never produced such a fluently sullen silence.

At length she grunted, "Fine. I'll just rearrange my life now, okay?"

"You're a star."

"Hey – if you get all like, beaten up and shit, don't expect me to come and rescue your sorry ass."

"Wouldn't dream of it."

"You gonna be okay?"

"Yeah."

"Aw Matthew," she sighed, "you're sweet when you tell the truth, and kinda crappy when you lie."

I went back to the hotel.

A uniformed man in a red cap and brass buttons was arguing at the front door with a beggar. " . . . I'll call the police if you don't . . ."

The doors closed behind me on that debate, and for the moment I thought no more of it.

As I took the service stairs up to my room, my phone rang. The number was unknown, but the voice was Kelly's.

"Hi, Mr Mayor!" she chimed, bright as a lighthouse on a foggy night.

"Hi, Kelly."

"I hope I haven't caught you at a bad time," she sang. "But I've got a few things I need to run by you . . ."

I fumbled for the key to my hotel door as she talked.

" . . . there's been a complaint of ensorcelment in Queensbury, a young woman claims her mind was stripped from her and her body ensnared in a web of enchantment by a local coven . . ."

The door beeped, swung open.

" . . . and I was hoping we could maybe look into the grave-robbing incidents only it seems that the corpses have been getting up by themselves before heading over to the dissection room and you know how this sort of thing bothers the council . . ."

Grey half-light was sneaking through the window. The bed was still unmade, my breakfast tray where I'd left it.

" . . . we do really need a final answer on the dinner for the Worshipful Company of Magi . . ."

In the bathroom the air was hot and steamy. It took me a moment to work out what felt wrong. My eyes wandered across the small white sink, the small white toilet, the small white shower, the white tiled floor, the white tiled walls and finally settled on the perfectly polished mirror set in its white tile frame.

" . . . and finally we've had a little problem with the dusthouses . . ."

And there it was. In the thick condensation clinging to the glass, far too much and far too thick for the time that had elapsed since the shower was last turned off, someone had written with their fingertip:

YOU CAN'T SAVE EVERYONE

I stared at it, my own reflection staring back from within the clear outlines of the letters. Then I wiped it away with my hand.

Kelly was saying, "Mr Mayor? Mr Mayor, sorry are you still there? Hello? Hello!"

I was already out in the corridor, door slamming shut behind me, heading for the nearest stair. "Yeah, I'm still here ... Sorry, right, bad reception. What were you saying?"

"Well, we've had a, um ... a minor incident with a dusthouse in Soho and I was wondering, seeing as how you were asking about fairy dust last night, if you maybe had heard something about what happened?"

"I don't know, what happened?"

"Someone, um ... someone destroyed it. The dusthouse, I mean."

"I didn't think that was possible," I replied, swinging down round the corner of the stairs and accelerating, taking them two at a time. "I've heard all sorts of stuff about armed bastards, about secrets and wards and protection."

"Well, it seems, Mr Mayor, that whoever did this got somehow inside the dusthouse and undermined their defences, because he – or she, I mean, it could have been a she too, I don't know why we let these patriarchal prejudices colour our opinions even now, do you? – but anyway, he or she cracked the floor beneath the house and brought it down like a stack of playing cards and, um, Mr Mayor, I was just wondering if maybe you'd, maybe, heard something."

"Sounds like an inside job," I intoned, pushing back a door that led past steam-filled kitchens.

Another door, marked 'Alarmed – Do Not Open'. I opened it; no alarm went. A narrow street, where lorries delivered fresh towels and little pots of jam.

"The fairy godmother is said to be a little annoyed ..."

"Well, that's a shame."

"Mr Mayor," – a hint of desperation was breaking through even Kelly's chipperness – "you are okay, aren't you? Only I know it's none of my business but I really do worry about you; I'm sure you're not eating enough ..."

"My God, Kelly, we've known each other for maybe twelve hours and you're only two words away from asking me if I've been to the toilet." I was at the end of the street, smell of the river close by, not sure where I was going but determined to get there fast.

"I'm sorry, Mr Mayor!" she nearly wailed down the phone, "but it is my job to be concerned and I really don't want to step on your toes and if you need a little space, then of course I'll give it to you, but we really must . . ."

I turned the corner, and saw her. Young, but face eaten up by more than time, pasty skin threaded with blue, thin mousy hair, thick faded duffel coat, heavy rucksack, sleeping bag stained with dirt and, even in the thick biting cold that ate away the city's other smells, even here, she had the beggar stink of doorways, ash and sweat. And she was waiting for me.

"Call you back, Kelly," I said.

The beggar looked at me, unimpressed. I looked at her, waiting. Then she said, "Domine dirige nos."

I held out my hand, the scars hidden beneath the fingerless glove, and we shook. "Sorry I missed your call," I said. "I was out."

Her eyes were pale and serious. "The Beggar King needs to talk. He's been looking for you."

"Sorry about that. It's all been a bit . . . you know."

"He'll be at Tottenham Court Road for lunch."

"I can do that."

She turned to go, then hesitated. "Hey – you really the Midnight Mayor?"

"I've got one of those faces, haven't I? Everyone seems surprised."

"We liked what you did to the dusthouse. Fucking stupid, mind, but doesn't mean we didn't like it." And before I could open my mouth to reply, she walked away.

I had some time to kill, before time came round to try and kill me.

Templeman had said to keep my head down.

The manner of doing so was left up to us.

And somehow, without quite knowing why, we found ourselves heading for the Underground, and the train out west.

Back to Westbourne Park.

Back to the football pitch with its wall of graffiti where, some nights ago, one kid had died and four had done nothing about it, and a shadow with claws had stretched itself thin across the watching eye of a post office CCTV camera, before vanishing without a trace.

Back to that all-white eye with its staring black pupil, painted onto the wall.

By daylight, the eye seemed brighter, too clean and clear. The brickwork showed through the rest of the paint on the wall, but not this. The painted-on eye had an unhealthy sheen to it, and where I'd written the words IT HAS CLAWS across its surface, they'd already been cleared away, leaving only the tip of the 'I' and the end of the 's' on either side of the eye. No local council moved that fast, or targeted any one bit of painting so specifically.

That was good; that was something we could use.

I looked around at the nearest houses, searching for a helpful pigeon or roaming rat whose eyes I might borrow for a moment, and was surprised to find someone looking back. A curtain twitched in a window of one of the better-kept-up houses. I went up to the front door, which was almost mirror-bright with fresh paint, and thumped with its polished knocker. Eventually the door opened, on a new brass chain, and a woman's voice said, "Yes? Who are you?"

It was a voice taught from an early age that what was said wasn't nearly as important as being heard. A pair of well-manicured magenta nails was visible, above the toe of a white fluffy slipper.

"Good morning, ma'am," I called out. "My name is Matthew, I'm from the local council; may I come in?"

"Do you have ID?" she asked, in a tone expecting the answer to be no.

"Of course, ma'am. Can't be too careful, can we?"

In my wallet I found a library card, and flashed it with one finger over the 'library' part. As she looked, we pushed gently against the fog of her suspicion, whispering to her to look away. The human mind is not an easy tool to work with; too many things are waiting to go wrong. But when it's focused, on the one thing you want to affect, manipulation becomes easier.

I smiled as she waved me into the hall, and kept on smiling as I followed her into a living room with shiny pink wallpaper bearing a floral pattern, and thick swagged curtains. There were prints of nineteenth-century hunting scenes, and a coffee table freighted with magazines on the perfect home. We sat down in lettuce-green armchairs opposite a vast TV. The place was saturated with the stench of air freshener. She said, "Is this about the complaint?"

"Your complaint?"

She was in her early fifties, with hair dyed to blonde so often it now looked stiff as brushwood. Her skin was freckled under a fading tan, and her watery blue eyes were framed by lashes longer and darker than a murderer's walk to death row. She wore a white towelling robe over a cream silk nightdress cut too low for comfort.

She said, "So it's not about the complaint?" I glanced around for salvation, and saw that one of the magazines, dedicated to sporting gear for the country gentleman, was still in its plastic wrapper and addressed to one Mr S. P. Dixon. I took a deep breath and said,

"Mrs Dixon . . ."

Seeing no doubt or anger, I plunged on.

" . . . I'm afraid I'm not here about your complaint, although obviously we take these things very seriously. I'm here about the incident a few weeks ago just across the street from here – you remember the one?"

"You mean the one I complained about?"

"Perhaps if you could tell me the nature of your complaint . . ."

"Which branch of the council are you from?" she asked, eyes narrowing.

"Special resources. About that complaint . . ."

"I blame the parents!" she exclaimed. "The ones who don't do their job properly. I mean, I'm sympathetic to their situation, I understand that not everyone can be born to do everything, but if you aren't going to look after your children, if you don't feel able to provide that level of attention, then you shouldn't do it."

My smile was locked and loaded. "So . . . you complained about the local kids?"

"Well of course. I mean, someone has to step up and take responsibility. They'd come round here at all hours shouting and drinking and intimidating passers-by. Do you know, one of them actually asked me if I'd go into the shop and buy him cigarettes?"

"Really?"

If she'd had any suspicions of me, she was now swept up by the sheer momentum of her indignation. "Naturally I informed the police, but they didn't bother, they never do. And the council – I hope you don't mind me saying this, but I feel very strongly on this point – the council never respond to a situation until it's too late."

"So the local kids had been . . . antisocial?"

"That's how it starts, isn't it?" she said. "I mean first it's drinking, and shouting at strangers, and before you know it you've got people being mugged and windows being smashed. There's an atmosphere of fear these days, and what are they afraid of? They're afraid of young, unemployed teenage men. Who are often black," she added. "I mean, I know it's horribly politically incorrect to say it, but I really do feel that until we face up to a few harsh truths in our society, we will never be able to cure it."

"The kids . . . mugged people?"

She hesitated before giving a triumphant cry of, "No, but it was clearly going to be their next step!"

Unable to make better sense of what she said, I demanded, "What can you tell me about the night of the murder?"

"A murder?" she echoed sharply. "I didn't think the police were calling it that."

"A boy died," I replied. "It was, by all accounts, not pretty."

She shifted in her seat, knees together, back straight. "One of them must have done it. I mean, of course one of them must have done it; even the police should know that."

"You think the boys . . . killed their friend? And they're just pretending to be . . . whatever it is they've become . . . damaged . . . in order to get away with it?"

"Yes," she said. "That's what I think. Logically, I mean."

We stared at her long and hard. Hers was the flat, spaced-out speech of someone behaving perfectly reasonably. The pattern of her thought had been laid out in paths which could only be followed in one direction. You couldn't argue with that.

"Did you hear anything?" I asked.

"No," she said. "Whatever they did, they did it very quietly. Cold-blooded, I'd call that."

"See anything? Something . . . out of the ordinary? Anything that perhaps you might not have told the police, because it seemed . . . too unlikely?"

"I'm afraid not."

"But you were in, the night they died?"

"Oh yes! I was the one who called the Neighbourhood Eye, in fact."

I paused, then sat forward. "The Neighbourhood Eye?" I asked.

"Yes. I'd seen those boys come down here before, and I knew their being here meant trouble, so I called the eye."

"Mrs Dixon," I said, taking it one word at a time, "I need you to tell me about this Neighbourhood Eye."

"It's a new thing," she explained. She reached over to where a fake crocodile-skin handbag sat on a table beneath a curling steel lamp. "I was part of the Neighbourhood Watch of course, but you really need the entire community to pull together to make those schemes work and, of course, these days no one's really heard of community, have they? So when I heard about the eye, it seemed so much more appropriate. Ah –"

She pulled out a card from her wallet, and passed it to me.

It said:

Neighbourhood Eye
The community support group for citizens
concerned about crime.

At the bottom it gave a telephone number.

"Where did you get this?" I asked.

"Oh," a tone of seeming surprise, the innocent discovering that the world itself isn't as innocent as they'd hoped. "From a friend."

"Which friend?"

"Rumina."

"What does Rumina do; who is this Rumina?"

"She's the wife of one of my husband's business partners. My husband works in development – have you ever had one of the protein drinks that they sell at gyms? They're trying to expand the market, make it more . . ."

"And what does Rumina do?"

"Finance, of some kind. She explains it sometimes, but not very well. I must admit I thought she was a bit of a trophy wife, so young, but actually she's surprisingly bright."

"Does the company she work for have a name?"

"Yes, but ..." a huff of irritation, "is this really relevant? Neighbourhood Eye provides an excellent service – a service, I think, which the council should be providing itself, otherwise what is the point of us paying our council taxes?"

"Mrs Dixon," I cut in, "if I was to say to you, 'witchcraft', what would you think?"

"I don't know. I'd hope you wouldn't, as I can't really see ..." Her expression was one of confusion, as she wondered exactly what manner of fruitcake she'd invited into her home. I changed tack, hoping the moment would pass too fast to register. "So on the night that the boys ... on the night whatever happened happened, you rang the Neighbourhood Eye?"

"Yes, I did. They were extremely supportive."

"So what did they do?"

"They said they'd talk to the police. They have connections, you see."

"And did they?"

"Well ..." she shuffled her chair, "I don't know. I assume they did. But all that ... the trouble ... clearly happened before the police arrived."

"What time did you call the Neighbourhood Eye?"

"I think around seven-thirty."

"And when did the first police cars arrive?"

"Around half past ten."

"But this was after the death?"

"Yes."

"How soon after?"

"I don't know. The first I knew of it was when the police cars arrived. I thought it was them, the Neighbourhood Eye, responding to my call. I didn't realise until they started taping off the area what had happened."

We sat pondering her words. "May I keep this?" we asked, indicating the card she'd handed to me.

"If you must."

"Rumina," we added.

"What?"

"We'd like to know what company Rumina worked for."

"I'll ... phone my husband," she stammered, moving towards the door.

"Good," we said, standing up. "We'll come with you."

She made the call.

We stood behind her as she did. It doesn't take a knife or a gun, or a promise of either, to make others afraid. When it's you and a stranger in an empty house on a quiet day, every floorboard is suddenly a blunt weapon, every kitchen fork destined for your eye.

She had called a switchboard, rather than her husband's direct phone, and asked to be put through to Mr Dixon. The receptionist didn't smell the rat that Mrs Dixon was trying to feed.

When she got through she said, "I'm very sorry to bother you in a meeting ..."

His voice was clear enough for both of us to hear. "I'm not in a meeting."

"Aren't you? I must have made a mistake."

Mr Dixon's voice was important and uninterested as he said, yes, she probably had.

She said there was a man who claimed to be from the council.

He said to tell this man to do something about the bins.

She said the man wanted to know which company Rumina worked for.

He said who the fuck is Rumina, what does this man care anyway?

She said, you remember dear, Rumina, Jeremy's wife, you remember Rumina?

He gave a too-big exclamation of realisation and said yes, of course, funny little woman. I watched the back of Mrs Dixon's ears burning as she stammered, well yes, Rumina, who does she work for, it's really important, perhaps her husband should come home and talk to this council man in person, yes?

He said don't play silly buggers I've got work to do I'm sure you'll handle it all perfectly fine wait a second ...

A pause on the line while he hollered at someone in the distant unknown of his office. We waited. Mrs Dixon smiled at me, the crooked, terrible smile of the mortally afraid.

Then Mr Dixon came back on the line and said he didn't know what all the fuss was about anyway but yes, he's got the company, do you need to write it down or something?

No, she didn't need to write it down.

He told her.

She said, please come home.

He said, have you been drinking? I'll be home at eight, and hung up.

She put the phone down with trembling hands and looked at me. Tears were beginning to well in her eyes. Alone in the house with a man who would not leave, who stood over her while she talked on the telephone to a husband who didn't understand, and who had given her a few words to say that could, for all she knew, be the last she ever spoke. Her lips trembled as she tried to speak.

I smiled. "Don't be afraid. I'm here to help."

She stammered, "R-Rumina works for a company called H-Harlun and Phelps."

I let myself out of the house.

The chain clanked shut on the door behind me.

Harlun and Phelps.

By day, financiers to the vastly overfunded and mysteriously well-invested.

By night, cover office for the Aldermen themselves, protectors of the city of London, guardians of magic, defenders and ostensible all-purpose good guys, battling the unnamed things that are out to get you, in the bleak and lonely corners of the dark.

Harlun and Phelps.

Corporate cover company for the Midnight Mayor.

The big white eye was watching from the back of the football pitch on the other side of the street.

A big white neighbourhood eye, on which no paint could dry, watching without blinking.

Had it watched, the night four kids lost their souls and a fifth was torn apart by a murderer no one had seen?

I walked without direction, and called Nabeela.

She said, "Hey, you got news?"

"Sort of. Look, you know when you went to try and get the Midnight Mayor to help before? At the office?"

"Yes . . ."

"Did you tell anyone there what it was specifically about?"

"I tried to, but they didn't listen, wankers."

"Nabeela, this is really, really, *really* important. Have you heard of a thing called the Neighbourhood Eye?"

"Uh, yeah, sure. It's like this group of local residents and stuff who look out for each other. They, like, call round if they think there's trouble. Why?"

"When you went to Harlun and Phelps, did you tell anyone about it?"

"No, why the hell should I? Hey, what's this about?" Her worry was starting to bleed through the telephone line.

"Trust me?" I asked.

"Dunno. Guess I don't have much of a choice."

"I need you to do two things. I need to meet, and I mean, soon, and I need you to absolutely, under no circumstances, say a single bloody word about any of this to any Aldermen, anyone connected to the Aldermen, or anyone you think may be connected to the Midnight Mayor."

Now her voice was ice-hard. "Okay, freaking me out now. What the fuck is going on?"

"What are you doing this evening?"

"I dunno, chilling? Watching the TV, having a microwave meal, chatting with my mates? I'm guessing you've got something particular in mind, right?"

An idea was forming; a horrible, cold idea.

It had a high-pitched sound that echoed inside my head, and when the street light cast its shadows along the twisted places of my mind, this idea had claws.

But first I had a meeting to attend.

I caught the bus into the centre of town.

Tottenham Court Road was the street of a thousand TVs, slicing past the heart of Bloomsbury like a strip of solder along a sea of silk. Clots of buses and cars lurched north from the tight corner of Oxford Street, too tight for the bendy buses cranking their way around it. By the same corner loomed the tower of Centre Point, where not so long ago my sometime teacher and I had discussed blood and betrayal and it had not ended well. To the north, University College Hospital sat like a child's picture of what a hospital should be, all green and white with big potted plants in the foyer and a shop by the door selling peanuts. On the stretch of road between, you could buy anything you wanted, so long as it sparkled, shimmered or beeped.

But so much affluence attracted others. In Warren Street Underground station, or pressed up by the walls of the big glassy banks, huddled in tattered sleeping bags or with bits of cardboard at their feet saying 'Hungry, please be generous', were the beggars. The city flowed around them like a river rolling over pebbles. Some passers-by would tut and proclaim, "Why should I give up my hard-earned wages for people who can't even pick themselves up?" – while the response from those who thought themselves not so much cruel as merely practical was, "They'll only waste it on drugs."

With individuals playing so poor a role, caring for the city's beggars fell to institutions. Behind a plot of tarpaulined market stalls, selling rucksacks, embroidered scarves, and mobile phone cases fallen off a lorry, a low red-brick church was half hidden by the bare branches of a group of plane trees. At the back, narrow steps led down into a small public hall, designed in the belief that versatility trumped character any day. Steam rose from a large vent and, inside the hall, long trestle tables stood in rows. The sound of conversation bubbled, and the smell of bread, leeks and tea washed over me like a hot shower on a cold night.

It was a soup kitchen. It even served soup, out of a great bubbling vat full of potatoes, but an effort had been made to diversify the menu, adding pasta in tomato sauce, and bread and butter. This was a place for the down-and-out of every form. Old men with vividly broken blood vessels in their bulbous nose, young women with tired eyes and ragged hair, men in donated suits far too smart for their perished trainers, women in two coats over a cardigan down to their knees who chatted about getting to the next place, and young men hiding the place where they'd recently been cut. A priest in black vestments and white dog collar moved between the tables, ready to hear stories and tell tales; two women in pink aprons and blue rubber gloves washed up dishes beneath a sign that said 'Jesus is My Light'; and by the door of the chapel a pair of plain-clothes detectives drank tea and talked quietly with the rector, trying not to look out of place.

A woman came up to me and said, "Can we help you?"

"I'm, uh ... looking for someone."

"Among the homeless, or one of us?"

Surprise showed briefly on our face, but her smile was innocent enough.

"I'll just look around for him," I mumbled. Our eyes swept the tables, but the familiar face was nowhere to be seen.

Something cold brushed by my arm. I jumped, fingers tensing, mind reaching out for the nearest source of power, ready to strike.

Nothing there.

I thought I heard ...

... a pair of footsteps, heavy hard boots moving on the floor ...

... and for a moment the rank smell of skin so unwashed that sweat and dirt had solidified into a secondary layer.

I forced my hands to my sides, and said at the empty air, "Don't muck about."

I heard the snap of a cigarette lighter just behind my left ear. He was leaning against the wall, hands cupped around the flame against a wind that wasn't there. His beard was big and dark, flecked with grey-white and dirt, his hair was scraggy and long, thinning to a bald patch, his eyes were stained with yellow gum, his skin so mulched over with the dirt of the city that it gave him an almost caffeinated quality, his clothes the remains of a once-pricey waxed coat, corduroy trousers worn shiny in places, and a thick sweater full of holes. The cigarette lighter was stamped with the words SMOKING KILLS, and as he dropped it into his bulging coat pocket he drew a long breath and snorted out a thick white cloud.

"Most people don't bother to look," he said at last, through crooked brownish teeth.

I followed him up the stairs to the outside world. He had a torn heavy bag on his back, all flaps and half-glimpsed tubs of 12p pot noodle and a smell that the open air did nothing to alleviate.

"How's being Midnight Mayor treating you?" he asked as we turned down a little street full of cheap mobile phone shops and the smell of chips.

I shrugged. "You know. Everyone's got a problem and muggins has to fix it. How's being Beggar King?"

"Cold for the time of year."

"Sorry I missed you earlier . . . "

He waved it away dismissively. "You've been busy," he replied. "Running, fighting, leaping, blowing up dusthouses, all that. But hey — try not to do it again, okay, it's not like I'm made of money or whatever, you know? You eaten yet?"

"What? No. No, I'm okay, though, thanks."

"Cool, because I wasn't offering."

We headed west into Fitzrovia, Bloomsbury's disreputable sibling, along a street of terraced houses, their grandeur diminished by the pizza parlours and sandwich shops in their gutted ground floor. The city was turning out for lunch: students queuing at little vans smelling of chilli and beef, men and women in sharp suits debating whether to go for French on the grounds of quality, or Chinese, where it might be quieter at the back, builders with steaming mugs of tea pausing beneath their scaffolds and couriers grabbing a quick sandwich.

"So you know about the dusthouse," I said.

"Of course I know," he tutted. "Bloody stupid, wasn't it?"

"Yes. I think that's fair."

"How long until you reckon the fairy godmother finds you?"

I shrugged. "He doesn't yet know that it was me."

"Don't be bloody dense. Phone rings in the middle of the night, hi there's this guy here says the Midnight Mayor is out to get me and whoops, what do you know, the dusthouse just sinks into a hole in the ground; you think he's not going to make a few connections?"

"I can hide."

"Not forever, you can't."

"You think he might hold a bit of a grudge?" We passed the open door of a curry house, smells of saffron and cumin washing out onto the street.

"You're funny, Swift," said the Beggar King with an idle flick of cigarette ash from his wrist. "Not many Midnight Mayors are funny — I like that about you."

"I'm guessing you didn't ask me to come for a wander just to talk about my career prospects."

"You know what? In my infinite wisdom and because I'm public-spirited, I actually did."

We rounded a corner, heading through the back streets south of Marylebone Road, houses growing taller, cars growing sleeker and parking enforcement even more strict. People passed us by and didn't even glance our way. It was something more than blithe ignorance; a slick turning away of the eyes before they'd registered the thing to avoid, a calm change of course that meant people crossed the street a good fifty yards away without fully comprehending what they did. And there it was, the smell behind the smell, something in the Beggar King's odour of dirt and sweat that was more than just biology, more than just time; it was a signal straight to the brain that whispered, *nothing to see, nothing to know, walk on by*. It was a spell of invisibility, rolling off the Beggar King, as natural as tears by the graveside.

"My career?" I heard myself ask. "What do you mean?"

He chuckled. "I like you, Swift," he explained. "I mean, you're about as fucked up as they come, but you're my kinda fucked up. You're a self-destructive infant with the power of a giant, but you've got respect for the little guy, for the fuck-ups like yourself, and I like that. Takes one to know one, and that."

"Thanks, I think."

"It'd be a real shame if you were killed too soon."

"I feel the same way."

"And thing is," he concluded, scratching his ragged beard with nails like thick yellow bone, raced through with dark grey fault lines, "I really hate the dusthouses."

I said, "Is it . . . the way they walk and the way they talk, or something a little deeper?"

"They fuck up lives," he replied, voice darkening. "I know what they say – if someone wants it, someone's gonna provide – but that's not it. They choose to provide. They look at the whole of human existence and go 'Yeah, we'll do that, and it's someone else's fault that they get fucked, because we don't make them take, we don't make them buy, we just provide.' And that is shit. That is a lie. That is the words of that man who isn't human, who isn't one of many, part of a city; men should walk lightly on the earth, for the millions of others who must follow where they have trod, and the dusthouses, they do not tread light."

I said, "Okay. So we agree. What now?"

"I need to know what you saw when you went inside. Into the dust-house. What did you see?"

"I saw . . . someone die. I saw men in overalls gather up fairy dust that had . . . I . . . we saw enough that . . . we . . . why?"

"I need to know if you saw my people."

"Why?"

"Did you?" he growled, and there it was, that sudden stillness in the air, that smell of something inside the smell; he was the Beggar King, he'd been in these streets since the first man starved for want of a coin and the first child wrapped rags around its feet to stop the bleeding, he was as old as the cobbles themselves – no, much much older – and he was glaring right at me.

"No," I stammered. "I didn't see any of your people in there. I'm sorry. I wasn't . . . I wasn't looking for them."

"Didn't figure as much," he said, and the moment passed.

We walked on past a Georgian square with tall railings, where men in overalls were blowing rotting leaves into great piles on the grass, while others hung fairy lights in the bare trees. He said, "When I heard you'd got in, I figured, cool, my favourite mega-mad sorcerer is getting his head in the game, I can use this. My people are everywhere, eyes on every street, but there are some places where they can't go. We are shadows on the street corner, not kung fu fighters or shit. We don't have the strength to go up against the dusthouses and win."

"Me neither. Last night was touch and go, by a means that probably won't work again." I hesitated. Then, "Why did you ask about your people? Fairy dust is expensive, from what little I know, as well as destructive. Why would your people be involved?"

"They wouldn't. Not with that."

"Then . . ."

He waved me to silence, took a final draw of his cigarette, and trod out the stub, exhaling thick smoke. "People go missing all the time. My people are not tied down by anyone or anything. Sometimes they go into a home, sometimes they find a friend, family. Sometimes they die. Some do drugs. Most don't. I'm not their judge. Then this!" He slammed his fist into his other hand. "I didn't think the dusthouses would be so stupid to try, but if they have then it is an offence against all my kind."

"Done what?"

His voice was low, but still carried clear. "My people ... my subjects, my kin ... we disappear and no one asks questions. No one asks where we went. But we see everything. It's been happening for several months now, a few people at a time. They wouldn't have run, they didn't fall through the cracks. I can judge the character of those who would, and these were not they. They just vanished."

"Murdered?"

"No bodies have been found."

"But you think ... ?"

"There was one. Her name was Ai. She was an illegal, who was tricked into this country and ran away from the brothel where they kept her. She found us on the streets, and we protected her. Then one day, she disappeared. We looked for her for three days, and could find no trace, but Ai was a woman determined to survive, and finally, at the end of the third day, we found her. Or rather, she found us. She'd escaped from a house in Enfield. She was dying. Her body was crumbling before our eyes, her entire form turning to dust. We tried everything we could, but the poison was already in her blood and within just a few hours she was dead."

"I'm sorry."

"That's cute, but kinda meaningless, so save it. The Midnight Mayor protects the city, not the people."

"So I keep being told."

"We went to the house in Enfield, of course, but it had been cleared out. We are not detectives or warriors, Swift, our skills are ... of a different nature. You asked for my help in the past, and I refused it, because it would have endangered too many of my people. Now I'm asking you for your ... " – the word filled him with distaste – " ... help. Fairy-dust poisoning takes months, sometimes years, to reach its ... inevitable end. Ai was clean when she vanished, and three days later she was dead. I want to find out why. Do this for me, and the beggars will forever be your friends."

As he gave me an address, I pinched the bridge of my nose, trying to drive back the fatigue from behind my eyes.

I asked, "Why would the dusthouses poison Ai?"

"That's what you're gonna find out."

"How long has this been happening?"

He shrugged. "Not so easy to say. The junkies, the runaways, the lost, the freezing, the ones who lie down and won't lift their heads up, I can be there for them, I'll sit by them when no one else will slow and be still, but there's gotta be a calling. Sometimes people wanna die alone. Makes it hard to judge these things. But as you ask, and since you're wondering, I'd say a few months. Maybe almost a year, silent and soft, like foxes on grass."

"A year?" I choked. "Why didn't you tell the Aldermen?"

"I did. They said they couldn't do anything."

"Did you do your scary face?"

He glowered at me, then gave a giant, crooked grin. "Hey," he said. "The Aldermen, it's all about protection of the city. Big maps, big boroughs, big cars and big streets. They forget about the dirty alleys and the quiet places, which is thick of them, because that's where the cruellest stories happen. But I guess they've been busy – I mean, you do kinda pull in the major-league trouble, don't you?"

"It's a chemical thing," I retorted. "Pheromones to attract psychos."

On the corner of a pedestrianised passage that ran down to the rumble of Oxford Street, the Beggar King paused. The air was cold; great plumes of white vapour were rising up from the heating systems of the buildings all around. He seemed about to speak, so I waited.

"Swift," he said, "there's a thought I should run by you, in a spirit of social-minded cooperation."

"Yes?"

"You can't win this thing alone."

"Is that it?"

"That's it."

"That's a real comfort."

"You've survived a lot of things that most wouldn't have; I respect that. But how'd you survive?"

I shrugged.

"You let others die for you," he explained. Our fingers tightened at our sides, something glinted in the corner of our eye. He smiled and tutted. "You mayn't want to hear it, but I'm the Beggar King, it's my gig to say it and my right. You can't win alone. Think about it." He let out a long breath and flashed a smile. "Well, that's it from me, nice to have this little chat with you, bye bye, so long, don't cock it up or be a stranger, wear your gumboots in the rain and all that, ta-ta!"

He spun with surprising grace and started striding towards Oxford Street. I called out, "Hey!"

He paused, glancing back. "Yeah?"

"If I'm alone then no one else gets hurt."

"Nice thought," he admitted, "but basically bollocks. After all, you can't save everyone!"

He loped off towards the end of the street, and the crowds parted without knowing what they did, and swallowed him up.

I walked.

Walking helped me think.

As we moved, our fingers caught at strands of magic trailing on the cold air, wrapping them as if with spiders' silk. Sorcerers went mad so easily, minds and bodies forgetting what it was to breathe, unless it was to breathe an air bursting with noise and smell, shared by a thousand lungs before.

I thought about the dusthouses.

I thought about the Neighbourhood Eye.

About the Beggar King and his warnings.

About my apprentice, Penny, and all the things I didn't want to happen to her.

About Templeman walking his dog.

Kelly Shiring on the other end of the phone.

Nabeela demanding to see the Midnight Mayor, so that he could solve all her problems.

Callum staring at nothing.

Morris Prince sweeping up fairy dust from the factory floor.

Meera.

Thoughts were measured in footsteps, not words; time, in distance travelled, not seconds lived.

Then we were at Trafalgar Square, looking down at where the kids sat, kicking at the empty air, on the four giant lions, waving proudly from above the signs saying 'Please do not climb'. Not long ago, I'd come here with my would-be-murderer and a ghost, and we'd talked about darkness, and regret and guilt and hell, and the outcome of our conversation was a death that shouldn't have been needed.

I thought about words written in steam on the bathroom wall.

YOU CAN'T SAVE EVERYONE

And without quite realising it, standing there and looking at a busy, bustling nothing of hundreds of busy, bustling people, I reached a decision.

I called my apprentice.

"Penny!"

"Yeah, Matthew," she replied, "not that I'm not, like, totally wowed to hear from you or nothing, it's just that when you call me usually it's to tell me to cancel my date because of, like, mega forces of death and shit, so sorry that I'm not more 'Yay' to hear from you, okay?"

"You're still annoyed?" I hazarded.

"I told Femi that your appendix had exploded."

"I see."

"He offered to come to the hospital with me to see if you were okay."

"Wow."

"That's what I fucking thought! I mean, you know how hard it is for someone, even someone as kick-ass as myself, to find a decent bloke? I mean, it's not just that I've got a few lifestyle issues what with the major-league magic shit, it's just men; I mean, *Jesus*, you'd not think we were the same fucking species, you know what I'm saying?"

"Penny, fascinating as this is . . ."

"I'm all like sat there giving out signals, and I mean, you know what my signals are like, I'm not what you'd call a wilting flower or shit, and they're all like 'so yeah, babes, see you when I see you' or whatever . . ."

"Penny!" She paused, her silence a sharpened blade. I flinched back from it and added, meekly, "Lovely, wonderful Penny, my amazingly wonderful and incredibly talented apprentice who I completely appreciate giving up an evening of romance and . . . well, romance . . . for my worthless sake . . ."

"Nice try," she grumbled.

" . . . lovely Penny," I went on desperately, "how'd you feel if I asked you to help me out with a little field exercise?"

Suspicion filled her voice. "What kind of field exercise?"

"Nothing too bad. A little summoning. A little binding. A little chat with a thing with claws."

She complained.

She said something about keeping a low profile from mobsters and how summoning monsters wasn't part of the brief.

She grumbled a bit more.

Then she said yes, just like she'd always meant to, and said she was hanging up now, to go and get supplies.

This was good.

This was the beginning of a plan.

We felt very . . .

. . . executive.

I went in search of the next step.

Marchmont Street was a second-hand place.

A place for second-hand books, on second-hand subjects. Tomes on the best skiing resorts of the 1970s, magazines railing against the Yom Kippur war, novels about sex in the era of Thatcher, thrillers translated direct from the Norwegian and tourist brochures to countries that still felt the need to mention their former Soviet status in diplomatic documents and, probably, the national anthem. Even the food felt second-hand, from Chinese noodles reheated behind a plastic screen, to solidifying cake proffered at £2.50 a pop. To the east, Brunswick Square was a pass-me-down housing project built in an era when jet packs were the future, and latex was the fashion-to-be. It was a place of mixing worlds, where the tides of the city's magics met and spun around each other like water vortexing around a plughole. It was loud and quiet, new and old, busy and still, a good place to find pretty much anything and nothing in particular.

The only sign to the place I sought was a board above a doorway between a minicab company and a video rental store. It read:

INTERNET CAFÉ
£2.50 an hour.
Free coffee.

At the top of a gloomy flight of stairs a door stood ajar. It led to what had once been an office, with faded white ceiling panels and scuffed carpet tiles, and which now held the paying public as well as the humming of computers. A desk by the door held, as advertised, a kettle, a box of teabags, two tubs of instant coffee offering the full range of flavour from caffeinated to decaf, and a jar of teaspoons, and a young man sat there behind an ancient second-hand PC, reading a book about Macroeconomic Development Policy in the Twenty-First Century.

I paid my money and helped myself to coffee, then retreated to the deepest, furthest corner of the café. Logging on, I went straight to the internet.

Aldermen believed in email. They went electric every time, rather than walk ten yards and say something to your face. To make us cooperate with this oppression, we had recently been given an email address and a password to Harlun and Phelps's internal mail.

My inbox was surprisingly full. Harlun and Phelps did a good job of blocking most of it, but some had slipped past them.

From: unknown
Subject: Great Opportunity!
Hey there, have you heard about this amazing opportunity to work from home and make money, money, money?
From: tllbppwb@bprmail.com
Subject: Limited offer – must end soon!
Worried? Nervous? Feeling your performance may not be what it should? For $50 this revolutionary treatment could change the way you feel about your body . . .
From: getgr8orditrying@helthyuz.com
Subject: Have you heard?
Hello friend, Im writing to tell u about a great oportunity to get fit fast, no pain no cost, just the new u and ur new amazing life . . .

I flagged it all, every bit of spam in the system. Then I kept on working.

The Aldermen's internal server had contact lists for all emails. I searched for Rumina, and got seventeen hits, all beginning with 'R'. I sighed, and started typing.

The first email I wrote was sent to myself, and it said this:

Rumina –
They know. They saw the eye, the white eye with no colour in
its middle, staring out from the wall, the eye on which no
paint will stick. They saw the claws, shadow claws in the
night. They spoke to the kids, the ones who survived, the
ones with no souls left, who spoke about the screaming that
only they could hear. They saw the bodies. They know what it
is. They have to be stopped.
 • Your Friend

I sent it to myself, waited for it to arrive, then pasted into the
address box every single name on the Aldermen's list that began with
'R'. Then I added a note at the top, and the note said:

Hey –
No idea which one of you lot is Rumina but I get shit like this
in my inbox all the time, so could someone please deal with
it, okay? The last thing I need is some pretentious wanker
spouting cryptic bollocks to make my bloody day.
Swift

This done, I looked around to make sure no one was paying too
much attention, got down on my hands and knees, and crawled under
the desk. The hard drive of the computer was tucked away down here,
padlocked to the floor, the fans whirring busily, a little green LED flashing brightly. I pressed my ear up against it, listening to the hum. It was
warm, a high vibration that buzzed at the back of our teeth. I pressed
my palm against the side of the machine, felt that particular tingling
beneath my fingers, and closed them tight, drawing power into my
hand. It took a while: what I needed from the computer was very specific. A spark, a shimmer of amber-gold magic, a whisper of energy
that, when asked if it felt like going fast, would answer that mere light
speed was for losers.

It was the magic that lurked just the other side of the Ethernet
cable, that buzzed behind the sound of the telephones, that crackled
when the radio was tuned to a new station. It was rich and ready and
ours to command and, as I drew my hand back from the computer, it

came with it, a tiny blob of snapping, spinning light which bulged and warped inside my cupped fingers, aching to be free. I crawled out from under the desk, slipped back into my chair with a nonchalance worthy of a mobster, opened up my email one-handed, and selected attachment.

The screen asked for a file.

I looked left, I looked right and, feeling unobserved, I pressed my palm against the screen. The sphere of stolen, fan-pitched power between my fingers spread out for a moment like a bubble about to burst across the screen, which blurred briefly from side to side. Then the stolen light melted into the screen with the quiet whoosh of drivers powering down. And where there had been nothing, now there was a definite something attached to the email, a file without a name, a spell sat waiting in the wire.

I shook the last of the heat of the computer from my fingertips, and sent the message on its way.

There was one more email to send.

I found as many spam messages as I could in my inbox, and copied them into one email. Then I huffed on the screen, so that a small cloud of condensation showed up any grease, and on this canvas I started to draw with my finger. I drew the signs of the circuit breakers and the viral wizards who liked nothing better than to make their monsters out of static. I drew the symbols of the cultists who heard gods in the radio waves and found demons lurking behind every other line of code. I drew ancient runes, of some thirty years' provenance, discovered by junior staffers at IBM the day someone chose 'abort' instead of 'retry' from the wrong menu, and the wrong thing came crawling out of the computer screen. For a moment we considered drawing the ultimate sign, our own: blue electric angels with wings made from the sounds in the telephone wires, which the ignorant mistook for interference. Sometimes, though, even we felt the need to be discreet.

When we were done, the screen could barely contain the weight of magic written into it. Pixels danced giddily, and the computer's own anti-viral program was starting to pop up warnings of errors so arcane it didn't even grasp if they were errors, rather than something close to evolution in progress. I copied in the email address of every Alderman on the system, and pressed send.

Just one thing left.

I went onto the internet, and printed out the address, with maps, of every major recycling and refuse centre within ten miles of central London.

It was, we concluded as we signed out of the system, a thoroughly worthwhile use of an hour.

I headed towards Aldermanbury Square.

But not to Harlun and Phelps.

Not yet.

Instead, I went to the office across the street, found the service entrance, and swaggered in with the confidence of someone who had every need to be there, every desire to be there and, above all else, every right to be there. The one bored security man having a fag by the back door looked straight over me, eyes sliding off the thin coat of enchantment that I wore: a spell of nothing-to-see-here more than of genuine invisibility. If some spells could only be woven with the correct gestures, this was an enchantment that relied upon a very special gait – neither too relaxed nor too hurried, but utterly confident of its purpose.

A gloomy concrete-floored corridor passed the kitchens and a buzzing server room. I found a set of iron-railed stairs down into a dark basement smelling of damp and mouldering insulation foam. Great pipes ran along the ceiling, clad as if by NASA in wire and foil; doors were unmarked and even the spiders had despaired of weaving their webs in the dirty corners, confident that no self-respecting life would be seen down here to be eaten up.

I found the door I was looking for by the quality of the tubes running through the nearby wall. Here they were great fat square things, neither humming with electricity nor hissing with heat, but carrying from their flaps at the bottom the unmistakable stench of the rubbish heap. The lock gave after some persuasion, into a room like an over-sized cupboard, lined with metal shelves on which sat bottles of pink cleaning fluids ordered in bulk cardboard boxes. Blue overalls were hung up behind the door, and unfastened lockers revealed sad collections of latex gloves, dust masks, ancient stained copies of free newspapers, and a woman's abandoned sports shoe. At the back of the room was a group of three vacuum cleaners – great beasts on four wheels each that could have sucked up the curious cat and its doings without even showing a bulge. They sat now, silent monsters, waiting for something interesting to happen in their lives.

And there it was.

That interesting thing.

Almost impossible to spot unless you were looking for it: in the third cleaner along, there was a bulge in the bag that might have been ...

... easy to imagine but no, definitely, look a little closer ...

... just might have been the world's smallest foot.

I pulled the vacuum cleaner away from its neighbours and rapped with my knuckles on top of the main body of the beast, where pipe met dust sack.

"Hello?" I said.

Silence.

"Look," I went on, "I'm just going to open up the bag, but I don't mean you any harm, so try not to bite, okay?"

Silence.

"Okay," I continued. "Going to open it up now."

I eased back the catches on the lid of the machine and twisted the pipe free. The grey fabric bag inside was swollen like a bloated toad, with twists of human hair around the place where it met the pipe. I prodded it with a finger and, when nothing happened, reached in my shoulder bag for my Swiss army knife. Opening up the knife, I cursed for a few moments as I looked through a mixture of mini-hacksaws and fish descalers before finding the blade I wanted; then, with a slow, shallow slice, I opened up the bag.

Dust.

Unsurprisingly.

Thick grey dust that had been compressed into solid lumps of felt, tangled in with human hair and bits of old coffee granule and the occasional shard of broken glass. The odd lumpen food remnant too – crumbs, bits of rotting salad leaf, here a tomato-coated bean, and the smell of a sneaky cigarette, the ash swept up in the medley; but, mostly, felt-like dust.

I said, "Don't make me reach in there and get you, okay?"

Silence.

"I mean it. I'm a genuinely friendly and approachable guy, but both those qualities get dented by rummaging around inside refuse sacks all day."

Then something moved inside the bag.

A small cloud of particles billowed upwards like reversed snow, hung in the air, then began to descend again. A thing as grey as the felt that surrounded it inched up through the depths and curled around the tear in the bag, so lightly as to hardly twitch the fabric. It was a finger, comfortingly dry, but grey and coated over with thick dark hairs that stood upright like the quills of a porcupine, in which all the dirt of the vacuum sack tangled. It was no bigger than a child's thumb, but had one joint too many in its little length. A tiny hand barely large enough to support the finger itself followed, then a wrist, also quilled over. Then a shoulder, skinny enough that I could have held it between my thumb and finger and still had room for a book on law, and, finally, an eye, the colour of rotting brown sludge, with an oval pupil of inky blackness. The eye was in a head which was almost perfectly round and possessed of tiny ears and more black quills, with a bare slit for a nose and a mouth far too wide and thin. This opened, revealing, first, two rows of pointed yellow teeth, and, just behind, a set of bristles not unlike the hairs of the vacuum brush itself, in which bits of old rotting paper and crunchy pieces of bone were tangled.

The eye blinked at me, first with one pair of eyelids, then with another, translucent one that oozed thin greenish oil. Another eye appeared, and from beyond the bared teeth came a low, long hiss of animal intensity.

"Hi there," I said. "How's it going?"

The hiss came again, every black quill standing a little stiffer on the creature's arm and head. It was an imp, no taller than a waste-paper basket and no wider than the head of a broom. Judging by the rustling beneath it in the bag, it was not alone in its den.

"Now, before you get the wrong idea," I went on, rooting around in my bag, "I'm not here to complain or anything. You guys want to make your nest down here, that's fine with me. I have no problem with imps per se, and if you don't mind me, I won't mind you et cetera."

It twitched a little in the bag, crawling a cautious inch or two higher, a bit of a knee visible, toes hooked into the soft sides of the bag.

Feeling that I had its attention, I smiled my brightest smile, took a deep breath and launched straight in.

"Have you ever considered the possibilities of a real-life relocation?" I sang out. "Have you been yearning for more, better, brighter, fresher garbage? Do you dream of making the pilgrimage to the rubbish sites where all good imps find heaven? Well today might just be your lucky day!"

I flashed my printed-out maps and lists of refuse dumps around the city, pattering on as the imp's head turned this way and that to follow the papers moving through the air. "This is an exclusive, one-time offer, a chance of a lifetime to move yourself and your tribe to possibly the filthiest, foulest, most dust-filled havens of London. Don't worry about the dangers of the trip, just load yourself up into the vacuum cleaner of your choice and you will be transported at no extra cost to your dream rubbish site. All you have to do in return is temporarily to move your nest one building over, and wait for the relocation team to give you a lift to your new nesting ground."

I paused. There were other things moving in the vacuum bag now – two more little heads were surfacing to peer up at me. "So ... uh ... sound cool?" I asked.

Three imp heads turned to each other for advice. Then the imp furthest out of the bag looked up at me and made a noise, a thin, high whine that was as much broken metal plates in a smoking machine as it was words, but which, over an agonising stretch of time, resolved into "W ... wh ... whhyyy?"

"Guys ..." I said, opening my arms in an expansive gesture of defeat, "I cannot tell a lie. I want to go poking around inside the offices on the other side of the street, place called Harlun and Phelps, and they've got wards and defences and CCTV and stuff, and I really don't want to have to muck around with all that, and don't get me wrong, it's cool because I'm their boss, but sometimes to be a boss, you've got to be a bastard, and it'd be really, really handy if, say, a whole tribe of imps spontaneously relocated – just for a little while – to their basement, as that might cause a little disruption which I could use to ... you know ... do my thing ... And obviously it would only be a temporary thing because, as established, you could ..." I thrust the maps of the refuse sites towards the imps again, "you could soon be living in your very own de luxe rubbish dump along with your mates, minions and spawn!"

The imps looked at each other again, then one reached out and carefully folded its overlong fingers around the edge of the paper. The A4 sheets were too large for the little hands that held it, and flopped limply in the imp's grasp, so that two of them had to grasp the sides to hold it steady. They peered in at the pictures, leant right up close, eyes blinking busily away at images of piled-up rubbish and shattered goods, rotting food and churned-up mud. Finally they lowered the paper, looked up long and hard at us, and said, "Ssss ... sswww ... swwweear?"

I pulled off the glove on my right hand, revealing the thin white scars, twin crosses of the Midnight Mayor, that some tit with a plan had once hacked into our skin. "I swear by the badge of my office, by the running of the water in the pipes and the singing of the electricity in the wire, by the red-eyed dragon that guards the city walls and by the blue electric fire of our blood, that if you do this for me, I will guarantee that you and all your tribe are given access to the rubbish dumps of your choice. Let me have no shadow, let my feet make no sound upon the stones, if I should lie."

Behind the little imp eyes, little imp minds contemplated this; black dust-tangled hairs rose and fell across their backs with every fast breath. Then, without any outward sign of change on their features, one gave a single nod and hauled itself out of the vacuum bag, spilling a cloud of dust, and hopped down onto the floor. The others followed, two, three, then a fourth, slipping out of the warm grey depths of the bag; and there were other sounds too, a rattling overhead and a scrambling underfoot. The imps waddled out into the corridor with the over-stretched gait of creatures not used to walking when crawling was an option and, from the pipes and dirty ducts of the building, the rest of the tribe followed.

They popped out from the torn yellow foam that wrapped around the heating pipes, slipped messily down the trash chutes and crawled out of the dumpsters against the grey walls, slithered out from the hollows behind the toilet cisterns and unfolded from the shadows above the boilers. They rolled off the dust-covered cable trays and popped out of the ducting in the floor which carried half-chewed bits of Ethernet cable and slime-smeared trucking. The smallest were barely rat-sized, the largest and oldest the size of a small Labrador. They scuttled along the walls, leaving greasy tiny finger marks; they waddled along the floors, trailing felt and grit as they moved; they slithered along piping in the ceiling, spilling a small cloud of dried-up dirt like wedding confetti on their kin below.

They carried with them the thick sweet stench of blocked-up drain-pipes and cigarette ash and, though they made no words as they moved, they clicked at each other busily, the little slither-snick of every sound you've half thought you half heard in the night, or the creak-crack of the cold pipe warming up, now mimicked perfectly from their tiny throats, and with surprising volume. A dozen, two dozen, maybe thirty, thirty-five imps came crawling out of the forgotten pieces of the building, following the one who still held in its hand the curling papers showing the route to their refuse dump of choice, like a sacred text pointing to the holy land. As they reached a small grate at the end of the corridor, this was levered up with practised skill by four of them, and feet-first the imps jumped one at a time, down into an unpleasantly warm darkness that stank of grease turned to sludge. I watched them, listening for the shuffling below the floor that the ignorant would have called water in clogged-up pipes or the sound of furniture scraping the floor. The one with the paper was the last to jump, shooting me a look of determination as he was about to slip into the darkness.

"Sss . . . sss . . . swee . . ."

"I've sworn," I answered. "I won't forget."

It gave a sharp nod, imp-to-imp respect, and dropped into the darkness below.

The sun was already starting to wonder what was the point, when I let myself out of the office across the street from Harlun and Phelps and went in search of a sandwich and more coffee. I was beginning to feel the weight of the day: a broken night of a few scant hours' sleep leading into a broken day that promised another broken night. My hours had always been erratic, but this mortal body we wore did not hold up well, and was infuriatingly prone to fatigue and injury.

I went to the same coffee shop where – had it only been yesterday? – I'd talked to Nabeela about monsters and the Midnight Mayor – ordered a sandwich and coffee and sat in the window to wait.

I judged that the imps would need at least twenty minutes to start making their presence felt, and a good forty to get the Aldermen's undivided attention. Imp infestations were more of an annoyance than a true menace to health and hygiene, but the arrival of a whole tribe at once could disrupt even the most flexible of organisations, and the Aldermen were not renowned for their out-of-the-box crisis management. I'd picked up a newspaper from a rack by the door, and skimmed the headlines. A climate conference had ended in failure in Mexico; a politician had been caught sleeping with the wrong person again and was very sorry to have done that to his wife, two kids and the public at large; the elderly were being pushed further down the priority lists of the NHS as government cuts meant there weren't enough nurses to go around; and someone called Micky had won some competition to sing the role of a giant insect in a musical version of *Metamorphosis*.

Across the street, in the glass foyer of Harlun and Phelps, the security men on the front desk were growing unusually animated as they talked to each other, phones pressed to their ears.

I took another slurp of coffee and kept reading.

Members of the public had expressed anger at delays on the Underground, price rises on the buses and the general state of the roads; a children's TV presenter was photographed puking into a gutter in Mayfair; an interviewer earnestly wondered whether the actor on the next page had found it harder to play a monster or the monster's maker; and Sally the Panda was finally pregnant, and expecting twins.

Outside, the world turned. Rush hour was approaching: a sharp buzzing on the air, a rumbling beneath our feet, the time of day when every sorcerer's heart beat faster, and your teeth ached like you'd washed them in vinegar. There were now Aldermen in the foyer of Harlun and Phelps, also on the phone, looking fraught. A gaggle of suited men and women was forming by the entrance, some holding briefcases, most with nothing, moving with the herd gracelessness of startled deer. More were arriving with every second, and now there were men in yellow bibs, herding office workers towards the main door like dogs controlling a flock of sheep. My phone rang but, seeing Kelly's name, I didn't answer. I watched from over my newspaper and, as the lights started going out on the top floors of the building, I couldn't hide my smile. Imps weren't usually trouble; but who could blame them if sometimes they nibbled through the wrong cable to the wrong circuit?

The building started clearing in proper fashion now, the men in yellow bibs acquiring signs that said 'Muster Point A' and 'Evacuation Officer' to wave above their heads. The street was a roiling mass of suits, only the black-clad Aldermen still inside; most of the workers were giving up right there and slinging their coats on. They began to disperse towards the Underground and buses, or bickered over who was first to hail a particular cab.

Around this scene of discordance the city flowed, not oblivious, but far too self-absorbed to give a damn, or worse, be *seen* to give a damn. Staring was for tourists, and this was not a tourist part of town.

Except . . .

Except, there were one or two men showing more interest than they should. Sorcerers are, regrettably, far too busy learning the mysteries of the arcane arts to catch evening classes in espionage, but find yourself hunted long enough and you start to spot the signs. Was it normal for utilities vans to be parked for so long on a double red line like that, next to a sign proclaiming 'Danger – Works in Progress', with no sign of a worker working on anything more than a mug of tea? Sure, there was the British work ethic to consider, which valued the cuppa more than myrrh or gold, but this was the Corporation of London, where tomorrow happened now, and yesterday was a land for losers. And how handy that the van was parked just opposite Harlun and Phelps, with an excellent eye-line to both the main door and the service entrance. And, now I looked again, was that woman in a suit really taking so long over one cup of coffee, when she'd been sat by the long café window for as long as I'd been here?

What had Templeman said?

Nothing helpful or precise, but he'd been afraid enough to warn us against the fairy godmother. Don't blow stuff up, don't do anything spectacular, don't get caught by the godmother.

Would they really be so pissed off that they'd try and lift the Midnight Mayor from under the Aldermen's noses?

It took a lot of balls to cross an Alderman, let alone a whole bunch of them, and as stake-outs went, it didn't get much more ballsy than this. If they were here for me, they'd be armed against the usual spells

I wore to distract the casually wandering eye. Something more extravagant would be called for. I reached for my mobile and dialled 999.

"Hi, yeah, um, look, I don't know if this is the right number to call or anything, but there's like, this van parked across the street, yeah, and there's been these men going in and out of it for a while now and I didn't think it was anything, I mean, it may not be anything yeah, but they've been like, parked there for ages now and I, uh, work just opposite yeah and they're like not working around here or anything and I just think they're a bit suspicious, you know?"

"How do you mean 'suspicious', sir?" asked the emergency operator.

"Well, you know, they're parked on a double red to begin with, I mean, what the hell is that about, and they've been like putting stuff in the back of their van in, like, this really odd way, you know, like, making sure no one's watching or stuff. I don't know, maybe they robbed a hardware store or something, because I saw some of the stuff they're putting in there and it's all like nails in these big big crates and big barrels of chemicals and stuff."

I prayed for a bright – and yet not too bright – operator, and struck lucky. "What kind of chemicals, sir? Did you see any labels?"

"I really don't know," I said. "I mean it's not like I stopped to look that closely, you know, I mean, they felt really hostile, like how you didn't want to get too close or anything. But the van smelt really funny, I mean like, you know um … like cleaning stuff? That really strong cleaning stuff, like um … ammonia or something?"

It took the police four and a half minutes to arrive.

They even brought armed response with them, surrounding the van with heavily armed bastards all in black.

Bomb disposal took only another three minutes, by which time the men in the van were lying in handcuffs on the ground, and the woman at the end of the café window had made a discreet exit.

I piled my dirty cup onto my used plate, folded the newspaper back onto its rack and, as the first bomb-disposal officer started to thread his fibre-optic camera into the back of the parked van, I headed for the goods entrance of Harlun and Phelps.

It was a building in distress.

Frantic men and women with tool boxes scurried through the

corridors as, across the building, systems that had functioned perfectly well an hour and a half ago creaked and groaned like a pregnant volcano. And there was something in the walls. No one was saying it, but at every little rattle or snap out of place, eyes flashed nervously upwards, fingers tightened around spanners, breaths were sucked in a little too fast. From the lower floors, where pipes met wires met dust, the imps were digging their nests. Loudly, disruptively and, above all else, unstoppably. Imps have little concept of distress or discomfort, and once they've got a mission they'll carry it through with thick-skulled relentlessness.

I summoned a service lift, but the button didn't light up. A man nearby in the white apron of a caterer was having a sneaky fag beneath an air-conditioning vent that sounded in a full fit of anaphylaxis.

"Whole fucking system's gone weird," he replied when I asked what was up with the lifts. "If it's not the fucking boilers then it's the fucking computers; some kind of virus got in and now everything's just gone tits up."

I turned away, cursing under my breath. I'd aimed for disruption when I spammed the Aldermen's email server; what I hadn't planned on was having to take the stairs up fourteen floors. I pushed through the doors to the service stairs, and started the long, dull climb up to the Aldermen's office.

Our knees hurt by the eighth floor.

At the fourteenth we stopped to gasp down air, hands on our knees, head bowed forward. When we felt less light-headed, I pushed the stairwell door and let myself in as quietly as possible to the Aldermen's office.

In my absence, no good had come to these orderly open-plan desks.

Computers everywhere were in distress. Some were merely off, their screens dead and black; some gave the high-pitched scream of smashed keyboards stuck on overload; some were actually smoking, black noxious fumes rising from their hard drive and flattening in a cloud under the ceiling. Someone had tried to fix things by pulling out the very cables from the wall cavity; but this had been too little, too late, and now the fluorescent lights were flickering and buzzing, in the kitchen the kettle was boiling dry, and the hot-air fan in the bathroom was switching on and off with giddying speed. The virus I'd sent had got into the system and then some. I let myself into my office in its tucked-away corner, and locked the door behind me.

I waded across to my desk through the mess of papers, and turned on the computer. Having thought for a while, my computer loaded, and sat patiently to attention. I opened the email and there it was: my original bit of spam, copied no less than thirty-three times from thirty-three different email addresses as it had replicated through the system and been bounced right back to me from other Aldermen's infected computers. It had worked better than I'd hoped, and we felt a stirring of juvenile glee as I deleted the messages, wiping their cursed symbols off the screen with the back of my hand, and tossing the sickly bubble of static and power into the nearest mains socket to fizzle out with a spurt of blue electricity and a burning smell.

I went to my sent messages log, found the email I'd dispatched to the seventeen Aldermen whose names began with 'R', pressed my fingertip into the screen just below the file attachment sign, and pulled my finger back. The attachment fizzed out loud as it came with me, a thick tangle of amber-gold light that coalesced back into a bubble in the palm of my hand. I closed my fingers around it, trapping it like a butterfly. Then I logged off, shut down my computer and, just in case, stood back and threw a fistful of rolling electricity up its power cord and into its hard drive. The back of the machine popped open, ejecting loose circuitry and a gush of dark smoke that made our eyes water. I wouldn't have it said that of all the computers in all the building, mine had been the only one that miraculously wasn't affected by the spam attack.

Back onto the main floor the Aldermen were too busy arguing in their office for anyone to pay attention to the open-plan space outside with its wrecked and smoking machines. I ducked nonetheless below the line of the desks, then felt along the floor until I heard the whispering of data cables beneath the thin carpet, and pushed my bubble of light down towards it. The light wriggled beneath my hand like a trapped worm, then burst outwards, liberated and splitting into smaller parts that rushed out across the floor like a cloud of frightened fireflies. I watched as these baubles of light writhed their way up cables and slithered round the edges of screens, bounced across the tops of computer drives and finally attached themselves like golden leeches to the back of a select few computers.

Seventeen computers, to be exact. With luck, the same ones I'd infected with the tracking spell, attached to the email and lit up for me to see.

I moved between the rows of machines, looking for one which stood out brighter than the others, and ducking behind desks whenever a door opened. At one point a team of people marched towards the lift, remembered it wasn't working and, grumbling, headed for the stairs. Later, a door briefly opened and I heard a voice say, ". . . imps don't just move nests during the mating season . . ."

I spent ten minutes skulking between computers, looking for the glow of my tracking spell. It was a piece of resonant magic that grew brighter when closer to similar enchantments. In theory, wherever someone had rashly forwarded the original message with the original spell attached, the spell was replicated, creating a brighter signal for the tracker to latch on to. All that was left was to hope that Rumina, whoever she turned out to be, had forwarded the email to all her friends.

Fifteen recipients I found easily, but couldn't detect much above a simple signature on the spell; no signs that the email had been forwarded by the reader or marked as anything but junk. The sixteenth proved to be an IT specialist, whose voice I could hear from fifteen yards away through his office door. "Stupid fucking firewalls can't even keep out fucking spam is this what we fucking pay subscriptions for NO I DO NOT WANT TO UPGRADE TODAY . . .!"

Finding the seventeenth and final computer took me another twenty minutes, and it turned out not to be on the fourteenth but on the thirteenth floor. A repair crew was already at work down there. They were a mixture of IT consultants in short sleeves and comfortable shoes trying to reboot the system's smouldering remains, and black-coated Aldermen attempting to exorcise any spam by less traditional means. The Aldermen weren't doing badly – they'd wheeled in a TV and were plugging it into every electrical appliance, with a coil of thick bare-ended wire, drawing out the spell into a whirlwind of static rage that hammered against the inside of the TV but couldn't quite break through the screen. It would be a laborious process, but in time they'd do it: then they'd start asking just who'd spammed their system, and how. By then we meant to be gone.

There was, however, no avoiding being seen. Giving up on subterfuge, I marched across the office with all the arrogance I could muster, beelining for the toilets and keeping my glances left and right for the glow of my tracking spell to a minimum. One Alderman looked up with the beginning of recognition.

I cut him off before he could speak: "Fixed it yet? No? For Christ's sake, what can be so bloody hard?"

Inside the toilet I counted to thirty, slowly, then set my face into a grimace of displeasure and marched back the way I'd come. I hadn't seen the glow of the tracking spell on my first sweep of the floor, and couldn't look again without arousing suspicion. The TV in the middle of the room was starting to smoke alarmingly, with cracks of light around the edge of the screen where the spam spell was breaking free. Several Aldermen were flapping in frenzy as they tried to incant the spell into submission.

No glow to the right, no whiff of tracking spell to the left, doors beyond, all closed, names, titles on little plastic plaques, Accounting, Logistics, Law Liaison, Finance, there was a wall ahead, we'd have to leave if we were going to avoid suspicion, where the damn hell was that last tracking spell?, more doors, more offices: L. Carver, Department of Demons, Shades and Shadows; I. Latimer, Office of Unlicensed Exortations; P. Ling, Non-Human Resources; R. Rathnayake, Treasurer.

I turned without thinking, without slowing, put my hand on the last door handle, thanked every god there was that it was unlocked, pushed and let myself in with the ease of someone who'd planned on just this turn of events. The door clicked shut behind me and I remembered to breathe.

The office of R. Rathnayake, Treasurer, was small and ridiculously neat. What personal touches there were – here a picture of Big Ben, there a photograph of a woman feeding pigeons in St James's Park – had been put up with such impersonal precision that they detracted from the soul of the place, leaving it more hollow than before. The in-tray was stacked medium high, the out-tray was filled to bursting. A stainless-steel mug stood on a cork mat and held a plastic filter. A computer sat on the desk, new and shining and, like all the others, hissing and spitting from the weight of enchantment trying to eat up its circuitry; meanwhile its keyboard was clean but worn, and the screen angled towards a large chair designed for maximum discomfort and a healthy spine.

I looked, and there it was, the glowing leech of my tracking spell, lurking in a USB portal at the back of the computer and pulsing gently as it fed off all the magic I'd emailed into the system. I prized the spell free with my thumb and snuffed it out in a little pop of power. Then I sat down in front of the screen and dragged out into my hand the thick static mess of enchantments corrupting the hard drive. It came free as another bubble of spitting electric-white chaos, and I chucked it into snapping oblivion via the nearest mains socket. That done, I found myself looking at a desktop of such precise organisation that we felt a part of our soul shrink to behold it. All the rogue files, random shortcuts and clips of odd tunes that cluttered the computer system of the average mortal had been filed away, under such catchy titles as – 'Committee Minutes, Preliminary', 'Committee Minutes, Final', 'Fiscal Reports 09-10' and 'Fiscal Reports 10-11', each of which contained yet more subfolders, and folders beyond that. I flicked through without knowing what I was looking for and, finding nothing exciting, opened the email.

My luck, always a fickle little madam, grudgingly gave the nod; she was already logged in.

And there was my email, flagged in red. She'd forwarded it to five people, creating the replication that my tracker spell had found so tasty. Three had replied: C. Caughey, L. Holta and T. Kwan. I knew one of them already: C. Caughey – Cecil, for who knew what crime his parents had chosen to punish him – an Alderman who took executive magic to its logical conclusion, choosing to spend his days ordering others to do legwork for him while he sat at the top of the office bewailing the trials of being in management. T. Kwan I'd also heard of – had there been a Tommy Kwan who'd once sent me a memo about waste in the catering department? Two hadn't replied – B. Fadhil and

and really it had been too good to last, hadn't it?

and R. Templeman.

I leant back in the chair, lacing my fingers behind my head.

Templeman.

An Alderman who actually bothered to talk.

Too good to be bloody true.

I read down.

From: R. Rathnayake
To: T. Kwan; L. Holta; R. Templeman; C. Caughey; B. Fadhil
Subject: Fw: What the hell is this?
Just received this. How does he know? What does he know?
Who's talking? There are clearly references to both the eye
and the culicidae here – does he know the rest? We need to
meet as soon as possible; tell no one else, we don't know
who to trust.
Yours,
Rumina

I scrolled over to the replies. T. Kwan was brief and to the point:

From: T. Kwan
To: R. Rathnayake; L. Holta; R. Templeman; C. Caughey; B.
Fadhil
Subject: Re: Fw: What the hell is this?
Usual place, at six?
Tommy

L. Holta had a lot more to say.

From: L. Holta
To: R. Rathnayake; T. Kwan; R. Templeman; C. Caughey; B.
Fadhil
Subject: Re: Re: Fw: What the hell is this?
Rumina –
What the fuck is this? What kind of stupid half-witted game is
this man playing? Does he know what he's dealing with?
Jesus this is a total bloody balls-up. Someone must be
talking to him. Let's just hope he's too bloody thick-headed to
understand what it means. Suggest we close the eye for now
until we can find what's leaking, and make sure the
summoner is out of town. The last thing we need now is Swift
getting his hands on the culicidae.
Lucy

Finally, C. Caughey, clearly not a man for whom crises happened, gave a more considered view:

> From: C. Caughey
> To: R. Rathnayake; T. Kwan; R. Templeman; L. Holta; B. Fadhil
> Subject: Re: Re: Re: Fw: What the hell is this?
> I'd say this isn't actually that bad. Of course it's a little alarming that someone is attempting to inform Swift about the eye, but the details they've given are extraordinarily vague and he clearly isn't taking them seriously. The only thing which I can foresee likely to make the situation worse would be overreacting now and provoking him into an actual investigation. All in all, a lucky escape.
> Yours,
> Cecil Caughey
> Chairman
>
> P.S. There's some sort of file attached to this email – has anyone else got it? My computer's playing up and the IT boffins are useless at talking sense.

No one had bothered to answer this last question.

I sat back in Rumina Rathnayake's office chair, nudging it from side to side with my foot. Then I went through her desk. For the most part its contents were depressingly practical – stationery, a packet of aspirin, a couple of over-the-counter pick-me-ups for when the day got hard, a shirt in a dry-cleaner's bag and, right at the back of one drawer, a pack of cigarettes, two of the dozen gone. I nudged the last drawer shut, turned back to the computer – and froze as, with a merry beep, the screen flickered and a new message appeared.

> From: R. Templeman
> To: R. Rathnayake
> Subject: Re: Fw: What the hell is this?

I opened it carefully, half expecting it to bite, a virus bigger and badder than the one I'd made, leaping out of the screen with tooth and claw.

Just words, nothing more.

They said:

Swift, I know you're there. I know you're reading this. Imps do not spontaneously move nests without incentive, and I can recognise a Trojan spell on my hard drive.

I apologise for the situation – it was not my intent to deceive you unnecessarily on any count.

I will call you this evening, if that suits you.

As always, I would urge you to desist from any rash action, and please be aware that this building is being monitored by the fairy godmother's associates. I assume that the business with the hoax bomb alert was your doing – it will not be enough. They will find you, unless you move quickly.

Rest assured I remain,

Yours sincerely,

Richard Templeman

I looked at the email long and hard.

Didn't bother to reply.

I shut the computer down, picked up my bag, and went in search of an exit before we hurt somebody.

The sun was down. Not the thick blackness of night-time down, but winter down, when office lights were still on and people still moved about inside, above the busy street. It was drizzling, in wisps of water too light for gravity to make much effort. Outside my office the police cars were gone; so too the van in which I'd reported a fictitious bomb.

Meanwhile, given such dubious calls on my old number, along with what I'd just read in Harlun and Phelps, I needed a new phone. I pulled up my collar, shrugged my shoulders forward against the cold wind, and headed for Cheapside.

Thirty pounds bought me what I wanted from one of the glass-fronted shops that gleamed along this bus-crawling street. As the man at the counter activated the sim card, I looked at reflections in the glass cabinets nearby that held the most expensive phones, the ones which told you how to look and what to wear, and regarded sending messages as a demeaning secondary function. I also watched the other customers in the store, and the people passing in the street. Waiting, I looked for patterns. If the fairy godmother was all he was supposed to be, a team of his watchers could easily avoid being exposed – what I needed was to force their hand. As the salesman laboriously printed a succession of receipts and failed to convince me I wanted a warranty, I slipped out my old phone from my pocket, and wiggled first the battery, then the sim card, free, just in case I needed them again. I slipped my new phone, still in its packaging, into my bag, turned to face the world again, and went in search of trouble.

I started in the Underground.

St Paul's station was only a few minutes' walk away, a shy subway beneath a cobbler's shop rattling with the noise of a key-cutting machine. The station itself was all dirty tile and curving underground concourse, crowds pushing their way towards the down escalators, all black shoes and drizzle-stained overcoats, beeping oyster cards on yellow readers, and the odd lost tourist wondering which way was out.

I went down to the Central Line.

Everyone, no matter how insensitive to such things, who commutes on the Underground has felt its magic. A thick, hot, dirty magic, a power that slaps you in the face like the winds carried ahead of the trains, or pulls you off your feet like suction down a tunnel. A magic that gets under your nails like the grime on the handles of the emergency stairways, that buzzes in your head like the hum of the PA system, that wriggles and twists around your feet like the lines on the Underground map. It waxes and wanes with the hour of the day, but always, and without fail, the Underground is burning with it. Here, more than anywhere else, we were safe.

The eastbound platform was heaving, the trains coming every two to three minutes, bursting at the doors. The trains couldn't take every passenger on the platform at once, so, like ocean waves, the crowds would surge forward and break against the passing trains as they came and went, only to be immediately resupplied from the passages feeding in from behind. Two great fans behind vents were chugging away, labouring to move air around and, though it was cold outside, the warmth on the platforms caused an instant prickling burst of heat. I sat on a bench and let three trains pass, looking out for any and all who weren't fighting their way to the front.

A girl in a woollen hat stood some way off, listening to music on a pair of oversized headphones and, as I looked her way, she finally boarded the train. The second the doors had closed I headed over to the westbound platform; it too was packed, with people heading towards Acton and the furthest, darkest reaches of West Ruislip. A man in a blue shirt and torn jeans followed me and, when I turned to look his way, changed course without a beat, heading for the nearest Tube map like one lost and suddenly aware of it. I waited for the train, got on, stood by the door and, as the alert began to beep, hopped straight back off. The man with the blue shirt was in the carriage behind. As the train pulled away he kept his eyes fixed on the map running above the doors, but there was a flash of irritation in his eyes.

I walked to the furthest end of the platform, and caught the next train heading west. At Oxford Circus I changed, and took the unmarked route between the Victoria and Central Line platforms, moving the wrong way, against the crowd through a one-way system. Here too I was followed, by a boy not fifteen years old, in a big green hoodie and a baseball cap. As I caught sight of him in a concave mirror above the steps down to the train, he lowered his eyes, and swerved onto the opposite platform from mine.

Paranoia and security are only ever a thin line apart.

King's Cross Underground was a mess of old and new, where leaving at the wrong end of a platform could involve walking for what felt like miles of white-tiled passageway. But a more knowing escape, usually by an exit barely marked with a friendly arrow, could, by one escalator and a quick turn to the left, take you where you wanted in an instant. Years of renovation, for the introduction of Eurostar next door at shining renovated St Pancras, had created a mass of shut-off tunnels and half-forgotten walkways that anyone in the know could dive into, in the sure hope that they would not be followed.

My chosen escape route brought me to a high chipboard wall, thrown up across a corridor of yellowing tile and posters advertising films three years out of date. A heavy padlock fastened a makeshift wooden door cut into this permanently temporary wall. I turned my back to the platform and the eyes of the crowd, and ran my finger over the lock, slipping thick, dirt-smelling underground magic, the black magics of the tunnels, into its core; then I twisted, and felt it snap open.

A metal staircase that stank of rat droppings led up through a metal door into a corridor linking the main terminal of King's Cross to its Thameslink neighbour, from which trains ran to such exurban spots as Luton Parkway and Milton Keynes. In the concourse at King's Cross I made my way out past a gold-plated coffee shop offering liquid caffeine in small cups for big prices, and turned east, heading up Pentonville Road towards Islington.

As I walked, I pulled out my new phone and dialled Penny.

"So yeah," she said, the sound of traffic loud behind her raised voice. "I just wanna check a few things with you, yeah, not because I'm not totally on it or anything, but because you know, you're my fucking teacher yeah so you should be like taking a proactive interest in this, right?"

"Hit me."

There was the sound of the phone changing hands, and we imagined Penny Ngwenya, list in one palm, phone in the other, checking off her inventory of goods. "So it's a can of petrol, yeah, a six-pack of beer, a couple of bottles of like, cheap cider or something, or like those alcopop things or whatever, two packets of fags, a can of spray paint, a switchblade knife and like, an abandoned car, right?"

"And some police tape."

"Yeah, I mean, *obviously*."

"Sounds perfect."

"Yeah – you know how hard it was to, like, get the guys at the impound to just *give* me some shitty abandoned car?"

"You're an ex-traffic warden; I thought you'd be up on this kind of thing."

"I just don't want you taking my total awesomeness for granted, yeah? How long until you reckon you're getting here, only I'm freezing and getting these weird looks, right."

"I'm heading your way now, just making sure I'm not being trailed by any mystic mobsters."

"Would these be the mystic mobsters you made me cancel my date for?" she asked sourly, as I turned a corner past a child's giant painted sign proclaiming 'Say No To Drugs and Bullying'. A picture showed a happy family all holding hands against a backdrop of crossed-out needles and pipes. Someone had drawn a pirate's moustache and eye patch onto the father, and blacked out two of the mother's teeth.

"That's them!" I sang out.

"You're supposed to sound way more majorly contrite and shit about that," she grumbled.

"Imagine my face."

"Yeah – that's the problem, innit."

"Look, Penny, there's someone coming to join us tonight . . . "

"Someone dishy and datable?"

"It depends on your point of view, I suppose. Her name's Nabeela, she's a social worker, and if you could try and be extra-polite and sweet-natured and not swear or curse or – or in fact curse in any way until I'm there – then that'd be lovely."

"Are you saying I'm fucking rude?" she shrilled.

I turned past a rack of locked bicycles, heading towards the local police station, blue light shining outside, doorway full of faces you wouldn't want to meet anywhere else. "I just don't want her to be overawed by your awesomeness," I explained.

"Uh-huh. You know, Matthew, you are so full of shit sometimes it's just like . . . "

"Gotta go now!"

"Course you have! . . . Bye!"

I hung up before she could melt the phone. Rounding another corner, by a shopping mall, I glanced in a plate glass window, to see

mother, two daughters, waiting for the bus

boyfriend, girlfriend, bags of shopping going home

one old lady with a shopping buggy

one kid in a blue baseball cap, baggy black trousers, grey jumper

and, bugger me, he was looking right at us

Could just be paranoia.

I went into the mall.

As such places went, it wasn't American in scale. It was a mall in that it had samey shops with samey lighting and samey music, and TV screens in the ceiling showing out-of-sync music videos. I went into a clothes shop at random, picked up a grey jumper and a black hat, went into a fitting room, and waited two minutes. In an out-of-sight corner I then put the grey jumper and hat onto a rejects pile, and picked up a blue jacket and a green jumper instead, bundling them inside my bag. The security guard wasn't paying attention, neither was the fitting room attendant. It was easier to set off the alarm by the main door than it was to disarm it, so I loitered nearby, twitching enough erratic current into the system to set it wailing a couple of times, before making my exit. By then the security guard had given up after stopping several perfectly innocent clients and was on the phone for a repairman.

From within a crowd waiting at the nearest bus stop I checked the people in the street and saw

Big Issue vendor, crutch under one arm, stopping a man with a beard

two women in suits trying to find a taxi

five schoolgirls bickering about the bus

cyclist in black skin-tight leggings unlocking his bike

kid in blue baseball cap, baggy black trousers and, of course, grey jumper, this time being far too careful to be caught looking directly my way, but no getting round it, he'd made me as well as I'd made him and the relationship could only go downhill from here.

I was beginning to understand the urgency in Templeman's voice when he'd warned me about the fairy godmother.

There was just one place, I hoped, where no tracker, however good, could follow.

I caught the bus to the Barbican.

The Barbican Centre was built after World War Two as a massive experiment in communal living. Here, so the theory went, was everything you could want, not merely to survive, but to live in a cultured and educated way. The original buildings had been bombed to obliteration, and out of this ruin had sprung an artificial lake, a theatre, two cinemas, a concert hall, a library, a music school, a secondary school, a conservatory, a gym complete with swimming pool, and an art gallery, all raised up into a complex of towers and walkways designed to give a sense that the Future Was Here Today.

With no fewer than four Underground stations within easy striking distance, the Barbican is a bastion of pedestrianised tunnels and passages, both exposed and interior, surrounded by a sea of busy streets that straddle the join between the studios of Clerkenwell and the financial edifices of the city.

It is also, as any urban magician could tell you, or anyone hurrying to find their way between Barbican and Moorgate, a place where the laws of space and time are put through the wringer.

Its origins did not bode well. Built on top of the old London Wall, it was a place where ley lines met: the stones far beneath still seethed with old magics that crawled out into the shadows at night, and played games with perception. During a time of plague, bodies had been dumped by the thousand in nearby pits, and while all sorcerers know that life is magic, all necromancers would be quick to point out that the cessation of life in vast quantities can often pull off the same effect. The resident population should have brought stability, but there was also a continual influx of people to see shows, plays and concerts, which never allowed the power of the Barbican to settle into one distinct form. It was a fuzzing, unpredictable environment for enchantment, like cold and hot air meeting on a storm front.

It was quiet now, up here on the main pedestrianised level, where the wind spun in sideways and the lights were coming on in the Barbican's three high towers. The scars on my hand itched as I crossed the invisible line of the old city wall, felt it jolt beneath my feet like a live wire. A lot more had been built into the London Wall than just bricks and stones, and just because the bricks and stones were gone, it didn't mean the magic had faded.

I was crossing the wide paved space that had once held an ice rink, before council cutbacks made it a dead zone, another unmarked path in the Barbican's core. Halfway across I knelt and ran my fingers over the paving, feeling for cracks and changes in texture. There were ways to move unexpectedly in the Barbican, if you knew what you were doing; ways to convince place A that it was really location B, and B that, really, it shouldn't bother its little head with things it couldn't understand. The Biker clan had a way of doing this, of moving without travelling, based largely on the theory that since so much of Britain's motorways looked to the human eye like every other bit of motorway, why shouldn't nature be fooled as well?

I felt it: a dip beneath my fingers, a softening in the texture of the ground beneath our feet, and if we just pushed, just right, just *there* . . .

Footsteps moved behind us.

Sound travelled well in this place.

Between the white globes of light on a nearby row of posts, a figure was moving; by his shape and size, a man, and probably one who thought you couldn't put a value on personal fitness. Also he'd brought friends. Here they came, up a wide flight of stairs leading from the main complex itself – the boy in the baseball hat, the girl with the oversized headphones, the man in the blue shirt from the Central Line. Others too, more than a dozen, now surrounded the area. They wore black suits and white shirts that were only a pair of wrap-around glasses away from screaming CIA.

One of them stepped forward.

He too was in black, and had a slightly too-small head on a too-wide neck, dark hair cut to a mere shimmer on his skull, skin that showed signs of having been tanned once, pale blue eyes, and just on the very tip of his chin, a tiny, thin, old white scar. His hands were too big and, as he moved, there was a stench of magic that came with him, a thick odour of iron and salt.

Then he spoke, and his voice was deep but soft, carrying without apparent effort.

"Good evening, Mr Swift. I would like to ask you to come with us."

The others seemed to be waiting for his orders. I wondered how many carried guns. I wondered how many needed to.

"You're from the fairy godmother?" I asked.

He nodded, and said, "May I please invite you to come with us?"

"In a couple of hours?"

"I'm afraid it must be now."

I sighed, still kneeling on the ground. "So you guys know who I am, right? I mean, you've cottoned on to the whole thing about this being my city, my heart, my place of power? I just ask, because it seems like it could be important for people in your line of work to know that sort of thing."

"We are aware, Mr Swift, of your inclinations."

"Then I'll do you a deal. You tell me your name, and how you're tracking me, and I promise not to go spontaneously mega-mystic in a way that would embarrass everyone involved."

"Forgive me, Mr Swift, if I doubt the integrity of your offer. Your reputation has you as one who . . . if you'll pardon my saying so, goes 'mega-mystic' as something of a default reaction to a situation."

I stood up, brushing my hands off on my trousers. I looked up at a narrow stretch of sky between the towering blocks of flats, then down at the cracks between the paving stones. "I didn't get your name," I said.

"You may call me Hugo."

"Hi Hugo," I replied. Then, "Bye Hugo."

They started to move, an instant too late. One of them had a gun half out of his pocket; another was pulling what looked suspiciously like a wand, all coathanger wire and rust, ready to fire. I raised my hands to shield my head and stomped down as hard as I could on the softness between the stones. Anywhere else, I would have hurt my foot, but this was the Barbican, where geography and reality had given up a long time ago.

The earth split beneath my feet, opened with the wide jaws of a blue whale, and swallowed me up.

I landed a second later, dropping out of the ceiling on the third floor, just inside the library, and slamming down onto the crime novel section in a dirtied flurry of paperbacks. The lights were out in the library, and the only sound was the distant noise of pre-theatre chit-chat from the concert-hall foyer. I limped a few paces as blood started returning to my feet, and was as far as the locked library doors when in the corridor outside the first of the fairy godmother's men appeared, barrelling down a glass-walled staircase. They didn't stop to look left or right, but headed straight for me. I cursed, turned, and ran for the nearest wall, where a yellow-painted panel had been welded into place, perhaps to hide trunking and pipes. I reached out for it as I neared, felt the air thicken and split in front of me, and passed straight through without slowing for reality.

There was a moment of giddy darkness full of sparks, a roaring in my ears, a taste of dirt in my mouth, impossible to breathe, then I hauled myself up into the cold open air of a walkway: posters on the walls advertising Japanese kabuki, a Bollywood movie season and kids' playtime club on Sunday mornings. I heaved down air, dragging dark-ness and shadows with me as I ran, wrapping them around me like a blanket, feeling static rise around my fingers and every step shudder through my body as the magic came.

And heard the howling.

It started behind us, then it was everywhere. I changed direction, hands over my ears. Flats below and above, well-tended window-boxes, electronically operated blue metal doors and ranks of faded-letter buzzers. The howling came again, closer this time, and I glimpsed something skidding round the concrete columns of the flats behind me, no taller than a bicycle, no wider than a coffee table and no less angry than a smoking hornets' nest. Eyes flecked with yellow and red above a black coat, and there were teeth, of course but there were teeth, and they were coming right for me.

I ran for the door to the nearest apartment block, reaching again for that slippery hole between what should be and what was, saw the light flicker in the stairwell behind the door, half closed my eyes, and pushed straight on through, staggering out the other side with my chest bursting and a whole construction site drilling at the back of my head. I was inside a hallway; small, square, ground floor, with a lift bearing a sign that said 'We Apologise for the Inconvenience'.

But it was not the same apartment block I'd run into; this was the other side of the lake, with the creature nowhere to be seen. I let myself out back into the night and ran the few yards onto the walkway high above the water. There were three men down there, eyes already turned up towards me and, at their feet, hackles raised and ears drawn back, was a creature that could only be a bloodhound; just not the kind that helped to seek out missing persons. Feed anything enough blood and magic, and you shouldn't be surprised at how quickly genetics adapt.

Cursing, I turned, and nearly collided with two more men, who must have run up the stairs from the lakeside. They weren't even out of breath, and had the rugged, determined look of people who'd long since sacrificed basic mental functions in favour of physical endurance. One carried a piece of glass and metal that might once have been the cathode ray tube from a TV; the other had gone for the simpler gun option. I swung instinctively, sending a blast of hot, vent-smelling air rolling out from the back of my hand. It slammed into the one with the gun, hard enough to spin him a hundred and eighty degrees with the snap of a dislocating shoulder. The other levelled the cathode ray tube at me, lips moving in the beginning of an enchantment. As the thing spat strobe-white fire at me I dove to one side, tasted metal and smelt the nasty smoke of boiling tiles just a few inches from where I'd stood. I ran, felt a weakness in the ground beneath me and dropped down into darkness just as another blast of too-bright light fractured the air overhead.

I landed in the apartment block below, the ceiling re-solidifying overhead. Two children with brown skin and curly hair were watching a TV near where I'd landed on a mass of sheet music and magazines. The smaller girl stared open-mouthed; the older, with more sense of propriety, screamed with the uninhibited vocal power of the young. I ran for the door as, further back in the apartment, a door slid back on rollers and a voice began with, "What is ...?"

... fumbled with the lock, slammed the door behind me. There were already footsteps on the floors above, and I could smell the still-smarting magic of the cathode ray tube, a nasty weapon for a wizard, a wand that was as much X-ray and unpleasant overdosed radiation as it was heat and light. I went downwards, the air growing colder and lights yellower as I descended, felt once again the shimmering power of the London Wall close by. A metal door opened into an underground car park smelling of urine and old oil. A pounding off to my right, and there was a woman and two men, their bloodhound off its leash and coming straight for me.

In the stark fluorescent light, I could see the hound clearly: cracked yellow fangs that pushed its lower lip back, revealing the soft interior of its mouth. Eyes stained the liver-failure yellow of any fairy-dust addict, for reasons that couldn't be coincidence, ears too small for the mass of black head that carried them. A neck thick enough to melt into the body without slowing for the joins, and black fur stained with something slippery, like oil on a duck, but thicker, viscous, and scarlet. The creature's eyes were fixed on me, its nostrils flared; I ran for the nearest upwards ramp, stretching my hands out as I moved, tangling my thoughts in the cars around me.

They rumbled and shuddered to life; first a few, then with brake lights flaring along the length of the car park. Dirty black exhaust filled the low-ceilinged space in moments: there was a haze, then a fog, then a thick smog of carbon-dry dust. I heard sharp claws scutter across the floor, right behind me — and swung round into the nearest pillar, plunging head first into the weakness between here and wherever there was going to be, so long as there was elsewhere.

A moment of spinning darkness, and the sound of barking faded. A burst of heat in the back of my nose, an unbearable ache as, for an instant, I couldn't breathe; then head first out the other side, slipping in a puddle of engine oil and stagnant water as I tumbled onto the floor of another car park, on the other side of the Barbican.

Our nose was bleeding, dry sweat burnt our skin; this body was not designed for so much movement without travelling. I wiped away the blood from my nose with the back of my hand, then smeared the back of my hand across the pillar I'd just fallen by, leaving a thin red trail. Then I ran, every step jolting something soft inside my head. I was at the entrance to the lift foyer before the first shout from the stairs above. I hurled myself into the lift, elbowing a floor number at random. As the lift started climbing, at the first floor I hit emergency stop, then clapped my hands together and pulled them apart, dragging the lift doors open. I was only crookedly in line with the first floor, and had to wriggle on my belly to get out. Finding the nearest toilet, I pushed my way in and looked around for what I needed.

Inside the brightly lit space, a door opened into a cubby-hole containing mop, bucket, packs of spare toilet paper, bottles of chemicals and a large sign saying 'Cleaning in Progress – Do Not Enter'. I grabbed the sign and wedged it in front of the door, then snatched up a roll of tissue paper and the most powerful chemical detergent I could find. Hearing noises outside, I fumbled for my Swiss army knife, tried to find the blade I wanted, got the scissors instead and used those.

A sudden fizzle in the air and the door rocked on its hinges. Though bent in the middle, it held. I looked the other way, then quickly ran my thumb over the sharp blade of the scissors. Another blast of magic slammed the door back; it dangled on one hinge. No time to register the pain; that would come later.

The first bloodhound bounded through, followed by two of its owners. I raised the bottle of chemical cleaner and sprayed a blast into the air. The creature was leaping at me; it took a blast of the stuff right on the muzzle and fell back, its slobber flecked with red. I hit the spray again, filling the small room with the smell of chemicals and, as the black-clad man and woman tried to rush me, I swept my bloodied hand through the fine droplets, gathered them into a fistful of burning acid and threw it straight at them.

It didn't impact; instead it burst outwards in a shimmering explosion of foul-smelling moisture, sudden as popcorn in a pan. The blood was running freely down my hand; I could see the bloodhound's fur stand up at the smell, its pelt oozing scarlet goo in recognition. One of the humans tried reaching through the chemical wall I'd thrown up. As her fingertips brushed the cloud of moisture she snatched them straight back. A second later, and she was screaming as their instant redness turned to bleeding.

As I turned to look for an exit, a voice said from the door, "Now Mr Swift, you are being very unreasonable."

Hugo, the man with the pale blue eyes and tiny scar on his chin, looked unconcerned at my makeshift barrier. I pointed at the yellow sign between him and me.

"Cleaning in progress!" I exclaimed. "Do not bloody enter!"

In response, the wall of chemical droplets hanging in the air contorted and shrank, forming a thick spinning bubble above the sign. As it began to boil I was inside the nearest cubicle and slamming the door shut. Outside were sounds of shock as the men there realised what was coming, and ran.

The spell exploded, splattering smoky chemical remains across most of the room. I ran at the bolted cubicle door, and through it and straight out into darkness.

Tightness, burning, falling, dropping.

In another place, I staggered out of a different toilet cubicle, and nearly walked into a woman wearing a dead fox round her neck, and obscenely large pearl earrings. She opened her mouth to say something indignant, saw the blood rolling down my hand, and went instead for a well-meant cry of "Help, someone!"

It was hard to breathe, as if all the slipping through walls had drained me of lung capacity. I'd stumbled into a box office area, almost empty now except for where a few ushers were setting up for the interval drinks. I made it to a wide flight of stairs, dragged blood across the brass handrails, heard the howling of a dog and doubled back. I sensed a softness in a patch of wall beside a screen advertising art from Soviet Russia and free pilates for the over-sixties, went through it, fell out of the other side onto my knees, gasping down breath: where now?

A ramp, mirror panels overhead, dull white light. At the top, a pair of golden face-masks were, respectively, laughing and crying. I headed for the sound of the street, for open air at the end of the passage. I was nearly there when the first gun was fired, shockingly loud, unrealistically loud, making me wonder if it hadn't been fired at all, if I'd imagined it, since it seemed absurd that reality might pull off that effect. I saw the bursting mortar as the bullet buried itself in the wall in front of me, ducked down, and made it round the corner as two more slammed into the wall, and struck sparks off a metal column. Running feet behind me; in front, a free-standing information kiosk, with a map designed to confuse and a large red blob declaring 'You are here'. I ran at the map, closing my eyes just before impact and skidded through to the other side of the darkness, heart pounding in my ears.

I felt a blast of cold, damp wind. For a while I lay on the ground heaving down air. At length I risked opening my eyes and leaning over to look down. A very long way down. We drew a sharp breath and recoiled: we were on the roof of one of the three towers, having fallen out of an air vent in a clustered mess of heating units and aerials.

Down was so far down that nothing came close to a similar scale of up. The city shone all around. If someone had taken the Milky Way, turned it on its head and spread it across the earth, it might just have competed with the starscape of city light stretched out around, disrupted by nebulas made from office towers lit up LED blue and green, or the dying sun of a sodium-orange-floodlit monument, sliced through by the silver-black ribbon of the river. We stared, feeling the icy blast rush at us and wash us clean. Then there was another howl below, far off. I reached into my bag for tissues, wrapping several round my thumb, my fist, my hand, until I looked like I had a beach-ball for fingers.

I felt rather than heard the movement behind me, the twitch of warmth as reality opened and closed in busy silence at my back. I was turning, a fistful of icy high-up air ready to throw, but he was already upon me, blocking out the light. He caught me a kick to the side of the head that bounced my brain against the inside of our skull and set off a high singing in our ears. As we fell he grabbed us by the hair and pulled us back up, only to hit us again across the jaw, sending the music in our ears to play in our eyes, our nose, our face.

For a moment, all we could see was Hugo's face as he said, not with rage or resentment, "Now Mr Swift, did you think you were the only one who could do that?"

I opened my mouth to make reply and he hit it. I went limp, and he let us go: we bumped with the impact of the roof, and our clumsily wrapped hand flopped out over the edge of the tower.

I managed to wheeze, "Could we talk about this?"

"Mr Swift, I would like to point out," he said, shaking his knuckles as if distressed by the pain *his* punch had caused to *his* hands, "that it was your action which precipitated this whole situation."

I rolled a little distance from the edge. We felt pressure behind our ears, as if they were trying to burst from the inside out. Hugo spared me minimal attention; having taken out his mobile phone, he was dialling.

"Good evening. I require extraction," he said cordially to the unseen recipient. I crawled onto my hands and knees, and as I managed to drag my hand from the floor, grey concrete dust came with it, surging around my fingers like iron filings to a magnet. I drew my hand back ready to throw – and he was there, too fast, much, much too fast, no one moved like that; but he was there, his foot coming up and straight into my midriff. I felt something hot explode inside and wondered if this was how it felt to drink boiling oil down one lung.

Show me that sorcerer who throws spells while hyperventilating, and I'll find a zombie who reads Proust. Our body was flesh; we gritted our teeth and looked up at a sky blurred by our own failing senses.

A voice muffled by all the other sounds hammering for attention in my ear – mostly blood and inaudible screams – declared, "I do apologise, Mr Swift. We will administer appropriate medical attention to you as soon as can be feasibly arranged."

The breath for speech was two lungfuls too many. I wheezed, turning my head away from him and looking down towards the drop, deep and long and into an uncertain darkness. A thought flared at the back of my mind, a thought so hideous that, briefly, we didn't even notice the pain. Somehow I was still wearing my shoulder bag, strung across my chest. It was trying to slip now, trying to fall from the edge of the tower, and only my body weight was preventing it. Hugo was putting his phone back into his pocket, apparently satisfied with his night's work. I felt blood seeping through the tissues around my hand. I tried taking a deep breath, and it turned into a gasp as the ribs on the left side of my body announced they weren't having any of it. I closed my eyes, felt the cold high air pushing back against the burning in my cheeks, felt the slow slide of my bag into the drop, and below – a very long way below – a certain peculiar darkness on the earth.

There was a rattling overhead, the sound of engines getting closer. A helicopter, heading our way. I felt Hugo's arm brush my shoulder as he said briskly, "Now Mr Swift, please let's not be difficult about . . . "

I rolled to the side, pushing myself with the palms of my hands, feet flopping first, then knees, until there was suddenly no choice about where the weight was going and, feet locked together and arms pressed to my sides, I fell off the tower.

Monumentally stupid.

Just about enough distance between here and there to think, monumentally stupid.

Right up there, in fact, for flagrant opportunism mingled with pig-headed imbecility.

Unfortunately, there wasn't time to mull much more on the subject, because there was the ground below and the darkness of the tower rushing by and Hugo looking down and just a moment before I hit and it was all over, there was . . .

. . . a darkness below, a softness in the join between the tiles . . .

. . . a crack in the ground . . .

. . . that opened as we fell . . .

. . . and swallowed us whole.

Reality had a moment of uncertainty.

Gravity had a very serious moment of uncertainty. It still wanted to do its thing, but suddenly the solid pavement that it had been intent on dropping me onto had become a darkness, a space between places, a hole where A met Z and decided that the alphabet in between didn't count. In that time the world considered what to do, then opened up a hole beneath me and dropped me feet-first onto the bonnet of a silver Mercedes.

Reality had a sense of style, if nothing else.

My feet gave out instantly, my knees buckling; the car alarm beneath me began to wail, as did those of its two neighbours. A large me-sized dent took up most of the roof, following an impact severe enough to shear the metal frame away from the windscreen and cause two windows to shatter.

But not dead.

Still not dead.

Somewhere between here and there, gravity had become confused and decided to let someone else sort it out.

I lay on top of the car, until its wailing got too much.

Then I fell off the car and lay on the floor.

I tried getting up.

In vain. Pain exploded across my ribs and down my spine, sent aftershocks into my knees and tingled at the funny bone in my elbows.

I lay back down on the concrete and focused hard on breathing.

Were they following?

Almost certainly. But while Hugo might have been able to move through the Barbican's magical gaps, he didn't strike me as being so monumentally

monumentally

stupid as to try replicating what I'd just done.

At the sound of the car alarms, a man with black shoes and blue trousers was now heading towards me. "Hey, what the . . . ?"

"Police!" I gasped. "I've been attacked, call the police!"

He hesitated, then cried, "Don't move, okay. I'll be right back . . ."

Time to move.

One leg at a time, one muscle at a time, holding our screaming sides as if they might develop mouths and express their pain independently to the world. I made it four whole cars towards the exit before I had to stop, and drag down air. Each gasp brought water springing to my eyes. A few more steps, another pause, then there was the exit and beyond it a short tunnel, with cars streaming to and from somewhere better. Out onto the pavement, which smelt of trapped fumes, and, with one hand pressed to the wall, I began the journey towards the end of the tunnel.

Smithfield.

Had to get to Smithfield.

Not far on normal legs; but tonight someone was doing high-temperature metallurgy in my lungs, and just how long would it be before Hugo and his bloodhound found where I'd gone, how much more time until the howling started again?

We pulled ourself up straighter, nearly shrieking at the pain.

Midnight Mayor.

This was our city, this was our bloody city, this was our place of power, it was ours!

I dug my fingers into the nearest wall, felt heat and dry layers of invisible soot, scratched my nails along and pulled it under my fingers, dragged it in. I let the sound of the cars flood into my ears, felt the engines beneath my feet, tasted the dirt of their exhaust pipes on the air, sucked in lungfuls of it, let the blackness fill me up from the inside. I could feel the rumbling of the Underground below in the pit of my belly, smell the garbage truck on its evening rounds, taste the sweat of the gym a few hundred yards away, hear the singing of the telephone wires, feel the crackling of the mains cables overhead and, below, brush the old ley lines of the old city wall, feel their power shudder up my spine.

My city.

I dragged it all in until my breath was turning soot-grey on the air, until there was a silver-metal shimmer to our skin, until our heart beat in time to the de-dum of the railway over the tracks, until our stomach grumbled to the frequency of engine noise, and then I dragged in more until our head nearly burst with it, until every breath tasted of it and flesh was nothing now, just a thing that had to be moved, a tiny dot inside an ocean, to be swept up by the tide.

I walked, and watched myself walking from the CCTV cameras, and in the yellow eyes of the pigeons, and felt myself walking in the dusty memories of the paving stones, and heard myself walking in the scratched surfaces of the tunnel walls but, in that instant, nothing about me seemed to matter.

Smithfield.

Smell of meat and sawdust.

Smell of coffee and tuna sandwiches.

Bicycle rack, not much traffic, the rumbling of the Underground where the trains briefly emerged somewhere down out of sight.

The Victorian meat market, restored to sparkling new, the dragon of the city watching over it.

St Bartholomew's the Great, hidden beyond a deep archway in its grassy churchyard. Black flint walls faced with white stone, a battlemented tower of red brick above the west door. A saint holding a model of the church looked down serenely, his hand raised in blessing as I limped my way up to the heavy door and pushed it open.

Smell of candles and polish.

Colder in here than outside.

Thin light, barely making the effort.

A thick door of blackened oak, tucked away in a corner and almost hidden behind a sweeping red curtain.

Down a narrow, sloping corridor.

A flight of steps, only one naked bulb shining above it. A ceiling so low, I had to duck my head.

Another door at the bottom, even thicker and smaller. Around it, within a square sculpted frame, ancient carved stonework. As a cruel joke, some medieval mason had included a grinning gargoyle, its tongue rolled out, eyes bulging, like it was being throttled.

This door was locked. I leant on the door for support, raised my fist and, clumsily, I knocked.

An eternity later, someone answered.

"Uh . . . yeah?" asked a female voice. It had the disbelieving tone of all decent people who, at three minutes into extra time with the score-line at 0–0, or whatever extremity was their equivalent, had been called away to deal with a spider.

"Help me!" I rasped. And, this job done, I collapsed.

The era of government cutbacks had not been kind.

In the good old days – and how magicians longed for the Good Old Days – magicians had got healing from wise old folk who knew the secret words to do the secret deeds, and all very lovely it was.

Then some bright spark had pointed out that, actually, most sagely healers only knew ten or so combinations of sacred words and, in this modern age, did you really want a spell cast over you to cure, say, gallstones when in fact what you were dealing with was appendicitis? It wasn't just bad medicine, it was bad litigation. Fairly soon there was a movement to have the practice of magical medicine institutionalised into a more sensible and, above all, monitored form.

Thus the NHS took over the running of medicine for the magically inclined.

The first ward was, by all reports, a shining triumph of modern magical engineering. From dialysis machines designed to leech curses straight out of the blood, through to scanners that could detect any form of parasitical sprite, modern medicine embraced the challenge with vigour and, of course, at taxpayers' expense.

Then cutbacks began. Soon the magical unit found itself downgraded to an abandoned wing of the Elizabeth Garrett Anderson Hospital and told that for anything less than life-threatening wounds, the patient should probably seek to go private.

When the Elizabeth Garrett Anderson was demolished to make way for union offices, the unit had to move again. In an act of institutional defiance, it made its way towards St Bartholomew's, the oldest hospital in Britain.

Not, though, to the hospital itself.

Far too indiscreet.

However, a transfer to the crypt of the church next door – that could be arranged.

I opened my eyes.

Somehow, in the time since I'd knocked on the door, a person or persons unknown had managed to drag me by, I suspected, the armpits, and haul me onto a stone slab. I looked up into a low vaulted ceiling lit medicinal white, from whose medieval corners the stone faces of various mythical beings leered, grimaced and generally took unnecessary satisfaction in the distress of all they beheld. The last time I was here, I'd been temporarily blind; now, I was beginning to regret the clarity of sight.

Then a voice by my ear said, "You know, you're only really supposed to come here if you're, like, being screwed over by magic or shit. I *am* a specialist."

At four foot eleven, Dr Seah was only a little taller than the height of her unfolded stethoscope, even given a pair of black high heels beneath her brilliantly white medical coat. Yet when she moved, the question was not whether Dr Seah could handle high heels – but whether the heels could handle her. Her obsidian-black hair was cut to a straight bob around the line of her jaw, and as she pulled on a pair of latex gloves, she wiggled her fingers inside them with a little too much relish. A stool nearly as tall as she was brought her up to slab-height, where she perched and treated me to a smile brighter than a meteorite and just as quickly gone.

I stuttered, "Being . . . followed."

"Uh-huh," she replied, winding off the tissues still wrapped around my bloody hand and throwing them into a bin. "And you thought 'I know what! It'll be totally groovy to, like, go bleed out on someone else's time, yeah baby!'"

"They've got bloodhounds . . ."

"Oh, I see," she cut in. "So you didn't think 'It'll be totally groovy to go bleed' or, shit – sorry about that, that was totally me jumping to conclusions there, when will I learn? – you thought 'It'll be totally groovy to go get, like, this major-league spa treatment on the NHS to throw off the bloodhounds so that I can continue on my shiny yet quaintly rugged way'. Am I right? I'm right, aren't I? I can see that I'm right; go on, am I right, yes?"

"Gist," I admitted.

"Well!" she announced, prodding my ribs hard enough to make us gasp. "Don't be a baby! I can see why you came here. Oh yes, because for a worried moment there, I thought you might have come to the magical unit, the place where we deal with, like, magical shit, for *mundane* complaints like . . ." She did a tally on her fingers. "Possible concussion, bit of light blunt-force head trauma, fractured ribs and a bleeding bloody thumb . . . instead of all the totally groovy things that I could be diagnosing you with." She leant forward, head bobbing earnestly. "Do you know . . . I have a syndrome named after me?"

"Uh . . ."

"It's the way to go. I mean, you train as a doctor for forever, and then it's like exams this year and exams next year and everyone's trying to work their way up the chain and it takes years to get to the top, so the thing to do, yeah, the thing to do is get yourself some sort of condition that only you know about. I mean, not get it yourself personally, I don't mean, like, infect yourself with these majorly weird things that combine into one majorly mutated super-condition or something . . . although actually, now I mention it, that sounds kinda cool . . . "

"Dr Seah?" I quavered, raising a hand. She saw the hand, gave an "Oh!" of realisation, hooked a trolley with one foot, pulled it across and, before I could squeak, started swabbing at my cut thumb with what felt like the spit of a basilisk dipped in Tabasco sauce.

"Vampirism," she explained as she slapped a large pad over the end of my thumb. "It's where all the new and exciting medical research is at. I thought about going into lycanthrope – I did write a paper about the eccentric meiosis of lupine cells in the renal system, you'll be excited to know – but you know what, and this is, like, really sad, but it's the smell. I can handle the blood and the puke and the piss and the moonlight and all that, but wet dog and me? It just cramps the style. Hold this."

I found myself holding the end of a long cotton bandage attached to my thumb, as Dr Seah rattled among the contents of her trolley, eventually finding a large pack of alcoholic-smelling tissues with which she started mopping away the blood on my hand and wrist. All the time she worked, she talked.

"You know, I had this one patient, came down here with a punctured lung, broken arm and radiation sickness, and when I suggested that what he really needed was A and E, he started shouting at me that since it was an encounter with a supercharged banshee that had caused the injury, this was the department in which to get treatment. I mean, it's like me saying that because your GI tract infection caused a blood clot in the brain, you need a gastroenterologist instead of a neurosurgeon; can you believe that?"

I nodded and smiled.

"Now," a prod to my screaming ribcage, "if I prescribed bed rest you'd give me one of those looks, wouldn't you? Don't bother denying it, I can see the beginning of a look, one of those 'would if I could but there's this epic evil out there and I gotta deal with it' kinda looks; I know your type. Then again, I wouldn't be doing my job if I didn't pre-scribe you bed rest, and I'd probably actually get into, like, major-league legal shit or something if I didn't write it down somewhere or something; it's just that I can't be held responsible for whether my patient acts on it. Actually," a thought struck her, as it seemed many did with more regularity than the chimes on a cuckoo clock, "I sort of *could* be held responsible, but only within reasonably defined terms, and anyway" – a flap of her hand as the thought was dismissed – "there'd be legal wrangling and bitching and everyone would be like 'what were we talking about?' or whatever, so basically you," another pointed prod, "need bed rest!"

I gave her a look.

She rolled her eyes. "Okay then. Painkillers!" A bottle was rattled somewhere above my head. "No more than eight a day or your liver will go all squishy, and there'll be talk – try to use less but, you know, I get it, you've got like, cracked ribs and those hurt, you know? Look out for concussion as well: you'll be feeling fine, fine fine, fine fine fine, and then everything will kinda stop making sense, and you'll be a bit like ... *whoa* ... " 'Whoa' was illustrated by Dr Seah swaying in a wide circle from the perch of her high stool, "... and then you'll, like, collapse. Whatever."

The bottle of painkillers was duly pressed into my trouser pocket, and two oval pills dropped neatly into the palm of my hand. A pink plastic cup of water was proffered and, as I drank, Dr Seah asked slyly, "I don't suppose you've got ... *complications* ... you need to tell me about?"

I drained the last of the cup and handed it back. She threw it at a bin with the same perfect accuracy of her previous attempts. "Um ... not as far as I know," I mumbled. "Why, should I?"

"No," she sighed. "Just one of those moments of hope."

"About being followed ... "

"Oh yes! Bloodhounds, wasn't it? I assume you left a false trail, bits of your own blood in odd places. Did you? Of course you did. Just hang on in there ... "

Dr Seah dropped down off the stool, clopped over to another tomb, this one depicting a man lying with a sword resting the length of him and a dog under his feet, and rummaged in a giant orange shopping bag that was resting on top of him. Things clinked inside. There seemed far too much depth to the bag, and far too much time spent exploring it, for just a simple shopping trip. I lay, trying not to breathe too deeply in case something exploded inside my chest. At last there came a cry of 'ah-ha!' and Dr Seah trotted back to the slab, holding a small bottle of something. She gave it a good shake, flicked back the lid with her thumb and – with a cry of "Best bit!" – threw a cloud of brown powder over me. I spluttered as the smell rammed straight to the back of the tear ducts.

"What the hell is this?" I squeaked, wiping the powder from my eyes and neck.

"Garam masala, of course." Dr Seah took a long, pleasurable sniff from the bottle. "I mean, when I cook, baking is where it's really at – but sometimes, on special occasions you know, it's just gotta be curry time."

"And you're throwing garam masala all over me . . . because you like curry?"

"Oh sweetheart," she said, face crinkling in disappointment. "If I *wanted* curry, I'd *have* curry. You know how vampires are allergic to garlic?"

"Yes . . . "

"And werewolves to silver?"

"Yessss . . . "

"And banshees to ginger?"

"You're making this up."

"I'm sorry, seven years' medical training," she replied, "and you're just some git with fractured ribs, so whatever. Only, you see, blood-hounds . . . "

"You are kidding me."

"Bloodhounds . . . "

"No, seriously."

"*Bloodhounds* just can't take their garam masala."

She let me stay long enough for the painkillers to kick in.

She wrapped my thumb in many layers of plaster, with a cry of "Just a scratch, but a stupid scratch and we don't want those nasty blood-hounds coming after you, oh no . . . "

Night in Smithfield.

Not yet deep night, not yet the night of silent streets made quieter still by the distant swish of traffic. A night of emptying restaurants and pubs, just on the turning point when it was no longer cute-but-strange of the man to walk the woman to the bus stop; at this hour it became chivalrous.

We hurt.

Lying still for so long had been a mistake; it had given time for the adrenalin to get out of our system and for our brain to re-establish communication with our nerve ends. Now they were reporting in an overload of information, and none of it was good.

It took a while to learn how to walk again. Limping helped with nothing, and slouching just made the pain in our middle feel worse. Standing up straight, hands pressed to our sides, seemed the only way to do it. I shuffled off into the night, towards St Paul's Underground.

There was one more thing left to do.

Part 3: You Can't Save Your Friends

In which an enemy is revealed, a monster is summoned, and a social worker lets down her hair.

The first place was Stratford.

The name often caused confusion. Americans seeking the birthplace of Shakespeare would jump on the Central Line train to Stratford and, instead of finding Tudor cottages, canal boats and mugs proclaiming '𝔜𝔢 𝔒𝔩𝔡𝔢 𝔖𝔥𝔞𝔨𝔢𝔰𝔭𝔢𝔞𝔯𝔢'𝔰 𝔥𝔢𝔞𝔡𝔢', would discover a bus station, a portaloo, a vast building site, and not much else.

Then there were the Olympics. For years the prospect of the Games had turned the whole area into a chaos of torn-up earth. If all went to plan, there would emerge a landscaped, integrated series of developments, pure if soulless; but to make the future, today, the past not only had to get back out of sight, it had to burn the calendar too.

In line with these ambitions, Stratford International station had also been upgraded, so that mainline, Underground, Docklands and overground platforms ran over and under each other like a sailor's knot. Here I caught the Docklands Light Railway, and headed south, towards where Canary Wharf was an arctic silver beacon, catching the clouds in its towers and lighting them from beneath. A motorway sliced through the overbuilt landscape, heading for the Blackwall Tunnel. The last mile of my journey was on a single-decker night bus, the public transport equivalent of a red wheelie bin for humans.

I got off by a half-acre of scuffed grass containing three benches and a litter bin. In an estate of newish terraced houses and struggling little front gardens, a ramp led down behind a row of derelict garages. An open patch of concrete was framed on four sides by once-white blocks of flats, raised up on concrete pillars. The doors to every stairwell had been bolted, and covered with a metal grille; the windows had been boarded over, and nothing stirred here but fungal spores, rats, and the occasional graffiti artist with a sense of adventure but not much audience. Grass was sprouting between the cracks in the concrete paving, and thick woody stems of buddleia forced their way through the brickwork.

In the middle of this had-been courtyard, someone had parked a car.

It was not a happy car.

At some point a head-on collision had collapsed half the bonnet, an incident that had probably convinced the owner to let the wheels rust, the paint flake, the windscreen and two of the windows to stay cracked, and the stuffing to burst out of the seats. The air bag in the driver's seat was still hanging down, a wilting white rag.

Sat on the boot of this car, sharing coffee and, from the sound of it, having altogether too much fun, were two women. One wore a purple headscarf. The other wore a bright pink woolly hat with a bobble on top, from under which a mass of black hair had erupted like pyroclastic flow from a volcano. Nabeela Hirj and Penny Ngwenya were laughing while drinking coffee from a thermos flask and eating take-away chow mein from foil tubs, as I rounded the car, resisting the urge to moan piteously.

Their laughter should have stopped at the sight of me, but somehow whatever joke they'd been telling was only enhanced by my appearance and it was a full fifteen seconds before my apprentice managed to say, "Hey, Matthew!"

Nabeela managed a little self-control as well, and added, "You look really bad."

I grunted, "You got any more of that coffee?"

Penny shook the flask. "Uh-uh. Sorry." Then, as I limped closer, she reeled back in horror and added, "You *stink!*"

I moaned and leant against the car as the two women shuffled up to make room on the boot. "Garam masala," I explained.

"Yeah, and why are you, like, wearing it as fucking aftershave or whatever?" demanded my apprentice.

I told her what Dr Seah had told me. There was a stunned silence. "Wow, that is totally ... wow," Penny murmured at last. Nabeela's chopsticks had frozen in mid-air.

"I'm sorry," I spluttered, "Can we try this again? How about 'Hey, Matthew, you're being chased by bloodhounds, you've been kicked in the head and cracked some ribs, you're having a really stressful day, sorry we drank all the coffee, anything we can do for you to alleviate your pain and misery in this hour of need?'"

Penny nudged Nabeela. "Told you."

"How long've you been his apprentice?" hissed Nabeela back.

"Oh God, feels like for-fucking-ever."

"And he's never . . ."

"No!"

"What *never* . . ."

"Not once, ever."

"Well."

"I know."

"Shame."

"Totally."

The two having shared this moment of sisterly understanding, Penny turned back to me and fired up her best radiant smile. We cringed. Penny Ngwenya, sorceress and ex-traffic warden, who once got a little upset and accidentally summoned the death of cities: my apprentice. She had skin the colour of deep-roast coffee beans, purple-varnished nails that could have lacerated diamond and an attitude towards the rest of the world that made Genghis Khan look shy. In roughly equal parts, she was my student, saviour, and punishment by a darkly comic celestial power for sins unknown and unforgiven. And worst of all, in Nabeela Hirj, herself hardly a wilting flower, Penny seemed to have made a friend. "So you and the fairy godmother not so pally, huh?"

"Who's the fairy godmother?" asked Nabeela.

"Bloke in a dress," replied Penny.

"Drug dealer," I explained.

"And you pissed him off . . . trying to find out what happened to the kids in the playground?" Nabeela asked.

"Well, no . . ."

"You just piss people off professionally?"

"Well, sorta . . ."

"Because," she went on, "you're the Midnight Mayor?"

There was a shuffling silence. Nabeela wore an expression of polite interest.

"Um. Yeah," I mumbled. Then, when that didn't quite seem to do it, added, "Sorry."

"I don't see why you didn't just *tell* me you were the Mayor." Nabeela didn't sound angry . . . just disappointed. Much much worse.

"Well, if you recall the occasion of our first chat, you had just been thrown bodily out of the Aldermen's office screaming 'Fascist pig' and it didn't seem like you were exactly on the Midnight Mayor's fan list or anything, and you know how it is when someone says their name at a party but you don't quite catch it but then they're talking about something else and they got your name fine and by the time you've got the guts to ask for their name again, you've been talking for an hour already and offering to share a taxi back and . . ." I saw their expressions, and trailed off. " . . . okay, so when that moment comes, let me know."

"It's cool," said Nabeela. "I mean, I get it. Midnight Mayor is a really pompous title for a guy to have, and the whole dressed-up-as-garbage look you've got going is probably a really good disguise, helpful, I'm guessing, in your work, yeah?"

"Well, I wouldn't go so . . ."

"Matthew," said Penny, "you're wearing garam masala and a lot of bandage; think about it."

"Yeah . . . But . . . Sorry . . ."

Before I could embarrass myself further, Penny stood up, thrust her empty tub of chow mein into a plastic bag and exclaimed, "Well, now that's all cleared up, why don't we get on with what we came here to do?"

My apprentice had come prepared.

The abandoned car they had been eating their supper on, she'd managed to convince a very nice young man to deliver based on her, like, charms like, you know?

The can of petrol we duly threw over the car.

The bottles of cider and alcopops we spilt around the car in a wide circle, before smashing the bottles against the ground in great snowbursts of thinly sprayed glass.

One of the packets of cigarettes we lit, and let burn down, leaving four of them as markers at roughly where we considered north, south, east and west to be on the compass of our alcoholic circle.

Another two cigarettes we lit, and put into two more empty bottles, quickly taping over the tops to trap the swirling smoke, just in case.

Then Penny took the cans of spray paint and, very carefully, drew an eye on the wall opposite the petrol-soaked car. The outer edge was white, the inner pupil was black, and there was no colour in the entire thing.

"And this will help us find out what happened to the kids in my borough?" asked Nabeela sceptically as Penny put the finishing touches to her handiwork.

"With any luck," I groaned from my perch propped against a clear-ish bit of wall. "Take this, will you?"

Nabeela took the proffered roll of blue and white crime-scene tape gingerly, as if afraid the handling of it might of itself be a criminal offence. The last ingredient of the spell was a six-pack of Polish beer, the cheapest in the shop. Penny handed us one can each, cracked hers open and took a long swig.

Nabeela hesitated. "My religion . . ."

I added, "I'm a bit whacked out on painkillers."

Penny rolled her eyes. "Oh, I see, like that, is it? It's all 'Penny do this, Penny do that, Penny make it happen' and you two just lounge back there. I mean, no offence to your religion or whatever, you know; I'm just saying, that's completely cool and I respect that; I mean, it's not like getting pissed is fun or cheap these days, but seriously, Matthew, when are you not whacked out on painkillers or something?"

She snatched the beer cans back, opened them and took several more slurps, then threw each one overarm at the petrol-soaked car and barked, "Okay then, let's do it!"

Ten minutes later we stood on the balcony of an abandoned flat, looking towards where the car was burning. The blaze by now was bright enough to make us squint, and if I turned away I could feel its heat on the back of my neck.

And there were figures around it.

They'd drifted in one at a time, out of nowhere. They wore grey tracksuit trousers and baggy sweatshirts, with hoods pulled up around their heads. White headphone leads ran down into the front pouch of their tops, and their hands were slouched deep into their pockets or wore logo-marked sports gloves to match their trainers. Moving slowly, they circled the fire, basking in its heat. And when they raised their heads, it was briefly possible to see . . .

. . . that they had no faces. Nothing at all, nothing but darkness and vacancy inside their hoods, nothing but what they were: spectres, walking shadows drawn to the summoning circle of burning alcohol and petrol, shattered glass and melting cans. Like life, magic too has its parasites.

Nabeela said, "Are they . . . safe?"

"Totally!" lied Penny.

"Not really," I admitted.

"But are they going to try and hurt *us*?" demanded Nabeela, keeping her voice steady through an exercise of will.

"Probably not."

"And if they did, we've got, like, the Midnight fucking Mayor to fucking defend us!" Penny declared, gesturing at me like a circus master presenting its lion.

Nabeela's brow furrowed deeper. "Yessss . . . but aren't you off your head on painkillers?"

"Oh, that's a good thing!" exclaimed Penny. "Matthew only gets truly mega-mystic once someone's stabbed him or shit."

"What Penny means is that I save my best tricks for when the situation is really bad. Which this isn't." I scrutinised the scene below for a few moments longer, then said, "I think I should make a call now. Penny – can I borrow your phone?"

Her mobile was pink.

"Don't give me that look; it was a present, okay?"

The number I needed was written on a card.

The white card I'd taken from Mrs Dixon.

A phone rang.

A woman's voice answered.

"Good evening. Neighbourhood Eye: how may I help you?"

"Hi there," I sang out, watching the spectres from the corner of my eye as they moved round the burning car. "I don't know if this is the right time or place, but I was given this number by a friend. Are you the community watch service?"

"We are, sir; how may we assist you?"

"I was wondering, do you have any legal powers?"

"I'm afraid not, sir; but we can expedite matters through our local outreach officers with both the police and the magistrate, and hope to provide a free, public service for any and all who are concerned about social issues presently affecting their community. In this day and age we have to look out for each other, don't we sir?"

"Well, yes, absolutely!"

"So how may I help you, sir?"

"The thing is," I sighed, pumping old-fashioned English embarrassment into every word, "there are these kids down on my local neighbourhood and they're really causing a ruckus. I mean, they've been drinking, and I know young people drink, of course young people drink, but I do think they're just working each other up into some sort of frenzy, what with not having a responsible adult there to defuse them and of course it's not a police matter, I mean, the police can never do anything until the crime has already been committed, can they? But that's too late for the victim, that's always too late . . ."

The woman's voice cut me off. "I think I see what you're saying, sir, and I completely understand. Why don't you give me your address, and we'll send someone down to investigate the situation, see if we can convince these kids to move on."

"Oh, I don't know if . . ."

"Truly, sir. We'll handle it."

I gave her the address.

When it was done, Penny took the phone. Nabeela was looking at me with an expression somewhere between surprise and, just possibly, respect. "You know, when you need, you're almost slimy. I mean, in some totally hidden, nice way."

"What now?" demanded Penny.

"Now? We wait for the Neighbourhood Eye."

It was a gamble.

No reason to think it would come. Whatever *it* would turn out to be.

No way to know if what we had prepared would be enough.

Spectres circling a burnt-out car, the smell of beer and broken glass, paint on the wall, a phone call. But no way to know if what we had prepared would be enough.

Penny said at last, "Fucking freezing."

"You're not good at uncomfortable silences, are you?" I said.

"I cook, I sew, I do my own DIY, I pay my taxes, I look after my nieces and nephews when my aunt's away, I can ask for the bill in French and order paella in Spanish, and can summon spectres like a fucking taxi cab, what do you want here: perfection?"

"We could play I-spy," suggested Nabeela. We stared at her. "I'm just saying."

"You don't think," remarked Penny, "that would undermine this amazing aura of impending doom that we've got going here?"

I was scanning the low courtyard, half listening to them both.

"Okay – I spy with my little eye, something beginning with 's'."

Watching the hoodied creatures circle the fire.

"Spectres?"

"I'm not gonna play with you if you're like that," grumbled Penny.

"Look, you chose 's', okay, and . . . You hear that?" I glanced up at Nabeela, curious; heard nothing but the popping of flames and the slow groan of heated metal. "It's like . . ."

She stopped mid-sentence, clapping her hands over her ears. Penny was flinching too, turning her head this way and that, as if trying to shake off a wasp. Nabeela's face was scrunched in pain, her body bending in on itself.

Down in the courtyard, the spectres too were cowering, their not-hands pressed over their not-ears, at a sound I alone could not hear.

"What *is it*?" pleaded Nabeela through her teeth. "What is it what is it make it stop!"

I looked frantically around but saw nothing. Penny said, "There's a . . . sort of . . . faint sound, high-pitched, can't you hear?"

"No! What am I listening for, where's it coming from?"

"It's . . . it's . . ." She gestured, encompassing several miles with a sweep of her hand.

"It's everywhere!" shrieked Nabeela, dropping to her knees as she tried to block out the sound.

Then I did hear something.

Not the high-pitched screaming that tormented Nabeela; not a whine; not an unnatural ringing that pierced the innermost ear. This was solid; lower. It sounded like the chittering of a thousand tiny parts moving together, and it came from directly overhead. My eyes met Penny's. Together, we leant out from the balcony, and looked up.

For a second, just a second, it hung above us. I glimpsed iron mandibles snapping at the air; beyond them, a mouth of brown swirling glass. Then it stretched itself upright on double-jointed steel limbs, and leapt.

I ducked behind the balcony for cover, as it plunged down towards the burning car, its body blocking the light as it passed us. It had an outer skin of broken chimney pots and smashed slate tiles, the pieces smoothly interlocked to create a flexible armour. It had three limbs of iron and concrete dust on either side of its body, itself segmented into two front parts, plus a larger, oval component with a pointed tip at the tail – three parts making head, thorax and abdomen. The wings, small compared to the rest of the creature, were fashioned from black smoke and drawn in, bat-like; and where its segments joined, there was only air and a spinning matrix of broken glass, which rattled and bounced against its slate carapace.

To me the creature seemed silent except for the rattle of its passage, but Nabeela was screaming now, and the spectres down in the court-yard were prostrate. The flames from the burning car swerved, then flared as, no wider than a dustcart and no longer than a truck, it landed in front of them with a neat little bounce. It reared up, opening its dark, steel-framed mouth; and now there was no mistaking what it was meant to be: a mockery of an insect form, a summoned thing which seemed to resemble, in its artificial parts, a living, giant, hungry mosquito.

What happened next was almost too fast to see. Its mouth, then its whole head, seemed to crack open, splitting wider than its whole body. Inside the darkness of its matrix, filled with whirling fragments of glass, flashed a giddy reflection of the flames from the car. The creature rose up on the back four of its six legs, seemed to shake its entire body, then dove down and, in a single gulp, swallowed one spectre whole.

The spectre's form gave way with a sonic thump, blasting out the empty remains of hoodie and tracksuit bottoms as it was consumed. The others were trying to crawl away, but the creature turned, the leisurely swing of its tail shattering one of them into a heap of soiled clothing and, with a casual hook of one claw, grabbed another round the neck, threw it into the air, and swallowed it whole like popcorn. The fourth spectre didn't even try fighting as the monster curled around it, obscuring it from sight; and when the creature was done, there wasn't even a shoe left behind.

I looked at Penny; she looked at me. She pressed something into my hand: a roll of police tape. I nodded an acknowledgement and crawled to the far end of the balcony. Penny scurried in the opposite direction and, at a signal to each other, we stood up.

The insect-beast was circling restlessly on the ground, shaking its head to and fro as if trying to work out what it was about its last meal that had been so unsatisfactory. Sensing us, it snapped its head. Black multifaceted eyes, made from the scarred remains of camera lenses, focused in, first on Penny, then on me. Grasping my police tape by one end of the roll, I threw the rest of it at the creature as hard as I could. Penny did the same. Both rolls landed a few feet short, unspooling along the ground. For a moment the creature regarded them, as a bear might examine a wandering mouse. Then its attention came back to us, and its body rattled with rising tension. I jerked the end of the police tape I held and, on the ground near the monster, the rest of it twitched too, shuddered, then, snake-like, began to uncoil. I gave it another tug and, as the end of the tape slithered towards one of the insect's metal legs, it sprang up, uncurling in an instant, and wrapped itself around the clawed limb.

Bewildered, the insect gave a tug, but the tape just wound tighter, writhing upwards and starting to curl its way around the creature's great thorax. The tape Penny held was also unfurling, making its way up the foremost leg towards the insect's head. The creature raised itself up to utter what might have been a roar of confusion, inaudible to me, and beat its black wings, trying to pull free. The force of its anger nearly dragged me off my feet. We held on to the tape with both hands, hauling the creature back down, and as it came, we called out into the night:

"You do not have to say anything!"

The tape went on furling around the flailing creature; my feet threatened to slide from under me as I leant back to keep up a grip. Pain shot up from my chest and down my arms and legs, bringing water to my eyes, as I wound the tape around my wrist and pulled tighter. "But it may harm your defence if you do not mention, when questioned, something which you later rely on in court."

The tape was thickening in my grasp, responding to our spell, becoming harder and less yielding, tightening in on the creature, pulling it down to the ground. Penny was half leaning out over the balcony, trying to keep her balance as her lips moved in recitation of the same spell. "Anything you do say may be given in evidence; you do not have to say anything unless you wish to do so, but I must warn you that if you fail to mention any fact which you rely on in your defence in court, your failure to take this opportunity to mention it may be treated in court as supporting any relevant evidence against you."

By now the tape was fully unwound around the insect, pulling it to the ground. The tail end of its abdomen twitched upwards like a rearing wolf, but the rest of the body couldn't escape the spell. Through gritted teeth, I exclaimed, "If you do wish to say anything, what you say may be given in evidence!"

I gave one last pull, dragging the creature down.

Its jaw clitter-clattered in distress; its helpless legs rattled against the concrete. Penny was clinging on to the tape tight enough to turn her knuckles white.

Silence from the creature, made deeper by the noise of flames.

Penny began, "Is that . . . ?"

Then the creature screamed.

It threw its head back and screamed, so loud and so furious that, though I couldn't hear it, I felt it. Instinctively I put my hands over my ears, letting the tape slip from my fingers, felt the sound vibrate my eyes, felt it stir acid in my belly, tasted it on my tongue. What glass was left in the windows of the car burst, snapped apart; then the street lamps exploded too, plunging us into a fire-warmed gloom. And still the creature screamed, thrashed and rolled, tumbling onto its back and lurching the tape out of Penny's hands.

Then a claw caught a piece of tape and slashed it in two. I felt the sickening backlash as the spell broke, the tape suddenly just tape, just plastic. There was a popping in my ears; blood was filling the barely healed hollows of my nose. Penny was on the ground, hands wrapped around her head. And as I dropped down below the concrete parapet I saw Nabeela, half raised off the floor. Blood rolled freely from her nose and ears; her skin was sickly white; her lips worked soundlessly. Something was moving beneath her headscarf, pushing up against it from the surface of her head; no time now to look. A shattering of slate on metal – and the insect's struggles had brought it down on the burning car, spilling a roar of sparks and flame around its thrashing body. The creature rolled again, the last tendrils of tape coming free, then shuddered upright once more. Bubbles of petrol smouldered and popped, clinging to its shell.

It raised its head and looked straight at me.

Even as I ducked back down, the whole building shook. The creature had rammed us, leapt head first at the balcony. Concrete dust tumbled all around; a crack in the floor was spreading beneath my feet from the point of impact. Then a pair of claws hooked themselves onto the parapet and the creature's head blotted out the light of the fire as it pulled itself up to eye level.

I grabbed the first thing to hand, a paint spray can from my bag, and as the insect opened that impossibly black jaw full of spinning glass, I squirted a blast of paint straight at its eyes, blocking out one entirely. It flailed against the wall, then crashed down onto its back. In a single powerful motion, however, it flipped itself over again as the paint dribbled away from the lens of its eye. I crawled along the balcony to Nabeela, grabbed her by the shoulder, hissed, "Come on!"

She just shook her head and whimpered.

The building shook again, hard enough to send more cracks spreading outwards like a chaotic family tree: the insect had head-butted the place where I'd been a moment before. I cast around for anything that might serve as a weapon, but the electricity had been cut off long ago, and the mains cables were buried too far below to be of use. Gas was closer to the surface, but what use were flames against a creature made from the remains of chimneys? Close at hand I heard a scratching sound: the monster had levered itself back up to the balcony.

It was too large to fit in between floors, but it was compensating for this by starting to bash out the balcony above with the arch of its back, splitting the walls and sending great slabs of concrete tumbling all around. As an old building, scheduled to be demolished, this was already a place of decay, ready to crumble.

I got down on my hands and knees, bending my fingers into the damp concrete floor . . . Something deeper lay there, a further dampness beneath the mere surface covering of drizzle. I pushed, and something answered inside the building; I felt it rise, and within moments it was there in plain sight: a greenish-yellow stain beneath my fingers. It began to spread outwards, crawling up the walls and erupting in a sickly bloom between the cracks in the concrete. Moving as swiftly as water, already it had reached the metal feet of the creature. I pressed my fingers deeper into the concrete, until the grey surface beneath me began to smoke and hiss; then deeper still, until the concrete was liquid, thick and cold. I pushed my arm in up to the wrist, then almost to the elbow, feeling through the clammy depths of the floor until my fingers sensed iron. I closed my fist around it, and pulled with all my strength.

The plague of lichen continued spreading. White and yellow encrustations burst across the skin of the insect, instantly spawning more growths, which then worked through the gaps, embedding themselves beneath the slates. The insect reared up like a poisonous creature wounded with its own sting as it tried to scratch and burn away this sudden infection on its body. The metal I'd seized from beneath the floor came free reluctantly, snapping loose and bursting upwards as suddenly as ketchup from a bottle, and knocking me backwards: a rusted iron bar once part of the building's framework. Still writhing back and forth, the creature was trying to chew off the lichen embedded under its skin, an itch it couldn't scratch. I ran towards it, and as it turned its head to look at me I hurled the bar with all my strength, point first down its open throat.

The sound, the not-sound that was a force itself, stopped.

The mosquito reared up, its body shaking violently, and clawed at its own head with two of its flailing limbs; then, overbalanced by the effort, it slipped and fell backwards from the balcony.

I peered down after it.

It was rolling and flapping, trying to pull the bar from its throat and rub the lichen from its back.

Not dead; maybe just annoyed.

I ran to where Nabeela was slowly uncurling, streaked with blood from her ears and nose, and helped her to her feet.

As I did so, she gave me a look. For a moment there was something in her eyes, something dark and animal and not quite right. But then she shook her head and it was gone. She wheezed, "The things I do for local government."

"Penny?" I called out as my apprentice dragged herself up by the cracked parapet. "You all right?"

"Do I look fucking all right?" she hollered. "Fucking monsters and fucking magic and fucking sorcerers who can't fucking bind . . ."

"She's fine," I reassured Nabeela. Then, "That thing's not dead and it's not happy. Shall we scarper?"

"I suppose you'll be wanting a fucking lift now?" Penny shouted.

"That'll be grand, since you mention it. Let's go, right now."

Penny's car was a few blocks away, by a row of shops featuring one off-licence, one pharmacy with a strong sideline in water pistols, and one greengrocer that sold mostly plantain and butternut squash. As we passed the pharmacy I paused, gasping between each breath at a shooting agony the painkillers had barely numbed, and said, "Whoa there a moment!" Penny turned to say something rude, saw my face, and hesitated.

"That bad, huh?" I asked.

She laughed, a little too loud, her voice reverberating in the empty night. "Don't worry, you always look bad." But she moved closer, the better to look at my eyes. "You, uh ... going to pass out or anything like that?"

I shook my head and indicated the pharmacy. "You okay forcing the lock?"

"You asking me to do something illegal or shit?" shrilled Penny.

"Yup."

"So long as it's you asking," she replied, and bent down to try coaxing the lock.

Nabeela said, "Are we cool with doing illegal things? Only I *do* have a regular job to go back to, and just because you two don't really work doesn't mean I can put my life plans on the line, you know?"

"Don't work?!" I squeaked. "Do you know how many perks you get as Midnight Mayor?"

"If I said 'lots' that would be a mistake, right?"

"Not even a bloody company car."

"Matthew doesn't need a bloody company car," said Penny. "He just calls me, isn't that right?" The lock clicked, a whiff of Penny's bright magic drifting away from it, and she pushed the door back with a triumphant "Ta-da!" She asked, "What we looking for? Painkillers, bandages, that kinda shit?"

"Earplugs," I said.

Enlightenment dawned. "Hey-hey! Get you, not totally a bozo. I mean, respect."

She roamed through the shelves by the glow of the sodium street lamps outside. Nabeela followed her, stepping across the threshold with a wince, as if her council pay cheque were dissolving before her eyes. The earplugs were found between verruca treatments and baby bottles; Nabeela counted out four pounds eighty-three pence onto the counter, mumbling that she'd make up the last sixteen pence at some point in her life, honest. As we made our way back towards the car, Penny handed out the plastic bags containing the plugs, thin green things we rolled between our fingers into tiny tubes, which expanded once inside the ear. I was trailing behind the others, finding it painful right now even to raise my arms. How many hours had Dr Seah said between painkillers? How many doses had it been?

Because I was moving slowly, I now heard what they didn't. It was a rattling noise, a sound of clattering from just down the street. We were only yards from Penny's car, the keys already in her hand and, as I turned, I saw it, lurching round the corner towards us. It was moving too fast for balance, and found itself propelled by its own weight into the side of a parked car, which started wailing. Righting itself, the creature charged.

I shouted, "Penny!", realised the futility of my action and tapped her on the shoulder. She turned, saw the creature, and instinctively threw her hands up in self-defence. Silver-white fire crackled at her fingertips, danced around the telephone lines overhead, and struck sparks off the alarms and aerials on nearby buildings. I grabbed Nabeela and pulled her down as, with a yell and a flare of light, Penny flung spitting electrical fury into the heart of the approaching creature.

The impact knocked it to one side, slowing it for a second, but didn't stop it. A black smoking stain marked its armour; glass continued to clatter and whirl inside its belly. As it opened its mouth to roar again, I felt the sound rumbling through the ground and tearing the air. Penny threw another blast of fire and once more it staggered, but still it approached, slower now, eyeing up its opposition. Car alarms were wailing all up the street, lights were going on behind windows, and then it raised its head and lifted up its voice. Windscreens cracked, window-panes fractured, and glass showered down from the street lights.

The monster was nearly on top of us now, opening its jaws before that impossible pit. Tottering from the weight of the magic she'd flung, Penny tried in vain to gather strength for one more fiery assault. We saw sapphire blue in front of our eyes, tasted metal in our mouth, fire in our blood, pulled ourself up as our hair began to stand on end, felt the electricity beneath our feet, and tasted the breeze of microwaves and radio waves carrying a thousand million voices through the air. I looked down and our hands were blazing with blue fire, stretching out across our skin, spilling its crystal light across the earth, and the creature was there, ready to burn, going to burn, and Penny was struggling, trying to force herself into another spell and

and a voice said, "Don't look."

The voice was right by us and, though it was familiar, it was distorted. A voice that should have been Nabeela's, but which was now something else; laced with electricity, it went through the earplugs like they weren't there; not sound, but still a hissing, straight into the brain. Involuntarily we started to turn, and she barked louder: an order. "Don't look!" I saw the beast drawing itself up overhead, ready to dive, felt fire and tasted rage and then . . .

The insect froze.

It froze, hanging above us, like a wave trying to fall. There was a discoloration in its eye, a greyness spreading from its eye outwards. It rushed over the surface of its slate skin, trapped the spinning glass within its mouth mid-whirl, took the sheen off its legs and slipped grey dull hardness round its belly and back. The greyness spread down its legs, crossed the empty gap without a pause between head and thorax, and was already spilling into the great swollen abdomen before the thorax was completely changed.

Penny staggered back, mouth open in surprise, turning her head to see what had caused this. I caught her and pushed her to the other side of the car, pressing her face against my shoulder. "For Christ's sake," I breathed, "don't look."

The greyness was all across the creature now, locking it rigid; and it wasn't just a colour, it was a texture too, rough and grainy. "Phone," I breathed. "Give me your phone."

Wordlessly, Penny pressed it into my hands. Her body was shaking, whether from exhaustion or fear we couldn't tell. Her phone had a camera, which could be angled away from the phone itself, so I twisted and turned it so the camera could see what we dared not, and we could see the screen. "There," I whispered. "Look at this."

She looked at the screen and together we saw the thing that had frozen the monster – more than frozen, transformed; turned this creature of moving parts and glass into a statue of old, grey, unadorned concrete.

We saw Nabeela.

She stood a few feet in front of the mosquito, looking into that obscene, wide-open mouth. Her headscarf dangled from one hand, and on her head was revealed, not hair, not human hair, but something else, something that writhed and jerked and spun like living things. Once upon a time, they might have been snakes; but magic had evolved with the times, and now these snake-things had bodies of metal tubes, laced with fibre-optic cable, and heads of little hooded camera-eyes that swung this way and that to survey the world, darting no less lifelike than their organic cousins, but hissing not with venom but with motorised cogs. And the mosquito had stared straight at them.

Penny breathed, "Is she . . . ?"

"Yeah."

"I mean a . . . ?"

"Yeah."

Silence. Then, "That is so totally fucking awesome, I'd like, kiss her, if my heart wasn't already given to a guy called Femi."

"You'd kiss Nabeela?"

"Jesus, wouldn't *you*?"

"I thought you had to cancel your date with Femi."

"You learn a lot about guys from how they handle rejection. He handled it in a totally cool way, which means he's got my heart and is going to be, like, the sexy sexy man of my dreams, when I'm not dreaming about monsters and shit. But yeah," she added, voice rising indignantly, "thanks for reminding me about screwing up my love-life!"

In the camera screen, Nabeela was putting her headscarf back on, quieting the roaming creatures on her head, easing them back to sleep as, methodically and with great care, she tucked the folds of her scarf back in place. I flipped the camera shut and handed it back to Penny, then called out, "You decent?"

Penny punched me gently in the arm. "That is like the most dork-ish thing you could have totally said."

Nabeela came back over. "Yeah. I'm fine." She stood uneasily, arms straight, hands clenched. "Um . . ." she began.

Penny burst out, "You are the most totally fucking totally awesome bitch ever! Yo, sister, give it here!"

Nabeela was surprised to find herself high-fiving my sorceress apprentice.

"This!" added Penny, turning to look at the frozen concrete statue still hanging over us. "This is like . . . it's like . . . it's like totally amazing and if we'd just fucking known then we could have skipped all of Matthew's wanky enchantment stuff and just gone straight to the earplugs and concrete shit, you know what I'm saying? Because this . . ." she punched one of the mosquito's protruding frozen limbs triumphantly, " . . . totally kicks ass!"

Something went, *pop*.

All eyes turned.

Where Penny had hit the mosquito, a shard of concrete had fallen away, revealing the slate underneath.

Penny said, "Uh . . ."

"Time to go!" I sang out.

Nabeela's jaw was hanging open. "But it shouldn't . . ."

From the space where the concrete had dropped, a crack appeared. It became a fault line that began to run the length of the insect's immobilised hide.

"Ladies!" I exclaimed. "Take it from a guy who knows about implausible danger: nothing beats running away."

They didn't need to be told twice. Penny was in the driver's seat and putting us into gear before I had the passenger door open. Nabeela was struggling to pull her seat-belt on as Penny swung us out into the street. Already cracks were racing across the creature's body, their growth speeded by a shuddering from within. We were swinging round the corner and accelerating as the concrete burst from the creature's wings.

Some people, when stressed, respond by drawing into themselves. Some do not.

We sat at traffic lights on Commercial Road as Penny screamed at a neighbouring car. "You call that driving, wanker? Do you even know what a box junction is?"

Some parts of London never stop; Commercial Road is one of them. It was a wide street of curry houses, garages and sari shops that sliced through the East End of London like a lava flow, carrying a sluggish stream of buses and lorries into the heart of the city from the Blackwall Tunnel and Isle of Dogs.

Some eccentric navigation on our part had, I assured Penny and Nabeela, probably shaken the creature. We agreed to say no more on the subject.

Where now? Penny had asked.

I'd taken a while to answer, and then decided: what we really needed was a safe place to stay.

I knew just the man.

There was nowhere to park in the grand Notting Hill square, but Penny, ex-traffic warden as she was, found the double yellow line that, she assured me, was least likely to be done come 8 a.m., and even if it was she'd just forward the charge to the Aldermen and let them do their shit, yeah?

Black iron railings framed the kempt trees and trimmed grass of a residents' garden. Around the square, stone steps led to porticoed entrances, each adorned with a brass knocker almost as heavy as the door itself. Great sash windows, nearly twice the height of a man, had lofty wooden shutters or swagged and tasselled curtains. The area had been Victorian London at its most confident, built to remind all future generations that the British needn't be showy To Be Great.

The lights were out in every house; all good people had gone to bed. But a motion sensor picked us up as we climbed the front steps in question, turning on a bright yellow bulb in a big black antique lantern overhead. I rang the doorbell and waited. A light went on behind the door. A chain was taken off. The door was eased back and a man with dark eyes, dark hair, almond skin and a sense about him of thick treacly magic opened it just enough. He sighed.

"You," he said. "Come in."

A hall too tall, a living room too wide. The house was decorated in a neutral style for neutral people, complete with magnolia wallpaper, fittings in beige, and paintings guaranteed neither to offend nor divert. A fire burnt beneath a wide marble surround, and a vast sofa and two button-backed chairs were turned towards it. One of the chairs was occupied. Its occupant said, "Good evening, Matthew. If you would mind not leaving the smell of curry on everything in the house, I'm sure its owners would appreciate it on their return."

His name was Dudley Sinclair.

He Knew Things.

No one quite knew how he Knew Things, or exactly what the scope might be of the Things he was determined to Know. But he was, as he described himself, a concerned citizen in a world where the general citizenry's lack of concern was, in itself, a cause of grave concern for him.

Information broker, negotiator, diplomat, master puppeteer, power behind the throne, call him whatever you wanted to, if you looked hard enough, there was Dudley Sinclair, looking right back at you.

A man well into his fifties, if not beyond, with a great rolling belly barely compressed into his pinstripe suit, he had the aura of a man born into a waistcoat, for whom pyjamas were a phenomenon that happened to someone else. Even at this hour of the night, if you phoned he would answer within a few brief rings; never asleep, never in bed, never off-duty. There was too much world to let Dudley Sinclair close his eyes for long.

We were each led by Charlie, his ever-present assistant, to a bedroom, every one larger than the first flat I'd rented. The beds were so deep that it was hard to tell where duvet stopped and mattress began, and the headboards were piled with enough pillows to start a tournament. I slipped out of my shoes and tried to rub a little life back into my feet, washed my face in cold water dispensed from a tap so clean you could see your face in it, in a bathroom composed of perfect and unforgiving mirrors, and did a quick inspection. Dr Seah had removed the worst of the blood from the side of my head, but my ribcage was coming out an interesting shade of violet. Feeling like an idiot, I rubbed a little more garam masala into the palm of my hands and round the back of my neck. I hadn't heard the howl of the bloodhound for a while; maybe Dr Seah did know what she was doing after all.

Sinclair was waiting for me in the living room, a finger's-depth of whisky swirling in his glass. The lights were turned low, the curtains drawn; everyone else upstairs.

I stretched out on the sofa and he scrutinised me, little eyes gleaming in a large head.

I said, "The Aldermen lied to me."

He took a sip of whisky, appreciated, swallowed, appreciated again, put his glass to one side and said, "Yes, dear boy, of course they did."

"There are dead people packing out the edges of this lie."

"Again, I query your surprise."

I fumbled behind my head for one of the sofa cushions, punching it and puffing it up into something resembling comfort, then shuffled deeper into the sofa. He waited.

"Did you know?" I asked.

"That the Aldermen lied to you? It seemed inevitable. The specifics of the lie in question – that, you will have to tell me."

So, I did.

I told him everything.

I told him about Meera, fairy dust, Morris Prince and the trip to the dusthouse in Soho.

About the fairy godmother, Hugo and his bloodhounds, a meeting at the Barbican, a long drop and a short stop, and why everything stank of curry.

The Beggar King, his problem, his subject who turned to dust, and not through her own choosing.

Templeman and his plan.

About Nabeela, and the five kids on one night in Westbourne Park, who found themselves four kids without a soul and one corpse, torn apart by claws no one had seen.

About Mrs Dixon and the Neighbourhood Eye, about Rumina Rathnayake, emails between five people talking about plans and lies, Templeman's name on the list. About the deserted estate near Stratford, and calling the Neighbourhood Eye and getting, for our pains, a monster with claws.

At the end of it I said, "So I guess this brings me back to my initial question: did you know?"

Sinclair sighed, put the whisky glass to one side, and said, "Some of it ... perhaps. One must always keep abreast of rumours; sort, as it were, the wheat from the chaff. Magicians do so like to gossip, but sometimes – occasionally – there is more than a little truth to their tales. In answer to your question, I can only assume you are asking me if I knew about the connection between the Aldermen, the Neighbourhood Eye and your monster that comes in the night. The answer is: no, I did not know. And while perhaps I can understand what the Aldermen may have been attempting to achieve, assuming that this creature is all that you say – and by your expression, Matthew, and somewhat, how to put it . . . dogged look . . . I shall take it that it is – I really cannot condone their actions. As for the rest . . ." He let out a sigh, which took its time as a great deal of lung beneath a great mass of belly deflated with a great whoosh of air. "Let us say, I had heard rumours."

"What kind of rumours?"

"The destruction of the dusthouse, of course. Everyone is talking about that. The rumour is that the Midnight Mayor was responsible, though no one fully understands why this usually so conventional figure is taking such drastic measures against an institution which, until now, has been reasonably tolerated within the city. And, frankly, I was a little surprised; I had heard that the dusthouses were indestructible."

"Dodgy foundations," I replied.

"Of course, of course, dear boy, how short-minded of the architects. As for the fairy godmother's involvement with that little problem of the Beggar King . . . I had heard rumours that the beggars were angered by, shall we say, members of their order going astray, with unexplained deaths and disappearances without bodies. These things happen all the time, in a big city, when you are alone, but the Beggar King watches his flock well. If he thinks that the dust is involved, well then, we would be reckless to doubt his word. And yet . . . "

"Yet?" I groaned, fatigued, pressing my hands against my eyes.

" . . . and yet there is no economic benefit to the fairy godmother in addicting beggars. They cannot pay for the dust, and while the resources are hardly wasted if the subject then dies and produces more dust in the process, there can be no need for the godmother to achieve a massive increase in the supply of dust. A drug that by its very nature kills the user has, of necessity, a limited market – high demand, limited supply, high prices. No, I see no economic incentive at all for the fairy godmother."

"I thought the fairy godmother had a monopoly on dust."

"Well quite so, quite so; therein lies the mystery."

We could feel him watching us, unafraid. I said, "What would you do?"

A pair of oversized eyebrows flickered up above a pair of undersized eyes. "I?"

"About the Aldermen."

"Is the problem that concerns you one of disloyalty, or an objection to their deeds?"

"I didn't expect loyalty."

"Did you expect their deeds to be clean as well?" he asked, struggling to keep the incredulity from his voice. "They are the protectors of the city, Matthew. Not of you or me, not of individuals standing on the corner. Theirs is a world of numbers and ideas, of big problems and bigger solutions, of what is best for the majority and of prices that must be paid. Of course they would go behind your back were it for the greater good. It is, frankly, what they would expect of you."

I scowled. "Great." Then, "What do you think I should do?"

"You ask me, dear boy?"

"Yes."

"I am ... flattered, I think."

"And I'm totally stuffed."

"Nevertheless, to be asked my advice by your good self, even in consequence of your being totally stuffed, is ... unexpected."

"Don't worry, I try not to make a habit of it."

"If you do want my advice, here it is: talk to the Aldermen."

"That's terrific."

"I mean it, most sincerely. You already have the fairy godmother after you and, as the state of your ribs can attest, I believe you have discovered for yourself that he is hardly a trifling enemy. You and your apprentice, the last two sorcerers in the city – which, if nothing else, is tribute to your survival skills – have failed to tame this roaming monster which is summoned by the Neighbourhood Eye. By your reckoning, the creature has already killed one, maybe more, and stripped the minds from many others. You have proven that the Neighbourhood Eye and the Aldermen are one; therefore, to solve the problem of the insect-monster, you must first speak to the Aldermen, obtain their knowledge of this enemy that you cannot contain. A medusa's gaze," he exclaimed, "failed to contain it! By the by," looking thoughtful, "are Kensington and Chelsea aware that they've hired a medusa?"

"Doubt it."

"A pity. Medusas, banshees, vampires, werewolves, goblins – they should all really be covered by local council anti-discrimination guidelines."

I managed to convert a goggle of disbelief into a mumble of, "Well, that would be nice."

"Matthew." His voice was still light, but somewhere I heard a warning. "Of all the things that you have told me tonight, do you know what most gives me concern?"

"More than the monster, the medusa, the bloodhounds and the lingering smell of curry?"

"Indeed, more than all those."

"Wow me."

"It is this warning from the Beggar King. There is no need for the fairy godmother to risk his lucrative business by ... experimenting, shall we say ... on beggars. On the lost and the lonely; there is no profit in it for him. Yet by all accounts, the decay of this beggar woman, Ai, as described by the Beggar King, suggests someone out there shows an interest in the dust that is more than just commercial.

"The fairy godmother is a businessman, Matthew; he can still be bought and sold, for all his power. But fairy dust is as much a weapon as it is a narcotic – a deadly weapon, to be sure, a weapon which in time will kill its user, but still a weapon in the wrong hands. I would not like to think what would happen if ever a magician were able to control their own use of it."

"You said yourself, it's a narcotic, one that kills the host."

"In its present form."

"You think someone might be trying to alter that form?"

"I think all possibilities should be considered."

"Great, because my day couldn't have got better."

He smiled, the infinitely patient smile of the kindly father watching a clumsy infant son trying to climb the stairs. "You should rest, Matthew."

"Yeah," I groaned, laboriously getting up from the depths of the sofa. "Thanks, by the way, for letting us crash."

"Who am I to say no to the Midnight Mayor?"

"Hell, everyone else does."

"That seems remarkably short-sighted of them."

"Goodnight, Mr Sinclair."

"Goodnight, Matthew."

I shuffled towards the door, too tired to care any more about the pain. I was nearly there when he murmured, "Matthew?"

"Mr Sinclair?"

"If you must use my name when bluffing your way into dusthouses, in the future please do so with a little less flair."

I grinned. "Yeah – sorry about that. But if it's any comfort ..."

"Yes?"

" ... all publicity is good publicity, right?"

"I try to feel honoured, Matthew, I truly do."

The bed was infinitely soft and infinitely deep.

We fell into it until there was no more light.

Not quite sleep.

The half-state between sleep and waking when we could feel our eyeballs roll back into our head and, by the very act of feeling, would jerk awake again.

And then, possibly, sleep.

Dreaming of Meera.

Should have been of a smile.

Voice.

Smell of the river.

Fingers.

Lips.

Wasn't.

Dreamt of Meera and dreamt of dust, and woke with the taste of it in our lungs, parched and out of breath.

Morning came too soon.

It brought tea, toast and marmalade, and cereal with nuts in.

Nabeela said, "I gotta call in sick or something. I've never pulled a sickie before – how d'you do it?"

Penny said, "I should probably call my aunt, shit."

I said nothing, and checked my phone: two missed calls from Kelly.

I sat on a wide step leading down to a walled back garden of mown grass and the smell of lavender, and called my PA.

She answered immediately. "Good morning, Mr Mayor, I'm so glad you're calling, I was beginning to worry that something had happened, silly isn't it, I know, but there are just a few things I need to run by you ..."

"Kelly," I interrupted, head resting in my hand, phone clamped to my ear, "I need you to do something for me."

"Of course, Mr Mayor, anything at all!"

"I need to talk to Rumina Rathnayake, Cecil Caughey, Lucy Holta, Tommy Kwan, B. Fadhil and Richard Templeman, somewhere away from the office, now. And Kelly?"

"Yes, Mr Mayor?"

"Make sure they're not armed."

Charlie gave us a lift in Sinclair's car, because Penny didn't think there'd be anywhere to park hers.

Sinclair himself explained he needed to "tidy up a few bits of paperwork, you know how it is, dear boy, no rest for the wicked and so forth."

Then, as we were heading down the steps to where Charlie was waiting, Sinclair caught my arm. I'd never seen him move more than a few inches at a time, like a giant that didn't want to risk damaging the delicate furniture of lesser creatures, but his fingers were suddenly tight above my elbow, his voice soft, a hiss short of a whisper. "Be careful whom you trust, Matthew," he said. "Those Aldermen who oppose you will not submit without a fight. And there will be more, far more, than just this creature you've described. Ask yourself why the fairy godmother is so powerful. Ask yourself why the fairy dust is not more feared. Ask yourself who stands to gain from experimenting on beggars. And then be careful – be so careful – whom you trust."

This said, he let go, and turned away as if nothing had happened, gliding one careful step at a time back into the house, a light tweaking of the wrist at his side the only symptom of a goodbye, as the door slammed shut behind him.

The car smelt of fresh leather and stale air freshener.

I watched London go by. Bus stops busy with commuters, Underground stations churning forth a continuous stream of men and women, skins of every colour, clothes in every style, some walking the confident walk of the worker who has been this way a thousand times; some the shuffle of the nervous tourist wondering which way is up on their two-pound public transport map. The way people walk in a city tells a lot about them: local or lost, visitor or regular, tourist or resident, coming or going, afraid or at home. Thieves look for the quality of the walk as much as anything when picking their mark.

Penny was silent.

Penny wasn't usually silent.

As we neared our destination, Charlie started looking to avoid the endless one-way systems and perpetual 'no left turn' signs that were the bane of every inner-city driver's life. We made our way to Long Acre, a street of clothes shops catering to fashionables who surfed the very breaking wave of trend, perpetually unfulfilled in their quest. Outside Covent Garden Underground we scrambled out, Penny, Nabeela and me; and, as Charlie drove away, we paused.

Penny said, "You sure this is a good idea?"

"Sure I am," I lied. "It'd be bad form to shoot me in front of tourists. There'd be letters."

"He always thinks someone's gonna shoot him," Penny told Nabeela. Turning to me, she added, "Same old same, isn't it? Penny, come save me from monsters, Penny, I'm being hunted by mafia dudes and smell of curry, Penny, there's a big bad wolf and I left my magic cape at home ..."

"I'm going now," I sighed, "since it seems I can't count on any pro-active intervention here. Just remember how bad you'll feel if I do get shot."

"Come on, Nabeela," muttered Penny as I crossed the road. "Let's go find somewhere to keep an eye on Matthew, and get a *really expensive* cup of fucking coffee, yeah? Because we're keeping the receipts."

A few paces later, and the crowds of Covent Garden had swallowed them up.

Covent Garden.

Once a place where you could indeed find all the produce of an English garden, from courgettes not yet turned purple-black to cabbages with only half their leaves eaten by caterpillars. In recent years this sometime wholesale flower-market and traditional den of iniquity had been transformed into a tourist-trap paradise. Within its pillared arcades and vaulted glass-and-iron roof you could buy hand-made soap for only £15 a bar, hand-painted pictures of famous landmarks at only £25 unframed, or silver jewellery sold by an Irishman who delighted in explaining why this Celtic knot, yours for only £150, embodied in it all things rich and ancient about the Gaelic way of life.

The neighbouring market, only a few pennies less expensive, dealt in a wider range of goods, from leather jackets to paper lanterns, packs of custom cards to hot dogs swimming in grease. And everywhere you went in Covent Garden, there was entertainment. From acrobats juggling on stilts, to string quartets playing in the vaults beneath the market, to the sheng player by the Royal Opera House recreating the songs of ancient China, every other step brought you to a different kind of music or the spontaneous applause of a crowd.

The crowds were why I'd named this as a meeting place, along with its many exits into the busiest part of the city. Another reason was its large number of vantage points. From the Royal Opera House bar, to the balconies of restaurants and coffee shops within the roof of the market, there were several places where an observer might see without being observed.

I went up into one such restaurant, bought myself a large pot of coffee and a small, too-sweet biscuit for a price that sent shivers down my spine, and waited.

They were late, and they came separately.

Five Aldermen, watching each other's back. Only one of them, a man I guessed to be B. Fadhil, was wearing the full Alderman's black: long coat fastened too tight around the neck, buttons all the way down its front, black hat. He positioned himself beneath a columned arcade, in front of a shop inviting children everywhere to come and find their perfect teddy bear.

A blonde woman with short hair and a grey suit sat with a newspaper in front of the glassy entrance to the London Transport Museum, trying her very best to look innocuous, and failing – Lucy Holta, at a guess.

I recognised Tommy Kwan, arriving with another woman who I guessed must be Rumina Rathnayake; the two of them headed beneath my balcony, into the market itself. Finally Cecil Caughey, whose face I knew, stepped out of a cab on the corner by the Royal Opera House, briefcase in hand, wearing a black suit, blue shirt and silver tie, and as assured as a royal peacock at a noble wedding. He strutted towards the meeting place I'd assigned: a coffee shop with outdoor tables that would mostly be empty at this time of year. It faced a shop whose windows featured liquid chocolate being freshly dipped with strawberries, cherries, raspberries, before being packaged in little gold boxes as the ultimate indulgent gift.

Caughey didn't bother to order coffee, didn't bother to open his briefcase or make any show of reading a newspaper, but sat upright, one leg crossed over the other, a headmaster waiting for a naughty pupil.

We felt a stirring of personal dislike amid the generality of our rage. Even in watching each other's back, they were ignoring our request.

A waitress approached Caughey; he dismissed her with a curt shake of his head. Looking flustered, she went back inside.

A voice said, "More coffee?"

I barely glanced round, opened my mouth to say no, and he was there, right beside me, one hand resting on the back of a chair. His eyes had followed mine down to where Caughey sat. Templeman, in a charcoal-grey suit and shirt with no tie, smiled his thin smile at my look of recognition.

He slipped into a chair, asked a passing waiter for coffee and a menu, and went back to his study of Caughey in the café below.

"A pompous individual," he remarked. "When your message came to us via Ms Shiring, Caughey insisted that he should be the one to talk to you alone, as he, and only he, would make you see sense. I believe he referred to you as 'that silly little man', at which point, I must admit, my limited respect for Cecil declined to an absolute low."

His eyes narrowed and looked up at mine so suddenly, I nearly pulled back. A paper-thin smile curled in his pale face. "I naturally considered it unlikely that you would be at the meeting place specified by Ms Shiring, and am only a little ashamed that I declined to inform Cecil of this fact."

The waiter returned, laying out steaming coffee in a stainless-steel mug, a new bowl of sugar, jug of milk and undersized coffee cup, as well as a couple of menus. Templeman said, "Have you eaten? I think, considering the circumstances, it should be my treat."

"I'm fine, thank you."

"Eggs Benedict, two toast, and some fresh fruit if you have it, please," murmured Templeman at the waiter, who nodded and scurried away. "Well," he said, pouring coffee before leaning back in his chair. "You've found us."

"I don't fully understand what it is I've found."

His eyebrows arched like cathedral doors. "Really? As you've come this far I suppose it will all come out anyway. May I ask how much you do know? Not in that I wish to curtail your knowledge, but so that I don't have to retread old ground in our discussion."

I forced myself to meet Templeman's gaze. "I know about the Neighbourhood Eye. I know it's run by you and your colleagues. I know that the night Callum's friend was killed . . ."

"Callum?"

"A kid in Westbourne Park."

"You are referring to the incident, some weeks ago, in which four youths were . . . incapacitated . . . and a fifth died?"

"Yes."

"Ah, I see. I am very sorry for that incident; I was not aware you were investigating it. May I ask how it came to your attention?"

"Sure, but you're not getting an answer any time soon."

He smiled again. The spoon did a single slow circle in his coffee, chinked once more against the side of the cup, and was laid to one side. "Of course," he said. "I do understand. Please, continue."

"I know that when that kid died, a local resident of Westbourne Park called the Neighbourhood Eye, not the police. They hadn't done anything wrong, nothing illegal, so the police wouldn't have intervened, but she . . . she . . . " I hesitated, trying to find words that wouldn't become a shout, " . . . she didn't like their attitude. She called the Neighbourhood Eye, they called you, and you sent a monster to deal with it. How am I doing?"

"In terms of broad facts, so far you are correct. But what of the implications?"

"Coming to that," I snapped. "The insect is your tool, your creation. I don't yet know how you control it or what its exact purpose is. But from what I've seen, it targets . . . shall we call them cases of antisocial behaviour? A woman phones up and says 'There are these kids causing trouble' and a guy calls up and says 'Hey, there's these boys drinking and making lots of noise and I think they could be a problem' and you . . . what? You send in the creature to kill them?"

"Not kill, no," corrected Templeman sharply. "It was never intended to kill. That was an unfortunate one-off, an incident which, I believe, will not and cannot be repeated."

"What, then?"

"I believe the term was ... pacify."

"Isn't that what the Americans said about the Iraq War?"

"Only once they'd started to lose it," he replied. "No, the creature – the culicidae, we call it – was created to fill a very specific need. This world we inhabit – the secret world, if you will, a place of magicians – moves through the material world but is not of it. We expect our bins to be emptied and the buses to run on time, but through magic we contribute nothing to the actual functioning of society. The Aldermen have been receiving pleas for hundreds of years to assist in mundane affairs, and recently, what with the threats that have been so successfully dispelled from our city – the Tower, the death of cities, Blackout and the Neon Court – a few of us judged that the time was right to take a more active interest in how our abilities might help the community at large."

"So you created this 'culicidae'? What kind of rubbish name is that?"

"Latin," he replied, sipping from his undersized cup. "I personally think it's rather pretentious, but Caughey said it gave the creature a fine sense of learning and traditionalism. It was manufactured on a purely trial basis. The purpose of the exercise was to determine whether we could create a device which would target a very specific problem group within our society. You said yourself, the police only intervene once a crime has already happened. By creating the Neighbourhood Eye to report crimes before they could happen, and the culicidae to ... neutralise, shall we say, the perpetrators, we hoped to remove deviant members of our society before they had a chance to harm others."

I laughed. I couldn't help it, and I could scarcely stop. Templeman waited, the smile fading.

"Can you hear yourself?" I blurted. "Pacify, neutralise 'deviant members of our society'? Fifty years ago you'd be hunting homosexuals; a century back, you'd be going after suffragettes!"

"I think you will find that homosexuals and suffragettes – well, *suffragists* at least – have been of no danger to society. The youths to whom the culicidae is tuned have no qualms about hurting others. They have no code of honour, no future except one of crime and punishment. The purpose of the culicidae was not to harm them but, rather, to effect a cure."

The calmer he sounded, the more the horror seeped into my voice. "Cure them? Cure them of what? Of youth, of bad dress sense, of drinking, of drugs, of smoking, of sitting on street corners, of trying to pull girls, of spotty skin and swearing? Cure them of *what*?"

"Of ... too much of everything, I suppose," replied Templeman. "The culicidae was not designed to hurt them. It is a finely tuned creation, meant to draw from the subjects certain aspects of their nature which cause distress to others, as in, for example, their rage, fury, resentment, fears. So you see," he concluded, his voice calm and level, "our intentions were thoroughly utilitarian."

I was breathing fast with anger and disbelief. "Well your intentions suck," I exclaimed. "Your intentions aren't just on the stairway to hell, they're in the lift shaft and greasing the cogs of the fucking elevator!"

"Intentions are ... "

"It's killed!"

I'd shouted loud enough for heads to turn at tables nearby. Templeman studied his napkin, waiting for me to calm. I repeated softly, "It's killed. And I don't know if you've bothered to look at your reformed teenagers any time soon, but the one I met wasn't just stripped of rage. He'd lost everything. Head, heart, soul. He was an empty shell sat on the edge of a bed and you ... no intentions can justify this."

He paused, considering his words. "I admit that, as the situation currently stands, the culicidae is not ideal. It is, after all, a work in progress. But it prevents harm to the majority – doesn't merely punish, but prevents. Tell me what could be more important than that."

"I dunno," I said. "Due process? Rule of law? Innocence until proven guilty? How about the last thousand years of thinking about this shit and coming up, at the end of the day, with a big banner that says 'Don't go screwing around without the consent of your fucking peers'? Besides!" – he was on the edge of a rebuttal, and we hadn't the time – "I couldn't give a flying monkey's about your intent. I called the Neighbourhood Eye last night – last bloody night – and reported a bunch of kids who I said *might* cause trouble, who *might* be a pain. And you, even knowing that your stupid bloody stupid sodding science project had *killed*, sent it after us. Not just after a bunch of spectres I'd summoned and dressed up as kids, but after *me*."

A twitch of doubt creased Templeman's otherwise untroubled brow. "After ... you? No, it was not supposed to pursue you. If I'd been aware, in fact, that you were the one making the call, I would never have permitted its dispatch."

"It has claws and it bloody used them!" I snarled. "We tried to fucking bind that bloody stupid monster of yours, we did bloody bind it and it tore through the spell like tissue paper! It came after me, Penny and Nabeela with long claws and a really big mouth and it wasn't sodding stopping for anything. What kind of creature of bloody law and order doesn't bloody stop for the Midnight fucking Mayor!"

I was shouting again. A few of the café's more civilised customers muttered disapprovingly. Templeman let me breathe hard for a while, then murmured, "The culicidae is not designed to pursue people like you."

"And what are people like me?"

"Individuals ... outside a certain age range."

"What?"

"The culicidae is designed to neutralise aggressive tendencies in the young. We wished it to target the same tendencies in adults, but the variables were too great, the effects too hard to predict. Yet, curiously enough, in the young we were able to identify a pattern of behaviour, a loss, as it were, of control, which allowed a very precise tuning of the culicidae to their behavioural patterns. There is a sound ... "

"A high-pitched sound?"

"Quite so."

"I couldn't hear it; Nabeela was screaming."

"It is only audible to the young. As you age, you cease to hear certain high frequencies of sound; by the time you are, say, twenty-five, there are some which to you will be inaudible, but which cause distress to the young."

"So I'm too old to hear what Nabeela heard?"

"Exactly so. The culicidae should not have targeted you; even provoked, it is bound and commanded to disperse and dispel, to cause no harm until it is next summoned. That it did not obey is a cause of some concern."

"It killed a kid, and that didn't concern you?"

"Of course it concerned us; it concerned us very deeply. But in all other respects the culicidae has been functioning within acceptable parameters. There were some within our number who advocated a period of observation, to monitor the development of the creature – I was one among them – but I was outvoted. We are very democratic."

I drew in a long, slow breath, feeling the pressure of it down to the pit of my lungs. The fire in my ribs had reduced overnight to a throb that merely shot agony to my fingertips whenever I moved too fast.

"Okay," I said. "Here's the question of the moment, the reason we're all here, the bank-breaker, whatever. Who the hell are 'we'?"

Templeman registered a thought unseen. "We, Mr Mayor, are your Minority Council."

First Interlude: The Minority Council

In which a brief explanation is offered.

Templeman said, "Let me cast your mind back.

"Let us recall your inauguration.

"Your predecessor in this office, Nair, was one of us. A wizard who had, in time, found his way to the ranks of the Aldermen and, again in time, been chosen through fair debate and council as the most worthy candidate to be Midnight Mayor. When his predecessor died, and Nair succeeded to the power and responsibility of this office, there was general satisfaction, for Nair was, if nothing else, a safe pair of hands. Reliable, upright. University degree, seven years in the civil service, another eleven in finance; a conservative but essentially sound practitioner of magic. He even played golf, if you enjoy such things, and when an issue became too heated for discussion in the office, he would invite the concerned parties to join him for long walks, by the river in Kew and Richmond, to cool heads. He made no remarkable decisions, but he made the decisions that needed to be made.

"And yet, in time, there came a feeling that Nair himself was dissatisfied with the office. He never spoke of it; he was an intensely private man. But whereas he had accepted the role eagerly, as the years went by he seemed more withdrawn, taking to walking the city streets late at night, by himself, talking to things unseen in the shadows. You have not been Midnight Mayor for long, Matthew; you do not yet, I think, fully grasp its implication. You are part of the city now, and for a while you may feel as if nothing significant has changed within you, but in time . . . to serve a thing so big, so magnificent, you must be prepared to give up that part of yourself that is small, petty, and which in being small and petty is so very human. It is a lonely thing, to make the choices you must, and fight battles that no others can, without thanks, and with death the only certainty – for it is very rarely that a Midnight Mayor dies peacefully. You will find all this, I think, in time.

"Of Nair, then.

"In his last years of office, his isolation from the Aldermen grew ever more pronounced. Some thought it was a natural part of his power, that he was achieving a state of awareness that surpassed our mere comprehension – for me, this was too theological an interpretation. Others said the burden of the decisions he had to make, as a price paid for the greater good, was weighing on him. Others said perhaps he just knew his time had come, that he was growing older and that his safety could not last.

"Whatever the case, all agreed that things changed when you came back.

"Or rather, when the other part that is you came back.

"For some time we had been monitoring the activities of your former mentor, Robert Bakker. We knew about the Tower, about his organisation to monitor and control magicians for his own ends. We knew that sorcerers had been dying in the city; and while we could not link these murders to Bakker himself; nonetheless, as many died and he survived, a process of elimination seemed to confirm what we had always suspected: Bakker was killing sorcerers – Bakker had killed you. You were the first, you see, the first sorcerer to die in the purges he began, and your death was unremarkable, as your life had been.

"And then, two years later, the blue electric angels stopped singing. We monitor all spirits whose activities concern the well-being of the city. So we were listening when the blue electric angels vanished from the telephone lines. One minute they had been dancing their dance in the static of the wires, and the next . . . nothing. Gone. Just a dialling tone to empty air. And not two days later, Matthew Swift, Bakker's dead apprentice, is walking around London, apparently alive and well, and his eyes are now blue, and his vengeance is unlimited, and he is doing what no one else had dared, no, not even Nair, and striking out against the Tower. We watched you raise your allies; watched you battle Bakker's peers, then Bakker himself. We saw your blood burn blue, and began to suspect what you were.

"There were some who said we should ally ourselves with the Tower; that no matter what evil Bakker had done, he was still a force for stability. I do not say, for good – no one could deny that by this time he was quite, quite mad – but he kept the magicians of the city quiet, and afraid, and that kept them from doing others harm. A benevolent tyrant, a casual dictator. Yes, there were Aldermen who would have allied with Bakker, to remove from our streets what seemed to be the far greater threat – you.

"Nair would not authorise it.

"The debate on what to do with you, as your battle with Bakker reached its peak, was one of the most divisive to have reached my ears. A sorcerer – a dead sorcerer at that – and walking the earth together with the blue electric angels. And your campaign of retribution against the Tower hardly gave you a glowing press.

"But Nair said, no. You were not to be touched. It was then that I began to realise – he wasn't afraid of you; he didn't consider you a danger to the city. He was envious of you, Matthew. He was envious because you were standing up and doing the things that he could not do. Not that he lacked the means, but that the burden of his responsibility forbade him from doing what his heart longed to achieve. We all want to defeat evil, Matthew, all of us. But too often the greater good asks us to let a little evil live, for the good of us all.

"I think it was then that Nair decided to make you his heir.

"He told no one. He knew, I think, the outcry that would have followed. Perhaps he knew also that there were worse things out there than Robert Bakker, and that you, if angered, might be one of them. I think he chose you as Midnight Mayor to guarantee you would never be the city's enemy. It was a canny choice, and a dangerous one.

"I confess, our previous animosity towards you may have made us too hasty in judging you. Your current apprentice, Penny Ngwenya, ignorant of what she was, in rage summoned a creature we know as the death of cities. First it targeted the Midnight Mayor, and moved so fast, and so quietly, we did not understand what it could be, and when we found Nair's corpse, the things that had been done to it ... there were only so many creatures in the city capable of such power, and such cruelty.

"You seemed a likely candidate for having killed Nair – powerful and dangerous, your human mind, we thought, long since gone, subsumed into the fury of the blue electric angels, who know no laws and have no concept of our mortal morality. Our pursuit of you was violent, and the discovery that, far from our enemy, you were now our new Midnight Mayor, was traumatic for many.

"There was a vote taken.

"I believe it was the very first ever taken in the history of the city.

"We, the Aldermen, who are chosen by our peers, not by mystic forces and dead men's wills, voted on whether or not to kill you. The Midnight Mayor can control his heir, but you – you were only a few hours into your new position, you had not yet been inaugurated into its power, did not understand its strength – the risk of the power moving to a new subject seemed marginal compared to the risk of keeping it with you.

"We voted on whether to kill you.

"I must admit, I was surprised, when the decision was made, how close it was. You were saved by two votes. I'm afraid you misunderstand me – my surprise was not that you were saved by two votes, but that the numbers willing to save you at all were even close to the majority required. I had imagined the Aldermen would kill you at once and be done with it.

"Two things, I believe, saved you. The first was the fear that the Aldermen permitted themselves to feel at the time. After all, their Midnight Mayor was dead, murdered without the killer batting an eye, and the defences of the city were falling like sandcastles before the sea. Under such circumstances, if, say, one of our number should become Midnight Mayor, who was to say that the fate which befell Nair would not befall him or her instead? Dangerous you were – you are – but if that danger could be channelled against our mutual enemy, then it seemed a risk worth taking. The second thing that saved you, in my opinion, was the respect the Aldermen held, even then, for Nair. Few of us understood it, few of us appreciated the rationale behind it, few could believe it, but Nair had chosen you as his heir, had made the conscious decision that when he died, the phone would ring and you would answer it, and nothing would be the same again. Perhaps you were what we needed.

"Perhaps you were the right decision after all.

"You did defeat the death of cities. Few can make that claim.

"And when Blackout came, burning out the eyes of all who looked on it, you stopped Blackout as well. You brought peace between the Tribe and the Neon Court, for as long as it will last, and you found us: the culicidae. You took down a dusthouse. No one takes down the dusthouses.

"But, Matthew, you do not see the bigger picture.

"Penny Ngwenya, the woman who summoned the death of cities – she should have been killed. You had the choice to kill her and you rejected it, and dozens more died for your deeds. She is dangerous, unstable, afraid of her own power and what she will do with it.

"When Blackout possessed your friend Oda, you should have killed them both while there was time. Instead you let the city shrink to a bubble of light in a sea of darkness, let the streets tear themselves apart, all because of some misguided notion of saving your friend, which you could not achieve.

"When the Neon Court asked you to honour their alliance, you went instead to their enemy, the Tribe, compromising yourself and your office. The rule of law, the obligations of our treaties, they are what drive the office of the Midnight Mayor. There was nothing to prevent the Tribe from killing you outright at a time of crisis and yet you went, alone and without warning. These are not the deeds of the Midnight Mayor. And yet, because we are the Aldermen and you carry the scars of your office, you are obeyed.

"You asked us who 'we' are.

"This then, is your answer.

"We are the Minority Council.

"We were formed after the vote, to observe and monitor. To carry out the duties of the Aldermen regardless of your own deeds. We carry the tradition of what the Aldermen have been, of what the Midnight Mayor should be. We are not your enemies, Matthew, for we perceive now that you are as important a part of this city as any of your predecessors. But we do what you dare not; what you do not have the courage to do. We see the big picture. We protect you, even if it has to be from yourself. I cannot tell you how many there are in our membership. I can only tell you that we are as much a part of this city as you are, and to fight us is to fight yourself."

After he'd finished speaking, I was silent.

Down below, Cecil Caughey was fuming over his briefcase, the redness of his face visible even from where we sat. Templeman leant back in his chair, steepling his fingers, waiting.

I said, "Shut it down."

"The Minority Council isn't for ..."

"Not the Council. I'm not interested in them for the moment. Right now, I'm talking priorities. The culicidae, this ... thing you've summoned, this stupid bloody project, shut it down."

"There was a great deal of investment in the culicidae. Time, money, effort ..."

"This was never a profit-making thing anyway. This was you and your ... colleagues ... thinking 'wow, let's go stick our noses into local government and hey, what the streets are really lacking is a creature that eats the souls of our kids!' And it's failed. It's been a cock-up and it's failed and now you are going to shut it down."

"Matthew –"

We slammed our fist on the table hard enough to make the sugar jump from its bowl.

"Is this the fight you want to pick?" we demanded. "We don't know what else you've been doing, but there's going to be much, much more that you've been hiding. Of all the things we are going to tear down, is this the one you want to defend?"

He sighed loudly, a reasonable man confronted with the intractability of the insane. "Do I take it then that, when this is done, we can have a conversation – a measured, open conversation – about the Minority Council's future? One that is open to the merits of our work?"

"Find me a merit, and I'll let it stand."

"We did it to help you, Matthew. Someone has to take responsibility."

A thought hit, and was on the end of my tongue before I could stop it. "You can't save everyone."

"Indeed," murmured Templeman, an empty sound to meet empty sounds as he turned towards the waiter. "The bill, please."

A voice that might have been mine added, "You can't save those who don't want to be saved."

He wasn't listening. "We should also, at some point, discuss the dusthouses."

"Is that another one of the Minority Council's pet projects?" I demanded. "Bring down the dusthouses and if I get topped in the process then hell, two birds, one stone, hurrah."

"Please be assured, we never intended harm to you personally. The benefits of having a suitably ... radical figure ... are known even to those among us who can hardly be counted as your greatest fans. And no, since you ask. The Minority Council do not approve of aggressive action against the dusthouses. Such action, they believe, would risk upsetting the delicate balance we currently have with the fairy god-mother and must, at the end of the day, prove futile. The assistance I gave you was entirely mine. I ... somewhat compromised myself ... with my actions."

"Wow, you went out on a limb, how sweet."

"I can still help you, Matthew. If you'll let me."

Templeman paid.

We went down to the street together.

Caughey didn't spot us immediately. When he rose, face flushing, he proved a large man, with a big voice to match. But what nature had gifted him physically, it had taken away in other regards.

"Templeman, what the hell ... ?"

"Mr Swift and I have discussed the situation," replied Templeman. "And I believe we have it under control."

"I take it you think you're in charge," I said.

"I am the Chairman of the Minority Council," Caughey replied, looking at me as a crocodile might consider a lame mouse. "Templeman, for all we value his excellent work and service, is a sub-chairman."

"It's the way you say you're Chairman of the Minority Council as if it was a good thing. How do you do it?"

Before he could answer, Templeman cut in.

"Mr Caughey," he said, "the Midnight Mayor and I have had a

productive discussion and I will fill you in as soon as is feasible. But right now, I'm afraid Mr Swift must insist on moving on quickly, as there is a lot of work to be done."

As we strode away, Caughey didn't exactly yield.

He just couldn't quite keep up.

Templeman's car was parked round the corner. He'd got the worst of the sewer stench out of it from our last expedition, and now it smelt of lemons and aloe vera. I strapped myself in, flinching at the pressure of the belt across my ribs. Templeman didn't seem to notice, but he said, with his eyes on the street as we pulled away, "Have you seen a doctor?"

"Yes."

"Is it serious?"

"She prescribed bed rest." I added, "I'm surprised you care."

"I hold you no personal animosity. There is no room for personal feelings in our positions. Yet who you are, and what you are – they remain two separate entities."

"That's very pat. Where are we going?"

"To see the man responsible for the culicidae."

"There's one specific guy?"

"Perhaps I should say, responsible for the technical aspects of the culicidae. The realisation, if you will."

We headed south, towards Waterloo Bridge. For a moment, above the river, the pale blue sky was open and bright, with here and there a layer of high wispy clouds. Then the city reasserted itself, as we drove past the glassy side of Waterloo station and the clipped grass framing the Imperial War Museum. I got out my phone, called Penny.

There was the sound of tinned pop music in the background. "Hey Matthew," she said. "Not dead yet?"

"Penny, where are you?" Templeman glanced at me from the corner of his eye as I talked, but said nothing.

"Look, it was all going fine with you and these Council guys, wasn't it? I mean, you're cool, yeah, it's not like they're killing you or nothing? We saw you get into a car and you didn't look like you were being held at gunpoint or nothing."

There was giggling somewhere beyond the other end of the phone. I took a deep breath and said, "Penny, are you shopping with Nabeela?"

Silence. Then, "I have no idea, yeah, how you can have, like, so little faith in me."

"I'm going to go."

"It's not like I get to go to Covent Garden every day anyway ..."

"Hanging up now."

"... and we're not buying, we're just looking ..."

I moved to hang up but, God, she could be loud when she wanted to; even Templeman heard her shout down the phone, "Hey, Matthew?!"

I held it a little away from my ear and mumbled, "Yeah?"

"You call me if you get, like, shot or shit?"

"I'll do that. Have fun."

Distances changed meaning south of the river: stations were further apart, the trains faster, the journeys longer, the streets smaller, the buses slower, the boundaries between rich and poor, business and pleasure, thinner. Transport hubs south of the river were fewer and further between, but what they lacked in regularity they made up for in scale. Few rail passengers heading south could long avoid Clapham Junction; no dedicated bus user would ever truly steer clear of Brixton; and, for the motorist, there was Elephant and Castle, God's dire warning to man in roundabout form, framed on all sides by architecture the UN ought to have banned as a crime against aesthetics. The area had a vibrancy of its own, a magic of its own, but it was a power of survival, a hot, bright burning taste to the air that urged all travellers to pass straight on through, not to linger.

We made for a quiet side street in Kennington, another sly corner of town where good intentions had been raised up in brick and stone, and bad circumstances had knocked over the trash can on the doorstep outside. One of these good intentions was an estate made of shiny varnished red brick beneath a black sloping roof, with the sign of the Corporation of London stamped on the outside, and a noticeboard informing you that you were arriving at the Fryer Estate, a Peabody Trust property built by good men with nice ideas and not a huge deal of foresight.

An inner courtyard contained five parking spaces for the fifty flats that looked down on it, doors on shared balconies, and stairwells garnished with damp litter. On some balconies, metal grilles marked off *this* flat from *that*, behind which were children's bicycles, empty washing racks, long-dead potted plants and the obligatory broken plastic water pistol in a sand bucket by the door.

At ground level, there was one door to each apartment block, a thing of wrought iron painted pinkish-orange and baby blue. Templeman buzzed flat twelve, and waited.

The voice that answered through the intercom was deep, gruff and bored. It said, "Yeah?"

"Good morning," sang out Templeman. "I'm from Harlun and Phelps, and I'm here to ..."

"Come in," grunted the voice. The door was buzzed open.

The chipped front door to flat twelve was standing ajar. Templeman knocked politely and pushed it wide. We stepped into a hall that smelt of cigarette smoke. The walls were pale green, the floor was linoleum, coming up at the edges, and from the end of a narrow corridor there was the sound of a TV. A man appeared, one arm half into a black uniform jacket, flies undone and tie hanging loose around his neck. He saw me and grunted, saw Templeman and grunted again, with what might have been recognition.

"I'm late, okay, so you'll see yourself out when you're done?"

"Of course," replied Templeman, with a half-nod that in quainter times might have become a bow.

The man vanished into the room from which the sound of TV came, slamming the door behind him. Templeman smiled thinly at my expression. He turned to another door, painted a stronger shade of green, which bore a large sign in red crayon:

If you come in here without my permission you will get warts.

Seriously i mean i know you think you won't but you will.

And they won't be like verruca warts or shit they'll be, big and black and everyone will look at them and say 'wow, he's got warts uck' so don't fucking do it, even if you think your doing the right thing or something because your not and im serious.

Beneath this someone else had written in pencil.

I'll leave your washing on the machine.

Templeman knocked ...

He knocked again, louder, and called out, "Alan?"

A muffled voice exclaimed, "Go away!"

"Alan, it's Mr Templeman."

Silence from inside. Then, "Hold on!"

Sounds. Maybe the creak of a bed. A bare foot on a wooden floor. A wardrobe opening. Clothes hangers rattling. A drawer slamming. A thudding that might have been someone hopping about into a pair of too-tight trousers. A shirt, perhaps, was being pulled off the back of a chair. Then, "Just one more minute!"

A scurrying as of things being pulled off the floor and thrown into a corner. A sliding noise as of a window being opened, perhaps to let out smells that had no name. A scraping as of other things being pushed under the bed. A rattle, as of a chain being pulled back from the door, and then the door itself was opened and I gazed upon the face of the man responsible for the culicidae.

And the face had acne.

We sat gingerly on the edge of a single bed.

Behind us, the duvet rose like a camel's hump, hiding beneath it we dared not speculate what. A poster showed various species of dinosaur; nearby was a hobbit-sized cardboard cut-out of Frodo Baggins, complete with ring of power, looking like he'd just had an unnameable accident after a dodgy meal.

On the one chair of the little room, in front of a desk sagging with the weight of overpowered computer and computing equipment, was the greatest summoner in the world.

I knew he was the greatest summoner in the world because a large sign had been stuck up above his bed that read '!!!!Greatest Summoner in the World!!!!', complete with a picture of this same individual posing proudly in front of a spray-painted summoning circle with trapped troll inside to prove he'd done it. I knew he was the greatest summoner in the world because, as I'd shuffled dubiously into his bedroom, Templeman had said, "Matthew, may I introduce you to Alan. Alan did the technical work on the creation of the culicidae, and is widely regarded as one of the greatest summoners of the age, by people whom I trust to know about such things. Alan, this is the Midnight Mayor."

To which Alan had replied, "Yo dude, you look kinda shit."

I looked at him, he looked at me. He was maybe seventeen years old, with peroxide-blond hair greasily slicked back, crumpled grey T-shirt and pale skin glowing with unfulfilled hormonal stress. At some stage in his life he'd decided that having piercings was cool, and slotted a bolt into his lower lip to prove the point. When he moved, he trailed elbow and knee like the tail of a meteorite; and he sprawled across the bedroom chair with the discretion of a hand grenade.

We blurted, "*This* child summoned the culicidae?"

Alan was in there first with an indignant cry of, "Yeah, man! What, you saying you don't think I look up to it, or what?"

"Alan is ... very talented," murmured Templeman.

Alan pointed with both index fingers at Templeman, nodding vigorously in agreement.

"So," I mumbled, "you ... picked up summoning at school or what?"

"Uh, yeah, I like totally attend after-school classes, *not.*"

"Matthew *is* the Midnight Mayor," crooned Templeman, flinching. "I'm not sure if you're familiar with the office, but ..."

"*You're* supposed to be the protector of the fucking city? No fucking way!" exclaimed Alan. "I mean, like, no disrespect or nothing man, but you look like, you know ..." A gesture encapsulated what words could not express.

"The culicidae," I groaned, trying not to be distracted by the thought of painkillers. "Big, bad, brain-sucking monster, let's talk about that, shall we?"

He brightened. "Did you like it?" he asked, spinning in his chair. "I mean, it was, like, a total mind-fuck to create or whatever; I had to spend, like, hours planning and stuff and when it actually came together at the end I was, like, whoa, this is the shit, this is where the money's at, this is like, this is like King Kong on the Eiffel fucking Tower, you know what I'm saying?"

"No," we said.

"Hey hey hey hey." A snap of his fingers and Alan started rummaging through a drawer, babbling as he went. "I've been working on, like, these new mods for it too, you know, like these subroutines we can upload to like, the central matrix, for like, feeding patterns, hunting patterns, advanced ambi-mystic regeneration patterns, serious mega stuff."

Socks that were only a damp radiator away from evolving and walking off on their own went flying out of the drawer; dead batteries and crinkled magazines in torn plastic bags were turfed out onto the floor. I asked, "You do much of this? Summoning . . . things?"

"Yeah, you know, I dabble and shit. But some guys, you know, it's all like, 'elemental this' or 'demon that' and I'm like, guys, I don't know what kinda world you fucking live in, but me, I've gotta get on. I've got plans, I've got things to do, I mean, I'm gonna be twenty in like three years or shit and I'm planning on being dead when I'm forty because it's all downhill then and I can't be bothered, you know yeah?"

"And the culicidae . . . how'd you get involved in summoning that?"

"Oh, you know," he explained, finally producing from the back of the drawer a large green bag bulging with scrap metal. "I posted on a few forums, followed a few blogs, yeah, until I realised that, like, most people who talk about the magic shit on the internet are just losers with candles and stuff, because you know, magicians are so fifteenth century about technology, I mean, guys, Wikipedia, it's there, like, what are you doing with the whole books in cowskin shit?"

"So I guess you're proud of your work."

"Man, there's so much more I can do, I mean, the culicidae was just the start. Magic is life, yeah, I mean, life is magic, wherever there's fucking life there's like magic just waiting to happen and I, I am the guy, I mean, I'm Captain America, I'm the stretchy guy from the Fantastic Four, I'm like 'Da Vinci? Who is this guy?' I mean, what the hell was he on about, two guys with their arms sticking out in different directions, like what the fuck is that all about, hello? Here!" A broken bulb was held aloft in triumph, the glass smashed out at the top, and the filament glowing a gentle red. "Oh, man, when we plug this in it's gonna be like, I mean it's gonna be like . . . I don't even know what it's gonna be like but it's gonna have, like, nitro!"

I put on my best smile. "Alan," I said. "Don't overreact here, because I can tell you're committed to your work, but we might just have to put that on hold for a moment."

His face began to fall.

"Alan," I went on, all smiling firmness and thoughts of painkillers. "The culicidae. Very impressive, very good work, you should be proud, very grateful for all your efforts, and that. Now tell us how to destroy it."

There was some shouting.

Then there was some wheedling.

Then there was a bit more shouting.

I leant my head against the wall, wrapped my arms around my ribs and let Templeman handle it. There was no winning an argument against Templeman; words washed over him like water over diamond.

I tuned out of the argument all the way to a cry of, "I don't see why you need me anyway, yeah, I mean it's not like I didn't give you every-thing with a fucking manual for, like, dorks."

"There's been a complication," said Templeman. "It's not acting within its basic operational parameters."

Stunned silence. Then a defensive flailing of hands and a cry of, "And I hope you're not gonna try and, like, blame me because, sorry, what I made was ace and if there's something wrong with the system, then I'm gonna tell you, it's a wetware, not a software thing okay man?"

"Can we just go back to the part where you said that the Council could deal with the problem?"

Alan looked surprised to hear me speak, then blurted, "Well, yeah, because I, like, gave them the remote control and I mean, duh, it comes with an 'off' setting so I don't see why they can't just, like, fucking turn it off, you know."

I looked at Templeman, eyebrows raised.

"Mr Mayor ... we could turn the culicidae ... I think 'off' is a little vague, but we could control it to a degree. But as your own encounter with the creature has demonstrated, its behaviour has been ... erratic. It shouldn't have attacked you, to begin with, and now ..."

"Whoa there!" Alan was on his feet. "Did it, like, attack you?"

"Yeah."

"And you're, like ... how old?"

"Everyone's old when you're seventeen, and I'm not," I snapped. I turned back to Templeman. "Define 'erratic'."

"In its dormant state, the culicidae doesn't have a fully embodied physical form," said Templeman. "It reverts to its constituent parts: glass and slate, mostly, allowing it to be stored in a couple of dumpsters for deployment around the city."

"And can I just say, yeah, that it was, like, pure fucking genius get-ting it to do that," said Alan, adding, "It *attacked* you?"

"That's right."

"Way out! And you're not dead — that's like mega. You know, respect, man. Respect."

"Let's stick with how everything's gone wrong, shall we? A couple of dumpsters, dormant state, okay; what's causing the problem?"

"When recalled," went on Templeman, "the culicidae should return to a fixed location and decompose into its dormant state. Last night, after your ... encounter ... we called it back and it ... didn't return."

"You sure you did it right?" asked Alan.

Templeman glowered. "We did it exactly as we have done every procedure so far. To be frank, recently there have been ... a few glitches. The return to a dormant state should, for example, according to your notes, render it completely inert. But even in its decomposed mode, the culicidae has been moving."

Alan gave a shriek, hands going to his head. "Oh, my God, you guys are like ... you're like Dumbo on magic mushrooms, you're like Bambi looking at the big bad wolf and going meow, you're like ... you know what you guys are like? You're like thick, that's what you are like."

"I'm with Alan on this one," I offered, as Templeman allowed himself to look exasperated. "Sorry."

"I told you this might happen! Did I not, like, say," shrilled Alan. "Don't overfeed, don't overexpose, go easy in the first few months, you know? What have you been doing to my baby?"

"I fed it on spectres," I volunteered.

"Course you did!" exclaimed Alan.

"And it killed a kid."

Alan's look of shock darted from me to Templeman and back, daring us to call it a joke. Then he tried to insist, "Uh-uh. Doesn't kill, no death, that's not what it's built for. There'll be all sorta conflicts in the main matrix, it'll be like ... I mean it'll be like, I don't even know what it'll be like, so let's ignore any other shit and just focus on the bad. Big, big bad."

"How big, how bad?" I asked.

"Like ... like mega bad!" exclaimed Alan. "Life is magic, dumbos. I mean, you put enough of life into anything and sooner or later it's gonna pop, too much of anything too much, too much vitamin C is like, poison, you know what I'm saying. Too much sunlight you get skin cancer and too much feeding on the rage of, like, screwed-up kids who don't know how to, like, chill and talk to girls, and you get ... you get *boom!* The culicidae was supposed to have a cooling-off period, it was supposed to have time to discharge all that shit it's feeding on. You overdose it on too much stuff and of course things are going to get bad, it's gonna fuck around with the internal wiring, you hear what I'm saying? You feed it on rage and rage is what you're gonna get, haven't any of you guys seen *The Empire Strikes Back?*"

"With you so far on the academic theory – now, how do we fix it?"

Another sweeping gesture of 'damned if I know'. "Hey, I gave you, like, the full specs when you asked. If you went and screwed around with my baby, I can't, like, be held responsible for your pig-brained acts, you know?"

I smiled faintly. "You don't really get how this is going to work, do you?" For a moment, Alan's eyes met ours, and his Adam's apple rose and fell.

"Okay," I went on with a cheery loudness I did not feel. "Let's work on basic principles. The Neighbourhood Eye has been so brilliantly successful that they've overfed the culicidae on the drained brains of kids across the city, and now it's got enough juice in its system to allow it independent action, free from its usual control systems, as well as, while we're on the subject, making it mad enough to kill with claws. So I'm guessing that textbook solutions are out. The question now becomes: what is it going to take to destroy it?"

Alan cringed. "That's kinda a serious ask ... "

"I'm asking."

"I'm just saying ... "

"We're *telling*. What do we need to kill it before it kills someone else?"

The boy's face twisted. "I guess ... you'd have to summon it first."

"I'm good at that."

"And then you'd need to, like, bind it ... "

"Tried that, didn't work."

"Yeah, what'd you use?"

"Police warning."

"Well, *duh*, obviously that wouldn't hold it," grunted Alan. "It's like, designed to feed on the kinda stuff that makes kids ignore coppers, you know? Rage, fury, fear, these aren't, like, major-rational things that're gonna make you listen to a cop, I mean, you asking for trouble or what?"

"Then what would you recommend to use to bind?"

"I dunno, I was just saying, yeah, police warning – really crappy idea."

"Let's say," interjected Templeman, "that we manage to bind it. How do we destroy it?"

"Oh man," groaned Alan, "I mean, I built it really well, you know? I put a lot of mean mother cool shit into that baby, she's not going down easy."

"Hypothesise," I growled.

"Man, I don't even know what you're fucking saying, but I guess, if you were serious about decommissioning my baby, and I'm like, you know, major overreaction or shit, but okay, if you were serious . . . I guess the only way to, like, guarantee it would be to find a way to, like, bind it, because she's built on a separable organo-runic matrix so, like, chopping her up isn't going to hack it, unless you've got time to bury each individual piece in like, concrete, I mean, duh, no . . . what was I saying?"

"If I was serious about killing it."

"Oh yeah. I guess you'd have to, like, crack open the casing, yeah, and like, wear really big gloves, yeah, and maybe, like, find a way to pull out her heart. 'Cos that's where the spell got written, you know, I mean, that's where my best work was at. The rest is just, like, show."

"It's got a heart."

"Sure, yeah. All the best summonings gotta have a core, a focal point, something to make it all go *splat*." Fingers waggled to explain 'splat'. "That's what makes them great, you know. I mean, it's also what makes them weak so I, like, buried the core in the middle of the thorax, you know, behind as much armour and glass as I could find so, you know, make it hard to kill. Sorry." He tried a smile, charming as a shark.

"So your advice, just so I can make sure I'm absolutely clear about this, is to summon the culicidae somehow, bind it somehow, open it up somehow, reach inside a spinning mass of glass and death somehow, and pull out its heart."

"Uh . . . yeah, basically."

"Anything else?"

"Ohohoh! The heart'll be kinda crispy. I mean, like, hot, you know? I tried to make it more energy-efficient, get a couple of new resonance points shipped over from the States to try out, but it's always that payoff, you know, between mass and efficiency and, at the end of the day, I figured, let's go mega-big awesome cool, and screw the environment, you know?" He grinned the hopeful grin of a child caught stealing candy. "Hey – look, if you don't, like, get killed or something doing this, then can I, uh, can I have the heart?"

"What?"

"Seriously, man, it's like major cool work and I'm really, like, it's like my really best thing and – oh and yeah! If it, like, fell into the wrong hands it could do major-league-shit damage, because I'm telling you, it's like got 'go boogie' written all over it in, like, runic form okay, so uh . . . can I have it back?"

"Did the Minority Council pay you to summon this thing?" I asked.

"Uh, yeah."

"Then no, you can't have the bloody heart back."

His face fell. "Oh. Okay. Would you have given it to me if I hadn't been paid?"

"If they hadn't paid you I'd have given you a thick ear."

"Dude, that is, like, so un-cool and, like, totally not the mature thing."

I staggered up, leaning on the bed-head. "'Dude'!" I exclaimed, dragging down a ragged breath. "You're the guy who summoned a creature that sucks the brains out of kids your own age, and can I just take this moment to say that while I'm not exactly grammar 101 guy myself, you suck. I mean, you really do. I've been chased, kicked, clawed at and generally had a really shitty couple of days, and you're calling me 'dude'? Which part of me is so dude-like in your eyes? Is it the guy who stands above the coffins as they're lowered into the ground, the sorcerer with blood on his hands, the friendly bloke being hunted by bloodhounds with teeth of acid and claws of crimson, the Midnight Mayor with a scar on his palm and the eyes of the dragon at his back, or the electric angels blazing fury in our blood? Just what are you so pally with? And you – you're seventeen and the monster you've summoned has sucked the souls from we know not how many innocent kids, and you think you can speak to us at all?"

Alan began an incoherent splutter; a look from Templeman cut him off. I shuffled to the door and let myself out, forcing us to breathe long and slow, driving back the sapphire rage that blurred our vision. The cold air outside was a relief, a slap to the senses; and as we marched downstairs to the car the shadows scuttled out of our way.

Templeman followed a few minutes later.

He didn't start the engine, but sat behind the wheel, looking at nothing much. Finally, "Do you have a plan?"

"I'm getting there."

"Do you think summoning this creature is the right move just now? You are hardly at your best."

"I'll be fine."

"Matthew," insisted Templeman, leaning back against the headrest, "you can't be a hero for everyone."

"This is just good housekeeping."

"Then we can help you," he said.

"And you bloody will, too! You, Caughey, the whole bloody Minority Council, you are bloody going to be there when we deal with this thing and, for all I care, you can bloody stick your arm into its belly and go rummaging around for a burning heart, because there's nothing quite as heroic as an amputated arm and death by decapitation."

He let me seethe a bit longer, then asked, "Where would you like to go now?"

"Enfield."

"Enfield?" he asked, unable to keep the surprise from his voice. "Why – what's in Enfield?"

"A problem I've been neglecting."

"Can you share?"

I thought about it.

Thought about the Beggar King, and heard at the back of my mind the rolling voice of Dudley Sinclair, the sudden pressure of his hand gripping my arm.

"Maybe later."

We drove north in silence.

I leant my head against the window and looked at nothing much and everything in particular. Green Lanes was a suburban road that stretched for miles, crawling past traffic lights until the road signs started offering directions to motorways, to giant shopping centres clinging to the edge of the metropolis, and, all-purpose, to 'The North'.

In Enfield, Templeman asked, "Is there somewhere particular you want to go?"

"We're looking for Windmill Lane."

"What's at Windmill Lane?"

"A house the Beggar King mentioned."

"The Beggar King? What has the Beggar King to do with this?"

"Hopefully, nothing."

We turned off into a network of back streets, the kind that are a rat-runner's dream and a council nightmare: cars parked on both sides, creating just enough room for one vehicle to go one way and get stuck behind a garbage truck. Houses of red brick, with white-painted woodwork around the front porch and the bay window, looked out onto a street built just too early for garaging. To a cursory inspection, nothing in these roads marked left from right, north from south; but look closer. Here, a family with children of an age that liked painting and pasting had filled the windows with cut-out fairies, and cats with crayon eyes. There, a woman who loved lavender had filled her entire front garden with the stuff. Next door lived a family who believed in designer landscaping, as evidenced by zen pebbles and a stone vase. There, a house turned into flats, a worn buzzer by the scruffy front door; here someone with a belief in privacy, thick net curtains and a privet hedge eight feet high; next door a family who'd had experience of crime, bars on the ground-floor windows and another gate across the porch. Round the corner, and there was the house of the obligatory nationalist family, a Greek flag flying in splendour atop a pole in the front garden; two houses down, another family had felt the knee-jerk need to fill their windows with tatty Union Jacks. An upstairs window carried a scarf proclaiming the wonders of Enfield Town F.C., for this will be the year that they are promoted from the Ryman League Division One North to the full glories of the Conference South.

And there was Windmill Lane, a street like any other, uphill towards where once there might even have been a windmill and where now a sixth-form college invited attendees to Be All You Can Be.

The house where we stopped looked unremarkable. A tall laurel hedge had grown wild, and one of the numbers on the front door hung crooked by a single nail. The one black dustbin was empty, its lid greasy with rotting leaves from an overhanging lime tree. Templeman said, "What's here?"

I didn't answer, levering myself out of the car one cautious limb at a time.

The windows were dark, barred and shuttered on every floor. A frosted bathroom window had been broken on the first floor, the glass uncleared on the ground below. Broken from the inside, glass falling out.

At the front door I jiggled a set of keys in the lock until one of the right make fitted, and coaxed it to assume the right ridges and dips, metal moving at my command until, with a click, the lock sprang open. The hall was cold; the door slammed heavily behind. A tiled hall, high ceiling, wallpaper peeling away. Someone had left the mains sockets on, but I couldn't taste power in them. There was a no-smell; not dirt or bleach, dust or mould; not smoke or cooking, or any warmth that suggested people had been here. Wide rooms led off either side of the hall, but held no furniture. A flight of stairs led to a first floor as bare as the one below. We ran our fingers along the cold walls, feeling for electricity in the wires, sounds in the telephone, the warmth of someone else's skin staining the sense of the place, and found none of it. A minimum of light crawled round the shutters. In one room, a fireplace had been boarded up. Finger marks had been scratched into the top of the ply: white ragged dents in lines of four. We traced our fingers into those lines and our tongue went dry, thick leather in our mouth, and we tasted dust. In the bathroom, greasy tidemarks were layered above a hair-filled plug. A spider scuttled away down the hole of the sink, and where there should have been a mirror in a frame, now there was just a pale patch on the wall.

Downstairs, the door to the back garden was bolted shut, the garden itself overgrown with stinging nettles, buddleia and brambles. I cast my mind out for the usual tribes of rats and burrowing foxes that thrived in these places, and found nothing. Not even the limp-clawed grandfather rat that scuttled through the back gardens of the city without fear, not even the mangled pigeon with nowhere better to hide; nothing moved or answered my call.

Templeman murmured, "What is this place? Why is the Beggar King so interested?"

We made no reply. The cold was more than a condition of the weather; it was a thing that came from the walls, that had been scratched into the wood with bloody nails, raised up where a mirror should have stood, crawling out of the cracks between the broken tiles on the floor.

A triangular door in the side of the staircase opened into another, steeper stair to a basement. Here there was no light past the low ceiling, and where there should have been more rats and the dripping of busy pipes changing temperature, silence. I summoned a bubble of sodium orange light to my fingers, lobbed it ahead of us and, one hand on the ceiling and the other on the wall, eased down the stairs.

The basement was one room, in which my bubble of light merely thickened the shadows in the corners rather than dispelling the dark. The floor was concrete, smeared with a fine white grain of dirt. Heavy furniture with square hard legs had been dragged through the concrete recently, taken chips out of the stairs and scraped along the walls. In the centre of the ceiling a bare pendant sat where a light-bulb should have hung; a fuse box squatted with its door hanging.

Where the basement met the front wall of the house, there was bare brick, the mortar exposed and crumbling. There was a taste on the air, a buzz against the skin, that went to the brain without asking permission of the nerves. It made our teeth itch, the little bones inside our hand ache, each part with an individual distress.

Templeman stood at the bottom of the stairs, unsure where to go or what to see. We said, "Do you feel it?"

"I feel . . . something."

"Why would the fairy godmother experiment with dust?"

"I don't know. Perhaps to increase its potency. But that would also kill his clientele faster, so I do not think that could be it. Maybe to reduce its lethality? Just how does this place connect to the fairy godmother?"

I looked round at the bare walls, scratched my heel into the empty floor. "I'm not sure that it does."

Our gaze drifted back to the cracks in the wall. Even in the little light from our spell, there was something visible between the bricks, something about the way the mortar crumbled, a scattering of fragments on the floor. I edged closer, scratched my fingers along the gaps, peered at the dirt in my nails, licked our lips and tasted . . . a place where taste should have been, but wasn't.

"Careful," rasped Templeman. "There's something here that shouldn't be."

"I never thought I'd hear you say that," I replied, running my fingers over the bricks. More mortar dust fell away, tumbling around my feet; and there was something more than mortar in it. Something pale, yellowish, embedded in the dust, which, as it fell, tumbled across the concrete floor a bit too far, and rolled in just the wrong direction. I rubbed some between my thumb and finger, breaking down the larger lumps of mortar until there was just a yellow stain.

And looked down, at the faintest of rattlings.

At my feet, where the dust had crumbled from the wall, making a sad little pile on the floor, some of it had starting to bounce. The fragments of mortar and dirt tumbled around each other like water bouncing in a puddle during heavy rain. I took a sharp step back, and the cracks in the wall began to spread, running through the mortar, and there was something in the crevices, a whooshing, a pulling, a pushing all at once and, just on the edge of hearing, what might have been the start of an animal scream.

I heard Templeman shout and ducked down, covering my head with my arms as, bursting like steam under pressure, the mortar crumbled and the dust shot out, in great yellow billows. It exploded from the wall in a shower of broken masonry; unmistakable, though, the smell of it, the taste of it, the feel of it on the skin, oily and dry at the same time: thick yellow clouds of fairy dust filling the room.

I held my breath, pressed my sleeve across my nose and mouth, and tried not to look. But there was a noise with it, a more than natural noise, more than dust roaring as it burst out of the cracks. There were

voices in the dust

screaming voices all of them screaming at once trying to be heard and for just a moment as we opened our eyes, we looked up into the yellow roaring mass and saw

faces

just a moment.

Just an instant.

There and gone, swallowed up whole into the dust but there were eyes moving in that cloud, made of that cloud, eyes as yellow as the dust itself and mouths that opened to scream but had no throats to swallow and fingers that clawed at the air and were the air itself and as soon as you looked, they were gone, consumed back into the mass.

I heard Templeman shouting something, heard the crack of concrete under strain, felt a hand grab me by the back of my shirt and there was a thing spinning out of the darkness

and then darkness absolute.

He was saying, "When the Beggar King calls, of course it's important. No. I understand that. I understand that, but what you need to understand is this: the beggars have eyes everywhere and if they've found . . . I know that. Of course I can arrange that, I understand. No. No, listen. Yes. I understand. I'll handle it."

I risked lifting my head. Instantly he was there, phone vanishing into his pocket. His clothes were smeared with dirt, but somehow Templeman had cleaned his face and hands back to their usual polished selves; and his expression as he looked down was all concern. "Mr Mayor, are you all right?"

I considered the hypothesis.

"No," I concluded. "Not really, but what's new?"

Templeman had somehow dragged me to the top of the basement stairs. Below, only a few feet below, the basement floor was a mess of broken bricks and shattered concrete. I shook off splinters of mortar and patted dust from my clothes. He flinched as the yellow stuff rose in the air. "Please do be careful, Mr Mayor. The circumstances were less than hygienic."

He held out a hand to help pull us up, and we were not so far above our own distress that we refused it.

"The wall," he explained as I felt my head for a new patch of crusting blood. "There was fairy dust in the mortar. Somehow our presence must have disturbed it, and the reaction was . . . unfortunate. I pulled you out of the basement; it seemed the least that could be done."

"Fairy dust in the walls of the house," I acknowledged. "And in the floors and ceiling, I'd guess. Dust everywhere, and doesn't it love to scream."

"I am not familiar with this phenomenon," he admitted. He stood at a tactful distance, a man ready to catch a fall, as I limped towards the door. "By my understanding, fairy dust is inert until activated by an interaction with human physiology."

"They were experimenting."

"'They'?"

"That's what the beggars said. Find a house like any other in a street with not much going for it, and you'll find some bastard experimenting with fairy dust."

"The fairy godmother?"

"I dunno. Not many guys with guns, are there? Not many braying bloodhounds, not much in the way of sheet plastic on the floor or a big dollar sign above the door." I hesitated, glancing around the quiet interior of the house. Our mouth was dry, eyes itched. Templeman was looking at me closely, rigid at the knowledge of this too-still, too-empty place where the dust had come crawling out of the walls. "Thanks for pulling me out," I said.

He nodded in acknowledgment of the deed, but his eyes were elsewhere, running over the cracks and torn wallpaper, listening for something that shouldn't be. We opened the front door, and the world outside was too bright and too natural, possessed of too much normality to be true. I fumbled in my pocket for the painkillers, swallowed two of them dry. The ache in our head made it difficult to think, the fire in our chest, hard to breathe. I leant on the side of Templeman's car and closed my eyes against the light. Templeman was there, always right beside me but never too close.

"Are you all right?" he asked, in the concerned voice of a man who knew the answer.

"The Beggar King said they were experimenting on his people. Tramps, junkies, runaways, the lost. Dragging them off the street, locking them up, feeding them on dust, dust to dust. Three days ago I didn't know a bloody thing about fairy dust and now look at this!" I gestured behind me at the silent house, reluctant to look. "What a bloody mess. What is the bloody point of being bloody Midnight Mayor if I can't even stop this?"

"You're stopping it now," he said. "You can't save everyone and everything."

"What time is it?"

"Just after lunch. Why?"

"Bed rest," I groaned. "It's going to be a busy night."

He gave me a lift to a hotel.

Our silence held as far south as Turnpike Lane. Then we said, "Do you know why we are part of this? This . . . thing we've just seen . . . and the dusthouses?"

Templeman shook his head, not taking his eyes from the road.

I didn't realise I was speaking until after the sounds had entered my ears. "There was a woman. Her name was Meera. We met on a boat and she performed a spell that should not have been performed, a magic that even we, though we do not fear these things, would have called forbidden. Forbidden in that it could not have been, forbidden in that it should not have been, forbidden in that it can unleash things that cannot be contained, consequences whose causes are forever unreachable. And she did it . . . because it was beautiful. And because it was splendid and it was bright, and because when she wove that spell, she was part of the city, a buried deep part of that city, roots in time as well as place. Glorious. Bright and brilliant and glorious.

"And when it was done, she said, 'Come with me,' and we did. There was no reason why; and there was no reason against. For the first time in . . . in we could not say how long . . . there was only action without cause, wishing without consequence, no cries of men or deeds of monsters to force our hand either way but merely us, and her, and the chance to choose. We imagine you would call it pure. In the time we have lived this life, been in this world, we have never encountered purity. Do not think we have built her up to be more than she is. She was a witch, and an addict, and her magics were dangerous, and thoughtless, and beautiful, and mad. But she made us feel . . . human. And nothing else has."

We slowed for a set of traffic lights, behind a bus driver contending with a taxi cab where two lanes became one, a cyclist trying to edge by. Templeman said, "The fairy godmother would argue that she also chose. She chose to take the dust."

"Yes," we said. "We know."

"Then . . ."

"Vengeance is human. When one you care for dies, vengeance is what humans do. It is the human thing that must be done; it is what makes the difference between humans and everything else. It cannot be defended before the wise, it cannot be explained in a court of law, it will not stand before the theologians who believe in judgement day, but it is very human. We want to be human. What you want from the Midnight Mayor, what you think should be done, what needs to be and ought to be and should be ... sometimes it's good to remember that we are ... I am human.

"Anyway," I sighed, too loud, "that's me. That's why I'm here. What have you got against the dusthouses?"

Templeman hesitated, then the corner of his mouth curled into what might have been an animal smile. "Vengeance," he said. "Just like you."

"Is it something I'll find in your file, when I eventually get round to reading it?"

"No."

"Is it something that's going to get in the way?"

"No. At least," the smile softened, widened, "no more than it does for you."

"Okay then."

The road was widening in the traffic-crawl up to Manor House, a crossroads almost American in the width of traffic fighting through its lights, where red was a five-minute experience and green happened in the blink of an eye. Shifting uncomfortably in my seat, I said, "About the experiments. In that bloody house. What do you make of it?"

"If the motives for the experiments were not financial, then that leaves only so many options." His voice was matter-of-fact, at the end of a worthwhile and simple thought train. "Do you really have no idea who was behind it, if not the fairy godmother?"

"No."

"The Beggar King has eyes everywhere," he pointed out.

"They were busy."

"But if he knows about the house ..."

"An escapee."

"Ah," he breathed. "I see. And where is this escapee now?"

"Dead."

"I'm very sorry to hear that."

"Please," I groaned. "Like you didn't taste the death dribbling out of every inch of that bloody house."

"Did she say anything?" he asked as we turned off the bottom of Green Lanes, heading for the centre of the city. "There must have been something."

"Nothing concrete. A place, a warning, and a bad death."

A thought scratched at the painkillers smothering my brain, fingernails over a blackboard. When I tried to pin it down, it danced away, like a fly escaping a spider. I rubbed at my eyes, and felt uneasily at the back of my head, where kicks and bricks had been doing their merry best to knock out my brains. I asked, "Do Aldermen spend much time getting the crap kicked out of them? I mean, when you sign on, is there a training course or anything? Two days' magic, two days' manipulation, and a week and a half of getting kicked to shit?"

"There is an induction week," Templeman said.

"There's an induction week?"

"Yes. Junior Aldermen are assigned to more senior members of the establishment, introduced to useful contacts, taken out on a few duties. Naturally the basics – spellcraft, enchantment, observation, combat magics and communication skills – are all assessed pre-admission."

"Evening classes?" I asked.

"Only in advanced weapons skills."

"Funny."

"Is it?" he asked blithely. "I suppose it must be."

The thought was back, annoying, a thing just out of reach, an impulse I couldn't name or satisfy. I tried to grab at it but Templeman was saying,

" . . . specific I can find?"

"Hum?"

"The culicidae," he repeated. "I assume you have a plan?"

"Oh, that. Yes, I've got a plan. I mean, it's no blitzkrieg, but yes. There's a plan." I grinned. "And you're going to hate it."

I told him.

He hated it.

I said, you got something better, jimbo?

He was silent.

No one did silences like Templeman; they were the place between the notes of fine music, the pause before the crack of drums, the lightning that preceded the thunder. They were beautiful, tuned and elegant, and when it was done all he said was, no. No, he didn't have anything better.

Fantastic, I said. Now get on that little phone of yours, and find me a nice big bit of railway line and some willing volunteers. And make sure that the volunteers are Minority Council, thank you.

He agreed.

Not happily, but we weren't looking for inspirational. Not today.

There was time to kill between then and now.

There was a hotel.

This one was part of a chain, tucked in behind the wharves and con-verted jetties of Rotherhithe, at the place where fashionable river living met unfashionable urban life. I showered while Templeman sat on the end of the bed, making calls. I tried the water very hot, then very cold, then regretted the cold and went back to very hot. Somehow my ribcage had come out the colour of rotting aubergine. As injuries went, it had two disadvantages: it was painful enough to inhibit action, but discreet enough to limit sympathy.

The extractor fan in the bathroom had been working overtime and still couldn't clear the steam. I wiped away condensation from the mirror above the washbasin and looked at my bright blue eyes, which had once been brown, and realised.

It hit like an ice cube lodging in our throat.

There it was.

The thing that was wrong.

So tiny as to barely make a mark, but itching like a mosquito bite. A hum just on the edge of hearing.

I stood for a while, unable to think, then sat on the edge of the toilet with my hands between my knees and tried to construct patterns of thought from the gabble in my mind.

Templeman knocked on the bathroom door. "Mr Mayor? Are you all right?"

It took two attempts to answer. "Yes," I stammered. And added, "Fine."

"I'm going downstairs for a second, to check a few emails."

I listened for the sound of the door slamming, then came cautiously out, checking round the room shadow by shadow, looking for anything, listening for anything out of the ordinary. My satchel was on the end of the bed; I opened it up, reached instinctively for my mobile phone, hesitated.

Be still and think.

Be still.

I sat on the edge of the bed, turning the phone over and over between my fingers.

Perhaps nothing.

Perhaps everything.

No easy way to be sure.

I pulled my clothes back on, socks and shoes, and was struggling one aching arm at a time into my coat, when my phone rang.

I jumped, not knowing why.

I didn't recognise the number, and let it ring for almost half a minute, wondering whether to answer.

We did.

A voice on the other end said, "Hello, Mr Mayor. My name is Oscar Kramb. Some people call me the fairy godmother. I heard that this would be a good time to call; am I bothering you?"

Fairy godmother.

Not exactly the sugar plum fairy, not about to take Cinders to the ball.

A voice with the hint of a northern accent reduced through years of snobby voice training, sliding over its words like oil across a crystal pool.

Magic gone mobster.

I heard myself say, more defiant than I'd meant, "Really? Heard it was a good time from where?"

A creamy chuckle. "Naturally, Mr Mayor, I have friends; but don't worry, I'm not phoning you to let you know that your life is about to end, though obviously that was my first instinct. You are, for the moment, safe."

"I suppose your friends gave you this number?"

"I really couldn't say."

"Hold that thought," I said, and hung up.

I thumbed off the phone, pulled the battery from the back and the sim card from behind that, and put the various components in separate pockets. Then, moving with deliberate slowness, I finished struggling into my clothes, slung my bag over my back and headed for the nearest exit.

Look, and be still. Unobtrusive and quick. Any pain was briefly forgotten.

Down the stairs, past the kitchens, out of the back door, into the street. Eyes open for pursuers, the aroma of curry clinging to my clothes like an old friend. Two things we believed: firstly, that if the fairy godmother knew our location, we would not be walking free, but secondly, that even the most medieval-minded of magicians could track a man through his mobile phone.

And there it was again, that cold certainty, the sickness in our stomach that out-annoyed the burning pain in our chest. Kramb had even said as much: you didn't randomly collect the mobile number of the Midnight Mayor, you didn't just happen to catch him on a tea break. Had we made a mistake, talking so soon to the Minority Council? Had we blown open too wide a hole in our defences?

Walk, and be still.

Thoughts fell into the straight lines of the paving stones.

Get help.

We looked for the places where the beggars would go, unwatched ATMs and local churches, anywhere cash or kindness might be in supply. Rotherhithe was not necessarily a corner of town where you'd expect beggars, but once you started to look, sooner or later you would find.

So long as it was sooner.

And there she was, a girl maybe twenty-five, going on fifty, with faded tangled hair and a big green waxy coat, huddled between an ATM and a greasy chicken shop, a torn coffee cup at her feet and a long-tongued mongrel keeping lookout by her side. I scuttled straight towards her and she cringed, not knowing what to make of this. At her fear, we held out our hands, placating, stopped a few paces away and sought frantically in our pocket for any money, paper or coin, didn't matter, no time for it to matter. I still had most of Templeman's three hundred pounds; we put twenty into her cup and, as she mumbled 'thanks', squatted down in front of her. "Domine dirige nos," I breathed. "Domine dirige nos, you understand? I need to see the King. Help me?"

She bit her lip; the dog, curious, wagged its tail. Then she held out her hand, palm up. We hesitated, then reached out, peeling away the glove that protected our right hand. With dirty fingers ending in yellow curling nails, she traced the twin scars cut into our palm, the two crosses of the Midnight Mayor, one inside the other. She smiled, folding our fingers over our palm and pushing our hand gently away. "Got something you need to say?" she asked.

"The Aldermen have betrayed me," I answered. "I don't know how far it goes, but I can't trust them. And . . . "

She raised her eyebrows but said nothing. Her hands made fists, to keep warm.

"And," I sighed, "and I never told Templeman that the beggar who escaped was a woman. So how did he know?"

A silence, as the words settled like snowflakes. The dog wagged its tail again. "Okay then," she said.

"Thank you."

I dragged myself up a limb at a time, catching my breath. Bed rest, Dr Seah had said. I wondered if we were passing the point where that would really cut it.

Time to move again, taking it one step at a time. I paused at a little closet of a store nestled between a barber's and a painter's shop. It sold rip-off ink cartridges, rip-off computer monitors, rip-off money exchange to foreign parts and, above all else, rip-off mobile phones. I bought a pay-as-you-go phone with a bright pink cover adorned with butterflies, and dialled Penny's number instinctively.

She took a while to answer, picking up with a cautious "Yessss?"

"Penny, it's me. Nabeela still with you?"

"Uh, yeah – you okay, you sound kinda rattled?"

"I'm having one of those 'Oh shit' moments. Might be nothing. Might be everything. I just wanted to make sure you're . . . okay."

"Jesus, Matthew, I'm like kick-ass awesome! Why the hell shouldn't I be? There's even these Aldermen guys trailing us, and right monkeys they are at being discreet, seriously cramping the shopping style you know, and what the fuck is happening with you?"

I told her my plan, that night, for the culicidae.

"You want us there? Backup and shit?"

"No," I said. "Tonight, all things considered, I want you as far away as possible. And, Penny, you think anything's wrong, you think any-thing – anything at all – feels out of place, you run, okay?"

"This the fairy godmother again?"

"No. Well, yes, but no. This might just be something worse."

One more call to make, from my new mobile phone.

I rubbed a little more garam masala between my hands, and headed for Canada Water. When the moment came I wanted to be near the Tube, with options for escape.

Canada Water's Underground was a shiny new Jubilee Line station all in grey tile and grey glass, servicing a shiny newish shopping centre with all the charisma of herpes. I found a corner out of sight of the ubiquitous CCTV cameras, and followed the faint singing in the hol-lows of our ear until we came upon a small green telephone-exchange box. It resembled an upright suitcase bolted into the pavement, between a recycling point and map explaining the fastest way to the local garden centre. I plonked down on the pavement beside it, reached for the parts of my old mobile phone and began the work of reassembling. Inside the exchange box the telephone wires sang their tinny songs, clicker-clacking digital business from here to there, a whole world just waiting to be unleashed.

I reconnected my old phone and turned it on; as it warmed up, I pressed my thumb into the screen, until the image wobbled beneath it. As I drew my thumb back again, I dragged with it that tiny part of the telephone noise that my phone produced. A thin stretch of grey-white light tangled around my fingertip, pulled up from the screen like melted cheese. I flicked it at the green exchange box, and with greedy insistence it merged with the mess of wires and calls. My mobile phone flickered in doubt, the screen flashing on and off a few times as it tried to work out what it was and where it had come from, before finally giving up the ghost and displaying a single word:

Connect?

I connected, the signal bar jumping wildly as the tiny spell flickered between phone and telephone exchange, and redialled the number of Oscar Kramb.

He answered on the third ring, a rising lilt to his voice that converted irritation to surprise. "Good afternoon, Mr Mayor. I didn't think you'd be calling me back."

"I didn't think you'd be picking up," I explained. "Sorry about earlier. I just figured, what with your guys beating the shit out of me, and my guys having gone behind my back to supply my personal details to casual killers, I'd take a walk, for a more private chat."

"Mr Mayor, your paranoia is almost admirable."

"Mr Kramb – or should I call you Mr Godmother?"

"Oscar, please, and I'll call you Matthew."

"Isn't that fluffy?" I murmured. "And, Oscar, as we're such good mates can I say that if I'm paranoid it's only because your reputation is that impressive."

A businesslike guffaw that ended too quickly. "Matthew, I am so glad we could have this chat! I've been such a fan, and of course I wanted to let you know how sorry I was about the little incident with my people. They were under strictest orders to treat you with the proper decency and dignity according to your office, and they assure me it was only your reluctance to behave in a reasonable manner that led to them beating the shit out of you, as you said."

"You can't get the staff, can you?"

"Alas, no. But that's a problem we've got in common."

My grin was locked in place for no one to see. "So tell me, Mr Kramb," I said, "to what do I owe the pleasure?"

"Ah, now yes," he exclaimed, a cheerful man who's only just remembered the tragically dull business of the day. "This little business between us of the dusthouses – it was you who destroyed one of my dusthouses, wasn't it?"

"I heard something about that. Something about how some random guy went in and ripped the earth in two beneath one of these places where some psychotic bastards find economic satisfaction in turning human beings into narcotic substances. Is that what we're talking about here?"

"Fairy dust is not an illegal trade, Mr Mayor; I think my lawyer would like me to remind you of that."

"I think your lawyer would tell you not to bother with the debate at all," I replied sharply. "Get to the point."

"Mr Mayor," he sighed, "how do you see this business ending? You must understand, your own people will betray you, it is simply a matter of time. You cannot run forever."

"How about until next week? Next week would be good; I'll clear some time for you then."

"I'd heard you were funny – did I mention I was a fan?"

"Yes, and I ignored it as being creepy."

"Perhaps we can both find an amicable solution."

He waited, so finally I said, "You know, when a man responsible for the deaths of countless ... I won't say innocents, but definitely people ... talks about amicable solutions, I can't help but feel a part of my soul die."

"You would rather choose blood and violence? I can do blood and violence, of course, but I was hoping we could work this out some more civilised way."

"Okay, fair point. How about this? You stop. You quit. You pack up your stuff and you get out of town, no fuss, no blood, no violence, and you do it now. Amicably."

"Matthew," his voice was full of disappointment, "when did you become so absolute? There are few things in this life to be absolute about, and this is not one of them."

"Death is pretty absolute. Anyway, you're obviously not going for my amicable solution, so I guess we don't have anything else to talk about."

I moved to hang up, but he exclaimed down the phone, "Mr Mayor!" I paused, listened. "Matthew," he said, "are you not interested to know who has been poisoning beggars with fairy dust?"

I wasn't surprised.

Then I was surprised at how unsurprised I was.

"I'm guessing you deny all knowledge of it," I said.

"Not knowledge, no. I have been ... aware of the situation, shall we say, for some time. But it's not me, if that's what you're asking. What would be the point? The current market situation is ideal for my operation, and if we have learnt anything from this latest cock-up of a recession it's that massive outlays beyond your available assets only ... I was groping for a financial image that you would appreciate and understand, but I'm not sure if you are the right crowd for the gag."

"You know, I'm always impressed at how many ways people find to call me stupid. You'd think I'd be getting bored of it, but since I'm that mind-numbingly thick, there's always that twinge of novelty as I try to work out what's being so wittily said. Are you trying to buy me off? Only that doesn't seem in character."

"Not at all, Matthew. I wouldn't presume! If we were to kill you, and that's of course still an option, it would cause a great palaver with the Aldermen. Not for personal reasons – personally, I'm sure you know, you are disliked – but it is considered bad form to assassinate the Midnight Mayor. Precedent, you see. No, what I am proposing is merely an arrangement whereby we both benefit."

"How's that work?"

"Simply – I tell you who is responsible for experiments on the beggars, and you give me some guarantee that you will never again interfere with my business. I can even give you the details of several Aldermen who are, shall we say, less than you might wish them to be? I'm sure you could find such information valuable."

Temptation.

Just for a second, just there, just a moment.

But it was merely an instant of thought – cold, clinical, rational – and didn't stand a chance. "What kind of guarantee?" I asked, suspicion slipping into my voice.

"Say . . . a pint of your blood and an oath upon the twin crosses of your office?"

We just managed not to laugh out loud. "Wow! I'm not just thick, I'm clinically thick! Would you like one of my kidneys while we're at it? They're a bit shot through on painkillers right now, but I'm sure you could give them a good scrubbing."

"I wouldn't use your blood for anything but a guarantee of your behaviour, since . . ."

I cut in, soft and sharp. "What has Richard Templeman got against you?"

His silence was too long to be artful. Then, "Maybe I won't have you hunted down and dismembered. Someone will probably get there before I have the chance."

"That's what I thought you'd say."

"Think about my offer, Matthew."

"Were the long dead hours of the night made for anything else? Bye, bye, fairy godmother. Going now."

"Goodbye, Mr Mayor. Soon, I hope, we can talk under better circumstances."

Somehow, in the minutes my phone had been on, I'd missed two calls.

One from Kelly, one from Templeman.

I called Kelly first.

"Mr Mayor!" Her voice exploded with enthusiasm down the line, loud enough to make me flinch. "How are you?"

"Beat-up and grouchy, how are you?"

"Is there anything I can do to help personally? I've heard that lemongrass is a wonderful . . ."

"Kelly, please think hard before you extol the virtues of herbal remedies. I've had a bad couple of days."

"Ah, yes." She reset the brightness on her voice from dazzling down to shiny. "Just a few quick things to clear up. I've said 'yes' to the Worshipful Company of Magi, Maguses and Mages for next Thursday, I really hope that's okay with you, but they do do an excellent dinner and it wouldn't have to be a long speech . . ."

"If I'm still alive next Thursday, I'm sure I'll appreciate it. What else?"

"Well, we, uh, we had a little problem with an imp infestation . . ."

"That's a shame."

" . . . but I think it's in hand now . . ."

"Don't be too harsh on the imps; it's only nature, right?"

"Yes, Mr Mayor, of course, that's very public-spirited of you, I'll be sure to pass on the note. There was also a spamming issue . . ."

"Don't you hate computers when they go wrong?"

" . . . but we've got it fixed now . . ."

"I knew you would."

"I've been given a note from a couple of my colleagues advising that the fairy godmother may have hired some bloodhounds to track you down . . ."

"Really? That sounds messy."

" . . . but I'm sure you've got it perfectly in hand!" she babbled. "And finally there's this business of your attempting tonight to unsummon a creature made of slate and glass!"

"Hey, you know, if it hadn't been preying on my mind, I would have completely forgotten about that," I groaned. "What about it?"

"Well, Mr Templeman called to fill me in on the event – sounds very complicated, by the way, Mr Mayor, I'd love to read the summoner's reports afterwards – and I understand you want full Aldermen support teams in place when you bring down the creature?"

"Considering that last time I tried, it nearly took my head off, yes please, a bit of support would be nice."

"Now, when you say *full* support . . . "

"Caughey, Holta, Kwan . . . "

"Rathnayake, Fadhil and Templeman; of course, you requested their attendance specifically. Do you mind if I ask why?"

"Sure, ask away."

"Um . . . why, Mr Mayor?"

"Because they're the senior members of the Minority Council, a group of Aldermen dedicated to going round behind my back and taking decisions without consulting me, which may or may not – and in this case did – result in the death of innocents, any other questions?"

"No!" she exclaimed, in full-lunged horror. "I had no idea!"

"I imagine I'll be hearing that a lot."

"I can see why you might want them there!"

I pressed two fingers into the place between my eyes, trying to force something, anything, into my brain that wasn't pain and fuzzy bewilderment. "Kelly," I croaked, "if I hadn't actually met you in person, I really wouldn't think you were real."

"Oh, don't worry about that!" she laughed. "Everyone says that! Now in terms of the rest of the support . . . do you think you'll need light arms cover?"

"You're joking?"

"I would never!"

"In that case . . . no, I don't think light arms will hack it."

If at all possible, she brightened. "Heavy arms? Demolition team? Evokers armed with tamed elemental spirits, perhaps?"

"Every little helps."

"How about catering support?"

"Is that an option?"

"Of course, although I don't recommend the vegetarian menu."

Time to give up doubting; only madness would remain. "Sure, why not?" We never say no to free food. "Anything else I can do for you, Kelly?"

"Now wouldn't be the right time to discuss your health insurance, would it?"

"Can a silence be stony over the phone?"

"I think, Mr Mayor, that you might be able to make it so. Although there's always the danger that someone will just think you've been cut off, and they'll start shouting, and that will undermine the moment. If, I mean, if they couldn't already sense the stoniness of your silence. Which they probably could."

There was a long, slow rush as she let out the last of that breath down the phone. I waited for it to pass and asked, all sweetness, "Anything else?"

"Um . . . nothing that can't wait."

"Delighted to hear it."

"Do you need anything else from me?"

"I dunno, Kelly; I think that depends on whether you're cheering for the Minority Council and all their crap."

She sounded almost indignant. "Mr Mayor, I'm your PA! At the end of the day, it doesn't matter where the cheque comes from or what the work is; my role is to assist you and you alone. That is the duty of the PA, it is the covenant, it is the . . ."

"You make it sound like a rite of passage."

"I take my work very seriously, Mr Mayor!"

"How would you feel if I said the problem's not you, it's me?"

Indignation turned to dignity. "I would be gravely understanding of your situation, Mr Mayor."

"Bye, Kelly."

"Goodbye, Mr Mayor."

She probably didn't mean for it to sound so final.

The other missed call, from Templeman.

I rang him back, but it went straight to voicemail.

I left him a message saying I'd gone to get something to eat.

Part 4: You Can't Save Yourself

In which we cease to be me, and I forget how to be ourself.

Willesden Junction.

A dump.

Londoners have intense loyalties to the areas from which they come. Those born in Croydon will argue that theirs is a borough with access to the green belt, excellent shopping and wide, pleasant streets, while the rest of the city flatly knows that Croydon is a soulless hole whose only redeeming feature is the novelty of the electric tram and a large DIY store with reasonable parking. Likewise, those from Hackney would contend that their borough is vibrant and exciting, instead of crime-ridden and depressed; those from Acton would argue that their suburb is peaceful and gentle instead of souldestroyingly dull, samey and bleak; and the people of Amersham would proclaim that their town is the ideal combination of leafy politeness and speedy transport links instead of, clearly, the absolute end of the earth.

However, no one, not one mind worthy of respect, could defend Willesden Junction as anything but an utter and irredeemable dump. It is where journeys pass through each other: a mess of bridges and cuttings, a dirty canal and too-narrow one-way roads, as well as railways for the high-speed express and the crawling commuter train.

We stood on a pedestrian bridge that spanned the line to Wembley, eating dubious kebab with soggy chips, and listening to the trains rumble by. Trying to get anywhere in Willesden Junction for any purpose other than changing trains is a game of hugging walls and ignoring signs. Like the Barbican, there are places here, between the scrapheaps and the marshalling yards, where the borders between spaces grow thin.

This we knew. We could feel it, taste it. The smell of the city, that sense that goes straight into the stomach without asking permission of the brain; in these streets, even here, it had power, its own distinct character. It was a magic made from the rattling of wheels on old railways, from the electricity in cables overhead, the bumping of pram wheels on cracked paving stones, the cacophony of a dozen different languages which sometimes dipped into English for words like 'asbo', 'texting', 'Twitter' and 'iPhone' before darting away again. Listening long enough, hard enough, and the mind would start to snag like cobwebs in the bare branches of a winter tree, and for a moment all that there was and all that there needed to be was

pigeon wings, weight above, weight below, pushing one against the other to soar upwards from the screeching of

neighbourhood cat smell of fox frightening, smell of packaged food behind, a door slamming in the dark as someone calls their pet home to

house where TV plays in the living room, out of tune, football results, favourite side lost again, drowned briefly by

bus engine rattling needs to be serviced parts creaking inside just get to the end of the line and turf the passengers off,

beneath telephone lines chattering oh God yeah you won't believe what he said to me yesterday I mean can you believe it he was actually like babe I don't find you that attractive any more

bbbeeeeeeeeee

says the dialling tone

beeeeeeeeeeeeeee

change in the texture of the sound as Underground trains nose up into the open air whoosh almost now the change in darkness outside the windows of the Tube making the light inside the carriage seem more dim, dazzling fluorescent in the tunnel and

seagulls don't even raise their heads from the rubbish yards as the train rushes by and

"Matthew?"

and listen hard enough and there it is, the smell of gas in the pipes beneath our feet and the water running downhill towards the river in the sewage pipes and in the plane overhead a woman looks down at the city and wonders if she can see her house from here and

"Matthew? Mr Mayor? Are you all right?"

We let out a long breath and, with it, everything else: sound, sense, the weight of air and the humming of minds, blowing away to nothing. Glancing round, I said, "Hello Templeman."

"Are you all right, Mr Mayor? You weren't at the hotel . . ."

"Needed something to eat."

"For five and a half hours?"

"Needed to think."

In his face I glimpsed what might have been concern. "Are you sure you're all right, Matthew? Something hasn't happened?"

"I'm fine. Everyone here?"

"I believe so."

"You explained what we're going to do?"

"Yes."

"They going to play sensible?"

He gave a probably humourless smile. "I believe I have convinced my colleagues that this particular enterprise is, perhaps, not worth preserving."

"I bet they're all giddy about that."

"There will be a reckoning at some stage, Matthew," he warned. "Maybe not tonight – to be honest I think the speed of your action has caught them unprepared – but at some moment, there will be a reckoning. The Minority Council can't be ignored."

"*You're* the bloody Minority Council," I snapped, pushing past him and marching towards the end of the bridge. He fell into step a few paces behind. "And if you look closely, you might just see that the last thing I'm doing right now is ignoring you."

"You're not all right," he murmured. "What happened? Why did you leave the hotel?"

"Personal stuff." I saw his face. "Don't give me that look. What's that thing Shakespeare says? When things get crappy, they get crappy all at once?"

"I believe Shakespeare dressed it up a little."

"Jammy git. Come on."

A flight of metal steps down to a metal footbridge which ran into metal fences framing metal ramps down to the streets. Nothing human about Willesden Junction was built to last; it was a place for machines to reign triumphant and man to service their needs. A rush of air knocked us, from a snake-nosed train as it picked up speed towards the country; elsewhere a flash of blue-white electricity lit the dark like a camera flash, from a commuter train passing overhead.

There were Aldermen waiting at the foot of the ramp; at first glance

I counted twelve. They all wore black, and I suspected the large metal case that two of them were sat on didn't hold playing cards. They stood as I approached; a quaint gesture from a traditional kind of bastard. Caughey pushed his way to the front. His coat was a little too small, the buttons straining. Someone had had stern words with him, because he managed to spit out, one consonant at a time, "Good evening, Mr Mayor."

We ignored the disgust in his voice. "Good evening, Mr Caughey. I'm sorry I missed you earlier. Did you get the minutes of the meeting?"

"Mr Mayor!" A voice exploded from the back of the crowd, full of delight and excitement. Moments later, the owner of the voice pushed her way through, her arms sagging under the weight of plastic bags.

Kelly Shiring.

Because you had to see it, to believe it.

"Mr Mayor I'm so sorry I'm late I was just on the phone with Transport for London and they've agreed to clear all maintenance crews tonight from the area and reassign to Kentish Town West until we give the all-clear. And I know you don't necessarily need it, but I've got . . ." – she rummaged in her plastic bags – ". . . egg and tomato, ham and cheese, BLT and tuna and sweetcorn, and a flask of tea and a flask of coffee, and crisps. I could only get cheese and onion or ready salted, is that okay?"

I realised my mouth was hanging open. Likewise the mouth of every Alderman assembled.

"That's very considerate of you," we said. "We'll have BLT, and coffee, and cheese and onion, if that's all right."

Her face lit up, in a grin flashing wide enough to collide with her ears, and she delved into the plastic bags in search of supper.

We turned to the Aldermen. One or two of them had the decency to look away. "Okay," I said, a little too loud. Then, getting control, "Let's get this said, just once, and then we won't have to deal with it again. You lot suck. You really do. I mean, I know the arguments. Greater good, bigger picture, think of the city, not the streets, the crowds, not the people, the whole is greater – much, much greater – than the sum of its parts. But your project killed a kid, and sucked the souls out of Christ knows how many more, and you know what? You don't have the right to decide that your right is all that matters. So, guys, here's the news – you screwed up, and we're going to fix it. Let me add, right here, right now, that I screwed up too, and when all this is done we should have a chat about that.

"So, let's dismantle this cock-up monster thing before it can rip anyone else to bits."

Small hours of the morning on a railway line.

Against the silence I could hear the humming of electricity in the cables overhead, loud and busy, waiting to be tapped; smell the scrap-yards and rubbish dumps that orbited the marshalling yards and busy tracks, like lava moons around a burning planet. Separated off by a chain fence, a foothill of crushed cars, compressed to splinters of metal and glass, stretched upwards like a pharaoh's tomb against the stained night sky. Once, proud owners had polished the windows of these cars and waxed the bonnet on a Sunday afternoon, before rust and time had eaten them up from the inside out.

The Aldermen were waiting.

They formed a ring of men on bridges and women in the shadows of the sleeping cranes, watching entrances and exits, as much to keep strangers out as monsters in. I hadn't needed to be told when the last train had pulled out of the station. I'd heard its engine whining the final song of the day, felt it drawing power, and known, in the pit of my stomach, that was it. No more.

When the moment came, it was disappointing. We'd hoped, at least, for a little light and fire when they summoned the culicidae; but the five of them – Templeman, Fadhil, Holta, Kwan and Caughey – simply stood together in the middle of the tracks, clustered round a wand that looked, from afar, suspiciously like a TV remote. Maybe when Alan invented the creature he did have a sense of humour, to make up for other absences in his soul.

When they were done, Templeman came over to me. The four others moved to the shadows at the edge of the track.

"We all set?" Instinctively, I glanced towards the scrapyard, where the metal yellow claws that crushed the life out of cars beyond their time sat, bent down like giraffe necks.

"As we can be."

"How long does your pet take to come?"

"Not long. In its resting state it doesn't exist so much in a physical form, as a place where physical form might be. Therefore when travelling to a new target, it can remain largely unencumbered by the basic laws of physics until the final moment before its arrival."

"Out of interest, how much did you pay Alan for this thing?"

"Grand and a half."

I stared at him. "A grand and a half? For a creature that puts Isaac Newton through the wringer, a grand and a half?!"

He gave what might have been a shrug. "Alan is seventeen. We could have paid him a hundred pounds and for him it would have felt like a victory."

"What did you do before you were an Alderman?" I asked.

"I was a tax adviser. I still am a tax adviser, in fact. The stipend as an Alderman is very small. Why?"

"It makes a sort of sense. How'd you get involved in the Aldermen?"

He gave an almost imperceptible sigh. "My brother ... became involved in regrettable forces. He was unlucky in the job market, and not academically successful, but he always had an ear for the city, a sense for it that I did not share. He fell in with warlocks, bondsmen of the Regent, a spirit with a less than salubrious reputation who draws his power from the waterways. Like so many young men who try to dabble too fast with forces beyond their comprehension, he made mistakes, and enemies. He drowned, in the end, his lungs full of dirty canal water, though there was no canal nearby where his body was discovered, and no water on his skin or clothes. I suppose you could say I became involved in this world to understand why."

"You tried to save him?"

"No, it was too late. Much too late. I suppose you could say I tried to save him at the time, before I really understood what was happening. But he didn't want to be saved. And I couldn't do it, even if I'd known how."

I had nothing to say. We stood together and listened to the wind picking up speed down the open tracks of the railway line.

Templeman said, "May I ask you a question?"

"Sure."

"If you could give it up, walk away from this position, from being Midnight Mayor, right now, with no price to pay, would you do it?"

Down the empty railway, the lights were burning red, warning trains that weren't there to beware of dangers on the line. I said, "If you'd asked me a few months ago, yes. I'd have said yes without hesitation. I never wanted this. Never asked, never was asked. I'm not very good at it, and there are plenty out there who want it more; Christ knows why, because it's a lousy job."

"And now?"

"Now . . . now I'd say that I'd want a serious consult about who got the job after. It's not about the power, it's about . . . what the power does to you, I guess. It's the same thing that sends sorcerers mad. Spend enough time concentrating on the big picture and, sooner or later, you'll forget about being human."

Templeman was about to speak, then changed his mind. I heard a scampering and looked up; but it was just a fox, picking its way over the ballast of the tracks. Its head snapped round and, for a moment, with its tail straight out behind it and its ears high, swivelling like radar dishes, its eyes met ours. Then it looked away and trotted under the sleeping bulk of an empty freight truck.

The truck itself was little more than a metal platform on wheels that had been shunted away from the mainline tracks. It was part of a chain of pallets locked together, such as you saw sometimes in the urban night, rolling through empty stations of the suburbs for minutes at a time. The rolling stock making up this train included the usual unknown things: metal containers with bolted doors, drums for oil, open wagons for scrap, and empty double-deckered modules, for brand-new cars on their way to the dealer.

One shape in all the rest, I couldn't make out. It was crumpled, lumpen, and sprawled wider than the pallet that held it, all corners and curves. The only light that fell on it was thin and diluted, making it little more than a silhouette. How long had it been there? Had I looked and not seen?

I stepped down onto the railway track, pulling a sphere of fluorescent white light with me to cover my way. Templeman moved to follow; I motioned him to stay. Juggling my bubble of light above my head to cast a circle of illumination, I edged towards the darkness of the goods train.

Thirty feet; twenty. We wanted to drag the electricity out of the cables overhead, our fingers itched with it, we could taste it on our lips; but I kept our hands still, drove the rattling of our heart out of my ears.

It twitched.

The thing on the train twitched. Shuddered from top to bottom, something glinting in the half-light, a thing that might have been a metal limb. I froze, the breath sticking in my throat. Sparks danced along the cables overhead, across the tracks at our feet, as we braced ourself to draw the power – and yet, did not do it.

I heard someone shout on a bridge overhead, heard the clatter of feet running on ballast, but it was all a long way off. As the creature drew itself upright, I could see that the last pieces were still coming together, slate locking against slate to form its armoured shell, glass shimmering up into the cracks between the joins before they clapped shut, its six metal legs trembling as they snapped into place, the bends flexing. And there it was, a sound that wasn't a sound, a thing that only the internal organs could sense, getting richer and bigger without quite becoming audible. It made the wires rattle overhead, set lights flashing on cars parked near the track, sent ripples shimmering across standing pools of water, made cascades from broken bits of windscreen and old suspension boxes.

Then the culicidae gave one last, great shudder, two of its legs scrambling off the side of the train, raised its head, and looked straight at us.

For a moment, we stood there, and stared right back.

It was motionless, its lens-eyes twitching this way and that as it focused on us, trying to determine if we were friend or foe. I opened our fingers, quieting the power in them that threatened to run free, and took a step towards it. It drew back, head rising up, impossible glass mouth opening and closing like a valve, but didn't strike, didn't move. I took another step closer, heard the low hum of who-knew-what night-time machinery powering up behind me, saw the creature's head twitch in alarm, its long abdomen swish through the air behind it, the tip standing upright like a peacock's tail. We raised our hands towards it, as you might try to quiet a frightened animal, and its eyes snapped back to us, reflecting the bubble of fluorescence hanging over us.

Only a few feet away now. Someone had filleted the bones from my legs. The culicidae's head craned down as I approached; then down a little further, its body blocking out the cables overhead. We reached up, fingers shaking, and whispered, "Hello, you."

Its head was bent so close we could almost touch slate, see into the spinning glass within its throat and belly. We could feel heat coming off it, a strange oven warmth, dry, crawling out from its solid skin. There was no expression that a human could make out in that not-quite-insect face, nothing cartoon-readable about it, as it wondered what we were and why we were not attacking, and I wondered much the same. Yet one thing was certain: the culicidae, this summoned thing of glass and stone, was alive, aware.

"What have these foolish creatures done to you?" we breathed and, as it drew its head back as if it was trying to understand the question, our fingers brushed one edge of its slate head and

For fuck's sake Mum that is so fucking

What you saying, man?

Fuck off okay, just fuck off

They don't understand

You'll never be anything if you carry on like this

Do you know how much I've sacrificed for you and now you throw it all away

Are you having problems at home?

Go away!

God you're a right loser carrying on like that

That is so sick, man

Burning.

You ungrateful little bastard, you shit, is this what I gave up half my life for, is it?

They never understand

Until you learn how to buckle down you'll never amount to anything

I see a dark future for you, young man

Do you know how hard it is out there in the real world?

You want to be treated like an adult but you act like such a child!

Burning?

It's your life, waste it if you want

Get out, get out of this house, get out right now!

How dare you talk to me that way?

You're a failure
You're never going to be
Give up then
Do you know what happens to young men like you?
Burning!

I snatched my hand away: the fingers were burning, raw down to the knuckle. The culicidae drew up its head and screamed its silent scream, loud enough yet to shatter the glass in the parked cars and make the railway tracks hum with it, a single note reverberating up and down the line between the canals and under the bridges, and I ran, cradling my burning fingertips to my chest, ran as the culicidae slammed a claw down into the place where I had been. And there was something human about it now, something we could recognise and name, and we named it rage and anger and all those feelings born of incomprehension that didn't know any better than to be both of the above, sucked out of the minds of all those children who hadn't been given a chance to move on, grow up and get over it.

We ran, and now nothing held back the power: electricity danced from the cables overhead, stabbing down all around us like lightning, searing holes into the earth behind us, smacking into the shell of the culicidae; but still the creature kept coming, roaring its silent roar. The tracks began to sing with electricity as we leapt over each one; the culicidae landed one claw on a rail and its whole body arced as current rushed through it, sending black smoke pouring out of the cracks. Then, with a great snicker-snap, it pulled itself free and reared up, leaping across two tracks at a time, springing like a cat. The ballast spun into whirlwinds as we passed, whipped up and round, forming a wall between us and the creature, which just smashed past it as if through falling blossoms on a spring breeze. The movement of stones beneath our feet made the ground slippery, a living thing; the air stank of burning metal and slate, of black smoke; and we felt something move behind us, and dove just in time, wrapping our hands around our head, sending up a column of spinning, rattling stone to deflect a swinging blow from the culicidae's claw.

Then its weight was on top of us, pushing us down, and we dragged our knees to our chest and felt the air pushed from our lungs, and our skin begin to cake over with another layer, begin to roughen and turn silver-grey, a sorcerer's defensive concrete wall growing around us and the light going out as the culicidae pressed down on top of us with all its weight, forcing us deeper into a cocoon of darkness and liquid concrete that swelled up around us to try and shut it out, but of course, in shutting it out, it shut the air out too and I felt the beginning of that suffocation that begins with a heart pounding in the chest and becomes a pressure behind the eye and a seizing in the stomach and a collapsing in the lungs and a burning in the ears and a bursting in the throat and . . .

. . . and then the weight was gone with a loud thump overhead and I crawled upwards from a pressed hollow in the earth, shedding dust and cracked concrete in time to see a great claw, bigger than the culicidae itself, swinging overhead. It was silver, on a yellow-painted arm, and it swung and struck like a thing alive. Now there were two others, coming to life behind the iron fence, bending and stabbing down to try and capture the culicidae in their metallic fists. These were the claws that crushed the cars, with bits of internal wiring and scraped-off rust still clinging to their three fingers, and the stench of oil leaking from their internal hydraulics. I ducked as one swung, spitting oxide-red magic, to slam into the side of the culicidae with all the force that, by day, could crush a truck in a single grasp. The culicidae was rocked off its feet, legs flailing briefly, comically, in the air, and no sooner had it flicked itself upright than another claw stabbed down from above, grabbing it by the abdomen, slate crunching beneath the impact, before the culicidae wriggled away. I peered towards the metal fence that separated the railway from the car-crunching dump, and there they were, Aldermen, half a dozen at least, black figures against a floodlit background. Playing over their bowed heads and their fingers, spread wide, were the same rusty-red magics that sparked off the shells of the metal claws circling overhead; and I remembered why people feared the Aldermen.

Then the culicidae saw me and, associating me with its distress, swung round and charged head first, mouth gaping to reveal a pit of glass. I hurled the first spell that came to our fingers' end, and in that instant all I could hear was the roaring of trains and the scraping of metal wheels on a metal track, felt a rush of wind against my back that stank of tunnels and diesel and grease and that nearly knocked me off my feet, felt around me the dancing shadows of a train, ghostly and blurred almost to nothing, driving past me, through me in the night, and straight into the culicidae.

For a moment the creature was paralysed, its whole body warping at the force of the spell: sound and noise and shadow slamming into it, passing through it, and for a moment I wondered if this might be enough, if it might not burst in two from the force of the magic; but the spell was only the length of a high-speed train passing by, broken almost as soon as summoned, and I sagged to my knees, gasping for air from the force of it, and the culicidae was staggering drunkard-like towards me.

I made it up onto one knee just as a claw from one of the crushing machines slammed down between us, smacking into the culicidae's head hard enough for the place to be briefly visible where skull and thorax met, and sending splinters of glass whirling outward from the join. The fingers of the claw closed around the culicidae's skull, pushing it down, making its claws scrabble against the earth like the wheels of a lorry churning soft mud. I struggled to my feet, hauling down breath, and another mechanical arm swung round, thrusting the culicidae down harder yet. It burrowed and writhed, but a third claw was making its turn, the machine that drove it clattering with the strain of what the Aldermen were making it do, and even as it looked that the culicidae might pull free, the metal fist came down and spiked the writhing tail of the beast, pinning it to the ground.

Lenses flickered in those multifaceted eyes, jerking this way and that, mouth opening and closing noiselessly, deafeningly, as slate shattered and glass spilt, and even we could perceive pain. The tracks were singing it, a high-pitched angel hum, the wires were shaking it, cables swaying overhead, the yellow claws pinning the culicidae down were crying it in little runs of dirty oil, and the culicidae screamed and screamed and screamed, as the claws around it closed tighter.

We stood staring at it, I don't know how long.

The Aldermen stood together above the track, rusty light flaring off them as they struggled to control the spell. Someone shouted my name, and we ignored it. Someone shouted again, "Matthew! We can't hold it long!"

We looked down at our burnt fingers, felt the creature's screaming in our gut, looked back up at the culicidae, its mouth opening and closing wildly, legs still scrambling uselessly at dirt.

The boy had been right.

Even the foolish mortal summoner, a child playing with toys, had been right.

It was beautiful.

"For God's sake!" someone shouted. "Kill the fucking thing!"

We limped towards it. The movement of the creature's mouth slowed as we neared, its eyes fixed on us. We reached out with the scarred palm of our right hand, holding it a centimetre above its hot shell. We wanted to make the comforting noises mortals make to soothe their animals, or parents make to calm a child, but did not think the creature had the wit to comprehend. It had not been summoned with soothing in mind.

I don't know why we thought of it, or even if what we did could be said to travel such rigid paths as thought, but as our hand hovered above its skin, I found ourself making a sound, to match the singing of the rails. We couldn't achieve the pitch, but there was a point, a few octaves lower, where we could match the sound of the creature in distress. We hummed, starting at the bottom of our lungs, letting the sound grow, catching a corner of that sound and watching it shimmer down our arm, tingle at our fingertips, scald the air between us and it, the trapped creature. It grew inside of us and we thought, as it grew, that the culicidae seemed to respond, eyes growing less frantic, the open–shutting of its jaw slower, the whirling of glass inside it becoming still. Its legs beat a little less against the ground, the writhing of its body inside the claws grew slower. But between our fingertips and it we could still hear,

You're a failure, good-for-nothing, and that's all you'll ever be
Sorry babe, but I just don't want to waste my life on nothing
Hey hey man it'll be cool you know it'll be totally cool
I'm no coward
You talk big but you don't do shit about nothing
People like you always end up alone

Still humming, we felt again for the dryness of concrete over our skin, dragged up a protective sheath of it from the earth, let it wrap around our legs, spin around our outstretched arms, coat our hand in thick heavy dust, but leave our face free; and still we hummed, and the culicidae became quiet. Its head sank forward onto the track, its legs lay down to rest their joints on the ballast. Heavy with the weight of my concrete armour, I stepped aside, letting the humming fade. There was silence.

Neither the cables sang nor the tracks buzzed, no alarm wailed or metal clashed.

Only the slow creaking of the culicidae's shell gave any proof that it was alive.

"Sorry," I whispered, and looked down the track.

Two dots of white sprang into life, where before there had just been railway darkness heading out to nowhere. An engine hummed somewhere, far off. Nearer, a set of points snapped from left to right. A red lamp switched to green further down the line, spilling a cheery emerald glow across the track. Then another, and another behind that. The culicidae tried to move against the vice that held it, but finding no point of weakness, it lay back down, still and passive. The sound of wheels beginning to move against the track was like the screech of witches; venomous blue-white electric sparks started spurting into the night. We reached out towards the creature again and hummed, at the same pitch, with the same harmony, as the culicidae's silent scream, stilling it for a while; and the heat coming off its shell was almost bearable, merely enough to make the air ripple and warp around it, a burning off from

You have a responsibility and you've failed

Can't be a child forever

To be honest, I don't think he's going to get good enough grades

Grow up, damn you, just grow up!

Have you considered that he might be dyslexic?

Move along, okay, this isn't the place for you . . .

Move along . . .

It was clear now, that thing on the tracks, a black face with two white eyes. A squat freight engine hauling empty trucks, the kind that at night rattled through sleeping suburbs at twelve miles an hour, hauling twenty, thirty, forty wagonloads of steel, sand and oil between the backs of terraced houses. At that slow speed it could still move a ferry-load of goods; at thirty it could smash a brick wall without needing to slow, and at fifty a lead-lined vault wouldn't have stopped it.

I think the culicidae saw it coming.

It kicked and it struggled, but not, we thought, as hard as it might have.

Perhaps it didn't understand.

I stepped back at the last moment, letting the concrete shield complete itself, covering my head and mouth, blocking out the light for a few hot, suffocating seconds. The speeding freight train, trailing white sparks and black smoke, its driver's compartment empty and its lights flickering like a dying firefly, slammed into the culicidae. It shattered slate and spilt glass, snapping one of the mechanical claws that held the beast down, and sending razored debris shooting out across the tracks. I felt the heat through my shield, the snap of broken monster striving to batter against me. Then, muffled and far off, all I could hear was the engine quietening, wheels slowing on metal, and the clink of falling shell. I let my concrete armour dwindle, until only my right arm was covered, as far up as my elbow.

The train had rolled to a stop fifty yards away. Its rear lights were red and dim, its engine burping a periodic dying rumble, like a tape machine running out of batteries but unwilling to give up the game.

The culicidae had been cut in two. Broken glass and splintered slate tumbled across the railway track. A metal leg had embedded itself in the support of a signal box; one glass eye lay broken in its crib, the shattered lenses still twitching. Torn in half, but not dead, not yet. Glass still spun weakly inside what was left of the slate shell; three of the creature's remaining limbs scrabbled feebly at nothing; and I heard a little hum, like pings from a submarine, as it struggled to find its voice, its twisted jaws gaping in distress. One of the two remaining claws suspended overhead was dangling from its mechanical arm by a few wires, the spell that held it broken.

I picked my way across broken glass and torn slate towards the monster, searching for a gap in the torn black shell. Cracks were trying to heal already, bits of broken blackness twitching this way and that as the culicidae's internal mechanism tried to fix the torn puzzle of its own body. Thin, sickly yellow light ran between the cracks beneath the shell; I found one thicker than the rest, wriggled my concrete fingers into it until it parted, then pushed deeper, up to the wrist, then the elbow. Even with the creature in two pieces, glass whirled inside it, tearing at my shell almost as fast as I could renew it and thicken the concrete, to stop my arm being cut to shreds. The heat went straight through the concrete, an unpleasant throb rising to all-out shooting distress that only got thicker the deeper I went. Even as the crack my arm was in began to close, I went on flailing around inside the creature. The glass at its core was thicker than water, making movement sluggish as I tried to shove it aside and find the source of the fire now running up my arm. Aldermen were coming, running, but they were still far off and our arm felt huge now, bundles of nerves made bigger than the rest of us by the volume of their distress and ... There was something there, something ragged that got knocked a little out of reach as we strove for it, and we reached again, the edge of the wound in the slate starting to bite against our skin as we tried to find it and

there

There it was, our fingers tightened round it; the heat coming off it made the concrete on my arm begin to pop and simmer, splinters of glass stabbing through the cracks in it to scratch and tear at my skin. I felt blood run across my hand from where the creature's gashed slate shell had started to close on my arm, and we braced ourself feet-first against the side of the beast and closed our fingers around its heart and pulled, pulled, until the slate carapace snapped open again and we went tumbling onto the line.

The culicidae crumbled.

No final scream, no last twitch, no great explosion.

A thing that had been alive, a living, raging creature, was suddenly no more than glass and slate, impossible, a defiance of the laws of physics which, pissed off at being defied, now made themselves known once more.

It collapsed, tumbling into a thousand constituent parts that spilt like so much litter from a torn plastic bag across the track, with a hiss as the last of the heat rushed to escape, and the life went out.

I looked at the thing in my hand. The heart of the culicidae.

It still burned and smoked and blazed, too hot to hold except through concrete, and even that not good enough to stop the burning.

It was a bag, a plastic shopping bag, scrunched up to form a tight ball. Inside, just visible through the thin sheet: a broken mobile phone, a smashed couple of CDs, a torn-up notebook and a broken pen, a picture burnt at the edges and torn in three, a stained baseball cap, and the headless remains of what might once have been a child's action figure, the limbs melted to pinkish liquid goo.

Alan was a good summoner, too good; too much of himself had gone into this beastie, and then a bit too much of everybody else.

Then Kelly was by my side, and she had a cool-box, big, plastic, heavy-duty, as much about keeping curry warm as ice cream cold, and when she slammed the lid shut on the heart in its box there was a smell of magic as the wards snapped shut, sealing it in.

One or two of the Aldermen clapped.

In the excitement of the event, they seemed to have forgotten their default position of pissed-off bastards.

In the silence of destruction, Templeman swung into action.

Glass was swept, and slate removed, bundled up into the same dumpsters that might once have transported the culicidae in its dormant state, before the souls of a dozen angry teenagers sent it quite, quite mad.

I sat on the side of the railway track, staring at nothing, while Kelly tutted over my burnt hand and bleeding right arm. The glass hadn't penetrated far through the concrete, barely enough to scratch; but it had done a lot of scratching, and the black shirt Templeman had lent me after the death of my last had seen its final days.

A first-aid kit was produced from somewhere. Then a fresh cup of hot coffee.

"I do have milk somewhere . . ." Kelly proclaimed, looking around her.

"Don't worry about it," I replied. She tutted again, and went back to bandaging my arm. Kelly was a medic who believed there was no such thing as too much padding, and any hope of fitting my arm back into a coat sleeve was rapidly failing.

"You seem to have had quite a knack with that monster thing, Mr Mayor," she declared as a tube of alcoholic-stench burn cream was produced from her first-aid kit. "When you went up to it back then, I thought 'Whoops, that's it, he's gone,' but then it was really like you were bonding with it. I had a cat like that, you know, very shy of humans, probably had a bad experience in the past, rescue cats are like that, but if you let it know you weren't a threat and gave it its own time, its own place, it could really come round."

Through the haze of exhaustion, drugs and pain I tried to focus on Kelly's cheerful face. "You had a cat . . . like the culicidae?"

"Well, no, not exactly like the culicidae, I mean, not in the sucking-out-your-soul monster way, I can see how that might not quite work, but I think what I was trying to say was that sometimes communication doesn't have to be verbal to be poignant."

"Kelly," I asked, slowly in case the words came out wrong. "I don't mean this personally, and please understand, it's been a very stressful couple of days, but please tell me . . ."

"Yes, Mr Mayor?"

"Are you sure you're real?"

She chuckled, smearing burn cream across our scalded fingers in thick cool dollops. "Well, as the great philosopher would say, I think therefore I am and that is all I can know and in fact, since it is all I can know, sense data being prone to error and misinterpretation, the only thing I can say for certain is that I am real, whereas you might not be; but then again, you must think exactly the same thing so I suppose that doesn't help you, does it?"

Our mouth was hanging open.

I closed it, took another gulp of hot coffee, then drained the cup, put it to one side and murmured, "I'd like to have a holiday now."

"How about Swanage?" she asked.

"I don't even know where that is."

"That's the beauty of it! No one would look for you in Swanage!"

"You know what," I said. "You must be real. I don't have the imagination to make you up."

"That's the attitude!"

"Thinking of all things improbable," I added, "where'd you put the culicidae's heart?"

"We're taking it back to the office, Mr Mayor."

"Is that wise? I mean, it is a sorta burning core of bile and rage."

"Well, yes," she sighed. "That's exactly the problem. It's the safe-disposal issue. I remember one time, when there was a firedrake

summoned in Peckham, and the officers handling the case thought
they could just dispose of its bile gland down the sewer and I am telling
you, we were scraping off crispy parts for a month, such a mess! So I
think we want to avoid that this time. Unless, of course, Mr Mayor,
you have an idea?"

From anyone else, it would have been a put-down. Kelly's face
glowed with optimism.

Avoidance seemed only proper. "Where are the Minority Council?"

"Mr Caughey and Mr Fadhil have excused themselves . . ."

"Cheeky buggers!"

"Ms Holta and Ms Rathnayake are escorting the heart back to the
office to assist with the clean-up . . ."

"Are they supervised?" I snapped.

"Well, there are other Aldermen there," replied Kelly, a little taken
aback. "And besides, I'm sure that everyone understands the necessity
of tonight's situation, the need to deal with this culicidae problem
before it got out of hand; everyone's completely on board with the
message, Mr Mayor."

"And Templeman?"

"Is waiting for you by his car."

"Good. Do I have a schedule thing?"

She sat back on her heels, wearing an enormous grin, a woman who
couldn't quite believe her ears. "A schedule? Why yes, Mr Mayor, of
course you have a schedule, and, in fact, you've even got an app to
monitor your schedule remotely if you'll just . . ."

"Tomorrow afternoon, me, the Minority Council, a sit-down chat,
sandwiches, coffee, no guns, no offensive sorcery, several reasonably
impartial witnesses – give Dudley Sinclair a call, tell him it'll be dead
miserable and right up his street – maybe a few biscuits – no, maybe
a lot of biscuits – sound good?"

"Of course!" She was looking around now for tissues to wipe the
gunk off her hands, folding each one into an immaculate triangle when
done. "I'll have it put into your diary and a room booked right away.
Any particular kind of biscuits? I mean, I usually get the family selection, something for everyone, but Mr Nair liked butter shortbreads and
I know that some people think the family selection has too many
artificial flavourings . . ."

"It sounds fine," I groaned, dragging myself to my feet. How could pain still feel so novel? "No, wait, actually ... Can you do custard creams? And those chocolate things; the ones with layers? The ones you break in two and lick the bit in the middle off, you know them?"

"Of course, we can do any biscuit you want ..."

"We want those," we said. "And maybe ..."

"Yes?"

" ... those kind of cheese twist things ...?"

She walked with us, up towards the street, getting out a pen to take notes with as we went on our way.

Templeman was, as promised, by his car.

As I approached, with Kelly taking down the last of tomorrow's menu, he waited, until she'd scurried off to find a taxi and a catering company still trading at two a.m. The Aldermen began to leave, for whatever duties called them in the cold hours of the night. No one paid us much attention; the assumption seemed to be that if Templeman thought something was okay, it was. Questions were put to me, but answers were looked to from him. The fact that they pretended to ask me anything was an improvement of sorts.

When, finally, we were alone, I said, "Thanks."

"What for?"

"Making all this happen. Getting them to stick with it and deal with the culicidae. I know they wouldn't have, if you hadn't made them."

"The culicidae was a failure," he replied. "They would have seen that in time – I merely helped convince them a little faster. Besides, in all good relationships there must be some give and take."

"I know, I know. I just don't like committee meetings. Christ, there'll be minutes, won't there? And that thing you get where some guy keeps saying 'can we stick to the agenda please' and someone else saying 'if we can just discuss the issues here' and ... God it'll be crap. Do you think anyone would mind if I ran away?"

"Many people are surprised you haven't run already," he said, and added, "I mean, in regard to your other problems, rather than as a personal reflection on your character."

I groaned. "Oh Christ, yes, the fairy godmother. Hold on – before the good feeling goes ..." I felt in my pocket for my phone, flicked it on, dialled Nabeela.

Templeman watched me, and as I listened to it ring he asked, "Someone at this hour?"

"Oh, this social worker who put me on to the culicidae in the first place. I figured she'd want to know it had a happy ending. Sort of."

The phone kept ringing.

"Maybe she's asleep," suggested Templeman. "It is an unsociable hour."

"Yeah," I muttered, thumbing off after longer than I'd meant. "Maybe it is at that."

Then I pulled my phone out again, dialled Penny.

It rang, and kept on ringing.

I let it ring for a whole minute.

Then two.

No answer.

"Problems?" asked Templeman when I hung up to the still busy sound of buzzing.

"Maybe. Maybe not. What were you saying?"

"Would you like a lift? Whatever retribution the fairy godmother is planning, I'm sure we can keep you safe for a few more hours."

"That would be good. Thank you. I . . . no, wait." I dialled Penny again, let it ring, still no answer, hung up, dialled again, no answer.

"Matthew?" Templeman's voice was polite and neutral as ever.

"Penny would answer," I snapped. "She would answer dammit, she would answer! Or if she didn't, Nabeela would."

"You think the fairy godmother has them?" he asked quickly.

"I don't know, I don't know! Maybe. Jesus, but Penny is . . . she knows that he's after me, she's not thick, she's got skills, she's been trained, she summoned the death of cities for Christ's sake! Wait wait wait . . ." I stood still, forced us to be still, mind racing. "Wait," we breathed, taking control. "If the fairy godmother has Penny and Nabeela – which I'm not saying he does – but if he did, then he'd use them against us. He will attempt to trade them for us, their safety for our blood. That means they are unharmed. Which means there's still a chance."

Then Templeman softly said, "The fairy godmother won't give them to you alive." Our eyes locked onto his as he said, "I have experience dealing with the fairy godmother's ways. He knows your record, your personality. If he has taken your apprentice, then he knows you must destroy him, that you will destroy him. They aren't hostages – they're bait."

"Bait?" I echoed. Our mind was racing, too much, too many thoughts, all at once, tumbling together. "How the hell does that even work?!"

"He hopes to trick you into submission, into making a mistake. Matthew, you cannot let your personal feelings get in the way of . . ."

"Damned be to personal feelings and damned be to the Midnight fucking Mayor!" I roared. "She's my apprentice, she's my bloody apprentice; I've already lost one apprentice and I'm not going to . . . if he's got Penny and Nabeela then he's going to let them go or we swear that he will burn. The dusthouses will burn and we do not care what forces of God or nature he throws up in our way!"

I marched round to the car door and wrenched it open, but Templeman was already there, putting himself in my way. "Listen to me," he said, and his voice was low, urgent – had I ever heard Templeman urgent before? "I can help you get your apprentice back, I can help you fight the fairy godmother, but you have to listen to me. The dusthouses are powerful but so are you; I have means that will help you, ways to help you bring them down, get your apprentice back, but you have to trust me."

We dragged in a slow breath, let it out shuddering; and now, when we met his eye, he flinched. "'Did she say anything?'" we asked, soft now.

Confusion stirred in his face. His mouth formed a question that wasn't spoken out loud.

"'Did she say anything?'" we repeated. "We said, a beggar escaped from the dusthouse in Enfield. A beggar ran and a beggar died. And you said, 'Did she say anything?' Perhaps it was just a slip of the tongue, perhaps that's the way you think, only it's not, is it? It's not how these things work. Even women ask 'Is he okay?' as a default position when they don't know gender; it's just one of those social things, same the world over.

"And you hate the dusthouses, I mean . . . really hate them. But that story about your brother, you told it cold, dispassionately, a lecture in bad politics, not a tale of death and horror. What could you have against the dusthouses that is so much worse? To go behind your colleagues, to help me without another thought, to question nothing too far but the right things so specifically . . .

"Prince made a phone call to an Alderman while I was in his car, did I tell you that? He made a call to check up on the Midnight Mayor and I thought 'This is it, I'm done for,' but somehow he heard what he needed to hear and I remember thinking at the time 'That seems lucky' and I am not a lucky guy.

"Who ignores the Beggar King, seriously, when he comes knocking and says 'Someone's killing my people'? You don't ignore him, but somehow the Aldermen did, and, say what you will, Templeman, you are great with the Aldermen, I mean, they all look up to you, they all do what you say; it's an amazing trick you've got going and I wish I had it. And yet I'm glad that we don't.

"And the fairy godmother offered to sell me the name of the man who'd been dabbling in fairy dust behind his back, the man who's been experimenting, and you know what, I hate the dusthouses for preying on the needy, but we truly despise those who prey on the helpless."

His breath was coming fast now, short shallow puffs in the cold night air.

"So you see," we concluded, "we return to this: 'did she say anything?'"

My words hung there.

Stretched.

His face frozen, his breath lingering in the air.

Then he smiled, and it occurred to us that we'd never seen him smile quite like that before.

He said, "I apologise, Matthew. I had hoped we had more time."

We felt something bite us in the crook of our arm. Small and sharp, so brief we almost ignored it. But Templeman's eyes had darted aside, and we followed his look.

The hypodermic was thin, barely more than a safety match of clean fluid, the last droplets vanishing through our shirt and into our arm. As I tried to pull free he grabbed my hand, easily as holding a puppy by the throat.

Someone's knees buckled, and I guessed they were mine.

Someone's throat was dry, but that was a long, long way off.

Someone was tasting something bitter in their mouth.

Someone was turning out the lights.

Templeman caught us as we fell, eased us down onto tarmac, supported our head as it came to rest against the back of the car.

Not my head.

Someone else.

I heard him say to a stranger, "I'm sorry, Matthew," and it occurred that Matthew might be me, "you can't save yourself."

That was all.

Waking, we thought we were with Meera.

Her flat had been near Waterloo Bridge.

The night we stayed, a south wind had carried the sound of the trains in the early morning.

Her fridge contained a microwave chicken tikka, a lump of goat's cheese past its best, a half-bottle of nondescript 'tropical fruit drink' and two eggs. Breakfast had been a sausage sandwich from the greasy spoon across the street.

She'd spent too long in the bathroom when getting up, and locked the door behind her.

On the wall above her bed, someone with a sense of the Gothic had framed a dark green panel of fake marble, on which was written in small chrome letters:

> I am a stranger with thee: and a sojourner,
> as all my fathers were.
> O spare me a little, that I may recover my strength,
> before I go hence, and be no more seen.

"My aunt gave it to me," she'd explained. "She says it doesn't matter if you believe in God or magic or fairies or pixie dust. A good witch finds magic from the things they are inside, not the stuff around them. And that what they are inside is made by the stuff around them. My aunt said things like that."

On the bridge, saying goodbye, she'd asked us what we were doing tomorrow night, and we hadn't exactly lied, but neither had we said the right thing.

Waking, we thought we were with Meera, and we were not.

The city had changed.

It took us a while to place it, but now we looked, there it was.

The smell of the river; the silver lights of cloud-skimmed towers ahead; the flashing red beacon above Canary Wharf. Car parked by water, low black bollard and low iron chain, overhead gantry of the Docklands Light Railway; the rattle of steel rigging against the masts of nearby yachts.

Herons Quay, at a guess, looking north towards the money.

I twitched, and my body reported that twitching was bad. A crick in my neck might have been from time spent in a car boot, as well as pins and needles in my right foot. There was metal on my wrists, done up just tight enough to restrict blood flow. I was propped upright against the side of a car; no, against Templeman's car. By the cold seeping through my bones, I'd been there a while, even though it was still night.

A footstep beside me; to our shame, I jerked away.

Templeman didn't so much sit as fold paper-tight into a crouch next to me.

There was a needle in his hand.

The substance inside this one was cloudy yellow, the sickly shade of fairy dust.

We didn't speak, found we had no words.

He said, "The fairy godmother knows you're here. His men are on the way, and will collect you in a matter of minutes. In the meantime, I need you to listen."

As he spoke, he leant over and started rolling up my left sleeve. I tried to pull away but his fingers dug deep enough to make us gasp; there was a metallic strength to them, a reminder of his Alderman's power. The needle pierced our skin and something hot and thick started burrowing under it. I pushed our head back against the car, forcing us to stay calm and breathe slow. When it was done, Templeman rolled the sleeve back down to hide the mark, and carefully dropped the used needle into a plastic bag.

"I have told the fairy godmother I am delivering you to him in exchange for his silence. I have informed him that you are tranquilised and powerless; neither of these statements is entirely true. He believes that I am a fairy, addicted to the dust, and has been blackmailing me for some time to this effect. I am not, but, as you have correctly surmised,

I have been buying it from him for some time in order to further my studies. It was only a matter of time before he worked this out, and therefore his removal has become necessary. The substance you have just been injected with," he folded the bag round and round the needle inside it, dropping the bundle into his coat pocket, "is an experimental drug derived from my studies. Its effects on humans have been ... mixed ... but then, Matthew, you aren't human any more, are you?"

A laugh croaked at the back of my throat. I couldn't look at him, but stared out across the water, trying to breathe in river smell, river magic, river strength. Everything was muddy, a long way off, his voice the only constant.

"You will feel its effects in the next fifteen to twenty minutes. Then you should be inside the dusthouse. By now," he glanced at his watch, "your two friends will be dead. The fairy godmother will have killed them. His men will be watching you closely, despite my assurances that you are tamed; they will attempt to extract your blood, and bind and compel you. Even now the greed of the fairy godmother may overwhelm his good judgement – good judgement will have you killed, greed will have them drain your blood first. The blood of the blue electric angels will fetch a notable price, even if he has to sell it on eBay.

"The injection I've given you should temporarily allow you to overcome any reasonable opposition inside the dusthouse but, as I said, it is hard to know exactly how the drug will work on your physiology. Nevertheless, even if it does not act to full potency, I know what the blue electric angels are capable of, what the Midnight Mayor can be. You may not survive the experience, Matthew, but this is going to be the only chance to take revenge for the death of your friends. Do you understand me?"

I didn't answer. He put his hand under my chin, and pushed my face up to look into his eyes. "Matthew," he repeated, "whatever you think of me and what I have done, the fairy godmother has killed them. He has killed your social worker friend and he has killed Penny. I want the fairy godmother dead, so do you. This is the only way to achieve it. Do you understand?"

I felt too sick to nod or speak. He drew his hand back, unconsciously wiping it on his sleeve. "I had hoped we could avoid this," he said, straightening up. "I had hoped that we could find a better way." His eyes swerved towards the street we'd come down, a not-quite-cobbled road of few cars, between waterways. I heard an engine, off in the dark where there should have been none, sound muffled by buildings, carried by water.

"Whatever you think of me," he murmured, eyes fixed on the road, "remember – the fairy godmother has killed your friends. Pursue me next, if you must, but kill him first."

A car rounded the corner, crawling past the darkened purple lights of an expensive Indian restaurant and the locked front door of a private-members' gym. It was a blue people carrier, the outlines of heads barely visible against the glow of the night. Templeman pulled me up by the armpit. The injection site on our arm now registered a dull burning; there was mud in our mind.

The car stopped some thirty yards away, far enough to be safe, close enough to see. Three doors opened, three men got out. From the front passenger seat came Hugo, gleaming skin and perfect dress, a man for whom pyjamas were mere theoretical notions for the weak. A fourth man stayed behind the driving wheel, the engine still ticking over. Hugo scanned his surroundings: first Templeman, then me, then everything else, head turning upwards and round to look for shadows in windows, cars parked where there should be none, disturbances in the gentle slap of the water against the quays. All to his satisfaction; his gaze returned to me, then darted to Templeman.

"Mr Templeman," he said, his voice carrying without seeming to be raised. "It has been some months since we saw you last."

Somewhere through the sickly heat prickling the edge of our brain, we realised that Templeman was scared of Hugo. His hands gripped the top of my arm, pulling me forward with him. I staggered, bending, trying to remember which foot did what and in what order.

"You wanted Swift," he replied, guiding me towards Hugo. I found I couldn't look; the stones of the street were fascinating to me. "Here he is."

Halfway between his car and theirs, Templeman stopped. Hugo hadn't moved, hands loose and ready by his side. "The fairy godmother appreciates the token," he said. "And wishes to convey his grateful thanks. May I enquire how you managed to convince the Midnight Mayor to be so cooperative?"

Templeman tightened his grasp of my arm, a gesture of the hand to hide the look on his face. Then his whole body swung round, so suddenly I nearly lost my footing again. His fist came with it, a silvery coating on his white knuckles, and he landed a punch, not hard, but it didn't need to be, squarely on our cracked ribs.

We swallowed a scream and kept on swallowing, so hard and deep we thought we were going to suffocate with the effort of it. Somehow the world had gone from upright to lying down, the brain too overwhelmed to recall the journey; I lay on the ground and the ground was good and to breathe was to die, and not to breathe was to die and so I twitched and gagged and

We felt |
      | I was

and Templeman was saying a very long way off, "That's how."

Footsteps moved, beyond the edge of our sight. Hands caught us by the arms and pulled us back up; they were dragging us towards the car.

A wall of pain had inserted itself between brain and body.

I heard Templeman say, "All debts forgiven?"

"It is good business, to keep a promise," replied Hugo's voice. Someone opened the back passenger seat of the car, someone else pushed me in, hand at the back of my head like a copper, avoiding another knock. The door slammed shut, I smelt the thick dry smell of all clean cars everywhere, foam and grey fabric, mixed with a hint of diesel. The driver watched me in the mirror, someone else got in beside me and pushed my head down, keeping their hand on the back of my neck. I heard doors slam, felt the seat in front of me move. Hugo sitting. Hugo saying, "All right then. Let's go."

Second Interlude: I Can't Save Ourself

In which the fairy godmother explains
his business policy.

We felt something … | I wasn't feeling so good.
… that we hadn't felt before.

The journey wasn't far, barely worth the petrol it spent. Quicker to walk, once you'd taken into account the faffing with one-way systems and time spent at the traffic lights.

The Isle of Dogs.

Once a place of industrial dockyards and quays, then a place of decline, rotten council estates and empty wharves; now reborn as an almost-island of shimmering apartment blocks, expensive bars, high-end supermarkets, and sweeps of grass over formerly abandoned sites. In a word, money. The place had beauty, in its way, clean and crisp, in a land where litter did not blow. But it was a beauty of straight lines, of steel, glass and privilege; and somehow, for all its fluorescent twinkling glory, it was a desert place, where the magic was

slithering silver smooth | of illusions and glamours

rather than the raw fire burning elsewhere beneath the streets of London.

A yellow machine accepted the swipe of a wordless white card from Hugo's fingers. A curved jaw of steel slid away down in front of the car, a light turned from red to green, and we descended into an underground car park which, in keeping with the spirit of the Isle, did not smell of piss, and where the lights did not flicker, but whose shadows round the walls were nonetheless thick and deep.

It took two of them to help me, one on either side. There was a lift, a smooth thing of mirrors tinted beige, with buttons that lit up LED blue when you touched them. From a tiny speaker hidden in the reflective ceiling, someone slaughtered Sinatra on an electric keyboard. I expected to go to the top, but we rode only as far as the fourth floor. There, every light fitting embedded in the wall and every tweak of blue-black pattern on the carpet, every strip of white wallpaper and every polished oak door, was the same. It was the hour for all good men to be asleep, but as we neared the end of the corridor I could hear the creaking of pipes in the wall, and the muffled beat of bass music coming up through the floor.

A door like any other, except this one was guarded by a man in the same immaculate black suit that Hugo wore, who had about him the thick treacle stench of enchantment. He nodded, just once, as Hugo approached, and swiped a badge across a monitor. A click and a snap, and the door opened to a wave of warmth and sound, tinted with the smell of chlorine.

Someone was having a party.

Not a boisterous party, not a party of disco beats and roaring crowds.

This was the party of the casually indulged, of the kind of crowd who'd long ago realised that only the medium-rich flaunted their wealth on great spectacle, while the mega-rich let everyone else work it out for themselves. I half raised my head and saw

men in white shirts with the buttons undone, women, paid to be in bikinis and doing their jobs very well, chatting professionally on long green sofas and sipping champagne,

[idle curiosity turned to disdain in the glances of the people assembled, mortals thinking no further than their own sensory delight]

we see it all │ something happening to me

The sound of jazz played by a live four-piece band. It was a place where clearly the arrival of a handcuffed beaten stranger in the night was considered a brief distraction rather than a topic of debate. Several rooms had been knocked together into one long space behind a curving glass wall two storeys high, which led out onto festoon-lit balconies where there was relative quiet for the sharing of intimate secrets. The overall theme was white and cream: cream floors and white sofas, with the odd splash of colour from the skimpy clothes of the hostesses filling out the space. Low glass-topped tables bore champagne in ice buckets and nibbles on burnished plates; for the true punter, there were also boxes of enamelled jade and silver from which yellow-eyed revellers could pinch up dust, snorting it like snuff before reclining to smile and dream fairy-dust dreams. More than a few eyes in this room were stained liver-yellow from addiction, but not, I noticed, the men in black suits, standing round the walls with hands behind their back.

A wide set of white doors had been folded back at the far end of the room. Beyond, the music was quieter, with a pulsing beat that might at some point accompany French lyrics in a husky voice about love, disappointment and regret. The lighting was heading for ultraviolet, low and embedded into the wall. A brighter sky-blue glow came from the centre of the room: an oval swimming pool, too small for exercising in, but almost steaming hot, with bubbles rising in the middle. Men and women were littered around its edges, some with glasses in hand, others lying back in a yellow-eyed daze, while girls with tanned skin inclining to orange padded round the heated floor tiles bearing more drinks, more wine. The pool was set into a corner of the building, so that three walls were windows, each a dark glass that blurred outside light and looked across the river to the white glow of the Millennium Dome.

The men put hands upon us | pushing me to my knees

behind the not-quite-bald head of a man who reclined, in the shallow end of the pool, arms stretched out along its rim, surveying the scene like a king watching over his aquatic court. Hands pressed down on my shoulders, keeping me there, and one or two occupants of the pool spared me a look whose meaning was unclear. All I could see of the man was the back of his head, folds of fat on a short neck that joined a hairy white back, grey hair thinned to a half-tonsure, and flabby arms that formed a kind of cushion on the tiles. Not grossly overweight, but a man who received the occasional chiding from his GP, and orders to keep an eye out, please, just in case.

He ignored me. I stayed where I was, back bent and head bowed, trying to pin down

feel taste of sound of |
growing here | this sick feeling inside

Then, "I don't suppose you're the kind of man who appreciates cava."

euphoria and dust, dust and |
power | what has Templeman done?

"Personally," he went on, "I've always thought champagne was just champagne. I don't have time for people who talk pretentious twaddle about this vintage or that region. I imagine that before I die I'll insist on drinking nothing but rosé, or would it be ginger beer? Not much in keeping with what marketing men call 'image'. But I think that's a load of crap. Make the image what you want it to be, that's true power."

Smell of chlorine, heat of the swimming pool. Someone refilled a glass that wasn't empty; someone else laughed loudly at an insider's joke about football, or maybe rugby, in which the punch-line was an insult and the build-up was a smear. Who partied with the fairy godmother? The naïve or the guilty?

"I thought you'd talk more," he said, leaning back and giving me half a glance. "Everyone said you were a talker, the kind of man who, at great length, never says what he means. To be honest, I couldn't give a flying fart why you're here or what you think. You had your chance and you rejected it and I'd be a crap businessman if I didn't take the hint and say, well then, thank you very much, but that's it for you and me, journey over, job done. I'd have your throat cut right here, if it wasn't going to upset the guests."

He smiles at his own wit, at the instinct of the civilised host, and tilts his glass to his lips. The journey is long between his flabby hand and his open mouth; he drinks a sinful drink [uncaring guests glance at me and show no surprise], throat moving, up and down, cartilage and blood beneath the flesh [only so many ways to read a man in chains].

Guilty, then.

"I want you to look at it, Swift," he said, tilting his glass towards the room, encompassing the bubbling pool and the girls with the drinks, the musicians and the partying, the view of the lights on the river and beyond. "I want you to look long and hard and, while you're looking, I want everyone here to look at you. I want you to see everything that you could have had.

"You think all this is evil? There isn't evil in this world, not any more. There's no divine retribution, there's no absolute right and absolute wrong, God is dead and the world became too fat on its own over-feeding to keep to the narrow path a long time ago. There are always going to be the poor, the broken, the desperate, and there will always be the rich, the powerful and the ambitious. Not you, nor any like you, any pigheaded pompous crusaders who think that they have been chosen by Jesu upon high to come down and judge us busy men by their own petty standards, will change that. You're not some kind of fucking hero, Swift. You're deluded. You're mentally sick. You think that everything happens like a fairy story, a fantasy of perfect equality where all the happy bunnies roam and the grass tastes of chocolate.

You think that once you've killed the bad guy with the magic sword, that's it, problem solved, all the pixies will live in la-la land after and there won't ever be need and hunger and desire and revenge ever, ever again. You think people aren't people. You're fighting a war against the human fucking soul, and you know what, Swift? You weren't ever going to win. Do you hear me? Do you understand?"

| His words were meaningless to us. | I understood. |

"At this point people try to negotiate," he added. "Or are you too high and mighty to barter for your life?"

| We licked our lips, tasted dust and salt. Words were nothing, air rattling in our throat. | I licked my lips, tasted dust and salt. I tried to speak, but couldn't, had nothing to say. |

I couldn't even meet his eye, found my head bent staring at the lapping water on the edge of the pool as it sloshed overboard with the addition of a pair of women to the opposite end of the pool.

| We felt . . . . . . hollow | Something . . . hollow here . . . |
| And so alive. | |

Oscar Kramb, the fairy godmother – he seems to consider himself powerful. We want to laugh, and find that we were laughing, silent laughter that shakes our shoulders, makes our face ache. And now heads are turning, ignorant eyes in ignorant faces; they turn to stare at us, marvelling, wondering, and their faces make us laugh the more. And the fairy godmother [what a silly name] he doesn't speak, doesn't have any words to say as we laugh at him. He looks angry, as if he might want to skewer some piece of our flesh and eat it before his guests; act of pride on a cold night [place where warmth should have been]. He makes sounds, promises of pain, promises of death and we laugh the harder.

His hired helps take our arm, pull us to our feet. They whisper that they are going to take our blood. The blood of the blue electric angels.

Will you get high on that, mortals? Will you not choke on it? Will you not burn?

Well, it was a nice party while it lasted but hey, so it goes. No idea how you are going to get home after all this, I mean, have you tried getting a night bus from the Isle of Dogs at this hour?; seriously, they have letters in front of the numbers; that's always a bad sign.

A lift.

It's playing something twinkly. Sounds like falling glitter on cold stone. Fairy dust! Sparkle sparkle sparkle – make a wish! It makes me smile, and I look to the men – three of them – who are keeping me company. [They are going to take our blood.] The blood of gods and all that they can perceive from it is profit. Our head, turning as we are bumped into the lift, catches the eyes of one of the men. He has the thick arms of a man of the flesh, muscles fed on protein and pain. He tries to meet our stare. Then he looks away. His Adam's apple bobs in his throat. "Would you like us to tell you about death?" we ask. "Will knowing how it is make you less afraid?"

[. . . what the hell was I talking about?]

The mortal who calls himself Hugo, stink of slippery magic coating his skin, sighs and breathes, "Now Mr Swift, there's no need for that kind of talk."

Our head turns, our bones are full of air, our blood of heat, there is something inside us that was not there before, something wild and reckless and free. Hugo smiles, and smiles, and smiles as if willing it so; we can smell the stink of fear rising from them all. [I've got this splitting headache coming on. Do any of you have a paracetamol?]

The lift door opens, four floors below ground.

[Hello! Paracetamol?]

They pull us out and down a corridor of pipes and concrete, black and yellow warning signs to those scuttling slaves who have made it their business to tend to their master's welfare, their services hidden in the dark.

[No? Nothing? How rude.]

| There is a stench down here, pungent and sharp. It is a mixture of vinegar and | God it stinks! |

preservatives, detergents and chemical swabs. Somewhere a fan is turning, turning, turning and we feel the cold air on our face as if we were the rat hiding in the ducting behind it. We taste the dry bite of the dust, and as they pull us towards a grey metal door past men in white overalls and masks, we can feel it, the sun-dry tingle of the fairy dust on our skin

Someone should clean.

Something more as well down here.

like a living thing?

Infuriating mortal senses can barely perceive it, this dancing on the air; for all we can judge it may be no more and no less than a trick of light, a curious creation of the too-impressionable mortal brain.

A door at the end of the corridor. It, like all other doors, is anonymous, grey, metal. Mortals building things the same in the hope that conformity will set them free. Hugo unlocks it. It has a lot of locks. The door slams shut behind us and this room is a place for people to die in. The walls are coated with plastic sheets. So are the floors. When people die in this place, their dust is gathered in those plastic sheets like so much spilt paint.

[so thin I can barely see it but there it is, catching in the light, thin, eddies of dust and hello there! See how it swirls swirling swirling swirling]

It is a place for mortals to return unto the dust.

[it has faces too]

There is a chair set in the middle. There are chains attached to it. Chains for the hands and chains for the feet and chains for the neck. They have been kept clean and sterile, scrubbed down with surgical fluids so as not to affect the quality of death that shimmers down through their workings. [The dust has faces and it talks to me.]

They put us in.   Also, where do these people
Lock us down.   order their furniture from? Not

that I'm domestic man, but I'm
sure this stuff isn't from the Ikea
catalogue.

They bring over a tray of metal tools for playing games with mortal
bodies. Needles, knives, tubes and bags for catching the fallout. One
of them pulls up our left sleeve, observes the little mark turning to a red
bruise where Templeman stung us with his firefly needle of fairy juice.
They tie a tourniquet around our arm to force a vein to the surface. It
is fat and blue and ugly, a liquid worm beneath our skin; it repulses us.
The way our flesh goosebumps in the cold, the way our ribs still ache
through a cloud that encircles

some petty party of us | my thoughts

They disinfect our skin of germs before they plunge the needle in.
My thoughts! There's something a bit funny with my thoughts.
Comic funny? Comic funny. Comical. It's not a huge intellectual leap
to say that yes, all things considered, something a bit strange is going
down but well, shit, not like I can do anything about it and hey

push the metal tip deep into
                the vein | *ow!*

[why'd I get all the crappy sense data shit anyway?]

Hugo leans in close as they attach the first blood bag. He is looking into our eyes, trying to read our truth as if the soul of a god could
be understood by men. "Mr Swift?" he says. "Mr Swift, have you ever
taken fairy dust?" There must be something in our eyes more than our
burning blue.

"Mr Swift," repeats Hugo, "I understand that the present circumstances are less than ideal, but please be assured that, while
exsanguination is not the death we would wish on any man, we are not
savages in the dusthouses. I for one wish your death to be as painless
and comfortable as possible. Therefore I must ask again – have you
ever taken fairy dust?"

We watch our blood start to | Wait wait wait wait wait!
roll down the tubes. It is a sickly,
alien thing, fit only for meat.

| What was the question?

We laugh, but Hugo stays leaning over us, trying to read our eyes. We say, "We be light, we be life, we be fire!" He tuts, shaking his head at us, pulls away. "We be sunset blazing, we be heaven burning, we be darkness falling, we be sky cracking, we be earth shaking, we be ... "

"We don't need him awake," barks Hugo. "Just alive." A mortal advances towards us, a new needle in hand but his hand is shaking and we laugh the harder and turn our head upwards and taste

power in the palm of our hands, blazing blue power, and our blood was blazing blue in the clear plastic tubes, wriggling and writhing like a living thing, bursting into electrical sparking flames

electricity under my feet, how interesting and in the walls and in my fingers and that itches!

that eat through the tubing like acid and the lights are going out, not out, *in*, the lights are going in: we draw it inside of us, feast on the buzz of light and the stench of life and the smell of death and the heat of fear and the taste of dust and the humming of wires beneath us and the whisper of the gas overhead and the slipping of water and the beating of our heart and did they really think that their chains could bind *us*? Did they really think any mortal engine could bind us? The locks snap apart as if they are afraid to be on our skin. And though the lights are dying in the room, in all the rooms of this sinful palace, still we blaze with a sapphire glow that makes the veins stand out on the chalk-white necks of Hugo's men, burning from every inch of our mortal anatomy as if it might crack apart from the inside out to reveal our splendour.

"We be wall cracking, we be glass tearing, we be skyline tumbling down!" we bellow, rising to our feet, and the floor burns beneath us, the air shimmers from the heat rolling off our skin. They're running, the mortals are running, and as one of the men in white overalls reaches out for the handle, scrambling to escape us, we reach out with our fist [itchy itchy itchy!] and grab him by the insides, by the heart, wrapping raw fingers of electricity around the soft places inside his chest [like when the sole of your foot is itchy and you can't scratch it?] and squeezing, squeezing until we smell him cooking from the inside out and wisps of carbon-black smoke roll from inside his mouth [itchy like that]. His body arches in death, head rolling backwards and spine twisting like a bridge, pulling his whole body back until he balances, ballerina, on the end of his tip-toes. We hold him there for a second, letting the others see the blood bursting behind the corpse's eyes, then let the body go.

"Come be we," we snarl and now they are all running, animals kicking each other out of the way, to try and get out of ours, "and be free!"	"Look, it's okay," I try to say but there's something wrong with the sound coming from my lips.

They try to pull the door shut from the outside, lock us in, one left inside scrambling at it, screaming at them to let him out and we can see Hugo striding down the hall, back to us, calm in motion but not in mind. We grab the straggler by the hair; he screams as the electricity in our fingers bounces down the spine, lighting him up from the inside out like a glow stick and whatever Templeman has done this is wonderful! This is glorious, this is freedom, this is a drug of lava, a pit without end, liquid heaven, this is . . .

Majestic!	
	So yes, I think I might be a little stoned. I mean, not in a bad way, just you know . . . a little bit . . .
We are majestic!	

The world cannot conceive of what we are. Our right hand drips blue burning blood from the twin scars etched into our skin. And what repulsed us before is, now that we see it burning, oddly beautiful. We look up towards the door, and they were too slow to lock it, men are fleeing now down the open hall. We trace our fingers through the air, watching the electric afterglow dance on the back of our eyelids, then kneel, press our bloody palms into the floor and reach down for the things below. Our mind passes through dirt upon dirt that was itself once wood compressed beneath stone crushed by brick smashed by concrete, dirt of dirt made from mortar dust and time, smashed up then turned into unseen now. Twisted iron, foundations laid over dead men's work, the stench of old chemical works, the place where bombs once scarred the earth, a century of piss spilt onto a millennium of slime, the dead detritus of a human city beneath our feet, fermented into samey unseen sludge, so easy to reach out and grasp it now, to catch the whitened bones of what once was and heave it to the surface and it is here! The floor cracks with it, the building shakes, let the earth crack, let glass shatter, let steel split, let stone melt; we rise and the earth rises with us, it bursts upwards, the foundations of the building twist and rise upwards, jagged spikes of brown iron that smash through the walls, the floor, the door, piercing it like spears and we can hear them screaming all around, and we raise our hands higher and let the walls break! Let the ceiling split in two, let electricity dance like burning snakes between the gaps, let it writhe and wrap its tendrils around men's flesh, let them for a moment be seared with blazing light and the earth has opened beneath them and those who did not flee are trapped. Some are impaled on the foundation rods that lanced up from the ground itself – him upon a spike that has passed straight through his belly, pushing him off the ground like a doll [that's just disgusting]. She with a leg caught where the earth has cracked apart, trying to pull it free as if she could disconnect her body from the bone. We pick our way between the bodies, some dead, some dying, none meriting our attention. The cables have fallen from the ceiling, spitting fat electric sparks and here a man – the man who dared to push a needle into our veins – whose flesh has been burnt to the bone, thin clear fluids and yellow slime dribbling down across his skin, as if blood when boiled lost all its constituent parts [look at it! It's all squishy!]. At the end of the corridor, a woman dressed in white is clawing with a broken hand at the lift, which we dismiss from coming. Her hair is smoking [don't judge], and she sobs as we draw near, begging for her life, as if her life or her death was of any consideration to us then we see

a room to the left

I taste it.

The door was destroyed
when the walls began to bend,

an alarm wails behind shattered
steel. There are two doors,
forming an airlock between this
bloody corridor and what lies
beyond.
We think we can hear ...

Singing?

[Listen to them singing! Push it back, push it back and see ...]

A technician all in white scrambles away from us as we approach, mumbling empty incoherent words. We toss him aside with a flick of our wrist, his body is picked up and slammed through the air, impacting head first against the opposite wall. Dead or alive, doesn't matter, only the door. It opens before us. There was once a lock but it doesn't fight.

The lights are all out, but we see from the burning blue shining off our flesh. It is the place where the dust is kept [oh God], stored in airtight boxes that have begun to leak where the cables came down and the floor came up, factory-like, yellow dust, as far as the eye can see [why am I crying?], dust that was once human skin.

What is this?

We walk between aisles labelled with numbers and letters, batches of dust, and more dust and dust again, a thousand euphoric corpses, a thousand thousand blissful snorts on life-giving, soul-feasting death.

This species disgusts us.

[Not crying. Eyes that must cry and have no tears. The air here is too dry to cry – and *listen*.]

We listen.

[Can you hear it?]

There is something ...

[Life is magic, can you hear? I hear ...]

Dust to dust

... walls singing 'lalalala'
No, wait, not good enough, not
the way to describe it all the
words are foggy and faint they
come foggy and faint and far off
and I raise my hand

We raise our hand and let the fingers tangle in the air, feel the dryness and the dust that is spilling out, taste it on our lips, breathe . . .

(and even that seems far off)

Repulsion! Spit the taste of dust onto the floor!
Yellow spit on yellow floor!

We force ourself to be still and listen.

Listen!

The way the dust moves across the floor, stirred by a breeze but there is no breeze there. I saw sand move like this once, on a beach when I was a child. The beach stayed solid but the surface moved, sand in my socks and in my pockets and I did not then understand how the wind could dance on the earth.

We hear . . .
. . . so far off . . .

The dust moves, though there is nothing to move it.
[I raise my hands to my face but they don't come.]

We understand.

Oh God.
This is it.
This is your monster moment, universe, this is your cry in the dark, this is the mad cackle as the lightning strikes, are you sitting comfortably, world, have you got the popcorn ready?
It's alive.

It's alive.

It's alive.
God, but it sings of life and

Perhaps not yet with a form and

a shape, perhaps not yet conscious, but within the dust, there is movement, motion against the current, direction and purpose. This sick dead thing is a sick living thing. Alive.

It's alive.

magic, of death and damnation, of how the dust came, of how they died, of all the thousand voices that were silenced, a thousand last breaths trapped in a rolling yellow exhalation.

[I want to go now.]

And no living thing should be tamed.

We hear a sound behind us, off to the left, and turn instantly, raising our hands in defence. We had thought Hugo had fled with the rest, or died with the rest, but the mortal's pride held him back, denying him realisation of the futility of his actions and he is there in the dark, a gun in one hand, finger already tightening around the trigger. [Whatever happened to the good trip?] The gunshot is deafening but we are already moving with electric speed, diving down behind one of the great yellow vats. The bullet passes too close to our head, we can hear its passage, feel the air torn up by our face, a high-pitched whining in our ears, inconvenient sense data!

[See the way the dust danced when the bullet struck? It ripples and ripples back on itself, pebble in a pond.]

Hugo fires again, has some kind of automatic weapon, and though he is too proud he is also scared. As if bullets will stop us now. [Is this awareness?]

We extinguish all light, clenching it down and down to a bubble in our hand, a pea between our fingers, and pinch it out. He keeps firing for a few seconds longer, the star-pattern flash from his muzzle dazzling in the blackness.

[Stop.]

Stops.

Can you see in the dark, mortal?

[My eyes hurt.]

A shuffle-thump in the dark as perhaps now, only now, Hugo begins to comprehend that he is not the only hunter in the room.

We move silently, so silently, feeling our way between the great vats of dusted-down death, fingers tracing our path, head low and back bent.

[My breath hurts.]

The body is but a tool – sense data such a human failing.

['Cracked ribs' sounds dull when you say it – hey guys, I've got some cracked ribs, and a six pack of beer! – but what did the doctor say? Somewhere between cracked and fractured there's a moment of over-excitement just waiting to become a punctured lung.]

He thinks perhaps he has found us, fires eight shots in a sweep to our right, but they are wide, burning gnats chewing air, and all he has done is reveal his position. He tries to move in silence, but we hear his steps, his breath, his terror, feel the sweat prickling on the back of his neck.

Now he begins to understand.

He thinks he has found us again, fires, and this time he is closer but we press ourself into the ground and the shots travel high. It would be easy just to bring the ceiling down, the building down, the street down, the city down, the sky down . . . . . . but we want to look into Hugo's eyes as he dies.

I want out *now*.

This is a sick game the world is playing, normal guys don't dance when the music is this out of tune, normal guys don't walk *towards* the sound of gunfire, normal guys don't look down to see blood on their hands

blood on my hands?

I pull my hands away but they don't come.

We move closer, circling in towards him, smelling the oil-silk silver of his magics. He is attempting to throw up wards around himself, his voice a gentle low whisper on the air as he invokes defensive symbols, scratched into the ground and spun out of the air. They give a little silver-golden flicker as they embed themselves on the ground, creating just enough light to illuminate the shape of his back, the dance of his fingers. [Dust ripples at my feet, spinning around me in little eddies and

I did not say to move.] So close now – we are not five yards away from him, a silver shimmer on the air the only thing between him and our fingers popping out his eyes.

He looks up as if he can sense our approach, but does not turn his head to see, and we already have fingers in his mind, digging down through the soft part of his brain, blocking out sense. He calls out, "Swift! We don't have to be enemies! I have information about the fairy godmother that may be of service to you! I know things about Templeman!"

We feel a tug of pain in the pit of us, but shake our senses free of its tangle.	I try to speak and the words stick in mythroat.

"It is clear to me that we have underestimated you, that you are dangerous beyond our understanding. Pragmatism alone compels me to offer you my services and, I assure you, I have no higher loyalty than pragmatism."

We slide a step closer, splitting one of his silver wards in two, a shimmer of silent falling sparks parting beneath the palm of our hand. We can see the back of his neck, thick and ugly, see the pulse in a small blue vein from collar-bone to jaw. What piece of human anatomy would die if we pushed our thumb into that bloody cable?

"Your quarrel is with the fairy godmother, not with me!" he babbles, but the gun is still in his hand. "Let me help you."

So close now we can reach out and touch him.	
	I *hurt.*
The electricity crackles back to our fingertips.	
	Listen!
We reach out for the back of his neck.	
	Listen to me!
"If you must kill me," he breathes, "I would politely ask you to make it brief. I hate waiting."	Listen to me please listen to me listen you have to run please

So be it.

His petty wards snap apart around us and our left hand closes around his face, we feel the contours of his nose, the softness of his lips beneath our splayed-out fingers and our right hand grabs the wrist that holds the gun and we let it burn! Electricity blazes from every part of us, the black dark of the room split in two by the sapphire glory that dances off our skin, electric strobing flashing sparking brilliant fire it burns, and burns and he's screaming though his lips are starting to dissolve and his face is spilling blood, the gun rattles in his hand as the trigger finger convulses, bullets bouncing along the floor and still he's screaming and screaming and we laugh

his body goes limp, the bullets spent from the gun. We toss it aside, watch it fold in on itself like wet paper.

He's still alive. A creature without a face, a face become a red map of unknown

listen you have to run right now listen to me LISTEN

Stop it!

Stop it!

STOP!

No, please, please don't do this, please, please, don't have to, there's other ways, there's walking away, there's running away, there's not please no please don't

Please!!

I beg I beg I beg please please don't please!

IT'S NOT HUMAN!!

territories, but he's still breathing, still alive. If he had hair, it would probably be smoking with the rest of him.

Little dances of beautiful electric snakes ripple and earth off the remnants of his flesh. His eyes are open, reflecting our blue fire and perhaps, with what little of his senses remain, he sees us. He tries to speak, but his throat is a blistered tube. We kneel down beside him to better study the quality of his death, and his body is too weak to flinch away.

Enough he's broken he's beaten he never stood a chance please enough

please

He wheezes, "I ... I ... I ... " Tries to blink blood out of his eyes, but it is as washing away the ocean while swimming. "I ... I ... didn't ... " [I'm sorry.] "They're ... I did not ... " [I'm so sorry.] "I did ... did not ... " [I couldn't make it stop.] "She isn't ... " [She isn't?]

We wonder what it would look like to burn out the nerves behind his eyes.

No, no! Listen, please, listen, if there is anything left worth the name of thought, then just here, just now, please, be still.

"She isn't ... "

We force ourself to be still, to listen to his rattling dying breaths. [Please.] It comes slow and hard, blood and air mixing even as he says it. [Please.] "Kill me ... quick?" he begs.

"Why should we? What is there in your soul that merits mercy? What is there in your life that was not coming to an ending in death? What is there in your departure that is not insignificant? Not means, nor fate, nor deeds done and gone before, make you worth our pity."

Our hand twitches though we did not bid it move. We clench our fingers tight, press them to our side. A flicker of pain inside us, curse flesh and all its failings. Then he says,

Don't be stupid listen! Listen to him, listen oh God I want to . . .

"Penny"

We grab him by the throat

shake him like the paper thing he is.

Penny.

I lean in close

pull him up.

"Penny!" My words are nearly a scream, nearly impossible. "Tell me!"
"She . . . she . . ."

Electricity flickers between our fingers

blood on my hands

"She . . . she . . . mercy?"
"Tell me now!"
"Templeman took her!"

Templeman took her.

Templeman took her.

see the horror in his eyes

squeeze a little tighter

Just enough air to confess and die

I press my hand into his throat, feel the pulse beneath my fingers

what must I look like to him?

"What do you mean . . . Templeman took her?"

"We never had her," he says. "We never had your Penny. We never took her. Templeman has her. Templeman had her all along."

We hurt.
Penny?

Penny?

I'm so sorry.

"Please," he says, "please ..."
How long will it take him to die?

Minutes?

Let his body burst from the inside out, let him scream and scream and scream until there is no breath to scream with and then let him scream still in his dreams until there are no dreams left to dream with

Hours?

Days?

The end of the road.

"Please," he says, as if we should care.

I close my fingers around his throat, reach my mind down through the ravaged remnants of his nervous system.

Let him rot, let his body be eaten by the maggots and the worms, the fungus and the sickly green creatures that wriggle up from the earth with mandibles chittering, let his eyes be the last to go, let them stare and stare at the needle of the fly as it penetrates into the soft black ink of the socket

His heart is burnt, barely beating, "Please," he says.

I close my fingers. Feel his

heartbeat in the palm of my hand.

Why should gods be shaped by men?

Snuff it out.

His eyes close.

There.

He breathes his last.

Done.

What now?

Time to go.

That's all?

That's all.
I pick myself up.

We stagger up and feel . . .

No thoughts. Move.

[. . . feet heavy, shoulders stooped, arms dangling, belly sickly, ribs burning, breath aching . . .]

Feet shuffling through a tomb made of boxed-up dust. Breath through lungs that shudder when they shrink, burn when they grow. [Hate this hate this hate this!] Do not stop and do not think and do not stand and do not breathe. Corridor four floors beneath the ground where the ceiling has ruptured and the earth has cracked. [Make them pay we'll make them pay all of them we'll make them pay pay all of them pay for it for this for her for them for everything!]

Dead. [We can finish it just because you are afraid doesn't mean we cannot finish it we can end it all right now burn it all burn them burn the fairy godmother tiny tiny man go upwards and kill him we can we can we will we can.]

All dead.

Do not think.

Do not look.

God but do not look.

These are the stairs that lead to the open air.

Up a floor.

And another.

A sign says 'fire exit' in big green writing, but someone has raised wards across the hall in front of us. Thick red wards sculpted from flecks of paint scratched from the stop sign, the air thickens as I approach, trying to keep us in, pin us down. On the other side of that door there are

[little human minds they are so afraid we press our ear to the door and we can hear them even through their feeble wards, hear them breathing, men with guns and men with spells as if either can hold us back now]

Unnecessary opposition.

[wards break easily beneath our hands, we slice them through and the blood on our fingers only makes it easier]

I stand back from the door and call out, "Hello you there!"

Silence on the other side [but we hear their fears]

"I'm leaving this place now!" I say. "Please don't get in my way."

We can destroy them! |
                  | Too much death.

"Okay then!" I say. "Coming now!"

This is me letting

us step back a pace and smile, raise our hands and feel the power, the pressure of the air, the weight of it

[only for a moment]

as we spread our fingers wide and let our arms open and the air runs by us smelling of old cooking fats and the hot blast of the dirty air-conditioning unit pumping out at full volume. It slams into the door and blasts the frame straight from the wall, a flying piece of metal that picks two of the little men off their feet and sends them spinning legs dancing in the air, arms flapping like clowns.

[Kill the lights.]

Snuff out the light on the other side of the door and it was a foyer to this place, all potted plant and paper lampshades, and now it is a killing field, a death trap and there are five of them still standing, the fairy god-mother's men, armed with spells and guns and we laugh and say,

"Is this the best you can do? | I told you to run!"

And we raise our hands and there is the fire
Which I snuff out

Burning?
Darkness.
Burn them all.
Absolute darkness filled with the rising smell of smog.

Simpler if they die.	
	No more death.
They would not spare us, if they had the choice.	
	No more death.
We have the power, we have the means, we have the will ...	
	My choice.
We could be magnificent!	
	Not me. Not today.

This is my spell, this is the stench of London smog, of dust mixed with river vapour rising from the floor. This is the cloud that infects the mind, this is the addled brain drunk on river-stench, this is the stink of the East End, the slime beneath the silver steel sheets, this is the enchantment that infects your brains.

They stand like puppets, limp, caught in the tangle of our magic. Their minds are open easy things, made limper by the terror that has loosened their muscles and made their knees bend. Their fingers open, their jaws hang like gargoyles', their eyes frosted with the glaze of our spell-throwing. Not one, but not one among them had the strength to resist for more than a moment. We walk between them and they do not raise their heads as we pass.

	Is this not better?
This is nothing.	
	Is this not human?

Well then, there is the door to the outside world and here is the glass beneath fingers and there, high overhead, a party is still raging and I –

we could kill the fairy godmother now and no one could
stop us

	but plenty would try
and fail	
	and die

– step outside to this open world and here the smell of the river, cold air on our skin, in our eyes, in our throat, our lungs, snap-drying the blood between our fingertips and

What had Meera said?

Sometimes people come here to get clean

Washing away our sins

He'll only come after us	
again.	
	Blood on my hands.

Walk towards a bank of shrubs and concrete stones.

Water runs between them, pumped from an underground tank to twinkle between the moon-white lights of this artificial patch of nature.

Kneel down on carefully raked gravel and dirt.

Run hands through the water.

My hands.

The water comes away red.

Then pink.

Then clear.

The skin turns white and numb.

My skin.

What did we do?

[Something magnificent.] | [Something vile.]

Something both.

The spells I've woven will break soon enough.

Someone will find the bodies.

Bloodhounds will howl at the night, sirens will wail, and all of this will have been for nothing.

Penny.

('Templeman took her!')

We stand up.

Fingers drip.

(I mean, have you tried getting a night bus from the Isle of Dogs at this hour?)

Time to go.

Look round at silver lights inside silver walls of silver steel and silver glass, of silver water lapping against silver stone, a beautiful tomb, a soulless palace, a place where all the evils are tucked quietly away.

Time to go.

We walk away.

Part 5: It Is Not You Who Must Save Me

In which the nature of the Midnight Mayor is finally explained, proven, and ignored.

It was a bus with a letter in its name.

We rode it because it was there, and neither knew nor cared where it was going.

I pressed my head against the glass and felt the cold of it and knew I was shuddering and couldn't stop it and didn't care.

The place hurt where Templeman had broken our skin with his needle. A dull slow throbbing.

Motorway became A-road, which yielded to wide city street. Name such places, then see if you can taste the stories that come with them – Mile End, where the city had once stopped and which was now firmly, officially, inner city; Victoria Park, by day, at least, a lake and ducks and playing children; Bethnal Green, where the rural cottage had become the urban slum and now, after a hundred years of neglect, the comfortable middle-class idea of a cottage.

On Mare Street, the magic tasted of the local food, sweet potato and chilli and ginger, a medley of unreconciled senses. It was a place for spells of old black time and new sodium streets, where old met new and didn't like what it saw.

The bus terminated at Hackney Central, at a car park framed by raised railway lines that carried only freight at this hour of the night, and one-way systems laid out to tangle the senses.

Where and why didn't matter.

No buses, no trains.

I put my hands in my pocket, and walked.

Somewhere between Templeman and Oscar Kramb, I'd lost my bag.

I walked, westwards.

The orange indicator board behind the gates of Dalston Kingsland station proclaims it to be nearly four in the morning. In the locked-up hardware store along the street, a disco ball spins perpetually, sending out dots of purple and emerald light. In the window of the local library are invitations to attend first-aid courses, take up pilates, learn jiu jitsu, read this week's book of the week on this month's theme of American Noir, sign a petition to Save Our Library.

The hairdressers in Dalston will give you any cut you want – so long as you want Afro. For an extra £12 they'll throw in nails and, for £25, you can have the complete nail and pedicure indulgence. Sets of nails without fingers are lined up in the windows, arranged in rainbow-arcs. The betting shop next door offers £15 free towards your first bet. The pawnbrokers, two doors down, guarantees you a good rate of return, should it all go wrong.

My hand hurt.

Somewhere between Templeman and Oscar Kramb, I'd lost everything.

I held up my fingers to a sodium street light and looked at the twin crosses carved into the palm of my hand. I turned my wrist this way and that, framing the bubble of sodium between forefinger and thumb, then pinched a little harder, catching it in the hollow of my hand, pinning it there. The street lamp I'd stolen it from hissed and whined irritably, trying to glow. I let it hum, and held up the bubble of stolen light close to my face until I could feel its heat pushing softly against my skin.

Silence in the city.

No.

Not quite silence.

Not quite.

Half close your eyes and listen, and somewhere underground there is the service train rumbling back towards the depot from a night of maintaining the lines; and put your head on one side and listen and there is the delivery lorry come from the warehouses to the north to drop off tomorrow's bread into the back docks of the supermarkets; and click your heels on the pavement and see if the sound resembles the sharp-snap footsteps of the woman trying to get home after he swore he'd give her a lift and then turned out to be such an arsehole.

These things do not break the silence but, like a coin in a well, are reminders of how far down it goes.

I snuffed out the light between my fingers, and stood in a puddle of darkness beneath the street lamp looking down a long straight road from one unseen horizon to another. In that darkness, the twin crosses on my hand still seemed visible, discolorations in the gloom, a different kind of blackness. There was blood on my sleeves. I looked away.

Need help.

Templeman took everything.

Then again, a nothing so absolute is, in and of itself, a powerful thing.

I knelt down on the paving stones.

Pressed my scarred hand into the dirty ground. Bits of chewing gum, dried and pressed to black, had been so walked on that they were now part of the pavement itself.

I could feel the pipes under my feet, see the steam curling around the sewer grating a few yards further below.

I could feel my heart beating in the palm of my hand.

I said, "Domine dirige nos," and felt the words shudder through me like hot sickness. "Domine dirige nos, domine dirige nos!"

Need help.

I pressed my head down to the ground, dug my fingers into it, into the cracks between the paving stones. There was a place between the cracks, a world just visible out of the corner of the eye, the thing that mothers invoked when they laughed at their children, saying, 'Don't step on the cracks' without knowing quite where they'd heard the warning told.

"Domine dirige nos," I whispered, a few centimetres from the stones. "Please, domine dirige nos."

Footsteps.

They were soft on the ground, but we felt them.

They started from nowhere, and got closer without seeming to grow louder.

There was no light to throw a shadow, but we felt the air move above us as the source of the footsteps stopped. Even had we not known, we could have smelt him. He stank of a life lived without showers, of cigarette smoke and ash.

I looked up.

A cigarette flared orange-red in the night as he drew in a puff of smoke, before letting it out in a long blast from the corner of his mouth and flicking the ash away.

"Hey, Matthew?" he said. "You're one screwed-up sick pup, you know that?"

If it hadn't been so funny, we might have cried.

"Please," I breathed. "Please help me."

He squatted down in front of me, blew smoke above my head, flicked ash into the gutter. "You've still got some blood on your face," he said. "You should be careful about things like that, you never know where that stuff has been. Haven't you been watching those government health warnings?" The glowing end of the cigarette stuck the air with each word, to undermine its solemnity. "Chlamydia Is Everywhere."

I looked up at him, hands still pressed to the ground. The sound the Beggar King made as he rubbed his beard was like snapping bone over splintered wood. "I don't do interventions for just anyone," he said. "Beggar Kings aren't just sprung into existence to solve your problems; only to walk beside."

"Templeman took Penny." The words came out fast. To say them slow would have been not to say them at all.

He sighed. "I'm sorry to hear that, I really am. She was a nice girl, you know? I thought she had balls, and I don't think that about many people."

"He tricked me. Used me."

"Come on," sighed the Beggar King. "Like that's so hard."

"He killed your people. He did it."

A shadow passed across the Beggar King's eyes, almost too swiftly to see. "Is that right?" he breathed, the flame burning steadily down on the paper between his dirty fingertips. "And by the looks of you, he tried a little something with your internal soft bits too?"

He straightened up, drew one last firm puff on his cigarette and tossed the butt away. Held out a hand. The nails were ridged yellow bone, cracked and ragged; the dirt was so deeply ingrained it had become part of the skin. His hand was cold as I took it, pulling me up. "Come on," he said, looking me over. "Jesus, what a mess." Then he grinned. "Let me take you to my masseuse."

On a road with a No Entry sign at either end was a low grey building that had once been a primary school. Its windows were boarded up; an area of neglected grass was littered with old plastic bags and coke cans; and wires hanging off the walls suggested that the electricity board had long since lost control over who powered what where.

But there were some new additions.

These were bright green signs that proclaimed the following:

Security Monitored 24/7

Danger – Children Do Not Play

Live-In Guardians Protect This Building

Next to this sign someone had written with bright red paint:

MY GOVERNMENT DOES NOT SPEAK FOR ME

Underneath someone else had written

X-CREW 11

Underneath that, someone had drawn a quizzical owl, all in black, who stared out as if surprised to find itself so far from the Hundred Acre Wood.

There was a padlock on the main entrance. Either someone hadn't bothered to lock it, or it knew not to argue when the Beggar King came calling. The hall inside was dark, the air heavy with the smell of rising mould and settling dirt. Its walls were covered with paint, sometimes pictures, sometimes words, moving in and out of each other, messages from

ANNE FIND ME

To:

CAZ WOZ ERE

And laced in between, in bright paint that had dribbled down to the floor:

MISERY LOST

TEK 33

HEROES WITH GRIMY FACES

SUFFER IN SILENCE

WE DO NOT FORGET

A gloomy orange-yellow stain of light at the end of the hall led off into a room, student-sized with the remains of a single bed, the stuffing long torn out to make animal nests. In the shell of a metal bin, a fire had been lit from old timber fragments, siphoned petrol and newspaper kindling. Four sleepers were huddled around the flames, on cardboard beds, faces and breathing barely perceptible under a mass of sleeping bag. A big nylon shopping bag stolen from a store offering designer bathrooms at cut-price rates, get your quote now, leant against the wall, its sides bulging.

The Beggar King put his finger to his lips and stepped round the sleepers to the bag, unzipping its top and rummaging through. Even from the door, I could smell it, a mixture of dried sweat and exhaust fumes. He pulled out an armful of clothes from a bit too far down in the bag for its depths to be natural, pulled the zip tight and moved back past the sleepers, a hand extended over their heads like a priest blessing his flock. At the end of the hall we entered another darkened room, where a fire was burning low in an iron stove. A purple bloom of mould was spreading across the walls, and a dark stain on the floor had been scrubbed and scrubbed and scrubbed, and would not be shifted.

Closing the door behind us the Beggar King put the bundle of clothes down on the floor and said, "You're not one of these guys who goes to the gym, are you?"

I shook my head.

"Didn't think so." He leant back against the driest patch of wall he could find, patting down his pockets for another cigarette, which he found in a mess of torn white tissue and old bits of plastic. He ran it lovingly between his fingers and put it to his lips. It waggled like a seesaw as he said, "Okay, lose the clothes, burn them, before the coppers do you. There's fresh ash on the floor, I suggest you use it and I got ..."

Another search in a pocket, and a small glass vial emerged, the label long since rubbed away. Even in the low light, I could tell the colour, and when he opened the lid I recognised the smell.

"Garam masala?" I asked weakly.

He grinned. "You gonna be the sweetest-smelling bum on the block."

I took the chipped glass vial. "I thought Dr Seah was making it up."

"Wouldn't put it past her," replied the Beggar King. "But sometimes even the truth is funny. Come on, chop chop."

I struggled out of my blood-stained clothes, huddling close to the stove for warmth. With the cooling ashes from the floor, I rubbed my hands, my arms, my face, my neck, my shoulders and my feet, working them in well. Sure enough, when it was done, I felt cleaner. The dirt beneath my fingernails was flecked with blood; I scratched in the cinders until they were raw and black, and threw my old clothes onto the fire, to wither and die in a lick of flame.

Then the Beggar King rose, and unfolded my new clothes.

"Kneel," he said, and I knelt.

He held aloft a pair of shredding jeans, stained down one leg, with the pockets hanging out.

"I give to you," he proclaimed, "the foul-smelling trousers of my clan. All who see you shall look away, and you shall bring shame, disgust and pity wherever you walk."

He handed me the trousers ceremonially, which I hugged to my chest.

Then, "I give you the oversized second-hand shirt of the great fat man who went on a diet and no longer fitted his old clothes. He walks now in pride in tailored suits, does not give the beggars change but will perhaps one day donate a pair of torn-up shoes. Wear it with gratitude and bow your head when strangers walk away."

I took the shirt. It smelt of chemical disinfectant, and something else, faint and sickly.

A large coat was flourished ceremonially.

"I give you a coat of infinite pockets and vile smell. The last man who owned this coat died in a church porch from exposure on a bitter night. But the vicar buried him in the yard beneath a stone cross, and the vicar's wife laid flowers, and, though she did not know why, one of the paramedics came who had found the body and pronounced it long dead at the scene, joints stiff before the sun came up. Though you walk by yourself through the city streets, may you never know the truth of what it is to be alone."

One of the pockets still held a battered plastic cup and the red felt-tip pen that had been used to write, *hungry, please help*.

A pair of trainers was held aloft. The uppers had come away from the soles, so that the last wearer's toes could stick out, and the laces had each been knotted together from many fragments.

"These are the shoes of the beggar who cannot afford the bus, who does not have the money for the train. They have walked north and south, east and west, laying their footprints upon the earth with the lightness of a feather. We do not walk as others do, we are not the busy clatter of well-shod heels, we do not march with the stride of the rush hour, we are not joggers in a park or running for the bus. Ours is an ancient walk, the oldest walk known to man, down a path that has not changed since the first stone of the first city wall was laid. We walk together, the city and the beggars, until only the city remains. Take them, and be nothing but the city."

I took the shoes, huddling them into my meagre bundle of possessions, and looked up.

The Beggar King's open palm caught me across the side of the face hard enough to knock me down, landing awkwardly on my elbow. He stood over us and for a moment there was an ancient darkness in his eyes, as deep and wild as the whirlwind. "You're one of us now," he said, and his soft voice filled the room. "Don't screw up."

I scrambled back onto my knees and, at his nod, started shivering my way into the stained clothes. They felt sticky against my skin, dozens of owners embedded into every stitch. When I was done the Beggar King said, "Can you walk without pride?"

I bowed my head and nodded.

"Good," he said. "Walk with me."

In the city, there are many ways of walking.

Let me name them:

Rush-hour scurry, retiree's shuffle, drunkard's ramble, frightened scuttle, tourist's wander, shopper's amble, mother's purpose, children's skip. Who needs to see knees-upwards?

This was the beggar's walk. It was the sideways winding of those who are not there to be perceived.

We walked south, zigzagging between residential streets sealed off from traffic to prevent the rat run, around schools with the lights coming on as the caretaker arrived for the morning, past shop-front shutters coming up. At this time of year, the city began to wake long before sunrise.

"Tell me about Templeman," said the Beggar King; so I did. "Yup," he concluded, when I was done, "I mentioned that you were one screwed-up pup. What you want to do about it? Vengeance? I hear you do a good line in vengeance."

"I want . . . we want . . . Penny. I want Penny."

"Well, that may not be rosily possible."

"Have to try."

"I'm guessing that Templeman won't be giddy that you didn't kill the fairy godmother. Not like you couldn't have claimed self-defence."

"But it wouldn't have been."

He waggled his thick eyebrows in demand of an explanation. I shrugged and immediately regretted it, pressing my hands to my ribs as pain shot through my chest. "Fairy godmother thought he could use our blood, sell it for a profit. Sure, bad idea, no question there. But what we did ... what we became ... it wasn't self-defence. Not that."

"You enjoy it?" he asked, not angry or sad, just words.

I swallowed acid and didn't answer.

He tutted, and picked up walking speed to just above comfortable. "Well, what you gonna do? Go after Templeman, spells blazing, cowboy style? Bang bang whoosh, 'You calling me a pussy' 'No I ain't calling you no pussy' 'You saying you ain't calling me a pussy' 'Yeah I'm saying I ain't calling you no pussy' 'So you is calling me a pussy' 'No I ain't ...' – you get the idea?"

"Don't know where he is."

"He's an Alderman, he thinks you're dead, where's the problem?"

"If I was dead," I replied, "then the Midnight Mayor would be dead. Some poor bastard would be waking up right now with a brand on the hand and there'd be alarms going off all over the city and memos and people would know. The fairy godmother, the dusthouses, everyone will soon bloody know I'm not dead and, in fact, not only am I not dead but there's a whole great pile of dead behind me that I didn't bother to tip when paying the bill."

We kept walking.

The Beggar King said, "You know, I gotta tell you, since you're one of the flock right now, it's crap." I tried in vain to read the meaning in his eyes. "You feel guilt because you think you're a good man, and good men feel guilt. But I'm gonna tell you, good men don't have to burn their clothes regularly because there's too much blood in them to wash out. Which isn't to say that you shouldn't do the guilt thing – it's better than, say, you just taking what you've done in your stride, because that would make you a psychopath – but Matthew, as a guy who's in the know, I'm here to tell you, you're not a good guy. Sure, it's sweet that you try, but don't trick yourself into thinking you can relax. Don't think that just because you're beating yourself up about it now, you won't do it again. You will."

We said, "We did not . . . " and stopped.

I said, "I couldn't . . . " and realised how futile it was.

The Beggar King tutted. "Hey, I'm just saying, you know. I was never here to judge."

His footsteps made no sound as he moved.

Neat trick that, if you can do it.

"Got anyone you can trust?" asked the Beggar King.

Penny.

"No," I replied.

"Lone hero sounds great in the ad, not so good in the picture."

"Templeman took Penny," I said. "And he can't have done it alone. Templeman . . . had friends, and they took Penny. The Minority Council. What kind of piss-poor bloody Midnight Mayor am I if I can't even sort out the office politics?"

"Hell, you've got other qualities," he said with a comforting pat on the shoulder. "You've got . . . well . . . you've got . . . " He shrugged, and gave up. "You've got a great sense of humour."

I thought hard.

"There may be one person left."

Her name was Kelly Shiring.

Because you had to see it, to believe it.

She lived in a flatshare in Maida Vale. Her flatmates were madly in love. He taught at a primary school, she ran sales for a specialist arts magazine. Neither of them believed in magic, and frankly why should they? Kelly was a PA in a not very interesting accountants office, and if she kept unsociable hours, what business was it of theirs to ask? She didn't clutter the sink, always took the rubbish out, and only ever watched the TV for her weekly dose of crime drama. Her hobbies were harmless. On Tuesdays she did 'hot yoga' at the nearby gym, proclaiming with wonder and amazement on her return from the sessions, "'I've already had a shower and I still smell!" as if in this single phenomenon, whole schools of medical understanding crumbled. Once a month she attended the local feminist book group, and on the bottom of a very old draft of her CV, underneath the courses in practical exorcism and intermediate spreadsheet software, she listed as her favourite holiday pastime off-road bicycling.

And so Kelly Shiring moved through the world, healthy, hearty, never late with her gas bill, never caught skipping a bus fare, a junior PA in a firm of not much note, the future not simply in front of her, but all around her, just waiting to be seized.

Finding her wasn't hard.

I lay in wait outside Harlun and Phelps, sitting on the pavement with my knees tucked into my chest, head bowed, hands open to the world, as the sun rose and the city came with it. In the city, with the horizon lost behind office walls, dawn was a shift in colour that happened too slow to see, and so fast you barely realised it had begun before it was finished. The orange-black of night became a deep blue stained with streetlight. The blue faded to grey, the street lamps dimming in comparison to their surroundings. Ribbons of gold threaded the thick sky, and the summits of the topmost buildings reflected a rising watery glow where the sun peeped from behind the horizon and the clouds.

I listened to the sound of a rising rush hour, to the rhythm of feet moving faster, cars jamming up bumper to bumper, voices growing, the rumble of trains beneath my feet and the clatter of bicycle bells. Automatic revolving doors began to spin non-stop in the expectation of a day of human traffic. A stream of people started moving into the offices of Harlun and Phelps: some of them Aldermen, most not, bankers heading in for the working day, either ignorant of, or oblivious to, the darker operations of the place.

There was magic here. Hot rush-hour magic, and deep old-town magic that went right down to the base of the Roman walls. And another magic, hard to identify, but there, just in the corner of my eye. Beggar magic. I sat with my palms turned upwards for change, and the eyes of strangers and those who should have known me, should have recognised the brand on my hand, slid straight on by. I was an oil slick on water, a spot of coal-black blackness on a soot-black wall.

And Kelly was nothing special; her eye went past me like any other. But as I saw her pass I raised my head and called out, once, "Kelly."

She hesitated, stopped, turned; but even with my voice in her ears, her gaze still ran over me, unwilling to process what her eyes saw. I stood up and she stared straight at me, straight through, and didn't seem to recognise me. Then a flicker of doubt crossed her face as even the magics of a beggar's smell and a beggar's coat crumbled in the face of determined scrutiny. But I was already turning and shuffling away, the beggar's shuffle without purpose or direction, heading towards Guildhall.

And though Kelly was young and quite possibly naïve, she was no fool. She glanced to her left, she glanced to her right, turned her eyes to the heavens in the manner of someone who's forgotten something vital and can't believe their own foolish mind, spun on her heel, and marched after me.

In the wide open square by Guildhall, stones had been laid that were centuries old, where the guildmasters of butchers, bakers and candle-stick makers had all walked, in the days when the guilds ruled the money, in that part of the city where the money has always ruled. In the streets nearby, dignified plaques declare that here is the Wax Chandlers' Hall ('The Truth is the Light') and there the Saddlers' ('Hold Fast, Sit Sure'). Where a few ancient buildings, in all their proud Gothic glory, had survived the bombs of World War Two, dragons with rolling tongues cling to their rooftops, and spikes of knobbly stone stick up for the pigeons to poop on. Sometimes you can see the rituals of the city still active in this place – clergy with long sticks who both know and care about parish bounds, or officers of the Lord Mayor of London, dressed in red and fur-trimmed hats who will, for £35 and a friendly chat, grant to you the Freedom of the City, bringing with it the right to lead your cattle across London Bridge, but which, please note, does not exempt you from parking tickets.

Linger long enough beneath the red eyes of one of the guardian dragons that look down from the rooftops and out of the carvings on the wall, and you could begin to feel the well of power buried just beneath the water-swept stones. Like the spire at Charing Cross, Speaker's Corner where once men had been led to hang, or St Paul's Cathedral in the quiet hours of the night; you could feel those forces that the druids used to call ley lines, bunching and breathing under city streets. It was a place where here and there, then and now, met and lost their way.

I found a doorway where I could huddle out of the wind, and away from the watching eye of the CCTV cameras.

Kelly strode into the square a few seconds behind me, walked by as if I wasn't there, then paused, bent down to check something in her briefcase, couldn't seem to find it, cursed quietly under her breath and, in a single movement that was all innocent frustration, moved into the gloom beside me, every inch the harried businesswoman accidentally sharing a corner with a stranger.

Without glancing at me, and with no change to her expression as she searched through her case, she exclaimed, "Good morning, Mr Mayor! May I say how glad I am to see you not dead today!"

"Morning, Kelly," I groaned.

"You're not here for your 9.30 are you?"

"My . . ."

"You have an appointment at 9.30 with representatives from the Church of Our Lady of 4 a.m.; something to do with a missing goddess and a dog. It *was* on your schedule."

"I'm really not here for that."

"Ah, well," she said, snapping the briefcase shut and glancing up, just once, with a gaze that encompassed the entire square. "I'm sure we can rearrange; did I mention that last night every scryer we have woke up screaming in the night, reporting symptoms ranging from an over-whelming sense of dread through to actual visions of death and destruction raining down upon the earth? I sent you an email, but I wasn't sure if you'd got it."

"Funny thing, I kinda haven't."

She barely flinched, smiling her way through her disappointment. "Something to do with — and I apologise for the vagueness of the details — a creature of light and fire suddenly becoming manifest on the earth and attempting to rip the heavens into hell, unleash damnation upon the earth and so on; you know I really must talk to the scryers about finding more precise and less melodramatic language in their reports, it only encourages hysteria."

"Did they say anything else?"

"They said it was in Heron Quays."

"Well if I was going to bring about Armageddon, that'd be the place."

"It went away again," she concluded. "Although, funny thing is, someone did mention something about the fairy godmother having some sort of investment interests in Heron Quays, I think there was a row with the council about building permissions for a swimming pool or something, anyway, this probably isn't helping you, I'll have someone check with the planning office."

She finished, the words all coming out in one breath, and, for the first time, turned and looked directly at me, her smile widening. "Mr Mayor," she exclaimed, having surveyed my present state, "have I ever spoken to you about the wonders of a health spa?"

"No."

"They're wonderful!"

"Really."

"I have a friend who does aromatherapy."

"I'm fine."

"Mr Mayor," she chided. "Last night someone unleashed magical forces like unto which the city has rarely seen, you stopped answering your phone and are now, if I may say so, dressed as a beggar in both body and magic, hiding outside your own office ... How about acupuncture?"

"Templeman took Penny."

The words happened a long way off.

Kelly's smile stayed fixed, but the light went out behind her eyes. Then even the smile began to fade. She looked down, bobbing her head as if to ease the digestion of this news. Finally she said, "Why?"

"He's been using fairy dust to conduct experiments on beggars. Making concoctions to enhance magical capabilities without killing the subject. He tried one on me. It's got a few side-effects."

"Are you all right?" she asked. "I mean, alternative medicine is all very well and good, but I really do think that MRIs are one of the most astounding scientific achievements of the age."

"I'm ... fine."

"You say that, Mr Mayor!" she exclaimed. "But you say it in your special brave voice and, you know, I'm really not sure if I can trust your special brave voice these days because, if you don't mind me saying so, Mr Mayor, there's a very thin line between being brave and six months of physiotherapy and liquid foods."

"Kelly! Please! I need you to listen."

She pursed her lips, and raised her eyebrows at me to go on.

"Templeman," I tried again, "did it. The culicidae, the Minority Council, fairy dust – he's there, just out of sight, moving through it all. He took Penny."

"Why? Why would he do that?"

It came out flat and fast now, tick-tack-tock, sharp and cold. "He was being blackmailed by the fairy godmother. The dusthouses supplied Templeman with the initial dust for his experiments, and in return the fairy godmother got what he thought was a tame Alderman in his pocket, someone he could rely on to do whatever he wanted and turn a blind eye.

"That's why, for so long, the Aldermen have been ignoring the dusthouses, why Templeman didn't dare move openly.

"Then along I come, and I start kicking up a fuss and the Beggar King gets involved and, suddenly, Templeman sees an opportunity to get rid of the fairy godmother without actually getting his hands dirty because what am I?

"I am dangerous," I spat the words, "unstable, reckless, quite possibly psychotic, the kind of Midnight Mayor about whom your hard-working Alderman can say 'I tried to stop him, I really did, but he's just out of control.'

"Templeman used me. He used me to destroy the dusthouse in Soho, and he wanted to use me to kill the fairy godmother, to end Oscar Kramb's hold over him without ever alerting the Aldermen to the fact that he, Richard Templeman, is a traitor.

"He sent us to kill the fairy godmother and we ... we were ... it was ... I could have done it. I could have I could have killed him, we could have killed them all, I could have and I ... he took Penny. He took Penny and let me believe that the godmother had her, let me believe that she was dead she's dead she's dead she's ... " I choked on the words, pressed my hands, tasting of ash, over my mouth to stop the sound.

Kelly put a hand on our arm, trying to say words she couldn't find.

"Where is he?" I asked at length. "Where is Templeman?"

"I don't know. Maybe he's at the office. I can find out."

"He's dangerous."

"You said he's killed beggars?"

"Yes."

"Then he's violated his contract. I mean, we don't like to talk about it, but sometimes Aldermen have to do jobs that would cause gossip at the Met Police; but beggars . . . and the Beggar King, I'm guessing he's annoyed?"

"You could say so."

"But he gave you his sacred vestments – that was sweet."

I glanced down at the ragged clothes I wore. After a while, I'd even stopped noticing the smell, forgot what I was wearing. "These?" I asked.

"Of course!" she exclaimed. "I mean, it's not my field, obviously not, it's not something I really specialise in, but I can recognise the blessed vestments of the austere and ignorant masters when I see them – you know, they'd fetch an amazing price with the collectors. If you don't mind the curse that would befall you if you tried selling them, that is."

In vain I tried to process Kelly's words. I said, "There's something else I need."

"Of course, Mr Mayor, anything at all!"

"I need the culicidae's heart." Though her smile stayed locked in place, her lips thinned. "What?" I asked, harsher than I'd meant. "What's the new disaster?"

"The culicidae's heart . . ." she began. "Now, about that . . . Mr Caughey and Ms Holta took it."

I pressed my head back against the wall, closing my eyes against the rising glare of the day. "I've been gone for less than twelve hours – *less than twelve* – and already two prats in black have gone and pinched one of the nastiest bits of magical pollution in the city?"

"Um, that would appear to be the case."

"Kelly, I'm going to use my special authoritative voice, and I want you to know this, so that when I actually do use it, you'll understand exactly what it is and not say anything annoying, or flap or ask stupid bloody questions; are you ready?"

"Yes, Mr Mayor," she confirmed. "Authoritate away."

"*Find them.* Find me the culicidae's heart, find me the Minority Council. And Kelly?"

"Yes, Mr Mayor?"

"Find me Templeman."

*

Kelly set to work.

At least, I assumed she did.

From outside the office, huddled in the shadows, it was hard to tell.

Businessmen and businesswomen passed me by and spared me not a glance.

A city constable on a bicycle, yellow jacket pulled over his bullet-proof vest, paused on the corner beside me, and looked down, and round, and through me, as if I wasn't there, and looked bemused, and cycled on.

("But he gave you his sacred vestments – that was sweet.")

A pair of tourists stopped not a foot in front of me and argued furiously in Spanish about the way to St Paul's. A child was with them. She was no more than four years old, and proudly wore a striped purple and green hat with knitted braids hanging down by each ear. She looked me in the eye and grinned. I smiled back. Her parents pulled her on, in not quite the right direction.

I sat until I was too cold and stiff to sit any more.

My knees clicked like castanets as I clambered to my feet.

The CCTV cameras looked away as I approached, moving to stare at an empty wall or a quiet street.

Though it was hard sometimes to recognise, through the plate glass and sounds of traffic, this was the oldest part of the city, where every bollard bore twin red crosses, the mark of the Lord Mayor of London, responsible for daylight things, and the Midnight Mayor, lumbered with all the rest.

Look hard enough and you could maybe perceive the anomaly of things beneath the surface. When life started moving to the cities, magic came with it, and when the magic started moving, so did all the creatures that lived within it. If you wait until the dead, dead hours of the night, when the only texture on earth is street-lamp glow, you might see the metal of an ornate lamppost part and the grey-skinned city dryads peep out into the darkness from their wiry home.

There, above a stone doorway built by men who believed in empire and cricket, the statue of a woman in classical drapes, face turned downwards to mourn an unknown loss and whose stone eyes, which should be sandstone beige, are framed with redness from weeping.

And just below the artificial waterfall that glides down black marble into a pool beneath an iron grid, a shadow moves in the water that might be an infant kelpie, its skin the colour of the copper coins, tossed in with a wish, on which it feeds.

Had I told Penny about kelpies?

Of course I bloody had; I mean, how do you miss telling someone about kelpies? Once creatures of the sea and shore, worshipped by the fishermen who taught their children how to whistle to secret songs, they had migrated first up the rivers, then the streams, then into the drains, then the pipes, then the fountains and secret pools of the cities, adapting to their new environment as readily as the elves had taken up casino management and the dwarves had learnt a love of the London Underground.

I'd told her.

Just because I couldn't remember, didn't mean it hadn't happened.

On Cheapside a security guard stood in the door of a delicatessen.

The windows were full of shining, egg-painted pastries and fresh breads.

The smell of rising hot yeast was being pumped through the store.

Men and women sat drinking coffee topped with whipped milk and sprinkles. I stood in the window, hands pressed against the glass, and watched the steam rise and fall around my fingertips with each pulse of my heart.

The security guard's eyes swept over me and did not see; but his nose twitched and his back stiffened as he detected the stink of my beggar's clothes. His gaze turned on me again and, now that he looked to see, he saw, with a look of instinctive hostility.

I ducked my head and walked on.

("Can you walk without pride?")

Hunger, thirst.

They must have been coming for a long while, but the sight of others eating and drinking brought such feelings to the fore.

I thought about the soup kitchen at Tottenham Court Road. Where did a guy even get a drink round here for less than ten quid?

I thought about stealing.

It would be easy – so easy – not an alarm would trip, not an eye would flicker; this was still my city, and I stood at its heart.

("You're one of us now. Don't screw it up'")

Maybe not stealing.

Not today.

What was Kelly doing?

Where was Templeman?

I drifted back towards Guildhall, sat down in a doorway out of the wind, and waited.

Kelly Shiring didn't come out of the office until half past two.

She walked briskly to Guildhall and, not seeing me there, paused to check her mobile phone, using this ploy to scan the square, seeking me out. I detached myself from the opposite side of the street, walked up behind her, then straight on past. Her eyes locked onto my back and, with a sigh at some unseen annoyance on her mobile phone, she fell into step behind me, keeping a careful distance.

The oldest streets of London hadn't been built for heavy traffic. On crooked lanes and narrow alleys, between grand office blocks, lay patches of ground too small even for Londoners to build upon. I led Kelly to one of these places, where wooden benches stood near a tiny fountain shaded by pleached lime trees. She sat down, swivelled to face me, and declared, "Now, first things first, Mr Mayor, crayfish with rocket or halloumi and couscous salad?"

A plastic bag was opened as she proclaimed this, and the objects of the moment brought forth along with a bottle of water, a bright green apple, and an oatmeal bar.

I ate like a deprived animal, taste forgotten, volume all that mattered.

Through the crumbs and bits of damp salad, I mumbled, "Well? Where?"

"Would you like a napkin, Mr Mayor?"

"No! Where are they?"

"How about a lemon-scented hand wipe ..."

"Kelly!"

She managed not to sigh, folding her hands in her lap. "I've got good news and bad news, Mr Mayor. I hope you don't mind if I start with the bad news, but my mother always told me to get the bad news first, eat the things you don't like before the pudding, and always try to do at least one unpleasant task per day so that it doesn't have to prey on your mind when you go to sleep at night, and obviously at the time I thought she was talking utter nonsense but now I realise that she was right. But anyway, yes, the bad news: Templeman has disappeared."

I paused on my last bite of sandwich. Then lowered it, wiped my mouth with the back of my hand, and said, cold and quiet, "'Disappeared'?"

"Yes," she admitted. "Isn't it funny how these things happen? I mean, at first he was just 'late for work', but then Templeman's never late for work, is he? Then he was 'not answering the phone' and then he was 'definitely not at home' and then it was 'by now he should have called' and then he was 'not at the local hospital' and then he was 'heavily warded from scrying attempts by a mass reflective shield spell' and then he was 'evading authorities' and then, I suppose, by a process of elimination, he was 'disappeared'. The police like these things to take forty-eight hours before they say as much, but you know, I think, considering the circumstances, we can maybe, just this once, but maybe, skip the procedural stuff? So long as it doesn't become a habit, I mean."

"And you're telling me," I said, "that the Aldermen, psycho-bastards extraordinaire, can't find him? That one guy, one murderous, murdering, murderer guy, can evade the lot of you?"

"Embarrassing, isn't it?" she conceded. "But then again, you did, didn't you, Mr Mayor? In your time. Which isn't to say that he's at all like you, I think even the Minority Council would admit that experimenting on beggars and betraying us all to the fairy godmother is, you know, a little out there ... I'm just saying, it can be done, by exceptionally talented individuals. We aren't Jedi." She paused to blow her nose on a small white linen handkerchief. As she folded it neatly again she exclaimed, "In fact, you know, a few people are beginning to wonder where you are. And I mean, I am just your PA, it's really not within my remit to authorise the kind of operation I had to put in hand to track down Templeman and besides, no one can quite believe he'd do all that stuff, I mean, a lot of people are really quite fond of him, so actually, all things considered, it might be handy if you ... maybe ... told someone yourself? Which isn't to say I can't handle it, I'm completely on it, but, um ... it's just a thought."

I stared at her, long and hard, until she turned away. Then I said, "Fuck it," stood up, and marched over to the nearest bit of blank wall.

I licked the end of my grimy finger, and on the stone surface began to write.

I wrote:

THEY THINK HE'S INNOCENT,
YOU BELIEVE THAT OR WHAT?

This done, I stepped back.

Where my finger had run across the wall, it had left a barely perceptible ashen mark.

A moment, a pause.

Then the mark began to deepen. It turned grey, grey-black, then solid coal-dust black, smoking black, burnt black, burning its way into the stone itself, giving off a dry, carbon smoke as it etched itself in deep.

We smiled and turned back to Kelly. "Someone will be by soon," I explained, "to let the Aldermen know that they're twats. What next?"

"Um ... may I ask, Mr Mayor, exactly why you don't just tell us personally that we're twats? I mean, obviously you're a great inspiration to us all and I'm honoured to be working with you, but you're not exactly renowned for not telling people that they're twats when you think that they are, if you don't mind me saying."

I sat back down on the bench and ticked the points off on my fingers. "Finger the first says that Templeman must have had help if he took my Penny.

"Finger the second says that help was probably from the Minority Council.

"Finger the third says that I still don't know who was or was not Minority Council and therefore can't necessarily trust a single one of you.

"Finger the fourth says that the fairy godmother is gonna be pissed at me and hunting and guess where he's gonna look? Nowhere is safer than the streets, nowhere more dangerous than prancing around in black.

"Thumb the after-thought adds, everything the Aldermen have done up to this point disgusts and repulses me: the culicidae, the fairy dust, everything; and I would rather trust in the enemies of my enemies than put my trust in those who tell me that they are friend."

Silence.

Then, "But you ... trust me?"

"I dunno. Guess I must."

The moment paused, wobbled on the tightrope, flailed its arms around, and moved on. Kelly's face split into a delighted grin. "Oh, Mr Mayor!"

"Don't get ahead of yourself."

"Obviously it's important for a PA and her employer to have a mutual understanding, a relationship of openness and appreciation, but I had heard so many things, so many people had warned me off and, you know, they were completely wrong! Positive thinking *can* win the day, a cheerful attitude towards all the world's vicissitudes, free and frank discussion, good sandwiches, decent coffee, these are the principles on which modern management should be based!"

I took a deep breath, let the words wash by. "You mentioned good news," I intoned. "Talk to me about the good."

"Good . . . ah, yes, good news! Yes, well, I'm sure this will help a bit in brightening up your day, Mr Mayor . . . "

"Something should."

" . . . we found Mr Caughey."

I sat up straight, food and drink forgotten. "Where?"

"Weybridge."

"Weybridge? What the bloody hell – no, actually, never mind, don't care. Have you approached him?"

"Not at all. I mean, I've been very discreet, it's all been 'Hey, has anyone seen Caughey?' and 'I've got this memo for Caughey' instead of 'I think the boss wants to throttle him' or anything like that, because you know how it is, people might take that the wrong way and no one likes office politics do they, I mean, it only makes for friction, but anyway. And I did a bit of scrying – not really my thing but you know how it is – and he's shielding but I realised that if I used his office keyboard, then there's all this hair and skin and stuff between the keys, it's really gross actually, I mean, things breed in there, but . . . you don't really want to know about how I scryed for him, do you?"

"Maybe another time."

"In that case, um . . . Weybridge." She handed me a folded scrap of paper. It bore an address written in the bold capitals of the very neat dealing with the genetically messy. "He's got this mistress who has this amazing house that she got from her second divorce and it's got this amazing garden and I think you can play golf near there on this incredible course which you need these little buggies to get round, but anyway, he went there and I think Lucy Holta's with him and you know, the Minority Council are probably gonna have dinner there or something because they're keeping their heads down after you shouted at them last night, so, um ... you know, you could just say 'Avengers Assemble!' or something and we'd be like, in there. I mean, I know how you can't trust Aldermen right now because of how you've been screwed over by the Minority Council, but I really think that Sean in finance would definitely be on board for something and, you know, Louis in the Department of Demons, Shades and Shadows always said that Caughey was 'this totally stuck-up prick and I hate guys like that', and you've got me!"

If Kelly had owned a golden fluffy tail, it would have taken this opportunity to wag.

I found myself almost smiling. "That's ... very nice of you," I said. "But if it's okay with you, just this once, I'll handle things ... another way."

"If you're sure ... ?"

"I'm sure."

"I just feel like I'm not being very helpful ..."

"You found Caughey."

"Yes, but like I said and, really, once you've got the keyboard it's all downhill from there anyway and besides, you're not eating right."

"Thinking of which ..."

She was already reaching in her bag, pulling out a purse. It was small, clip-closed, made of woven white and purple beads formed into a tulip pattern. She saw my face and blushed. "It was a present," she explained. "From my mother."

"I didn't say anything."

She opened the purse and passed me every note inside it.

"I don't need ..." I began.

"Yes, you do!"

"It's ... he asked, 'Can you walk without pride?' and you did say these are the vestments of the Beggar King; it's ..."

She put her hand to her mouth in sudden comprehension and snatched the money back. "Oh God!" she exclaimed. "You're so right,

I'm so sorry, I wasn't even thinking, you're wearing the sacred vestments! Wait a moment ..." The notes were stuffed into her pocket and the purse itself tipped out into the palm of her hand. Coppers were separated from silver, silver from tarnished not-ever-gold. She sorted through the smallest change, eventually picking out nearly six pounds fifty, which she dropped into my open hand. "I'm so sorry," she repeated. "I sometimes forget how these things work, you know, I mean, it's like inviting a troll to munch on ogre bones, it's completely disgraceful and I'm so, so ..."

"Thank you, I'm ... I'm grateful. I know it seems like ... but I am grateful. For what you're doing."

She beamed. "Just doing my job, Mr Mayor."

"No," I replied, tipping the fistful of coins into the seemingly bottomless pocket of my coat. "No – much more than that. I'll be in touch."

Weybridge.

Did the citizens of Weybridge even get to vote in London elections?

On the train out of Waterloo it was harder to stay unseen; the magic of the Beggar King was only solid in the street, in places where you were expected, and expected to be ignored. Here I was an anomaly, and people glanced at me with polite uncertainty. I had a group of six seats to myself, three facing three, and a table just big enough to lean on. A free newspaper, the crossword puzzle torn out, offered **Saucy Celebrity Gossip** and advice on **New, In, Chic – Get The Look For Your Home**.

Small factories and frugal-looking streets gave way to semi-detached villas, then golf courses and wooded commons. At Weybridge I was one of four people and a baby in a buggy who got off. The sun shone with winter clarity on a platform far too long for our suburban train. Outside the station, a wall-map included the road whose name Kelly had given me.

I walked.

It was a place where the magic of the city stretched thin.

Still there, still just there, but like the sound of the ocean heard beyond a towering dune, the smell of salt though you cannot see the water. We were close to the green belt, far too close for comfort; to that place where the magic of the city and the country met like hot and cold air riding a storm front. We knew of country magic, could sometimes even feel it, in the raw power of the wind on the cliff, or the rustling of leaves in the forest, but it was a thing alien to us, distant and untapped. Outside the comfort of walls and light, we were vulnerable, mortal.

At first there was no sign of any town, or even a suburb. The station seemed surrounded by forest. I followed a road that took me through a dense oak wood – but not past anywhere you might confuse with real countryside. A wide pavement lay on either side, and the traffic was fast and heavy. I passed bus shelters for routes across the centre of London, as well as notices declaring, 'Bridleway'. The paths beneath the trees looked as if hundreds of people, dogs and riding-school ponies trampled them each day.

I came to an area of large houses, many on roads announcing, 'No Thoroughfare' and 'Private Estate'. In some windows, half hidden by trees, I glimpsed Neighbourhood Watch stickers; with a shudder, I also saw a large black and white image showing a large, watching eye.

Three doors down, the words running in thin white paint, someone had written on a garage door:

It has claws

After more than a mile of turnings that announced names like Cedar Grove and Forest Chase, I came to the quiet side road I was looking for. It looked much like all the others. The house was pastiche Georgian, in the style of much smaller new homes on more crowded estates; it looked like it was made from giant plastic Lego, and included a three-car garage with white automatic doors. It stood in a half-acre of recently cleared woodland, and had a professionally tended garden of mown grass and dwarf conifers. An ugly rockery featured floodlights and a small electrically operated cascade.

I rang the bell, and heard a musical ding-dong from inside.

No answer.

I rang again.

Then knocked on the big brass knocker in the shape of a swan's head.

Still no reply.

I ran my hand over the warm wood of the door, pushing my mind between the cracks, testing for any form of magical defence, and for a moment heard

this is all your fault all your fault all

for fuck's sake Mum it's not like you can stop me!

you don't talk to me like that how dare you

It was faint, heard far off, but turn our head to the side and listen, *listen*, and there it was, the gentle background beating of the culicidae's heart, rage and confusion in a fistful of fiery heat.

I couldn't sense any wards.

But, this close to the countryside, I considered there might be other defences, spells woven, not from coils of wire but from the roots within the earth. I knocked one more time, and when there was no answer I headed to the back of the house.

There, a curving glass wall looked out on a patio with an ornamental pool, teak garden furniture and a mothballed barbecue. Inside was a spacious living room of plush sofas, and fitted carpet deep enough to take footprints. I smashed a French window with a rock stolen from the ornamental pool, bashed away a few splinters left from the frame, and unlocked the door from inside.

The house was silent.

Except perhaps for . . .

You never listen you don't care you never understand!

when I was your age we knew how to behave

you call this acceptable behaviour, young man?

"Mr Caughey?" I called out.

My voice was dulled amid heavy looped curtains and engulfing upholstery.

"Templeman betrayed you," I declared, turning to climb the wide stairs. "He betrayed everyone."

A corridor on the first floor, long and white, doors on every side, fresh paint shining on panelled walls. A wall table on the landing held thick clean towels and a vase of coppery glycerine-dried beech twigs.

"It's over," I went on, trying a door that opened into a bathroom, a dozen kinds of shower gel made from honey and mint, tea tree and strawberry, arranged along the side of an oversized bath. "There's no salvaging the Minority Council after this. You've screwed up. You screwed up the culicidae, you screwed up with the dusthouses and now

Templeman has screwed you for good. All anyone's going to say when they think of the Minority Council is 'Hey, weren't those the guys who got played by a traitor?' Because you were. We all were. Templeman played us like a fiddle."

A door at the end of the corridor, white like the rest, locked.

I could feel a warmth on my skin, a tingling in my fingers, as I tried the handle. I knocked, and thought I heard something move in the room beyond, tasted bitterness at the back of my mouth.

"He took Penny," I said, barely aware that I was saying the words. "He took Penny and told me she was dead. Used me. Us. But he can't have done it alone."

Silence.

No – not quite silence.

Not entirely.

I pressed my ear to the door. I could hear a gentle sound that might have been wind against a window-pane, might have been breath after suffocation, might have been whispered frantic words.

Listened.

" . . . told them told them told them told them fuck! Fuck fuck they never why would they never hate them hate them he wouldn't have he wouldn't have done to me FUCK OFF hate them hate them hate them don't understand don't understand don't understand why didn't they understand . . .!"

I stepped back, considered my options, then gave a good kick.

It probably hurt my foot more than the door, but I heard something splinter, and kicked again.

The door bounced open, revealing a room with one small window, one small bed, one small, unused jogging machine, one small, unplugged TV, and one not very large man, huddled around a small box.

The box was insulated, the kind of thing well-organised mothers use for taking ice cream to a picnic. It was encased within the form of a man dressed all in black. His face was flushed, his salt-and-pepper hair was wild, revealing how thin it was beneath its comb-over, his black suit was rumpled. As he knelt, arms wrapped around the box, his eyes darted to and fro almost as fast as the words tumbled from his mouth:

"Fuckers! Fuck fuck fuck bitch bitch never understood never understood I don't need it why should I care don't care don't care it's always them them telling me what they want me to be not what I want they don't understand what I want don't listen don't fucking listen . . ."

I squatted down in front of him.

His eyes swerved to me then away, his body tightening around the cool-box. At the base of the box, the carpet was smoking, and a brown-black stain was spreading from beneath it. The air was heat-hazed, smelling faintly of tar, and where Caughey's cheek rested against the plastic of the box, blisters were emerging, yellow-white on a roaring-red background.

"Cecil Caughey," I murmured, balancing painfully in front of him on my haunches.

His eyes darted to me again, and were gone as quickly. "If they loved me they wouldn't have left me left me left me left me no one fucking loves me and that's fine that's fine I'm okay with that because why the fuck should I care anyway about those stupid bitches who don't fucking love me they're all going to go to hell anyway shit!"

"Mr Caughey, Chairman of the Minority Council," I breathed, "did you read the health and safety leaflet that comes with this thing?"

I tapped the edge of the plastic box with a fingertip. The box itself was burning, a thin sticky layer beginning to form on its surface like syrup on a pancake.

"You take everything!" he wailed. "I didn't mean it I didn't I didn't mean it you always make it out like it's my fault my fault my fault when it wasn't it wasn't why the fuck would you listen to those fucking cunts anyway they don't know anything they don't fucking care it's just a job to them but this is my life!"

I stood up, dragging in breath as fire surged through my ribs. Tearing the sheets from the bed into strips, I wrapped them like fat gloves around my hands. I squatted back down in front of him, took the box in my sheet-swathed hands and tried to pull it free. Anger flared in his eyes; he wrapped his arms tighter around the box, the black fibres of his jacket starting to smoke at the increased contact.

"Mine!" he screamed. "It's mine it's mine it's mine! Fuck off!"

I hesitated, let go of the box, watched him huddle closer to it.

Then I said, "You probably won't recover, but if there is something in there which can hear this, I reason you should know. I'm going to take the culicidae's heart now. I'm going to use it to destroy the dusthouses. Not because I think I can win, that this war can ever be won. Not because of Penny. Or Templeman, or Hugo and the blood-hounds, or Oscar bloody Kramb. Their time will come. Not even for Meera, not any more. I'm going to do it because, at this stage, I have nothing else left to do. I have nothing that is mine. I have no one that I . . . there is nothing left of me but this. Nothing to do but finish it."

I seized the box again, and pulled it free with a single tug. Caughey cried out and fell onto the floor; scrambled after me with blistered broken hands, one side of his face oozing blood and clear fluids.

"Mine mine mine!" he screamed. "Give it back to me give it back to me bitch bastard slut cunt I hate you I hate you I hate you why did you give birth to me why did you if you didn't love me why why why . . . ?"

I stood up quickly, stepping aside as he collapsed in sobs at my feet. Even through the padding of the sheets I could feel the heat from the culicidae's heart, hear its beating in my ears, a relentless pulse that longed to be heard, fed on rage and loneliness and despair.

"We ought to kill you," we explained to Caughey as he beat on the floor with his fists. "Templeman cannot have done everything alone. But we realise now that death . . . it is not sorrow or grief or despair. It is not guilt and retribution, it is not justice and the cries of the lost. Is merely a not-ending. A stopping of all things. A blackness without feeling. We could kill you, and by now . . ." We grimaced at the thought. "By now we are so washed in blood that your life would run off our skin like spray off the surface of the ocean. You would never be on our con-science."

Caughey's thrashing about grew less; he wrapped his head in his hands, words trickling out with animal sounds between his lips, body shaking, tears mixing with blood on his face.

"Please please please," he whispered. "Please please why don't you listen to me why don't you ever listen I'm just a kid okay? I'M JUST A KID!"

We backed off into the doorway, cradling the burning box that held the mosquito's heart. Between sobs he was scratching at the raw places on his face. "This," we said, "is much better."

We walked away.

The strips of sheet I'd used as protection from the culicidae's heart were already blackening and turning crisp by the time I got downstairs.

A set of car keys sat on a table by the door.

They unlocked a silver hybrid car parked in the drive outside. I put the box in the back.

It had been a long time since I last drove, and I struggled to work out which complex part of the dash related to what. Even the indicator stick came with options, from turning on the radio to warming the driver's seat.

Suburban driving was a mixture of wide open roads where 70 mph was allowed but not recommended, and busy roundabouts where all things merged to a 4 mph slog. I could smell the back seat beginning to burn and, through the sharp stench of it, there was the inescapable beating of the culicidae's heart.

why didn't you

it's not fair!

she said she would never

i hate you!

time to grow up

I knew where I needed to go. It wasn't far.

I headed for the river.

Travel through London up the river and you see the Thames change its nature very quickly. Above the wide muddy estuary, it ebbs and flows in a controlled torrent of controlled water between tall stone embankments, sliced by the central bridges of the city. Further west, the banks are lower, and by the old riverside mansions of Chiswick and Richmond, where the cyclists and dog-walkers throng, the towpath is frequently flooded by the tides. Up towards Hampton Court Palace the water curls past more lazily: swans glide on its current, herons nest in tall trees, and small pleasure boats are moored at the end of long waterside gardens. 'Private' signs abound.

I parked on a dirt path between two walled-off white houses, where a sign said 'Trespassers Will Be Prosecuted', and unloaded my smoking treasure. One side of the lid was starting to melt; inside, drops of dirty plastic had fallen onto my rosy-tinted prize: the culicidae's heart. Seeing it only increased its pressure against my own mind; for a moment I tasted that bitter taste, that rush of adrenalin, in the mouth of all its victims as the culicidae had descended out of darkness to feast on their anger and rage, to drain them of all the furies of youth and leave them as hollow shells.

Between me and the river stood a wrought-iron gate fastened by an electromagnetic lock with a keypad. I snatched the electricity from the lock, holding it in the palm of my hand before shaking it away; the gate swung ajar.

Well-trimmed grass ran down to wet mud and the water's edge. A pencil-thin skiff, rowed by three men in matching orange sweatshirts, skimmed across the water. A cormorant, surfacing between dives, rode up and down on the boat's wake. I carried the box into the shallows, and let the water wash over my knees. Carefully, I lowered the box until the water slipped over its edge, and filled it.

Immediately it touched the heart, the water began to hiss and steam. I stepped in deeper, up to my hips, and pressed the box downwards until it was almost full, the culicidae's heart floating inside a bubbling mass. I unwrapped the sheets from my hands, pressed my fingers into the river mud, coating them with grey-brown sludge, then reached into the box of hissing water, pulled out the culicidae's heart, and plunged it into the river.

Heat.

Not just any kind of high temperature, but the burning sickly heat of feeling and disease. It was the fire a scream might have made, if it could burn; it was the fury of an ocean unable to tear apart the rocks; it was the stomach bursting from the inside out, the heart cloven in two, the eyes blinded by fatigue, the mind popping asunder under the weight of thoughts it could not comprehend. The water bubbled and boiled, steam rising up to sting my eyes and scald my skin, the heat running straight through my fingers and into the marrow of my bones, scorching out all other sense. And then came the rest of it.

Not just the fire, but the thing that made it burn. Our body arched as claws gouged our back, and our mind surged with a shrilling sound that went straight through the brain like an earthquake's roar through antique glass, and our nose bled and our ears bled and something ruptured in the thinking part of us and, for an instant that lasted forever, we looked up and saw the shadow of a creature etched in darkness, its jaws opening to feed. Above, as a lance longer than my body emerged from the pit of its spinning-glass throat, it moved with infinite slowness over less than a second, balanced for a moment between our eyes, and thrust straight through.

We screamed.

Or someone screamed.

They blurred into one, the voices in this creature's heart, the thoughts sucked out of them like blood from a wound. Didn't matter whose or what they'd been; all that counted was the pain, and the sense of loss when the creature withdrew, its jaws dripping with thoughtless nothing, from the hollow inside that could never be healed.

Someone fell forward, clutching a scorching heart, and it might have been me.

Water broke beneath and above me, rolled over my head, filled my nose and tickled, cold in my throat. The rumbling of the river rushed into my ears, and through it, far away, the rattle of a barge engine choking on cheap diesel, and the beating of great wings as a flight of swans made their way skywards.

Old Father Thames was real, as true a god of his dominion as the Beggar King and the Bag Lady, and there was more than a little truth to the rumour that, if you looked hard enough, at certain hours the river dragons could be glimpsed below the water's surface. The silver-skinned dragons of the Thames should have died when the cholera-infested sewage of the city began to taint their waters; in fact they had lived, evolved and would, one day, evolve again. Not stone or street had such power, not enchantment or prayer.

I forced open my eyes under the water, and in that instant I saw nothing but pain.

Closed them, opened them again, strove to look through the churning murk; saw the bubbles popping from the blackened heart between my hands, a bundle of broken plastic bag and shattered old childhood things. The fury of the water was turning, being tugged with the current, away, and, as I looked through my own blood staining the water shark-bait red, it seemed that something else was sliding free: an oily brown stain, thick and viscous and organic, slipping out from between the folds of the heart and rolling away.

I stayed under, holding out the heart at arm's length, until it became hard to tell if the pain in my chest was from ribs breaking, lungs bursting, fire washing or just an all-purpose exploding from the inside out. And when to stay under any longer was to pop like a boiling orange, I lifted my head up and gasped for air, and the culicidae's heart came with me, to rest on the surface of the water.

I hauled down air: one breath, two, three, gulping it like a thirsty drunk, and when the world had stopped pirouetting, I looked down, at the heart.

Traceries of oil were still peeling from its surface like starch from boiling rice, but the pain of burning was now merely a throbbing heart-red in my fingertips, a memory of distress running up my arms. The heat had baked the river mud, like potter's clay, onto my hands. I picked it off in chunks, and flinched as the skin on the palms of my hands came loose. I gathered up the floating plastic box by what I hoped was the least scalded part of my hands, and scooped the culicidae's heart and several litres of water back inside it. A pause, before leaving: I trailed my fingertips in the water held by the box, the heart floating inside, and listened for . . .

. . . nothing.

The thin layer of oil had vanished, drifting into the pull of the stream.

("Sometimes people come here to get clean.")

Meera on the river.

("It's where I'm me.")

Keeping my injured hands clear, I clasped the box within my arms and, dripping and squelching, I headed back for the car.

Wet clothes and fresh car seats do not mix well.

I took off my socks and shoes, and the foul-smelling coat of infinite pockets, and laid them out as best I could across the car's heaters, turned to full. Then I pressed my toes against the pedals and curled my fingers as best I could around the steering wheel, and went in search of medical aid.

I drove as far as I could, gingerly prodding the wheel this way and that, before giving up and parking, badly, on a double yellow line.

The joints of my hands were swelling up, making it hard to separate my fingers.

A shuddering was starting to eat through my body that wouldn't stop even as the temperature in the car rose higher and steam began to run down the inside of the windows. I staggered barefoot out onto the pavement, river water dribbling from the ends of my sleeves, and half walked, half fell towards a row of shops.

Before I could get there, the throbbing in my chest burst into full-fledged agony. I gasped for breath and slid down onto the pavement, clutching my side with my swollen hands and shaking. A mother with a buggy came towards me, saw me, accelerated away. A man on a mobile phone hesitated across the street, conscience fighting with caution as he wondered whether to help. Caution won.

I curled over on the ground, and now nothing could stop the shaking. Cold and heat and pain and a few things besides, a few terrible things that we could not name, pinned us to the earth and we just shook, head pressed to the ground, legs kicking, unable to believe there was no place they could be to stop this agony.

A pair of feet at eye level.

A voice said, "Um, excuse me?"

Male, middle-aged; the shoes were brown leather, clean laces. Above them, beige flannel trousers, neatly pressed.

"Excuse me, you can't stay here."

"Help me," I begged. "Please, help me."

"Mary!" hollered the voice.

Another pair of shoes snapped on the pavement. A pair of navy-blue pumps lined up beside the brown loafers. A voice said, "For Christ's sake, can't you see he's in pain? Hello? Excuse me? I'm going to call an ambulance."

I shook my head, whimpered, "No . . . no ambulance . . ."

A moment, a pause, in which thoughts turned and turned again and decided that no matter how they looked at it, they didn't like the view. "I'm calling the police," murmured the woman called Mary.

"No!" Our hand shot out and grabbed her by the ankle. She screamed and all at once the man shouted a wordless cry and kicked our arm, twice. We held on and she was still screaming, so he turned on us and, with a grunt and a limp flail of limbs, he kicked us in the belly.

Fireworks burst behind our eyes.

Something black and bright and hot wriggled its way out from the back of our brain and started boring its way forwards. A big squirm-shaped hole, eaten by worms, led to the place between our eyes where, if it had lived, the culicidae would have enjoyed sucking out our thoughts. There, something opened its jaws wide enough to blot out the sun, to engulf our head, our throat, our body and our all, before snapping us into darkness.

I thought I heard Penny's voice.

I thought I heard a lot of things, but Penny's voice was the only thing I wanted to remember.

I thought I saw a dragon.

Its black wings were folded time, its eyes a red endless pit.

It stood on the black walls of the city, silver claws curled round a blazing shield, tongue rolling out, licking the air.

There was blood on its lips.

Bones beneath its feet.

Then it looked at me, and I was tiny, and it was vast, and it was not impressed.

I staggered towards the pit inside its eyes, that great red falling pit of a thousand thousand years lined with a million million bones, and didn't fight it, and didn't argue, didn't even pause on the edge to catch my breath, lined with flame, but fell in, laughing all the way.

Someone was playing bad songs of the 1980s in another room.

The DJ called them 'vintage classics', which was never a good sign.

Someone else was unwrapping cling film from around my hands.

Funny thing, that.

The DJ said, "Now, we've got a request here from Sharon in Hoxton, who says this song reminds her of the time she first accidentally walked through a wall, and it's for all the gang in GCSE Chemistry who wanted to know why and never got an answer – interesting shout-out there, Sharon, not often we get that kinda request but then, you've asked for a classic of the 1980s and all afternoon we will be playing your Vintage Classic requests so here from Sharon to everyone in Chemistry class is your choice . . ."

Something cold was run over my skin.

It tingled to the touch, like icing sugar on a sore.

Somewhere else, a kettle was boiling.

A voice said, " . . . milk and sugar?"

Another voice, much nearer, replied, "Just milk, ta, and leave the teabag in."

I knew those voices.

The smell of tea drifted on the air.

Somewhere overhead – not so far overhead as it should have been – a jet plane locked its undercarriage for landing, or maybe unlocked it from takeoff, or perhaps merely came in low to have a better look at the seat. The dishes rattled in the kitchen at its passage.

I opened my eyes.

Dr Seah sat on the edge of a small single bed in a small single room, a pair of latex gloves on her hands, holding a fistful of white cream. She was chucking the cream at my hands and lower arms like a paintballer testing the quality of their ammunition, bottom lip curled in concentration. I was certain I hadn't made a sound but she said, without looking up, "Now, when I said 'bed rest', did you take this as, like, meaning the *bed* should get a rest, because I think we both know that wasn't what I was getting at."

I opened my mouth to answer, and regretted even that much movement.

Someone had made a corset of bandages and steel and wrapped it round my chest: mostly, I felt, to enhance the pain. I groaned and pushed my head back against the lumpy pillow on the bed. Dr Seah said, "Yup, that right there is what I'm talking about but do people listen, oh no. It's all 'I know my body' and I'm all 'You only think you know your body' and they're all like 'Hey who the fuck are you' and I'm all like 'Hey, you know what, it's your fractured ribcage, whatever' so, basically, I figure, screw it."

A footstep in the doorway to the room and the smell of tea grew stronger. A voice rang out, "Mr Mayor! You're not dead!"

Kelly Shiring – grinning hugely – scurried up, nearly dropping a mug of tea.

"Mr Mayor," she babbled. "You would not believe what happened, but I was just about to leave the office when . . . "

"Kelly?" I groaned.

" . . . when the Beggar King burst through the door! He marched right across the floor, stood on a table, clapped his hands together and shouted, 'Right! Which of you bastards thinks Templeman is innocent? Come on, stand up right now and let me kick you and your smug, polished white teeth in!' I mean I couldn't believe it . . ."

"Love a cuppa tea," murmured Dr Seah, taking the mug and circling it under her nose like a wine taster.

" . . . and then he grabbed poor old Rumina Rathnayake by the scruff of the neck and I thought she was going to cry poor thing, and he starts shaking her and shouts, 'I put the curse of the beggars upon you! May all eyes turn away from you in distrust and fear, may the cold wind find you in the warm corners of the street, may you be forever lonely in a crowd! I command the doors of the city to be shut upon you, all that you eat shall taste of the garbage from whence it came, all that you drink will be slewed with mud, there shall be no charity, nor no redemption for you and your departure will be cold, alone and unmourned, a headstone placed upon your tomb which reads simply "unknown" and he lets her go and she's shaking and he turns to me and I think, 'Whoops, that's it, I'm next,' but he just marches up to me, takes me by the elbow, pulls me over to the water cooler and says, 'Your boss is a stupid fucker who can't keep out of trouble and that's why I like him' and next thing I know he's sending me down to the Weybridge police station and I'm having to . . ."

" . . . are there any biscuits?" asked Dr Seah.

" . . . do the Alderman thing and pull rank and be generally, you know how it is, generally *ghastly* unpleasant and then here you are!"

"Here you are," concluded Dr Seah over her mug of tea. "I should probably add, I don't usually do house calls."

I looked from Dr Seah to Kelly and back again. Kelly's smile quavered, unsure if it was appropriate for the moment but hoping it would do. Dr Seah's face was one of pure tea-filled contentment.

I tried a deep breath, and regretted that too.

"You'll get that for a while," said Dr Seah, eyes not leaving her mug of tea. "*Bed rest*. Did I mention the bed rest and, oh yes, while I'm here, can I just add, *bed rest*."

I managed to wheeze, "Kelly?"

"Yes, Mr Mayor?"

"Don't think that I'm not grateful for the intervention – I am – but

I gotta ask a few questions and I'd like you, if you don't mind, to answer them succinctly, if not, in fact, briskly, is that okay?"

"Oh, sweetie, you have had a bad day," said Dr Seah.

"Go ahead, Mr Mayor!" trilled Kelly.

"I was in a police station?"

"Yup. Apparently you assaulted some woman. And possibly trespassed. And stole a car. Mr Caughey's car, in fact! And passed out on the pavement isn't really a criminal offence, might be a civil disobedience. But actually there's something . . ."

"Does some great curse befall anyone who arrests the Midnight Mayor?" I asked hopefully.

"Um . . . I don't know. Why, do you want one to?"

Dr Seah had put down the mug of tea and was looking in her medical bag for bandages.

"As a matter of fact, there is something you should probably . . ." began Kelly. She was interrupted by Dr Seah snapping on a new pair of gloves with every look of relish and demanding, "So which part of bed rest are you still not clear on?"

She wiggled her fingers inside the latex and waggled her eyebrows and grinned a malicious grin.

"I promise," I intoned, "that as soon as I'm not being hunted, chased, betrayed, abused and neglected, I will find somewhere, possibly with room service, and do the bed rest thing."

"Sweetie, it's your body, I can't be here all the time to stop you destroying it. I'm just saying, sooner or later you gotta take responsibility for these little things like, I dunno, *breathing*."

"Actually, on that subject . . ." began Kelly.

"Where's the culicidae's heart?" The thought struck too hard for me to let Kelly finish; the words just tumbled right out.

"Um, the . . ."

"The culicidae's heart, Kelly, the thing that I went to all this trouble to recover from Caughey, who is, by the way, completely mad."

"Mr Caughey is mad?"

"Well, yes. Bit too much exposure to the beating heart of a creature fed on bile and rage will do that to a guy, and I'm not one hundred per cent convinced he had a psyche of stone to begin with."

"But he only had it for a few hours . . ."

"He helped make it, helped create it, had a longer exposure to the whole affair, and besides, I only had it a few minutes, and here I am," I retorted, brandishing my scorched and gloopy hands.

Dr Seah tutted, swatted them back down. "Professional at work here!" she chided. "This is me, *bandaging* and all that crap, on a *house call* and all that crap, but don't you worry, I've got my professional face on."

"Which does raise the question of where *here* is," I added, looking round the room.

Baby-pink walls, featuring a total of two pictures – one a Japanese print of a wading bird in still waters, the other a faded photograph of a school gathered in their best bow ties. A wardrobe, white, shut; a dresser, beige, empty; and a large mirror, cracked at the edge and framed with plastic gold. Somewhere outside, but not far enough outside to be civil, the roar of planes passing overhead, wheels locked to land.

"It's a safe house," explained Kelly. "Basically, my ex-flatmate has a cousin whose boyfriend has a house . . . "

"Where in London?" I asked.

"Osterley."

"How the hell did I get to Osterley?"

"Well, I managed to convince two very nice young policemen to carry you from the station to my car, and then when I got here I convinced a passing dog-walker to help carry you from my car to the house, and then I convinced Dr Seah . . . "

"Have you found Templeman?"

"No, but actually . . . "

"What about the fairy godmother? He about to come storming in here, guns blazing?"

"Well, he might," admitted Kelly, "but actually you're sitting inside a very fine specimen of its type, a series of anti-scrying wards constructed mostly from wire ties, post-it notes and kitchen forks balanced together in that way, you know when you get three of them and they all support each other but don't really support each other, that kind of counterbalanced thing that boy scouts learn to do . . . "

"And Brownies," added Dr Seah. "Youth activities are all about the magic tricks."

"If we can call it a *trick* . . . "

"The bit with the forks is a trick. Obviously the anti-scrying ward is more magical but you gotta ask, where'd you draw that fine line between amazing tricks and basic magic? Or maybe you're not asking, but you should."

"Point being," concluded Kelly, raising her voice, "no one knows except you, me, Dr Seah, and my ex-flatmate's cousin's boyfriend where you are, so even if Templeman or Mr Kramb have sources still active within the Aldermen, which I must admit is a rather distressing thought, even if they did, I can't imagine they'll be doing anything about it soon. Which actually does bring me to my final point ..."

There was a thud from the end of the hall, the sound of a heavy door being shut. Our fingers tightened instinctively. A footstep in the hall, the sound of plastic bags being put down on a lino floor.

"You, me, Dr Seah ... and who?" I asked.

"I was trying to explain," said Kelly. "You see, the anti-scrying ward ..."

The footsteps came closer, a hand pushing back the door to the tiny bedroom. The fingernails were long and painted, the pads on the fingertips warm pink, the skin above the nails, deep-baked brown.

" ... wasn't actually cast by me ..." babbled Kelly.

A foot, wearing a boot laced up to the knee, a knee clad in black, an arm in blue denim, a head covered with an explosion of frizzy black hair. A voice.

A familiar, unbelievable voice.

It said, "Yo, what the sister's saying is that this ..." – a gesture taking in the shape of the room and its unseen defensive magics – " ... is no ordinary fucking spell. *This* is a totally *awesome* fucking spell."

Penny.

Penny Ngwenya.

Once upon a time, she'd stood on London Bridge and looked towards the east and said, as a curse, give me back my hat, and things had gone downhill from there.

Ex-traffic warden, ex-cleaning lady, six GCSEs, grades A–D, one higher education diploma in art and media studies, two years' experience in retail at her local supermarket, one point on her driving licence from that time when some total wanker, like, cut her up at the traffic lights or whatever; wannabe sorceress; my apprentice.

Penny Ngwenya.

She stood in the door and stared at me, and, by the look on her face, all the clever things she'd been practising saying weren't so clever any more.

I stammered at the others, "Out. Please."

Dr Seah was already at the door, pulling Kelly into the corridor with a cry of, "So where'd you get cake round here . . . ?"

She closed the door behind them on the way out.

Penny hooked her fingers into her pockets and said nothing.

Then, "Fuck it, I hate, like, fucking awkward fucking silences anyway, so I'm just gonna say, Matthew, you look like totally shit. Sorry, I know we should be all like 'It'll be fine' or whatever, but you look really crap."

We felt it was our turn to speak, and found we couldn't.

Penny blurted again, "So yeah . . . Templeman is, like, a psychopath. But I figure you've worked that out, right, because if you haven't then you are such a twat you. like, deserve to lose."

"We thought . . . I thought . . . we . . . he told us the fairy godmother had you. He told us you were dead."

Something swept over Penny's face, something I hadn't seen before, couldn't name. She nodded slowly, biting her lip, folding her arms. "Yeah," she said. "I guess he would. He lied."

Third Interlude: Sometimes, You Can't Be Saved

In which Penny tells her story.

She said, "It was fine. It was all going fine.

"I was with Nabeela, we were . . .

" . . . I was with Nabeela.

"We followed you to your meeting in Covent Garden. Watched you talk with the Aldermen, watched you get into the car with Templeman. Nabeela said, 'Uh . . . should we follow the car?'

"I told her you didn't look frightened or scared or enchanted, and it would probably be okay. And it was okay, wasn't it? You called, we talked, you said it was fine and we went shopping. I mean, I know it's a bit clichéd, okay, two girls, out together, going shopping, but it wasn't like we were going to buy anything and it's Covent Garden, you know; it's not like you can't really not go shopping in Covent Garden, everything smells of soap and chocolate, it's like going to Edinburgh and not having haggis. And I liked Nabeela. I did. She was cool. Sure, she'd got the medusa thing, but she handled it in a groovy way; I liked that.

"So we went shopping. And we must have pissed off so many people because we didn't buy anything. I mean, we tried everything on, moved it all around and messed it all up, but have you seen how much these things cost?

"I really think it was good for her, you know, what with her condition, she almost never got to dress down with the girls and there was one shop, and we were looking at the dresses and she saw this purple one with, like, long sleeves and this amazing skirt with these, like, waves sown onto it and she wanted to try it and we went into the changing room and there were these mirrors and we were the only ones there and she said, so long as you only look at the mirror you'll be okay, just look at the mirror, and so I did and she . . .

"I guess she 'let down her hair'.

"I hadn't really seen it, close up, I mean, before.

"I'd only seen it in that crappy mobile phone screen. But I stood right next to her in this tiny little changing room with these mirrors on every side, close enough to touch, and she said it was okay, because I was a girl and because I was a sorceress and I would understand.

"The . . . things on her head . . . they were part of her. Her hair was cables, thin and silver, each one ending at a lens, and they moved and writhed like living things, but where the cable met her skull it wasn't like it plugged in or anything, but like it just melted into her. Like, if you looked, you could see tiny wires running along her head like veins, before they vanished down deep, and if you touched one of them it'd twitch like a frightened rabbit, but if you ran your finger down it, it'd sorta relax, like a cat.

"She said, 'There's a recessive gene somewhere in my family. My great great great aunt had it too, but it wasn't like this for her. She had black iron snakes on her head that wheezed coal dust when they turned, and their gaze turned all who looked at them into carbon monsters. And her great grandmother before that, she had the whole proper snakes-on-the-head thing going, I mean, real proper adders and stuff, and the people would come to her for advice and teaching, and call her an imam, a teacher, one who knows the path.

"'We – I mean, my kind – don't have kids. My great great great aunt didn't have kids and I won't. It's not that we can't, I think, it's just . . . you know . . . you don't want to take the risk, do you? But the boys are carrying it, the gene I mean, and have you tried stopping boys doing their thing? I mean, God, it's so depressing.

"'My family's from Lebanon originally – well, we moved around a lot – but my grandmother wanted to move here. I think she thought, maybe it wouldn't happen in the city. Maybe it would be different, another land, another place.

"'And yeah, she was right, it was different. But it didn't stop. I was home-schooled until I was old enough to wear hijab. It keeps me safe. My Mum wears it too sometimes, when we go out to big dinners. She always said, when I was growing up, it was really useful – men would see it and they'd sorta talk to her, like she was a person, you know? A someone, not a *something*, without trying to get a snog or anything like that. Seems to me that guys my age are either so desperate to get off with you they can't say anything at all, or so busy thinking you want to get off with them that they still don't say a word. Now that she's married, she says she kinda doesn't feel like that any more. She loves my dad, and he loves her, and they're comfortable together, and that's all that matters. But she wears a scarf when she's with me. I think she does it to keep me company. Silly, really.'

"She looked at herself in the mirror, hair all writhing around her head, glass catching the light. She was beautiful in that dress, she had this figure, I mean, proper hourglass stuff. But she was sad, and she said: 'I will never have a husband. Too risky. One day, he'll want to see my face, touch it, and I'll turn the wrong way and he'll look at me and see and then he'll . . . it is a curse. I know that. But there must be a reason.'

"She started putting her headscarf back on, smoothing her hair back down beneath the cotton. I watched, and then I said, and I don't know why, 'I summoned the death of cities.'

"She looked at me, surprised, in the mirror, like, but didn't need to ask. Her face was doing the questioning.

""I didn't know what I was doing,' I explained. 'I was ... hurt. I was lonely. My friends were scared of me, they didn't understand what I was going through and as they became more scared, they stopped being my friends at all. And I had this shit job and I didn't know what I wanted or who I was or why all these things ... and then one day this total bastard hit me, and I was just doing what I was meant to, and he called me all sorts of shit things and I know it was, like, a little thing but you know how little things add up after a while? And a kid stole my hat. The kid was called Mo. He stole my hat and I was so angry and so confused I went to the river and stood on London Bridge all by myself and raised my hands to the sky and screamed, I just ... I just screamed it, "Give me back my hat! Give me back my hat give me give me give me back my hat!" And something heard. This ... parasite ... this thing that feeds on the death of cities, it heard and it came crawling out of the shadows, out of paper and rage and it ... it killed people. I didn't know. I swear I didn't know I couldn't have I didn't ... but it killed, and I made it. It killed the kid. It killed the last Midnight Mayor. It nearly killed Matthew but he ... he was supposed to kill me, you know? The Aldermen, those fuckers in black, they wanted to kill me, to break the spell and he just swanned up and said, "I brought you back your hat" and I was like, "What the fuck?" and he said, "I heard you lost it. I brought it back" and I knew ... fuck, I don't know what the fuck I knew but I knew ... everything. Everything that had been, everything that was, everything that might be. Not like God or shit, not like parting of the clouds stuff. Just something solid, here, inside. But the thing is, what I'm trying to say is ... I nearly destroyed the city. How screwed up is that? How screwed up does that make me?'

"She was quiet for a while.

"I guess it wasn't fair to kinda just throw that at her, but I hadn't told no one and she had told me and it felt right. The right thing. Not often you get to be sure.

"Finally she said, 'Thank you,' and I didn't really get what for, but I smiled, and she smiled back, and got on with pinning down her hair. And we had lunch at this Persian restaurant and I asked if Nabeela spoke any Persian and she said, my family's from Lebanon, so it'd be Arabic, idiot, and no she didn't, she was from Finchley, what did I expect, and we had humous and pitta bread and those little plates of stuff you get with like dates and vine leaves, and everything comes all at once so you look at the table and think 'Shit, I'm such a pig' and then somehow you eat it all and find yourself ordering more and . . . do the Aldermen do expenses? Only I've got the receipt somewhere, and it was a big lunch, you know what I'm saying? Anyway.

"I guess what I'm saying is, we got pretty relaxed.

"I mean, I'd spotted the Aldermen following us.

"Of course I'd spotted them.

"But fuck me, Matthew, they're supposed to be on your side. I mean, I get it, I get the Minority Council shit, I get how that's bad news, but, like, you're the Midnight Mayor. No! You're more than the Midnight fucking Mayor, you're the blue electric angels, you're the guy who said no to the Neon Court and pissed off the Tribe, the apprentice of Robert fucking Bakker, destroyer of Blackout, banisher of the death of cities, I mean, you may not look like much, but on paper you're really cool until people meet you! So what the fuck? How the hell were we supposed to know? And you taught me to be a sorceress. You taught me how to bind and compel, enchant and exorcise. Not what to do when some fuckers in a big blue van pull up beside you on St Martin's Lane and suddenly the two guys in front who you thought were just a pair of tourists have guns and the two guys behind who you figured were theatregoers in fancy coats are grabbing you by the arms and there's some guy in the fucking van pulling a bag over your head!

"You taught me that life was magic, that in all things that live there is not just power, but wonder and possibility, shadows and time, that magic is a reflection of layer upon layer upon layer of life plastered across this world like air; you taught me that and then went off to do the Midnight Mayor thing and these guys they just came out of nowhere, they came out of nowhere and they . . .

"They took us.

"And I'm no fucking damsel in distress, I wasn't going to scream, I was going to ensorcel their ass, but they had drugs. I felt them stick something into my skin and it burnt. And I felt sick and all my muscles went slack and then . . .

" . . . they drugged me.

"That's all I remember about then.

*

"They took us some place.

"It was dark when I woke up, really dark and quiet, like dead-night in dead-place black. They must have kept on drugging us, keeping us out for hours and hours. Maybe they'd wanted to keep us asleep until they killed us. Maybe they'd just run out of needles.

"The place smelt.

"It was a shed of some kind, a concrete shed, but you could feel it hadn't been lived in for a long time, all dark and damp and cold as the outside air.

"There wasn't any light.

"Someone had killed the power.

"Everything felt . . . a long way off. Slow. I guessed we were in the countryside; I couldn't hear traffic or planes or feel the city close or anything like that. They'd tied us up. They'd been real paranoid about it. They'd put handcuffs on, and cable ties around my feet and knees, like I was about to get up and cha-cha my way outta there, you know? They'd given me something and it made me sick. I puked. There wasn't anywhere good to do it, so I just did it there. I heard footsteps move outside and tried to wriggle away against the wall. They sounded like they were walking on more concrete. There wasn't a window, but there was a door at one end; I could see the outline of the grey. I tried to summon light but it was so hard, everything was so hard, so far away, and I couldn't see and my mouth burnt, tasted of acid. Then something else moved and I swear to God, that's the closest I ever came to screaming. There was something else and I thought at first it was a rat, but then it moved a little more and it was too heavy for a rat, and grunted as it moved; a woman.

"'Nabeela?' I asked, voice all sticky in my throat.

"'Penny? What's happening?'

"'Are you okay?'

"'I'm . . . there's tape, I can feel tape I can't move my hands I can't open my eyes I can't . . .'

"'Are you hurt?'

"'I feel a bit sick.'

"'Me too. Hey, it's going to be okay, okay? You're gonna be fine and I'm gonna be fine and we're gonna bust our way out of this like the kick-ass bitches we are, and even if we don't, which we will, Matthew's gonna come on down here like the kick-ass bastard he is and do the saving thing, and he'll be insufferable for a while, but basically cool, okay?'

"'Okay,' she trembled.

"'Hey, girl, we'll be okay, okay? It'll all be . . . okay.'

"I think I heard her nod. I tried to crawl towards her. It was hard, wriggling on the floor or something, like, head and shoulders banging against it and kicking with my knees. But I was glad she was there. Is that wrong? I was fucking glad she was there, because she was a medusa and I was a sorceress and between us we'd be okay, and because she wanted me to say it was going to be okay and I was going to do it. I was going to make it okay.

"I bumped into her head first and heard her gasp for breath. I said, 'It's me, it's me, we'll be fine. Hey, can you move?'

"'No,' she replied. 'There's . . . they used gaffer tape, they . . . they stuck it over my face, over my . . . my head. There's like, tape on my head or something; it hurts, I feel really weird.'

"I got to my knees and whispered, 'Okay, okay, like, move your head towards me or something, I'll see if I can feel anything.'

"I was close enough to feel the heat off her body; I leant down and I brushed my cheek against the top of her head. The fuckers had wrapped her like some sort of Egyptian mummy, they'd fucking wrapped her; they'd got this really cheap tape and they'd run it round and round her skull and under her chin and taped her hair down so it couldn't move, but even under the tape I could feel it moving, trying to press its way free. I said, 'I'll find an end. There's gotta be an end to the tape or something; maybe I can pull it free.'

"I tried to stand up properly, so I could feel the tape around her head with my fingers, but every time I tried I kept on falling back down until Nabeela said, 'Hey, try this.' And she lay down. I turned my back on her and she put her head in my hands and I felt around the tape on her head, trying to find a place where it was thin, something I could pull at. Every time I thought I'd found an end, it was just another long length of the strip, and the stuff was taped down too hard, too thick to just tear it, and I couldn't move my fingers. I tried to summon magic, tried to put it into my hands, make them stronger, harder, but it wouldn't come and I was scared of just scratching at it with my nails; I didn't want to hurt her or scratch her eyes or anything like that. But she was calmer now. She said, 'It's okay. I trust you,' so I kept looking, systematic like, starting just above her eyebrows where the first bit of tape was and moving my hands side to side across her head, trying to find a place where it was weak.

"And I found it.

"It was round by her neck, a place where the tape was weak. So I whispered, 'Hold on, I think I've got something . . .'

"But there was a sound outside. Nabeela gasped and sat up straight-away, which was smart because otherwise they would have caught us, and she pressed her back into the wall but I tried to stand up again and just fell straight back down.

"The door opened and there was this light outside, thin, grey light like really old moonlight, but it came from this flood above the door and there were two guys in the light and they wore black. One of them I didn't know; a woman, I think. The other was a man, and even with his back to the light, I thought I recognised him.

"Then he said, 'Good evening ladies. Actually, forgive me, it's more like good morning at the moment. My name is Richard Templeman. I'm very sorry for the inconvenience I've put you to. I hope your stay will be safe and temporary.'

"'Wow, that's so sweet,' I said. 'Tell you what, you let me go and I'll show you my sweet fluffy fucking gratitude with bells on.'

"'I understand your anger, Ms Ngwenya,' he explained, and his voice was all cold and telephone-like, I mean like a sound with no face. I wished he'd shouted, or dribbled or raved like a proper madman, but he just stood there so still and just talked like a sad headmaster or something. 'I can only assure you again that, if you are cooperative with this process, your stay with us should be as peaceful and easy as pos-sible. Please do not attempt to do anything unwise, as you will be forcefully restrained should you do so and it will only make this process harder. Matthew is presently aware of your situation and is doing everything he can to ensure your safety. You may be confident of free-dom soon, once he has cooperated.'

"I went cold at that, it was like it took all my words. But he waited, and I hated him even more for waiting for me like he was wise and I was just a child, and when he was done waiting it was because I shouted, 'What the fuck do you mean: "Matthew is presently aware"?

What the hell do you think you're doing? He's going to fucking kill you, I mean gut you, rip you to little pieces, when he finds out what the fuck you've done to us!'

"'I have no doubt that Matthew will seek retribution against me for my actions,' said Templeman, like it was a really boring thing. 'But at this present moment, his cooperation is all I seek and the removal of you both from the current scenario was the most suitable way to expedite affairs. Should he survive, I have no doubt he will seek my blood, in which case the preservation of you two as healthy, happy hostages would be to the benefit of us all.'

"He was talking balls so I started screaming, 'What the fuck are you talking about, you're talking like this isn't fucking real, what the . . . ?'

"But then Nabeela cut in, like, right in, and said so quiet, but so clear all at once, 'What are the conditions of Matthew's behaviour that will allow for our freedom?'

"I thought Templeman brightened at that, at hearing a voice that talked like his own. I guess everyone talks like that in local councils.

"'To put it simply, I require the destruction of the dusthouses. This is an ambition, Ms Ngwenya, Ms Hirj, which benefits us all. Leaving aside its current practical necessity, it could be argued that there is indeed an ethical benefit to such an eventuality. While I have no doubt that Matthew would have, eventually, taken it on himself to act against the fairy godmother, the pressures of the situation required rather more . . . drastic action . . . to expedite events. The godmother would have exposed certain pieces of information that would have compromised me, and our Midnight Mayor himself perhaps . . . overreacted . . . to a situation rather beyond his control. A speedy solution to our problems was called for. Simply put, you will be released once Matthew has killed the fairy godmother. Oscar Kramb's death will benefit many, including you, and Matthew, and me.'

"'What happens if he doesn't do it?' I asked. 'What happens if, like, he doesn't kill the guy?'

"'Alas, it is to be regretted by us all that Matthew does not sometimes engage in more radical solutions,' Templeman replied. He still hadn't moved, standing in the door. But now I thought I could see his eyes, and something else. There was something yellow in them, something that I could see though there wasn't enough light to see by, something sick and yellow, and a smell about him that wasn't just bad deodorant.

"'I am aware of Matthew's fondness for you, ladies, that's why you're both here. He is currently under the belief that the fairy godmother has you. I am hoping that this will inspire him to do what has to be done. Should he not . . . well then, as I said, there is advantage for us all if you are helpful.'

"'Not for us there's fucking not!'

"'Yes, for you,' he replied, and his eyes were too bright in that darkness. 'For see it like this, Ms Ngwenya. You could be dead. At this time, in this place, you could be dead, and you are not. It is within your power to remain alive, if not free.'

"He seemed happy with himself, a clever guy making a clever point to stupid people. He turned to go but then Nabeela said, 'May we know why?'

"He paused in the door. I think she'd surprised him.

"'Why?' he asked, not looking round.

"'You know, so that we can, like, get where you're coming from, understand your point of view, be better, nicer, more cooperative hostages. Do we get to know why?'

"I thought he wasn't going to answer.

"Then I thought it was something worse. I thought he was angry. There was something in his shoulders, this tiny thing, but like he was all stiff inside. But then he breathed it out and turned and looked at us and I knew what it was that was wrong with him, that smell. He stank of magic, but wrong magic, sick magic, the smell of rotting bodies and sand, things left out in the desert for vultures to pick. He was on something, he was fired up on it, and even in this place, where everything was too far to reach, I could taste it on the air.

"Then he said, 'We must evolve. Society evolves all the time, every day in new ways. That which was forbidden is now permitted, that which was magic is now science, that which was fiction is now fact, that which was unspoken is now sung from the wires. The world is changing, *mankind* is changing. We magicians take pride in the evolution of the spells we cast, our adaptability to this changing world. But we contribute nothing. We are . . . irrelevant. We must change. I will make us change. Do you understand?'

"'Yes,' breathed Nabeela. 'I understand.'

"I didn't know if she was lying. I hoped she was, because he was talking psycho-shit and I wanted to say it. But there was madness in his eye and belief in his voice, and if I know one thing from bitching with my aunt, it's that you don't never reason with true believers.

"I think I knew the other thing then too.

"He was gonna kill us.

"He was talking to keep us quiet, keep us sweet, but when you were done, even if you did it, he'd kill us.

"Were you gonna top the fairy godmother?

"I didn't think so.

"You'd come storming in here first.

"But that didn't mean I was gonna wait for it to happen.

"When he was gone, I turned back to Nabeela.

"She said, 'Perhaps we should . . .'

"'He's gonna do it,' I replied. 'You know he's gonna. He's gonna kill us.'

"'But he said it himself, if he wants to control Matthew then he needs us alive.'

"'Babes,' I explained, 'there's only two things you do with Matthew. You get on board with him or you get out of his way. You and me are on board. That means Templeman is in his way, and we do not want to be round here when that shit goes down.'

"'Will Matthew kill the godmother? Will he do it?'

"'I don't know. I don't think it matters. Moment he does it, we're dead. And if he doesn't do it . . . then he's not gonna change his mind just because Templeman goes "Hey, it's okay, I've still got these two bitches alive." And even if he does try that, he'll probably try to scare Matthew, try the whole frightening thing, and I'm buggered if I'm gonna sit around and let some psychopath cut off my toes or pull out my fingernails or shit. I'm gonna get out and find this really hot guy called Femi, and you're gonna get out and, like, kick local council ass, and we are *not* gonna let this happen, okay?'

"'Okay.'

"'Come on, I think I was getting somewhere with this fucking tape.'

"She shuffled back down and I felt around her head, blind, looking for the tape. I could feel her hair moving restlessly, feel it jerk whenever I tugged at the gaffer tape holding it down. Some wanker had really done a number on it; it didn't want to come and, in the dark, it was hard, slow progress. I found an end and pulled and at once she shouted out in pain and I said, 'I'm sorry babes, I'm sorry; you okay?'

"'Yeah,' she answered in that little voice that tells you they're not okay at all but are way too brave to make you stop. 'Just . . . be quick.'

"I started ripping the tape away, and I realised that, in this place, in the dark, I might be just one bad look from turning into a concrete statue myself, if I could get her free. There were more sounds outside, voices. I tried to move faster, to pick at the tape with my hands, but it was round her chin and she was nearly choking, trying not to cry out; I could feel her shaking with it.

"Footsteps at the door, a brighter light, a torch, flashed under it, and then I heard a key in the lock and I was only halfway there but some of her hair was coming free, I could feel it pushing up but the door was opening and there was this one guy in the light and he had a bottle of water in one hand and a little plastic box in the other and I didn't need to be bloody Einstein to guess what kinda needles a guy might carry in a box like that.

"He shone the torch right in my eyes and then saw Nabeela behind me and the tape I'd already pulled off on the floor and he opened his mouth to shout and I just charged at him. I mean, there wasn't much there, there wasn't anything solid to cling to, but there was that light in his torch and it was all I had, so I grabbed at it with everything I had and heard a pop as the light-bulb went and in that moment of surprise I guess he must have panicked because he dropped the torch.

"And my hands were still tied but I went at him head first, kinda jumping like a jack-in-the-box, and knocked into his belly as hard as I could and used my weight to push him down; the thing was to keep on biting and twisting and not give him a chance to realise how fucked I was. He went staggering back and tripped right over his own feet, falling on his arse, legs flying, me on top of him. I was going to head-butt him; I pulled my head back and, I knew, the trick was to go straight for his nose but he shouted out and got one of his hands under my chin, pushing it back.

"I tried to find something to hit him with, electricity, fire, light, anything, but we were in like this field, we were in a fucking field and I could see the lights of a motorway at the end of a distant hill and I guessed it was the M25 because there was this big blue sign with an aeroplane symbol on it and because the traffic was really slow, but then he rolled, got himself on top of me, legs out either side, and he was shouting for help and calling me a stupid bitch, and he clenched his fingers into this ugly fist, the bones all standing out at the knuckles like troll hills in rocky country, swung his arm up high and then . . .

"'Close your eyes.'

"It was Nabeela who spoke and there was this shadow behind him and I didn't need to be told twice. I mean, I was going to close my eyes anyway, because there was this fist heading for my face, but I closed my eyes proper now and I could hear the sound of tape tearing and felt his head turning and heard the beginning of a gasp, but it didn't have time to finish. He started to breathe and it was like the breath got stuck somewhere in his throat, didn't even make it to the lungs. And then I felt the rest of it.

"He'd been turning, the weight on one leg, but there was still his weight on me and suddenly it went from really fucking heavy to crushing; I mean, I couldn't move my chest, couldn't breathe in, just lay there gasping these thin little wheezes of air, and his legs, which had been warm, grew cold really fast, and hard, and where his thigh had bumped against my wrist, I felt fabric turn rough, ragged, grainy – like concrete.

"I just lay there, eyes squeezed shut, until Nabeela said, 'Okay, I'm going to turn my back.'

"I waited.

"'I've turned my back,' she called, and her voice was shaking. I opened my eyes.

"The guy was just frozen there, one hand still raised in a fist, his head turned towards where Nabeela stood with her back to me, his eyes open wide. Her hair was writhing like it was angry, dancing on the end of its silver wires, bits of tape still hanging off and the ends of the lenses pushing at it like they were annoyed, trying to pick each other clean. I crawled out from under the guy and there were more footsteps running towards us. The keys to the handcuffs had been in his bloody pocket, bloody turned to stone, and as the footsteps approached Nabeela said, 'Duck!'

"I wasn't arguing. I got down with my head on the ground and heard the footsteps round the corner, and that same sound – that beginning of air to shout or warn or threaten or whatever – then that sound just stopped. If a medusa turns you to stone, does everything turn? Blood, bone, blood, air, electricity in your brain, sense in your spine? It'd be shit if you kept on thinking as you died.

"Whatever happened, the footsteps stopped.

"'Okay,' said Nabeela. 'You can look again.'

"I looked up. She had her back to me, facing out towards the motorway. Two more guys were stone. I looked at them. One of them was an Alderman; I mean, the full, proper bloody Alderman get-up. I guess that was the moment I realised the other thing, the thing that was probably scarier than Templeman being a psycho. I realised that the fucking Aldermen were involved, that nothing and no one could be trusted.

"I looked round at where we were, taking it in properly.

"It was one of those commercial estates; you know, the flat-roofed buildings, the empty car parks, the old metal chutes that carry nothing from nowhere to a place where a lorry should have been. Everything was rusting up. A sign on our shed said, 'Gleeson's Printers – Digital Design for the Digital Age' and was covered in pigeon shit. There was another shed across the way that was for importing Turkish wines, and all the windows had been smashed in. Looking back behind us I saw a hill, and I guessed, if that motorway was the M25, the city had to be somewhere on the other side of it. There was just one road heading up, no street lights, but there was that city-orange glow beyond it, and I knew, I just knew, it was London.

"Then I saw a car moving on the road on the hill, coming towards us. I wondered how long it'd be before Templeman worked out what had happened, so I hopped up onto my knees and said, 'We gotta get out of here.'

"Nabeela just nodded.

"'Hey, if I close my eyes, do you think you can do something about this tape around my feet?'

"'I'll try,' she said.

"So I closed my eyes, and it was hard. I mean, when your heart races and your head is pounding and you're still breathless and scared and waiting for something to move, it's hard. But then, looking: that would have been harder; that would have been death. And she kinda wriggled round behind me and started scratching at the tape around my legs until it tore and my feet came proper free. We still had these fucking handcuffs but, with all the guys turned to concrete, I guessed there wasn't anything we could do about that and at least we could walk now, so I nodded towards the road and said, 'We gotta get going before they come looking for us.'

"'Perhaps you should leave me.'

"'Fuck that, babes, no offence.'

"'I mean it. If you look at me ...'

"'I won't look.'

"'If you look at me ...'

"'Babes, I love you, seriously, you're really sweet and that, but in case you haven't worked it out I am one shit-stubborn bitch and I'm telling you, either you fucking come with me right now or I don't move an inch, okay?'

"I thought she might say no, and then how fucked would we be?

"But she whispered, 'Okay.'

"'Great! Probably safest thing, yeah, is if I walk, like, ten yards in front or something. And I won't look back, and you won't say boo, and we'll be fine. Can't be too far from here to somewhere with proper civilised magic, right?'

"'Right.'

"So we went, past these three frozen statues, eyes staring at nothing, while Nabeela's hair writhed on her head, and made a noise like metal rustling against metal. I wished I knew something about stars, could find north and work out if we were outside Barnet or Croydon, Upminster or Uxbridge. But the sky was a fuzzy orange-pink on black, and there was nothing to focus on, except the tug of the city.

"I could hear Nabeela walking behind me. It made me stiff, my head locked on my shoulders, like I didn't dare turn it, like my own body wouldn't let me turn it, and the more I didn't look the harder it became. Your mind plays tricks, you start thinking maybe you can't hear Nabeela behind you, maybe it's someone else coming up behind, someone else gonna grab you by the neck and stick a knife in your ribs; that there's something there in the dark, watching you, laughing.

"I tried, like, a dozen different things to calm me down. I tried breathing slow and deep, but that just made me breathless because the deeper I breathed in the faster I had to breathe out, like too much time was wasted getting air into the corner of my lungs. I tried counting, one two three four, one two three four, but the numbers just got faster and faster, like my thoughts were out of control. I looked at my own feet and broke up my steps into rhythms, into groups of eight, but then I was scared of looking up, and then, when I looked up, I was scared because I wasn't looking down again. I mean, everyone says how you shouldn't be afraid but I'm, like, fuck that, you should be afraid, everyone should be fucking afraid, bravery is all about being scared and carrying on despite it. So yeah, I was scared. And proud of it.

"The road from the estate led up this hill. There were trees either side, not thick forest-like, but close enough that the light stopped way too fast. At one point I heard an engine start and I went to hide, and Nabeela did too, and we crouched, the pair of us, behind the trees, mud up to our ankles, squatting like we were having a really difficult piss.

"And this van went by. I watched it go down the hill, to where the sheds were. I saw tiny men moving against a little light, and then they saw the statues, and they moved faster, and the engine of that van didn't stop running, and then, I wasn't afraid. When it's all about staying alive, you don't have time to be scared.

"We ran.

"It was hard, keeping our balance with our hands behind our backs, but we ran. Every car that went by I shouted at, trying to get them to stop. The first two just sped up, I guess they thought we were having a prank, but the third slowed down in front of us. I could see this woman inside, turning her head back to look at us better, and she was getting out a mobile phone. Then, as we approached, she sped up again, drove away. We must have frightened her, and then I realised – Nabeela's hair. It was out, free, and that woman in the car was only one stupid fucking glance away from being frozen by it, one blink off being turned to concrete.

"And if she was calling the police, then how'd I know that the Aldermen wouldn't be listening, because that's what they do. They listen to the police, they use the cops, and now Templeman would be looking for us.

"We had to get off the road.

"I didn't know what time it was.

"I guessed by how quiet everything stood that it had to be early-late, the little hours of the morning. There was this muddy path between the trees, with a green sign saying 'Parkland Trail' and a bin for people to put dog muck in. We ran down it, and there wasn't any light, none at all; we slipped and stumbled on leaf mould and dirt. Eventually Nabeela held onto the back of my shirt and I tried to summon light.

"I pulled. I summoned light, a tiny twisted tangle of orange-pink that I dragged from the heat in my body and the pain in my head and the stain on the sky, a glimmer that drifted along at feet-level to mark the path, the weakest will o' the wisp as ever got made.

"After a long, long while, the trees thinned out. The path sloped down onto an open grassy place.

"But it was proper grass, proper contained grass, inside a proper fence, kept under control by stomping feet and pissing dogs, kids playing football and all that shit, and beyond the grass . . .

" . . . God, I nearly laughed!

"Beyond all those fucking miles of grass, the city. South London. I never thought I'd be so fucking pleased to see it. It stretched out like a pinky-sodium star-map in front of us, neat little streets with neat little houses where everyone knows their neighbours and the kids can always find a quiet place to smoke after school, not much in the way of bloody landmarks except the odd red-topped mast and mobile phone tower, and the odd bit of rising dark in places like Norwood and that, but still, all around, my city.

"It all came back then, like light that had been hiding just behind a wall, just out of reach; it went straight in through my pupils so hard and hot I thought I was gonna burn; but I felt it inside me again, proper city magic, big and wide as that ten-million-light horizon, deep as night and strong as street stone, and the light at my feet grew brighter and stronger and I almost started to turn to Nabeela, to hug her or something, before I remembered just how fucking stupid that would be. But I thought I could hear the metal moving on the top of her head and, to me, it sounded like excitement.

"'We're gonna make it,' I breathed. 'We are gonna bloody make it.'

"'I know,' she replied. 'I think . . .'

"And that was when Templeman shot her.

"I felt it, as well as heard it.

"Her blood was on the back of my neck.

"It was on my arms.

"She must have been standing close.

"You know how gunshots are supposed to be really loud?

"I guess it was, but I wasn't listening for it, and the sound just sorta spread out big across that big bit of grass, so I suppose my brain didn't connect at first. But my body did, because I turned and she was falling, already falling, and as she fell her eyes closed and all the hair on her head went sorta limp, wriggling down and dying around her, a few cables twitching but everything else soggy. Living, she'd been awesome; dead, and the freakiness of that stuff on her head was suddenly horrifying, blood curling round the places where metal met skin.

"He came out of the darkness behind her, gun in hand. It was a little thing, and he held it out to one side like a proper gangster. His eyes were flecked with yellow, only really visible when he turned his head too fast, like the flash of a reflective jacket caught at a funny angle, and he was breathing fast. He didn't speak, didn't have nothing to say, just turned the gun right towards me and I screamed.

"Not girl-scream.

"Not standing-on-a-table-oh-shit-look-a-mouse scream.

"I screamed a city. I turned my face towards him and I screamed from that place inside where all the light and the dark and the shadows went; I screamed the echo of a gunshot in the night and the look in Nabeela's closing eye, the taste of concrete and fear, the smell of streetlight and shadows, the touch of night and the cold of day; I screamed the rolling drops of blood running down the back of my neck, the straight pattern of the streets pressed against my back, the pain in my legs and the ice in my fingers, the shriek of the culicidae and chitter of slate legs on brick, the memory of a bridge on the river and the sound of falling paper; I screamed everything, so long and so loud that the lights began to go out in the streets beneath me and the red beacons on the spires behind grew to a point and burst into black. I screamed until the streetlight spun on the surface of the clouds and I kept on screaming because my friend was at my feet,

"And Templeman staggered back like a seagull against the wind, putting his hands to his head, chin turning upwards in pain, and I kept screaming until the blood rolled from his nose and from his ears and the gun turned red hot in his hands and he dropped it and the tears rolled from his eyes and the tears were amber-yellow, tree-gum goo and his body bent like I'd hit it in the middle and then bent again like I'd punched it in the stomach and then bent a third time and I had fingers in his lungs and I was squeezing, squeezing the breath out of him and making it mine, digging in deep, trying to pop him from the inside out, stepping over the body of my friend to move that little bit closer so I could see the eyes bulge in his skull and . . .

"(Give me back my hat!)

" . . . and I guess something in the way he looked reminded me of . . . I dunno what. His tongue was lolling out of his mouth and his arms were twitching at odd angles, and I remembered . . .

"Give me back my hat!

" . . . remembered the way it had been that night on London Bridge, when everything had hurt so much and everything had burnt and I hadn't meant to, but I'd made something bad, and this was the same, this was it, déjà vu, that pain again but so much deeper and so much more, and I knew I could scream forever and this time, nothing would be able to shut me up except me.

"And it was the hardest thing I'd done.

"Harder than not watching my back when scared of a knife.

"Harder than running through the darkness with a medusa at my side.

"Harder than looking at a guy with a gun and knowing he wanted to make me die.

"That was nothing.

"Stopping – that took everything I had.

"But I did.

"I stopped.

"And it was like I had nothing left; I just fell forward onto my hands and knees, and my foot fell on Nabeela's arm as I slipped down, but she wasn't complaining, her head turned to one side, blood and thicker lumps of stuff on her face. And, fuck me, but Templeman was still on his feet, curling round, his hands over his ears like the echo of the sound was still going through his brain, but he looked at me and there was something in the way he opened his mouth, a tightening in the air about him, and I knew, whatever it was, it wasn't over.

"Then he shouted right back at me.

"It wasn't a shout like I had done, it was something that came from inside him, and him alone, a force in the pit of his belly, and as he opened his mouth I saw something move behind his teeth, staining them yellow, and I threw up a wall between him and me on instinct, not knowing I had the strength to do it, and this stuff came from out of his mouth, this cloud of yellow dust, it burst out of him like a sand-storm and knocked back against my shield hard enough to make me gasp, the blood drum in my head, and there was stuff moving in the dust. There was water in my eyes I was like working that hard to keep my shield up, keep something between me and it, but I saw still, as the yellow stuff surrounded me, I saw the way it moved and it wasn't moving like a normal thing: it swirled and it danced and it spun, and sometimes, if you were feeling imaginative, you could say that faces screamed out of that cloud before they melted again into nothing.

"And it kept on coming, sound lost now, world lost now behind the dust.

"But Nabeela's blood was still on my face and I'd be damned if I got killed by some fucking psychopath in fucking Croydon. So I stood up. My knees shook so bad I couldn't balance on my left at all and had to try again with my right, hardly able to keep more than an inch of magic between the end of my nose and that roaring yellow stuff, hands still behind my back. But I got up and, for my next trick, I took a step, and then another, and then another, moving towards Templeman, and with each step I took, it got harder, and harder, until my head was bent forward double and the cloud of dust was sparking like welding iron off my shield.

"He was just a shadow in the storm, a fuzzy dark shape, but I pushed and pushed again until I couldn't see for the fire blasting off my shield as to where it met his spell, but I knew, I knew he was almost there, right in front of me, near enough that I could almost touch, and I took one last step and closed my eyes tight and took the warmth from out my skin and out my bones and I took the beating of my own heart and listened for it, for that de-dum, that moment between the beat and when it came again; I took the strength inside me and the rhythm of my blood and I threw it at him with everything I had.

"Something hot and bright and white burst across my skin, across the skin I wore just outside my skin, slammed into the dust-storm and broke outwards, with that sound exploding flour makes, a *whoomph* not a boom, a *vroom* not a bang, a sound that you can't hear because it's so high and so low and so everywhere all at once that the only part of you capable of feeling it is that squishy bit in your belly, and the hollow bit in your bones where it echoes up and down your body, and I was thrown right back, landing so hard I thought I had to have broken something, and he went flying back too, into the trees, landing with a crack against one of the branches.

"For a while we both just lay there.

"My head was spinning; all I could see were these dancing yellow stars.

"I think he tried to get up and then cried out in pain.

"The fucker broke something.

"Good.

"Hope it was one of those fucking breaks where the fucking bone sticks out of your arm, so you can like see all the little cracked ends and the veins and shit.

"Somewhere a long way off, a siren was wailing.

"I rolled over and I'd been lucky, I'd landed on grass made soft by rain, but I still fucking hurt everywhere and knew in my belly that that was it, game over, nothing left that wasn't the end of the world, that wasn't going to be more than I had to give. I'd taken the strength from a beat of my heart, and now the blood rushed back to the corners of my body like it was making up for lost time, and everything hurt.

"Blue light somewhere behind the trees.

"Someone had called the cops.

"Someone who knew more about what guns sounded like than me.

"I heard him try to get to his feet and that made me try to get to mine.

"I fell on my first go, landed right next to Nabeela, saw a place in the back of her head where the bullet went in, and wanted to puke. I crawled away on my belly and Templeman was trying to get up, shaking with pain. I didn't have much left in me, but I saw the gun, still warm from where he'd dropped it. I crawled towards it, rolled onto my back, felt in the grass for the butt of it, found it, held it tight. Its heat burnt, but a good burning. I sat up on the grass, turned my body to the side so I had some kinda shot at him, and pulled the trigger.

"I must have missed by miles, I couldn't fucking aim with the thing, but he didn't know that. I saw him stagger up, and I fired again and he wasn't waiting twice; he crawled away and I fired, and just kept on firing until the gun was empty and he was a fleeing shadow in the dark. Then I dropped the gun. He wasn't coming back. Coppers were coming and we were both fucked.

"I sat there.

"I should have said something smart.

"I should have cried or something.

"I should have . . .

" . . . something.

"I guess when you're a kid, you learn from your parents that you're supposed to smile at funny things. And then you learn that you're supposed to cry when you see someone bigger than you cry, and you learn that you're supposed to shout when you're angry, because that's what your stupid primary school teacher did that day you dropped the paint pot on her new trousers.

"I hadn't learnt what you do when your friend is dead at your side.

"I hadn't got lessons in how to look when there's blood on your face.

"So I just sat.

"She'd understand.

"After a while, the blue lights stopped moving.

"I heard people among the trees.

"I thought about sitting there longer.

"Or, I guess, that part that thinks with words thought about sitting longer. The part that thinks with words explained it all, said sorry, sorry, sorry to Nabeela, and didn't move. But the part that doesn't need a voice to speak said, shift your arse, woman, there's a dead medusa by your side and you are still totally screwed if you sit around, and it was right, so I moved, thinking still, sorry, sorry, sorry.

"I headed down the hill, towards the city.

"Sick and tired.

"I walked to that place where green belt begins to stop and city begins to start.

"Once-country lanes, big houses with big gardens on cul-de-sac roads, with alleys round the side that lead into football pitches. Retirement houses, new estates in yellow brick where Ideal People lead Ideal Lives.

"There was a church with a tower, and the tower had a clock put up there by the kind donation of Mr and Mrs Woods, and it said it was nearly six a.m. Even Croydon would start to wake up soon, from the weird dog-walkers who don't mind the cold to the kids with a long school run.

"I got rid of the handcuffs, finally, when I found the tram track. London isn't big on trams, but I kinda liked this route just because of that, because it was strange, and different, and new. There was enough electricity above the track for me to drag it in, enough that I managed to put some into my fingers and burn the chains between the cuffs. The things were still locked around my wrists, but at least I could move my hands now, and I figured that, in this town, handcuffs were probably just another fashion statement.

"The sun was coming up by the time I got to the central station. Croydon comes in three parts. There's the scummy shitty suburban part, full of people too skint to find anywhere closer to better things, who live in council houses that were designed to be ideal homes and haven't stopped leaking since. Then there's the posh leafy part, where the trees are tall and the cars are smooth, where in the spring there's blossom in the gardens and on the streets and where your kid can learn horse riding without having to drive for an hour and a half to do it. Finally there's the shopping bit, where every shop has a sale, and you just walk round and round and round trying to find your way out even though you aren't really inside anything, and where all the signs pointing towards the bus stops lie, and you're never more than fifty yards from a hamburger and a Diet Coke.

"I kinda walked round and round for a while there.

"Sure, even kick-ass awesome sorceresses get lost in shopping centres sometimes.

"And, sure, I didn't know where to go.

"Templeman had taken my mobile phone, my wallet.

"I remember thinking that Femi's number was in my phone, I didn't have it written down anywhere else; that's one hot date I'm not gonna make any time soon. Then I felt ashamed for thinking about that, when I should have been thinking about nothing except grief. Didn't seem right to do nothing but cry. Didn't seem respectful to do more than stand still in one place, until I was like stone too.

"But the sun was coming and the brain-that-has-no-words kept me moving.

"There was a public toilet in the train station. It stank and everything was lit blue to stop the junkies shooting up, but I didn't care. I washed at my face and my hands and the back of my neck, scrubbed with soap and then a bit more until my skin felt like barbecued bacon. Then I went to the first newsagent I could find and stole a bottle of water and a packet of crisps. I'd never stolen in my life before, but I did it now and didn't feel anything while I did it. I got pissed off after, because there wasn't any recycling bin on the station and that's just shit, because it's a railway station and there should be like some government directive saying there should be a recycling bin there or something because it's public property and we all use it and everyone drinks water on the train anyway.

"Then I got onto the platform by tricking the ticket machine; kicked it until it thought I had a ticket and beeped me through. Then I took the first train I could find. It was going to London Bridge and it was crowded, even at this time. I got a seat by using my elbows, and the woman opposite me didn't meet my eye all the way; she was afraid. There were those free newspapers. I tried to read one but kept going back over and over the same line, not taking it in. All I can remember is that Wayne has been seen on the piss with Rochelle, and I don't even know what that fucking means.

"London Bridge was too busy, too crowded, and I realised even the second I got off the platform my mistake.

"Or maybe it wasn't a mistake, I don't know; maybe there is like some higher power or something.

"Whatever, once I was there, I couldn't exactly not do it, so I walked out of the concourse and up onto the bridge proper. It's a crap bridge, you know. Nice at night when they light it up pink and stuff, but you've got Tower Bridge over there, which is all famous, and you've got Southwark Bridge over there, which at least has that kinda green nobbly thing going for it, and then London Bridge in the middle, which is just shit.

"But whatever. Let's pretend like we're not architects for a minute and go, okay, I walked out onto London Bridge. And even though it's just a flat bit of concrete, I could feel everything it had been, all the bridges that had gone before, right back to the days when it was sticks and stones and falling down for some fair lady. And I walked to the middle of it, to the place where the wind was strongest and icy cold and turns your ears first to pain, then numb, and I looked towards the east and breathed out, and remembered the sound of paper and the pain in my belly, and wished that it could just wash away with the tide.

"I dunno how long I stood there.

"Something about time.

"So much time beneath me, around me, in the water under my feet and in the place where this bridge ran, that minutes and hours kinda lose their meaning.

"I stood and I looked at nothing and everything, and the wind numbed my face and my hands, my body and my back, and I felt almost clean.

"I guess the rest isn't that great.

"I tried to find you.

"I thought about calling you, dialling your number, but then I thought if Templeman was fucking with you, he'd probably have your phone.

"Then I thought about the Aldermen – I mean, not all of them can be psycho-bastards, right?

"But just because one or two might be okay, didn't mean I knew which ones they were.

"Then I thought about trying the beggars, but I didn't know the rituals, the right way to start.

"I considered maybe a summoning. An electric elemental might know, or maybe the Old Bag Lady; see if she had any tips; but then I decided I couldn't take the abuse.

"Finally I went for the safest sorta option.

"I went to the Tower of London.

"Do you know how fucking expensive the tickets are to the Tower? And it's hard to just bluff your way in; there's magic in those old stones that doesn't like being tampered with, rock-deep magic that makes it really hard to trick the eye of the security guys on the door. I ended up having to go several streets away, pinch some cash from a banker whose wallet was, like, hanging out his back pocket anyway, and *pay* for an actual ticket at the Tower gate. And the sandwiches are stupid; I mean, they're not very good for starters, and then it's like five pound something for a bit of scrambled egg between two slices of rubbery bread.

"Then it was really hard finding what I needed to without getting shouted at, because I was still wearing these bloody handcuffs and I had to pull my sleeves right down and act all natural and people kept looking at me funny, but okay, whatever. I set off an alarm in the gallery where they keep the crown jewels and, when everyone went running there, I went down onto the grass beneath the keep and found a raven.

"It was bigger than I'd expected, and wore this tag round its left leg, but I figured if anything could bloody find the Midnight bloody Mayor in this fucking city, it would be a raven of the Tower. So while no one was looking, I tore my stupidly bloody expensive sandwich in half, and fed the raven one half, and it looked okay with it, and didn't puke or go for the eyes or nothing, and then I left all nonchalant like while the coppers tried to work out what the hell was wrong with the alarms, and went out along the river.

"And you know how in the centre of the city there's all those little churchyards left over, I mean, tiny places with stone graves where the names have been rubbed off and where a bomb must have dropped or something because there's maybe one spire left standing and no church, and it's all shadowed over by these great fat buildings? Well, I went to one of them and sat down and got out the other half of my sandwich and waited for the raven to come, and finally it did.

"I think all the ravens are supposed to be called after Norse gods or something, but this one looked like a Dave to me, and I fed it the sandwich and talked nice to it, and finally drew the symbol of the Midnight Mayor on the ground with a stick, and it seemed to get it, because it hopped up and started flying west immediately.

"And there was a bike hire place really close by, and I know how you're not really supposed to take the bikes out of the congestion-charge zone, but it wasn't like I knew where the raven was going to go so I sorta . . . borrowed . . . one of these bikes and started following the raven. It would fly a bit and then land and wait, and then fly a bit more, and land and wait, and keep on flying and, you know what, but this city is fucking big. I mean, I know it's not exactly Mexico City or got twenty million people in it or something, but as someone who has now, personally, cycled across most of it following this one stupid bloody bird, I can tell you that it's sodding huge and it's a fucking miracle I'm still walking.

"I followed that raven, then, from the Tower of fucking London, west. Embankment, Westminster, Victoria, Earls Court – some wanker in a van nearly mowed me down at bloody Hammersmith and a copper shouted at me for being on a blue Boris bike that shouldn't be outside the congestion-charge zone, but he was on foot and I just pedalled away. Chiswick, which was posh, Gunnersbury, which wasn't, and then all these samey streets with samey little houses and still this raven kept on flying on and by now I was shattered, I was ready for bed, but it seemed to know what it was doing until finally, about an hour ago, it stops above this bloody house in this place called Osterley, wherever the hell here is, and caws a bit and preens and looks pretty pleased with itself, and I go up and knock on the front door and Kelly answers it and she says, 'Oh my God! Ms Ngwenya!'

"And I can't remember what I fucking said, but she seemed to understand.

"So yeah. That's what I gotta say.

"The sandwiches out there, by the way, they aren't for you. I mean, I figured having flown from Tower Bridge to Osterley, I should probably give Dave the raven more than a shit egg sandwich, so all the shopping I've just got, that's mostly for him. And the coffee is for me, but if you're lucky you can have some, if Dr Seah says it's okay. And I guess I stole a bicycle. And a wallet. And jumped some train fares. Sorry. And Nabeela is dead. She's dead and Templeman killed her. And I tried to kill Templeman but he ran away. And he's on something, Matthew. I don't know what it is but he's on something big and bad and nasty and, if I were you, I'd be seriously scared. And I'm tired. I'm really, really tired. I think that's it. I think that's all I got left to say."

Penny sat, a rag-woman in muddy clothes, on the side of the bed, shoulders bending with each breath, and said nothing more.

I put my bandaged hand on hers.

She was still wearing the remnants of the handcuffs around her wrists. Blood had dried in little spots on the metal.

Night had settled on the street outside.

In the kitchen, the Vintage Classics of the 1980s were playing at a lower level.

The radiator ticked.

The radio went onto a different song.

Penny said, "I hate this tune."

"Why?"

"Everyone talks pretentious crap about it. Like how it's all about female enfranchisement and race and stuff, when in fact it's just another smoochy love song."

I listened a while longer. "Oh yeah," I said at last. "I get it."

"And people say like 'The music of the 1980s, it's so great' and I'm going 'Why's it great?' and they go 'Because it's so crap' and I don't get that. I mean, I know I wasn't around for much of the 1980s, but I really hate it when older people are all 'Things were so much better in my day' and you go, 'Yes, the world before the collapse of communism – wow what a place.'"

So saying, she fell silent again.

I cleared my throat, and regretted it, as pain referred its way down to my elbows. She must have seen me flinch, because she turned on the edge of the bed and said, "Hey, what is up with you and the, like, mega-medical action anyway? Only you don't exactly look like the living Apollo to begin with, but did you have to go get all Dr Frankenstein on me?"

"Frankenstein's monster," I corrected. "I mean, if we're talking looking like crap."

"What?"

"The monster wasn't called Frankenstein."

"What was the monster called?"

"I don't know. 'Monster', I guess."

"I can see how that might've sucked – like kinda not leaving you many career options, is it? Besides, you got what I mean, so don't talk like you've got an English Lit degree shoved up your arse."

"I'm just saying . . ."

"You're doing the avoiding thing," she corrected sharply. "So here's the real question, then. How bad was it, and do I want to know?"

I thought a while. Then, "It was bad. And no, you don't want to know."

"There'll be a day when you want to tell me about it."

"I know. But can we just put it off a little while longer?"

Silence again, but it was shorter, playing its not-noises to a different non-tune. At length Penny stood up quickly, looking anywhere that wasn't directly in my eye, and blurted, "So what the hell happens now?"

Kelly made dinner.

She said, "I'm really sorry, Mr Mayor, I didn't have time to stock up on the proper ingredients and the local shop was completely out of fresh coriander so that was that plan out of the window . . ."

Penny was already halfway through her third forkful and accelerating. I took an experimental mouthful. Then another.

" . . . honestly, I would have thought the kitchen would be better stocked but, essentially . . ."

"What is this stuff?" asked Penny.

"It's seared tuna with a glass noodle in sweet curry sauce, and fragrant sansho pepper, mango and shiso salad on the side with just a pinch . . ."

"It's totally bloody awesome!"

"And you found this . . . round the corner?" I queried.

"The trick is to be imaginative with your flavour combinations," Kelly explained, doing her best not to flap as she stood in the door. "It's not about many strong flavours all at once, but about several clean flavours which you can take one at a time, to complement each other during the meal as a whole experience. I also found some clothes which might fit you, Ms Ngwenya, if you want to change, and there's a hot bath running in the next room and I've turned on the radiator in the living room and I think that at nine there's a detective drama on the telly which might be worth watching . . ."

"Oh my God, is there ice cream? I love sitting in front of the TV, in a blanket, with the fire on, eating ice cream; it's, like, the only good thing about when someone splits up with you."

"I think there might be some strawberry ice cream . . ."

"Can we eat it from the tub?" demanded Penny. "I mean, don't get me wrong, this meal is like ... totally awesome ... but seriously, ice cream from the tub in front of the TV – what did you say was on the telly? It's not that one with the guy with the big hair, is it?"

"I'm sure at some point we're supposed to do something noble and brave about the state of the city," I quavered.

"Bloody hell, haven't you heard of fucking working hours?" shrilled Penny. "You're like that monster that doesn't even have a name and I'm shattered and Kelly here has, like, done the cooking and the washing up and I'm just saying, do you think a half-hour sit-down will kill us?"

We sat in front of the TV.

Kelly had the armchair, and flitted in and out with fresh tea, hot water bottles and a seemingly unending supply of biscuits and ice cream.

Penny sat next to me on the sofa, a blanket pulled up to her chin.

We dimmed the lights down low.

On the TV, a detective with big hair strode around the city untangling enigmatic mysteries and foiling deadly plots with a gusto that left me feeling exhausted.

Penny's head somehow ended up on my shoulder, her legs swinging round and tucking in on the sofa.

Her eyes were drifting shut even before it was revealed that the cabbie dunnit all along. Kelly sat forward in her chair, fingers pressed to the arms of the seat, eyes wide, mug of tea forgotten at her feet.

I pulled the blanket a little tighter around Penny's shoulders and didn't move.

Hero and villain danced around in an intricate and dazzling game of life and death.

Not even the final gunshot woke Penny up.

The credits rolled to the sound of a presenter inviting the audience to change channels now for a celebrity quiz programme on this week's special theme of male leg waxing.

Penny's head slipped from my shoulder and bounced against my chest. I started, dragging in breath, and the movement was enough to wake her up. She sat up, eyes rimmed with gum, and Kelly said, "Let me see if I can find a spare toothbrush ... " and led her upstairs.

I watched the TV a while longer.

On another channel, a different detective was solving a different drama. Two channels over, and two men and a token woman were talking about cars in the language of drunken magi who've seen the Christ-child but weren't impressed. One channel over from that, and three teenagers with Liverpudlian accents stood on the balcony of a council estate and screamed at each other, a proper circular argument with no beginning, no end, and a touch of mood lighting thrown in. The ice cream was reaching that melted consistency where refreezing would just create soft mush. It was a baby pink colour, with the occasional solid frozen strawberry trapped inside. I licked the spoon when I was done, and dropped it in the empty tub.

Kelly came back into the room just as the news was doing its regional recap of the Silly Local Story of the Day. Tonight it was a guide to the ten worst potholes in London – which local councils should we hold to account?

"Penny's in bed," she murmured, still-house soft.

"Sleeping?"

"Maybe."

"Good. You should go home," I said. "Go to the office tomorrow morning, carry on like nothing's happened."

"Something *has* happened," she replied. "Templeman ... the Minority Council ..."

"The Beggar King has cursed Rathnayake in front of you all. Templeman went up against my apprentice and the final score was nil–nil without extra time. There are three men turned to stone on a commercial estate outside Croydon, Caughey is mad and the culicidae's heart has been purged and is currently sat in the kitchen fridge. Penny was right. Time to breathe."

"The fairy godmother ... ?"

"You're a good cook, you know that?"

She hesitated, unsure whether to beam proudly or not. "Thank you."

"How'd you end up in this life?"

A smile teetered on her face, then broke free. "Well," she said, "with a degree in International Law and Economics and a Masters in Actuarial Science, it was either this or back to the checkout at my local Sainsbury's."

It felt like a while since I'd smiled and meant it.

"I'll see you tomorrow, Kelly."

"Tomorrow, Mr Mayor."

"And thanks for everything."

"Just doing my job!" she beamed.

I waited for the sound of the door to close and the snap of her heels on the pavement outside, before I turned off the TV.

In the bathroom I put my head under, first, the cold tap, then the hot, then the cold again.

I looked at myself in the mirror.

It was hard to use my fingers properly, but I got a fist around the handle of a toothbrush, and scrubbed.

I checked on Penny.

I didn't know if she was sleeping, or merely pretending.

Either way, I let her be.

My coat and shoes were in the bathroom. Someone had toyed with the idea of cleaning the vestments of the Beggar King, and changed their mind. I pulled them on, left Penny a note by the front door, found a bin bag at the bottom of a kitchen drawer, and opened the fridge.

The culicidae's heart was still, cold and silent on the top shelf, wrapped up in kitchen foil.

I put it in my bag, tied a knot at the top, picked up the spare keys to the flat, and let myself out.

There is a moment in all big cities when the traffic stops. It may only last a few moments, through a tiny pause, a trick of the traffic lights. But when it happens it is louder than an engine as it backfires, deeper than the roar of the double-decker bus.

It was there, as I stepped out into the dark Osterley night.

A moment when the traffic stops.

I tightened my grip around my black bin bag, pulled the coat of the Beggar King tighter around my shoulders, picked a direction that looked like it might lead towards a main road, and walked.

This was my city.

Midnight Mayor.

Light, life, fire.

Osterley was built from timber and concrete. The flagstones sang where they were loose in the pavement, the cars slept in tiny little drives, the newsagents were local, the cul-de-sacs were residential, and the roads were main.

I walked and the traffic fled before me, though the drivers did not know why.

The lights bent as we passed.

Pigeons watched us from their dens, the rats scampered beneath our feet.

As we moved, our shadow turned and turned again, a sundial's darkness moved by street glow, and our shadow was not our own. Sometimes we thought it had wings of black dragon-leather. Sometimes we thought its hands dripped, staining the cracks in the paving stones as it passed. I could feel the places where the bikers moved, those thin points in the architecture of the city where *here* became like *there* and it was possible to jump the gap without mucking around with the spaces in between. Ley lines crackled underfoot, following the passage of the underground tunnels, the old water pipes, the silent whirling gas, the dance of electricity. We put our head to one side and could hear the voices in the telephone lines overhead, far-off whispers of

Hey babe
So next week any
Sorry I didn't call
Missed you
Midnight Mayor.

This was our city.

We caught the last train of the night, heading east, back to where it began.

It was called Avalon.

It was still, against all expectations, a nightclub.

Some nights ago, I'd stood outside its doors and explained to a bouncer about my mega-mystical pinkies, because my mobile phone suggested that Meera's mobile phone was inside those walls, calling out to me.

Some nights ago, I hadn't even heard of fairy dust.

Look what had happened.

There was a new bouncer on the door.

I walked up the thin red carpet to the silver door, and he glanced at me and said, "Sorry, sir."

We looked him in the eye and saw the colour drain from his face. We whispered, "Walk away," and he carefully reached up to his armband, pulled it off, let it fall from his fingertips, turned, and walked away, to where we knew not.

At our back, our shadow twisted with pleasure, arms flexing, dreaming of flight.

Down the stairs, back down into the pounding, pulsing dark of the club, taste of magic on the air, booming music from the speakers, and drinks that fluoresced in the low blue light.

I looked, and didn't have to look long before I found a woman with sickly yellow eyes who split from her friends to go into the ladies' toilet. I followed her, using speed to make up for the incongruity of my appearance, shoved past a drunken woman in six-inch heels who half fell past me out of the door, marched into the glowing dark of the toilet, grabbed the woman with the yellow-tinted eyes by the hair and put my hand over her mouth before she had a chance to scream.

"You're a fairy," I breathed. "You're addicted to fairy dust. Scream and I'll break your neck, do you understand? Just nod."

She nodded, once, slowly.

"You're going to give me the name and address of your supplier. Then I'm going to let you go. First I'm going to tell you this. The fairy dust will kill you. You will turn into dust yourself and your body will be swept up in a nice, clean plastic bag, and sold onto the next punter to sniff. Quit the dust, don't quit the dust, I really don't care and doubt I can make a difference, but as a public service and just in case, I figured I'd let you know. Nod if you understand."

She nodded. Her little red dress had been zipped up so tight that a roll of flesh bulked over its low back. Now it shook visibly with the rest of her body.

"Right. I'm letting you go. Remember, if you scream, I break your neck. Tell me where to find your supplier."

She was an addict.

She wasn't stupid.

She told me where.

I let her go.

There was a taxi rank outside Charing Cross station.

The taxis came into the station forecourt, swung round the great neo-Gothic spike, adorned with sombre stone kings, that once marked the very centre of the city, waited, and then swerved back out into the stop-start traffic of the Strand and Trafalgar Square.

I queued.

When it was my turn, I let the people behind me take the first cab that came.

Then I let the next couple take the one after.

Then I waited a little longer.

The third cab that pulled up was black, like all its neighbours, with the yellow 'For Hire' sign illuminated above the windscreen, but there was a man already in the back.

He opened the passenger door as I leant down, and said, "You going my way?"

"Sure," I replied, and got in.

We pulled away.

Inside the cab, the man sat next to me was already busy, snapping open a large briefcase. He barely bothered to look at me as he said, "Okay, let's talk cash . . ."

Then he smelt me.

His nose twitched in sudden distress and he looked up and, for the first time, met my eye, and he recognised me and I recognised him. Fear spread across his face. I leant across the seat, clawing our right hand around his face, index and middle finger below each eye. The street lights filed peacefully by as the cab swung round towards Westminster.

He had the good sense not to move.

"Morris Prince," I breathed. "So you survived the Soho dust-house."

"Dudley Sinclair," he hissed. "Or whatever the hell your name is. You are a dead man."

We held up our right hand. He looked, and took in the scars carved into our flesh, the twin crosses, the badge of the Midnight Mayor, and his eyes grew wider.

"I'm surprised the fairy godmother is still talking to you," I said. "After all, you did let me destroy your business. Or is selling from the back of a cab your new demotion?" I saw the corner of his mouth twitch, and my smile grew wider. "Oh, it is. Well, can't look good on the CV, can it? Morris Prince, owner of the Soho dusthouse. At 10 p.m.

he was a smug murdering bastard with everything to live for, and by three in the morning he was just a murdering bastard. And why? Because he got played. If it's any comfort, we all get played. I've been played like pipes at a ceilidh – you barely made it to the tambourine." I reached past him and pulled the briefcase off his lap.

There was a little snap-click behind my head.

The taxi had stopped.

In the reflection on the rear windscreen, I saw the shape of the driver, gun in hand, turned in his seat, ready to pull the trigger. Our eyes stayed fixed on Prince's.

"Tell him to let us go," we breathed. "Or everyone and everything in this cab will burn."

"You can't be the Midnight Mayor," he whispered. "It's a bluff."

"Which part about it confuses you? Is it the power, the strength, the darkness, the magic?" Sparks coiled around our fingers, danced in front of his eyes; he flinched at the brightness. "I get it. You're confused by the outfit. You don't understand why a Midnight Mayor is wearing the vestments of the Beggar King. What crap luck you must have, to piss off every major power in the city. Or maybe it's our eyes. Maybe you look at us and know, deep down inside, that we were never human. Perhaps that's what you can't understand."

"A bullet will still kill you," he wheezed.

"Will it?" I asked. "What part will it kill? My body, sure, that will rot and turn to muck; but then again, will it? What are the blue electric angels, if not more than flesh and bone? What is the Midnight Mayor, if not a power as eternal as the stones themselves? You think it's worth it, then, sure, get your guy to pull the trigger. See if killing one out of the three of us is good enough."

"He'd never . . . " blurted Prince, then stopped.

"He'd never . . . what?"

"He'd . . . the Midnight Mayor wouldn't have . . . he wouldn't . . . "

"Our infinite patience, on which many an epic ode shall one day be written, has been taxed by recent events," we murmured. "The Midnight Mayor wouldn't . . . what?"

Our fingers against the hollows of his eyes were leaving red marks.

"He . . . he . . . he wouldn't have done all this for some woman called Meera."

We hesitated.

I smiled.

Wanted to laugh.

Hurt inside.

"You know what," I said. "I think you're absolutely right. A proper Midnight Mayor wouldn't have bothered, would he? I mean, look at all the shit it's caused. But then again," I pushed a little deeper, "do you want to meet the real me?"

He must have gestured, because the shadow with the gun turned away, the safety clicking back on. I eased the briefcase of little yellow packets away from his lap, tucked it under one arm, smiled at him.

"Screwed over twice in one week," I exclaimed, pushing open the passenger door and stepping out into the cold night. "You might want to consider a different career, Mr Prince."

I slammed the door, and watched the taxi speed off.

I needed somewhere to work, out of the wind.

I crossed the river, to Waterloo Bridge.

There was a place beneath the walkways of the South Bank centre. By day it was full of kids on skateboards and tourists ogling their tricks; by night, a place of paint and grey shadows. Its concrete walls were a graffiti artist's paradise, scrawled with colour and movement that bore tags as mundane as 'Police Grey' through to a more political 'No To Cuts'. They changed every other day, as new contributors came in with their dirty bags and metal cans to spray on top of the thick bright paint. Look closely, and you could see the work of the Whites, those magicians who found life and power in the signs on the street. Some of the stones themselves echoed hollowly beneath these bridges, where imps and mean-eyed, foul-mouthed pixies had dug their lairs into the embankment floor, drawn by the powers at work on the walls. There were runes and wards, curses and invocations painted here; it was a good place for any magician to work, safe within its tangle of spray-thick magic.

I opened up Prince's briefcase, pulled out the bags of fairy dust. So many – even now I was surprised – and money too, thick wads that I gave up counting after the first grand and a half. At the bottom of the case itself was a ridge in the lining. I felt along it, found the tracking spell scratched with a scalpel into the leather itself, and rubbed it out with the ragged ends of my nails. I kept on tearing until I found the GPS tracker too, plugged into a tiny lithium battery. Magicians aren't good with technology. I let this one be.

Then I opened up the bags of yellow fairy dust, covering my nose and mouth with my sleeve as I did.

I spread them out in a circle on the ground, large enough to hold a man, patting down the edges like a chef fussing over a piece of pastry. I pulled the culicidae's heart out of its black bin bag and placed it in the centre of the circle. I rolled my sleeve up and looked for the tiny scab in the crook of my arm where Templeman had pushed the needle in. I scratched at it until it bled, and held my arm out over the centre of the circle until a few drops of blood had welled and dropped onto the heart itself, which hissed as they struck. The red blood flashed blue for an instant on impact, before sinking into the plastic shell of the heart.

I rolled my sleeve back down, and stood well away from the ring of dust. I turned my hands palm-upwards and breathed in the river smell, let it fill me, then breathed it out again. I whispered,

"Meera."

A ripple ran through the dust.

"Meera," I said again, and the ripple danced round the rim of yellow dust and, in the centre of the circle, the culicidae's heart contracted and expanded, just once.

There was no spell, no symbols I could define, but there didn't need to be.

Here was the sound of the river, the memory of a ride on the boat.

Here was breath of her breath on the air, dust of her dust on the ground.

Here the place where once her feet had walked, and the recollection of the place in which she had died.

No one can come back from the dead.

Or rather, nothing human.

I said again, "Meera!" and raised my hands as I did and the dust seemed to dance in its circle, leap upwards like iron filings towards a magnet, and the heart in the centre of the circle beat once, then twice. I pulled again, and again the dust swirled and spun, and now, when the heart pulsed inwards, so the dust moved in, and as the heart beat out again, so the dust rolled away.

And here was my blood on the floor and dust of her dust spinning in its circle.

And once, perhaps, we'd shared something that only we had known about, and it had been one night, and it had been barely a few words and a little breath, but the taste of it was real, a lifeline to the world.

I didn't know where the spell came from, or how it happened, but the words were there now, on my lips, and the dust was dancing, and I called out:

"In the sweat of thy face shalt thou eat bread, till thou return unto the ground; for out of it wast thou taken: for dust thou art, and unto dust shalt thou return."

The culicidae's heart shook with the strength of its own beat and now the dust was rushing into it, clinging to it, wrapping itself around the heart like a swarm of tiny insects, hiding it from view.

"My heart was hot within me, and while I was thus musing the fire kindled: and at last I spake with my tongue; Lord, let me know mine end, and the number of my days; and verily every man living is altogether vanity. For man walks in a vain shadow, and disquiets himself in vain: he heaps up riches, and cannot tell who shall gather them."

I couldn't see the heart now, didn't know where the words were coming from, but the fog was rising at my feet, the thick white fog that Meera had made, and the heart was rising inside its shell of dust, the dust itself shaping around the heart, the circle obliterated, forming a new, writhing pattern in front of me. I thought I heard someone shout from the bridge but didn't look, couldn't look away.

"Take thy plague away from me: I am even consumed by means of thy heavy hand. For I am a stranger with thee: and a sojourner, as all my fathers were. O spare me a little, that I may recover my strength, before I go hence, and be no more seen."

A shape now in the dust, the heart was gone, vanished, consumed by the whirling fairy dust, but whatever it had become was solidifying, stretching outwards and thickening, forming something liquid but upright, solid but moving, and to stop speaking now was to explode, voices and sounds that were not my own coming out on my breath, my breath flecked with yellow, and I gasped,

"Earth to earth, ashes to ashes, dust to dust; in sure and certain hope of the resurrection to eternal life!"

The spell snapped. It felt like an iron bar landing across my shoulders. I staggered forwards, head pounding, hauling down air. There were footsteps around me, men running; I sagged to my knees and looked up at the thing in front of me, which, though it had nothing I could call eyes to see, looked right back at me.

Alive.

It's alive.

Skin of dust, hair of dust, eyes of dust; it could only be called human in that it was trying to grow legs out of a solid trunk, in that it raised up arms and sprouted fingers which at once melted away to dust, subsumed back into the living whole. Sometimes it had a head which opened a mouth as if it would speak, but the mouth collapsed like sand before a wave and the head vanished back into the worm-body before a new head grew, and sometimes the head had the neck of a man and the chin of woman, and sometimes its shoulders were round and broad, and sometimes thin and bent and always, all the time, the thing in front of me morphed and rippled, swayed and moved, as it tried to find a shape, and found instead a thousand. Only one thing about it was consistent, a hot place in what I supposed had to be called its chest, a beating pounding thing beneath its dust skin, a core that might have been a heart.

Then someone shouted and there were men running towards me, men in suits; some held guns, some held wands. I heard a footstep behind me and looked round and a man was already there. He slammed the butt of his gun into the back of my head, knocking me to the ground, then grabbed me by the collar and pulled me back up, gun pressed to my head. I went passively with him, eyes still fixed on this creature of dust that stood before me, and whose eyes, when it had such, I felt were fixed on me.

Then a voice breathed, "What have you done?"

He stood there, in a bright white suit with a yellow striped tie, leaning on a silver-topped stick. I almost didn't recognise him outside the pool and not on drugs, but his voice was the same, though flecked with fear. Oscar Kramb, the fairy godmother, pushed through his men and past the empty briefcase, its GPS tracker exposed to the sky. He was staring at the living man-woman-thing of fairy dust, which turned its unformed head to look at him. An arm was forming, which tried holding a cane, before crumbling back into its own swelling surface. Mimicking, like a child, I realised. Alive, aware.

"What is it?" he breathed, eyes still fixed on the creature.

"It's Meera," I replied, and even the act of speaking earned me the gun pressed deeper against my skull, bending my neck to one side.

His eyes turned to me, and it was as if the act of seeing caused him to remember his hate, face darkening at the sight. "What do you mean, 'Meera'?" he barked. The fairy-dust creature recoiled, as if surprised by the harshness of his words.

"I mean," I replied, "that it's Meera. Or, at least, that part of her that lived in her final breath, that was captured in the moment of death, that could be defined by heart, head, hand, skin, flesh, bone. It is Meera, solid and whole, fed on the beating heart of a monster, brought to life with just a little blood, and a little magic, since, all things considered, she didn't exactly die a natural death."

Kramb moved round to inspect the creature from every side, and it shuffled a leg, trickling dust, to watch him in turn. "Of course," I added, "it's also a lot of other things. There's probably a Bob and a Joe, and a Mary and a Sarah, in there too. I mean, I haven't met anyone called Bob or Joe or Mary or Sarah lately, but it seems a fairly good guess that of all the thousands and thousands of people you've killed, four of them had these pretty ordinary names."

Kramb's scowl deepened. He nodded at the man with the gun to my head, who kicked my knees out from behind and, as I flopped to the ground, pushed my head further down with the barrel of the gun.

"You'll be wanting to ask what happens next!" I blurted. "I mean, obviously you'll kill me because, shit, who wants to see the same killing spree twice? But you'll be needing to ask yourself, 'What is up with this dust creature anyway? Why the hell has this really annoying Midnight Mayor guy summoned it; is he still on something? I mean, wow he's gotta be pretty mental to just let me come and find him with all my armed boys; I wonder if I should let him say something. I mean, that's what I'd be thinking, if I had half a brain.'"

"Go on, Mr Mayor," growled Kramb. "Spit it out."

I craned my neck upwards so I could just about see the creature, and it turned and looked back at me. "Meera," I breathed, and for just a moment it had eyes, and it saw, and it, was perhaps, a she. "I mean, shit," I whispered, "you killed them. You killed them all, Mr Godmother, because it kept you in caviar. Don't tell me you were fulfilling a demand. You could have stopped, and you didn't, so they died. And it wasn't a good death. Christ, but it wasn't a good death . . ."

An instant in which the features of this ever-changing creature were feminine; a second in which a hand rose from the dust as if in greeting.

" . . . and the culicidae's heart, you see, it was designed to focus in on one very specific thing – on anger, on rage – and to drain it out of the souls of its victims. Well this . . . this thing I've summoned; this . . . *her* . . ." – fingers evolved towards me, but they kept melting before they made it to the fingertips – " . . . she's fed on the same magics, made from the same spells. She's programmed to find fairy dust, to feed on it like the culicidae fed on anger, and nothing you do can stop it. Oscar, meet Meera. Not five minutes old, she is, and she's going to destroy the dusthouses."

There was a moment.

I think, perhaps, he understood.

Then, having understood, he chose not to believe, and raised his head to his boys and barked, "Kill him."

It doesn't take long to pull a trigger.

It took a fraction of a second less for the creature of dust to raise up a blob that might have been a head, stretch out arms longer than a human's should have been, stretching and thinning like a rubber band, and scream. It had no lungs to scream with, no muscle to stretch out the air, but it had dust that buzzed like a swarm of bees, and if a giant's foot had crushed the head of the hive's only queen, it could not have roared with a greater rage and hate than this thing gave, fuelled on dust, heart and magic.

I covered my head with my hands as the creature seemed to burst outwards, in an explosion made from whirling grains of dust, each grain bearing a sting; pressed my head down and felt it roll over me, knocking back the men who stood all around, submerging them in a storm of dust that was twice, three times, a hundred times the size and shape of the meagre packets I'd spilt over the culicidae's heart. I felt it burn against my skin, tried to breathe and lost all breath, tried to open my eyes and couldn't do it, thought I heard someone shout, but there was only the roaring of the dust, the sound of it, the heat of it and perhaps still very very faint somewhere behind

just a . . .
didn't mean . . .
never understood
just a . . .
. . . please why won't you?
kid

Then it parted.

I felt it move away, and now the roaring of the dust was further off, a background buzz. I forced my eyes open, squinting in the gloom, and tried hauling myself to my feet. I couldn't see the lights of the city: neither the reflections on the river nor the glow of the north bank. A dark wall hid them: a moving wall. I summoned a bubble of light, but all it did was to cast a pinkish-sodium glow on a patch of circle of ground just large enough to fit a corpse. There was no one to be seen, only a spinning prison of dust.

Then something curled round our ankle. I yelped and clenched my hands, ready to call fire.

A face that had been a man's stared up at me, eyes yellow, skin burnt by abrasion and hanging off in tatters, hair blasted from the skull, clothes stained the same smeary yellow as his eyes. He stared up at me and managed to gasp with what was left of his lungs, breath bursting with yellow as he did so, "You . . . you . . . you make it . . . make it . . . make . . ."

I staggered away from Oscar Kramb, and the wall of dust moved with me. He screamed as it passed over his feet, consumed his legs; his body shook, his hands clawed at the air. The dust closed in fast, rising over his back and shoulders, swallowing them up in a thickness that left no room for seeing, until only his head was visible, and he tried to scream but his breath turned to dust and his skin was flaking off his face in yellow rags and he tried to say something, or possibly beg, or maybe curse, but the dust swallowed him whole, consuming him in darkness.

It ended as quickly as it had begun.

The wall of dust seemed for a second to freeze on the air.

Then it fell, drifting downwards like snow on a still winter day. It fell into a circle all around me, piled far thicker than it had been at the start, and lay there, a bit of refuse in an ordinary, undisturbed night. Buses passed on the bridge overhead. Seagulls competed for discarded chips by a dumpster. A tug hauling a barge of yellow crates rumbled towards the estuary. Of Oscar Kramb and his men, nothing remained, except the undigested scraps of yellowed clothing and the guns they'd carried.

A light breeze caught the circle of dust and blew it along the ground. I recoiled as it tumbled towards my feet. The grains kept tumbling, even when the breeze had stopped, pooling together in thickening clumps, rising back up with a busy rattle, re-forming a little at a time, a yellow ant hill become a yellow spire, which became again a warping fragment of humanity. When the last few grains had been absorbed into its form, I looked at it, and it looked at me, face changing from male to female, happy to sad, body growing and shrinking as it mixed and matched, moving through various forms.

I saw nothing of Meera in it now.

Something animal in the way it turned its head.

Something alien in how it looked at the light.

We said, "Pain is difficult," and its head turned towards us, neck rippling with the movement. We held out our hands, placating, adding, "Though you are of humans, you are not human. That is difficult too."

Its body shimmered with movement, but we felt that what might be its eyes were on us.

We said, "Feeling is difficult. Mortals have other mortals with whom to share their thoughts. They have built houses to hide in, words to protect them, stories to make them feel right. You will have none of that. It will be difficult."

A shudder took the creature throughout its body, shedding a small cloud of dust onto the ground.

"There are dusthouses in this city. There is fairy dust," we stammered. "It killed you. You can stop it doing the same to others."

The fallen cloud of dust had instantly begun to reassemble, wriggling back to join the fluctuating mass of its feet.

We said, "We have made you with three of the most potent forces we could find. Fairy dust, insect heart, angel blood. It will make you strong." We took a deep breath and added, "Stopping will be difficult – when you are strong, when you can revel in it. Being weak will be difficult. Choosing to be weak. Choosing when not to . . . choosing to be human will be difficult."

It hesitated, then formed a mouth.

The sound of little bones cracking, of pebbles sliding down a mountainside, of sand in a breeze.

It moved its head.

It might have been a nod.

It might have been a greeting.

It might have been goodbye.

We held out our hand in farewell.

Its fingers ran through our own, dissolving.

It turned away.

It managed a step.

Then another.

Its third attempt was less successful: it gave a lurch and its whole body spun forward, the human shape disintegrating for a moment into a yellow cloud, a grey shadow at its heart that might just have been, perhaps, the heart itself.

Briefly it regained a vague human shape, and took all of five steps before it span back into dust.

I called out, "Hey!"

My voice echoed back in the concrete pillars beneath the bridge.

It didn't turn, but we felt it was waiting.

I said, "Hey, you! You be good, okay?"

On what might still have been its face, a flash of something familiar.

Then it dissolved, and billowed away, dust in the night.

*

I went back to Osterley.

Got lost in the streets near the station.

Identical semi-detached houses in endless straight lines.

It looked different as the sky grew lighter, and eventually I found a small park that looked halfway familiar. I sat on one of the empty swings, and rocked a little.

The warmth of the walk became a chill, the chill became cold.

At this time of year, dawn was slow to come.

I slumbered for a while in the mind of a half-sleeping pigeon roosting at the cracked base of a chimney stack.

I rolled through the water pipes under the streets, splitting and dividing at every junction until I was as wide as the city and as thin as light.

Thought I heard Nabeela say: "Fascist pig."

And smiled, and felt guilty for smiling.

Hey, Nabeela.

Wow, you're like, Midnight Mayor. You're like, cooler and more powerful than all the little people, so everyone can fuck right off; I mean, don't you hate that?

Yeah, Nabeela. Right now, kinda do.

Well stuff it, you're still stuffed. Just saying. As one dust-stained corpse to another, you know? So come on, get yourself up.

I struggled to my feet.

Walked without thinking.

Walking without thinking took me back to the house.

Let myself in.

Penny was sleeping.

The house was grey and silent. Dead-hour morning silent, when the night shift start to think about breakfast, and the closed eyes of all day-shift dreamers jerk back and forth in response to stories due to be forgotten at the instant of waking.

I put the keys back on the table where I'd found them.

Went to bed.

Fell asleep immediately, and couldn't remember our dreams.

We woke to the smell of bacon.

There was a dressing gown in the wardrobe.

It was pink, and had the image of a small brown teddy bear sewn into one corner.

The smell of bacon sang its siren song.

I put on the dressing gown and went to find it.

Penny was in the kitchen. As I walked in she said, "I'm not like, domestic woman or nothing, and when I find Femi again and we start going out proper, I'm not even gonna to tell him I like cooking, I'm not even gonna tell him I can cook, until at least the sixth or seventh date."

Penny wore a dressing gown too. Somehow she'd managed to find a striped blue and white one with no teddy bears, and a pair of fur-lined slippers.

"So you're an equal opportunist?" I asked as Penny professionally cracked open a couple of eggs on the sharp edge of the pan. Simmering became a sizzle.

"Way I see it," she explained, kneeing shut a cutlery drawer with a brutal up-thrust, "there's nothing romantic about equal opportunities. 'Hey, you fancy me?' 'Yes, I do.' 'Do you feel like going halves on a meal?' 'Yes, how equitable.' 'I was thinking it might be nice to buy you some flowers.' 'Cool, keep the receipt and I'll be sure to get you something of an equal floral value within three working days.'"

She laid a plate down on the table in front of me. The bacon was crispy, the egg was perfect. "So, yeah," she concluded. "Basically, what I'm saying is don't get used to me making breakfast."

She plonked down opposite me, picked up a nearly empty bottle of tomato ketchup, shook it vigorously and squeezed. It made the noise of all plastic ketchup bottles everywhere. When there was no more ketchup left to come, she threw the bottle with perfect aim at a small green recycling bag hanging up by the sink, and speared a mouthful of sauce with a little egg garnish.

"Being shot at is shit for my diet," she explained through the mouthful. "I was all 'fruit and muesli' and now I'm like 'fuck it' or whatever. Jesus, I've missed bacon."

"You're on a diet?" I asked.

"I know," she declared. "You're thinking, my apprentice is already like, amazing already isn't she, so why the fuck should she need to diet? Thing is, Matthew, it takes *work* to be this sodding amazing. You're a weird skinny freak and wouldn't understand."

Somehow, even having started later, and with more ketchup, she finished before me. She put the kettle on, and watched while I got up and made a start on the washing up.

Finally, "You have fun last night then, sneaking off and shit?"

"Oodles."

"You gonna tell me about it?"

"You want to know?"

"Was it," she stubbed the table with her finger at each word, "disgusting, sickening, repulsive, icky, sticky, stupid or wank?"

I paused. "If I went for 'all of the above' would that be a good thing?"

"I wouldn't have to go far for my surprised face, put it like that."

"I summoned a monster."

Penny hesitated, teabag halfway to a mug proclaiming 'I Love Cake'. Then, "Okay. Because ... that hasn't caused major shitty problems recently, oh no."

"I used the culicidae's heart."

"And you're gonna explain to me how that's actually a shiny okay thing to do? I mean, instead of, like, a monumentally stupid fucked-up thick thing, yeah?"

I scraped at encrusted grease round the edge of the pan, watched it float clear.

"It was the only way I could think of to hurt the dusthouses. In a hurry, I mean. You don't win these kind of battles by just ... torching coca leaves or poppy heads or anything like that. You can't change people by pointing guns in their faces and saying, 'Yo, dude, your craving and your pain – deal with it already!' But the dusthouses *are* evil. Evil's a dodgy word, Midnight Mayors shouldn't say evil, it doesn't leave you much wiggle room after, but stuff it, it's said, there it is. And we were angry. It will be a long time before we are not. So we summoned a ... thing. A dust-storm. And it walks and it has ... awareness ... and it is made from the dust of all who died. It is made from those who were killed by the dusthouses. Because if there is a conservation of mass and energy in physics then likewise there must be a conservation of life in magic. And if I'm right, and if the culicidae's heart works like I think it does, then this creature will seek more life where it can, and its life is of dust, and so it will hunt down dust, and find it, and absorb it, and no one will be able to stand in its way."

Penny stood holding the teabag over the mug, mouth hanging open. She said, "Oh my fucking God."

I shrugged, putting the pan in the drying rack.

"No, but seriously," she said. "Oh my fucking God. You're fucking insane."

She was quivering with the effort of suppressed vehemence. "You've summoned the culicidae 2.0. You've given life to something that should be dead. And dead is dead and it's shit, it's shit and it hurts and it hurts to die and it hurts to live when you've seen someone who's dead when you've seen your friend . . . it hurts. But Jesus fucking Christ, Matthew. Would Meera want this? To be . . . sucked back, not herself, not human, just some fucking part of some fucking bigger plan with you in charge of it going 'Hey, you ain't got no life, no hope, no nothing now, just dust and more fucking dust, so off you fucking go.' Didn't you see? The Minority Council went 'Let's make a big fucking easy solution,' but there are some things – there are some fucking stupid, fucking painful fucking fucked-up things and they make you feel . . . like nothing matters any more, ever again. What have you done?"

I stared down at the dirty water and had nothing to say.

"Can you control it?" she asked. "This thing?"

"I . . . don't know."

"Can you destroy it?"

"I . . . think so."

Penny sat down with a quiet groan. I pulled off the washing-up gloves, and looked properly at my apprentice. Who looked away. Finally I asked, "You okay?"

"Yeah."

"You sure?"

"No."

"I'm . . . sorry."

"Don't be. Don't . . . I don't blame you. You get that, right? It wasn't your fault."

She sighed, stretching out her legs slowly under the table, letting her head roll back. With her eyes half closed towards the ceiling she murmured, "What you gonna do about Templeman? And don't say something as fucked up as what you just told me."

I scratched the end of my nose with the rough cotton of a bandage, and thought hard. "Don't know," I said. "It's . . . difficult. There's no courts of law for these situations, no prison service, no friendly supercharged coppers."

"There's the Aldermen," she replied. "I thought they were all, like 'We make the law, we enforce the law, we are the fucking law' or whatever."

"Yes . . ." I dragged out the word. "But . . . Alderman justice is hard, fast and absolute. Their only guiding principle is: what's best for the greater good? And sure, that's supposed to be the guiding principle of law, but it doesn't leave much room for redemption or understanding. Templeman has believed himself to be acting for the 'greater good'."

"You sound almost sorry for him." Penny's voice was unforgiving.

"No – no I'm not," I exclaimed. "He did things to people, to me, to you, to ... Nabeela." Then, "Do you want him dead?" we asked, so quickly I was surprised to hear our voice.

Penny's knuckles whitened around the tea mug.

"Would you do it?" we murmured. "Would you look him in the eye and make him die?"

"Yes."

Something thick and heavy flattened the breakfast in my stomach, turned the taste of bacon to the raw bite of meat in my mouth. But we reached across the table, wrapped our hand around hers, and didn't know why. "Don't," we said. "Dead is dead and it hurts until all you can do is hollow out the place where there's pain. But don't. Don't do it."

"Is that it?" she asked, not meeting our eyes.

"Yes," I replied. "Pretty much."

"Okay," she breathed. A smile. Perhaps the first I'd seen on her face for a while, faint, but true. "Let's go to the office and do that Midnight Mayor thing that you do."

Walking, after all that sitting, was a mistake. I felt my pulse throb in the eroded skin of my hands, and forced myself to breathe regardless of the shooting pain in my chest.

At St Paul's Underground, riding the long creaking escalator to the surface felt as much effort as if it'd been an ordinary staircase. The steps themselves moved slower than the rubber handrail, causing delight in a child who was leaning on it and found his body being perpetually stretched by the discrepancy and fury to a pensioner with a thick walking stick who cursed London Transport under his breath, loud enough for all to hear.

At Harlun and Phelps, out of instinct I headed for the goods entrance, looking round, as I went, for bloodhounds, gangsters, murderers, and medusas who had an angry agenda and strong feelings about local council politics.

Kelly was waiting at the bottom of the stairs. She sprang to her feet with a welcoming grin. A magazine offering the true secrets to avoiding wrinkles disappeared under her briefcase as she exclaimed, "Mr Mayor! How lucky I happened to be sitting here enjoying my morning break when you turned up, isn't that a coincidence? Please do come upstairs," she babbled, the chinchilla in her soul bounding to the fore. "We've got the lunch of your choice and there's a medic on call to have another look at those bandages and an acupuncturist as well if you need one and I don't know how you feel about chiropody but actually it turns out the whole body is this great interconnected mass of nerve endings . . ."

"That much I'd figured."

" . . . and there's some people who'd really like to talk to you . . ."

"Oh God, who?"

"Well, there's a representative from a group of individuals calling themselves Magicals Anonymous who are looking to set up a support agency . . ."

"Seriously?"

" . . . and there's a goblin shaman who keeps on insisting that the earth is burning all around and we just can't see it . . ."

"Should have stayed in Osterley!" sang out Penny.

"And of course your senior staff want to see you to talk about recent events."

"Great. Because that's not going to end in blood and tears, is it? Are any of them armed?"

"All weaponry within the building is kept under strict lock and key," recited Kelly. "Access to the armoury is fully logged, and the issuing of any weapons likely to cause structural damage in excess of £50,000 must be countersigned by a senior watch officer."

"How about a bed?" I asked as the goods lift rose up through the floors. "We've got a chiropodist, an acupuncturist, an armoury; do we have a bed anywhere?"

"No. But I'll look into it at once, Mr Mayor!"

"How about a snooker table?" added Penny. She saw my expression and shrugged.

Sure enough, Kelly gave a cry of, "What a fabulous idea! Obviously I'm all for the team away-day, but they come so rarely; a snooker table on the premises could really help the departments bond with each other."

The doors swished open at the top floor. We stepped out into a service corridor, past bags of recycling waiting to be taken down. "You have team away-days?" I asked faintly.

"Of course. Chocolate making was my favourite, although we also do the more traditional away-day sports – paintballing, rowing, ukulele playing ..."

I stopped so hard that Penny walked straight into me. "No bloody way."

"I'm sorry, Mr Mayor ..."

"No bloody way, ukulele playing."

"It's an excellent team-bonding activity ..."

I laughed, and it hurt, and I laughed anyway.

Kelly had prepared a meeting room.

Prepared in that there were extra cushions on the chair, extra sandwiches on the table and no one to watch me flinch as I eased my way into a seat.

Words were whispered at the door.

The door was too big, the room too wide, the ceiling too high, the table too long. Someone had laid out green leather mats in front of each chair. It made no sense to us. They looked far more expensive than the table on which they sat, so what was the point?

"Now, we're going to do this gently," explained Kelly. "I decided that you probably didn't want to observe the usual protocols of the workplace, so had the agenda put aside until next week. And obviously, owing to the sensitive nature of the meeting, no one will be taking minutes.

"So, if you're ready, Mr Mayor ...?"

Kelly opened the door one more time.

Aldermen came in.

They wore their formal black, and entered with heads bowed, hands folded in front of them. I could have been forgiven for expecting a coffin. They lined up, first five, then ten, then thirty, then too many for me to see, pressing in around the room until it wore them as wallpaper. Penny's fingers tightened on the back of my chair. Kelly waited until the last were inside, then closed the door quietly, walked to the opposite end of the table, put her briefcase down on it flat, looked me in the eye and said, "Domine dirige nos."

"Domine dirige nos," intoned the Aldermen, men and women, old and young, one voice, eyes still fixed downwards.

"Ladies, gentlemen," she declared, "we are here to say farewell to some of our brethren. I wish us to thank Rumina Rathnayake for all her hard work as Minority Council Treasurer, a post she is giving up after tireless labour in order to retreat into the countryside and seek a cure for the irrevocable curse of the Beggar King. She will, I am sorry to say, experience sorrow, loss, regret, disease and, above all else, loneliness over the coming years as the King's curse slowly blinds all the world to her passing, until she dies cold and alone, a frozen shadow on the earth. We thank her for all her service, and if you could all sign her farewell card on your way out, it would be appreciated."

"Lord lead us," intoned the Aldermen.

"Domine dirige nos," confirmed Kelly. "I'm sure you'd all like to contribute to the flower and fruit package that we will be sending to Cecil Caughey, President, Minority Council. He's currently confined in an asylum, on suicide watch after his overexposure to a burning heart of rage and fury of his own making, so please, if you do send him any gifts other than the fruit basket for which we will be accepting donations, I'd ask you to make sure they aren't sharp. Lord lead us."

"Domine dirige nos," they repeated.

"After due consideration, our colleagues Ms Holta, Mr Fadhil and Mr Kwan are all standing down for personal reasons. We are getting them all cufflinks to commemorate their years of service, but must buy them as quickly as possible as these are likely to be confiscated upon the start of their prison sentences for murder in the second degree. So please, again, if you wish to contribute to these gifts do make your donation by the end of the working day."

"Lord lead us."

"Finally," she informed us, voice light as a rising lark, "I'm sure we all hear with great regret about the actions of Mr Templeman. It is always a sad reflection on us when one of our own turns out to be a murderer, a traitor, a torturer of innocents, a manipulator of men, a dust addict, a madman and a danger to us all.

"I will be requesting a management review in the near future to discuss just how we managed to let ourselves be so utterly manipulated by a man who represents so much that is evil. Forgive the strong language, but I reiterate: evil. We have all been touched by it, we have all been used by it and so, in our ways, we have all been party to it, if only because we did not stand up and say no. Why, ladies, gentlemen? Why could not one of us, not one, say no?

"Our motto, the words that are burnt into the stones of this city, is Domine dirige nos, Lord lead us. We here gathered who do not believe in a god, we use these words of power to invoke something far more. We ask the city for guidance, for strength from its streets and its walls, its secrets and its shadows. We draw our power, our authority and our right-eousness from all that is around us, and in that process we forget that the city is no more and no less than those who move within it. We are not greater than other men. We are not wiser, we are not smarter, we are not worthy of more or less than those whose air we breathe, whose water we share. This truth is universal, but never more import-ant than within a city. Ladies, gentlemen, I propose that we have failed in our oaths. Our oaths to the city, to the people, and to the Midnight Mayor."

She held up her right hand, and then took her left across to it. Her nails were tinted silver, a silver sheen around her palm, a reddish glow to her eyes as they met ours. A wisp of blackness curled round her nos-trils; her hair wore a metallic sheen. She unfurled a thickening, curling nail that was, perhaps, growing closer to a claw, and in two swift cuts dragged it across the palm of her hand, top to bottom, left to right. The blood rose slowly, then didn't seem to stop, trickling down over her wrist. "Domine dirige nos," she breathed, showing no sign of pain, eyes locked on ours.

The Aldermen likewise raised their hands, and for a moment I anticipated blood and cleaning bills. "Domine dirige nos," they repeated, and there was a power in those words, as there had always been power: not god-power, not spell-power, but city-power etched in with time built on time. We all felt it. Penny's breathing was short and shallow, and the Aldermen as they stood round the table had a hint of crimson in their eyes, the fever-red of the mad-eyed silver city dragon that guarded the old London Wall, and their skins were stained with its metal taint, and the smog of the old city unfurled in the air as they repeated, "Domine dirige nos."

Blood rolled down Kelly's sleeve.

I could feel something thin and hot trickling over the palm of my right hand: blood was oozing through the bandages, seeping out in the shape of the twin crosses. I stood up, leaning on the table for support, then raised my right hand to them.

"Domine dirige nos," I repeated and, for a moment, something stood behind me, a shadow that writhed in the light of its own accord, and it had eyes of fire and claws for hands and it had wings.

Kelly smiled.

And it was gone.

The Aldermen lowered their hands and, without another word, they filed out, heads still bowed.

Kelly stood there smiling, eyes fixed on me, waiting until the door had closed. The blood was still welling up between her fingers.

The second the heavy door clicked shut she waggled her hand in the air and exclaimed, "Oh my God, that stuff really works!"

Penny said, for the both of us, "Uh . . . ?"

"I worried they would take too long to come in," Kelly admitted. "I mean, the nurse said it wouldn't last forever . . ."

"Your hand . . . ?" suggested Penny.

"Exactly! Hold on . . ."

She eased open her briefcase, and pulled out a plastic pack containing an antiseptic wipe and a very large plaster. It was bright blue, and carried a picture of Winnie the Pooh and Piglet walking hand in hand.

"I was a little worried it would show," explained Kelly, tearing open the antiseptic wipe with her teeth. "I mean, when the nurse applied it, it had this horrible smell."

"Applied what?" asked Penny.

"Anti-bacterial numbing cream," explained Kelly, wiping away the blood. "Oh, look," she added with a cluck of annoyance. "It's stained my sleeve; that's not going to wash out. Ah well, I never liked this shirt anyway. Ms Ngwenya, would you mind . . . ?" She waved the plaster at my apprentice, who dutifully peeled it open and applied it to Kelly's upturned hand.

"Numbing cream?" she asked.

"Oh God, yes. I really *hate* getting hurt," explained Kelly. "So I went to the nurse and explained I'd probably have to cut myself and what was the most hygienic, least painful, least-likely-to-leave-a-scar way of

doing it? And do you know, she had all these really amazing sugges-
tions. If I was going to self-harm, I'd completely get NHS advice first.
I mean, not that I'm suggesting that; the whole ritual is really rather
ridiculous, isn't it?"

Kelly snapped her briefcase shut, admired the bright plaster on her
hand with every look of someone who'd dreamt of the Hundred Acre
Wood as a kid, twiddled her fingers to test that they still worked and
exclaimed, "So, basically, I've asked every department – including catering – to help hunt Templeman down, and the Beggar King is going to
do a bit of nosing and I've bought the Old Bag Lady on board and I've
asked if the Seven Sisters wouldn't mind joining in and there's some
guys having a chat with Fat Rat and I was thinking we really should see
to actually appointing a consul to the Tribe, and the Neon Court kinda
owe us a favour sort of anyway so really, all things considered, I'd say
it'll be fine. It'll all be completely fine and in fact may I suggest that this
could be lunch? Lunch anyone?"

"We kinda just had breakfast . . . " began Penny.

"Lunch," we interrupted. "Lunch would be good."

"Maybe a little lunch . . . "

"Posh food always comes in small sizes," explained Kelly. "It's how
you know it's worth it."

So saying, she beamed one final burst of perfect dentistry, swept her
briefcase off the table and was out of the door before I could remember to breathe.

I breathed.

So did Penny. "She," Penny said, "is totally fucking awesome. What's
her job again?"

"She's my PA."

"You've got a PA!" Penny flapped with indignation. "You've got a
fucking PA; that's like . . . that's like you're going to get multicoloured
highlighters and then, like, maybe those file divider things in all the
different colours and that shit! Oh my God, you've got a PA!" She
clapped her hands over her mouth as if trying to contain a bad thought,
then slowly lowered them and breathed, "She's awesome. What's her
salary like, because you read all these stories, yeah, about how PAs get
less than the minimum wage and their bosses are on, like, a million plus
bonuses, and that sorta crap makes me sick."

"Penny, I don't get paid."

"Yeah, but you get expenses, right?"

The table seemed warm and inviting. I put my head down on it and asked it if it would be my friend. It seemed okay with the idea. "If I passed out right now, would that be okay?"

"So long as you don't cry. Crying would completely undermine the moment and, besides, I don't cope well when people cry around me; I get all puffy-eyed and don't know what to say and it's shit for everyone."

"No crying," I promised. "Just a bit of rest."

There wasn't a bed.

But there was a sofa.

The owner of the office it was in agreed to take the afternoon off to play golf, so I stretched out on it in my beggar's clothes and a clean black coat for a blanket, and slept. The half-sleep of daytime snoozing, where time crawls and flies, crawls and flies, like a drunken woodpecker on a lazy day.

Sometimes shadows came to the door to try and disturb me, to ask questions or make requests, and the shadow of Kelly waved them away, and I thought perhaps I should say something, or do something, or make some noise to show I was interested, and found I wasn't, and stayed where I was.

Shadows stretch and thin.

Between the glass towers of central London there are still some narrow views through which the eye can catch the city's weather-vanes. There a boy balanced precariously on one leg, staring at distant horizons. There a galleon, sails swollen at the full; there a tiny golden dragon; and here a black crow in flight. If you know where to look, they're still there, centuries on from when they once dominated the city, visible until the last light of day.

There were things to do.

I did them slowly.

Hauled myself down to the basement, Penny in tow.

It took a lot of bins, a lot of cleaning cupboards, before I found it.

Something moved in the bottom of the dumpster.

I knocked politely on the lid before easing it open, and looked down into the stinking depths.

"Hi there!" I sang out.

Something moved in the depths, sending down a small landslide of packaging and torn plastic. A trio of tiny yellow-stained fingers curled up from the depths, followed by an oversized pair of ink-black eyes.

"Penny, meet imps. Imps, meet Penny." Fine brown goo slid over the staring eyes from the bin, washing dirt with dirt. "Penny's my apprentice," I explained to the creature in the bin. "She really loves small furry creatures that stink of sewage, don't you Penny?"

"Yeah," said Penny, shuffling uneasily behind me. "Totally."

I took as deep a breath as I could, and said what I'd come to say. "So, in recognition of your clan's fine and sterling work in disrupting the interior of Harlun and Phelps, I, in my senior capacity as Midnight Mayor and keeper of promises, guarantee that should you and your kind be assembled here, at this dumpster, at, say, eleven-thirty tonight, a pick-up truck will come and transport you and all your kind to the foulest, most pest-ridden garbage site within the Greater London area you could possibly imagine. Your once-in-a-lifetime trip to the dream wasteground of your choice is coming here, now. Well, here, tonight. We good?"

A tiny head nodded, black bristles straightening across a felt-grey skull.

"Fantastic!" I exclaimed. "Tell all your friends. Harlun and Phelps – what a waste of effort. Landfill – hello!"

As Penny and I walked back towards the elevator, she was unusually quiet.

"Okay," I said as the doors slid shut behind us, "I may have incidentally promised a clan of imps a transfer to their dream rubbish dump in exchange for helping me out with a little problem."

Silence. It lasted four floors.

"So ... you've got, like, these kick-ass Aldermen suckers who are supposed to carry guns for you, and you've got, like, major-league mega-mystic powers, and you've got like, higher urban powers and all that shit on your side and you ... went to the imps and promised them a holiday in a landfill?"

The doors parted with a faint ding-dong.

She added, "Is there like a word for anti-style? I mean, in like the way there's antimatter which is kinda matter itself but sorta like not-matter so it behaves like matter until it hits matter and goes boom? Like that?"

"Mojo?"

"Don't kid yourself."

We paused by Kelly's desk. It was set not quite next to my office, like a guard dog daring a cat to pee in its kennel.

I explained to her the fact of the imps, and my promise.

Kelly blanched. "But imps ... rubbish dumps ... the breeding cycle ..."

"Yeah, I know, there'll be kids, there'll be a surge in seagull deaths, but I still think it'd be a lovely thing to do in this new and golden era of generous Aldermen with warm hearts. So if we could add it to the list of shit to get done, that'd be great. Thanks!"

I swept on by before she could argue.

I was getting the hang of management.

There was another duty to perform.

Penny went out and bought clothes.

It took her a long time.

When she came back, she was swaying under a weight of bags.

"So yeah," she said, "there's like ... shirts for formal shit, and T-shirts for like casual shit, and kinda sports tops for running shit because, you know, you do loads of running, I mean, not like a professional or anything, more like a guy scared of being shot, but seriously, I think if you're gonna make a habit of pissing off people with guns, you should take up running as a proper hobby, do this whole keep-fit thing. And then there's smart black trousers because you can't beat black; I mean, I know it's a cliché and that, but seriously, black works. Even on you, which is, like, a total fucking miracle or whatever. And then there's kinda less formal trousers which you can spill tomato sauce on and shit, because, hell I've seen you eat and I'm, like, what were you like growing up? And I got you lots of cheap trousers that you can get blood on because I realise now that you *never* do a proper wash or anything. Like, you just wait until you're covered in blood and then some poor schmuck has to burn your clothes and lend you something and shit, and actually you stink a lot of the time. I mean, you do, not personal or anything mind; I'm just saying."

I received each garment as gratefully as I could, and Kelly took the receipts, for expenses, with her smile locked in place.

Changing clothes was hard work.

Sweat and odd chemical reactions had glued the Beggar King's vestments to our skin.

Bandages stretched.

Bones creaked.

When it was done, I looked at my face in the mirror. The shirt was white, the light was cold; it wasn't a sympathetic place for a viewing.

I folded my beggar's garb and put it carefully into a plastic bag.

"Kelly, I need to go out," I said.

"Is that wise?" she asked. "I mean, obviously you can handle yourself, Mr Mayor, but right now do you really think you can handle yourself? I've heard that there's a point when the body is in so much physical pain that actually it stops hurting, that pain can become euphoria at a certain intensity, but I'm not a doctor, I've never tested this and I would feel so much happier thinking that you weren't personally trying to prove the theory tonight . . . "

I dropped the bag of beggar's clothes on the table and waited for her to work it out.

"Oh," she breathed. "Well, yes, I do see how that might be something you need to do in person."

"And alone," I added. "It's important."

She slumped, frowning in worry. "Oh, very well," she sighed. "But if you absolutely must, may I give you this?"

She opened a drawer, and pulled out a small black box, from which she produced: a mobile phone, a pre-paid oyster card, a small bundle of ten-pound notes wrapped in a rubber band, a pack of lemon-scented travel tissues, a pair of tweezers, a penknife, a packet of baby wipes, and a gun. I looked at the gun. It was black, heavy, semi-automatic. Kelly checked the magazine, clicked it back in place, pushed it towards me. I said, "I don't really do guns."

"They're a truly ghastly thing," she agreed, "but other people do guns, and that's always the problem, isn't it?"

"Yes, but that's kinda like saying other people do muggings and murder and rape, so get with the party."

"Mr Mayor . . . "

"I'm going for a very short walk through the heart of my own city," I interrupted. "You really think a gun and some baby wipes are called for?"

"Templeman does guns," she answered.

A pause. Moment to think. Then, "If the police do me, you're going to have to do the explaining, okay?"

She beamed. "You know, I've always had this amazingly good understanding with coppers. Some people don't get them, but I find if you're just willing to listen to their point of view and speak in a gentle tone of voice, they're actually very reasonable people."

I put the gun in my pocket. It was heavier than I'd imagined.

"Back before you know it," I muttered.

I walked through the night all the way to Holborn Circus before I found what I was looking for. A church that had somehow survived the wartime bombing protruded into a bottleneck of traffic that wound round a monument to great generals and the glorious dead, rifles turned down and heads bowed in prayer. Here, in a narrow locked doorway, the beggars huddled. Eyes flashed up from grimy faces as I passed, took in my clean clothes and washed face, my empty pockets and single plastic bag, and looked away again.

Round at the side of the church, I found who I was looking for, sitting alone on an old cardboard box that had been pulled apart to make a small mat. She had two sleeping bags, one inside the other – the first was bright blue, a camper's sack with drawer strings; the other was a duvet, sewn together, and rotted at the corners. She wore a grey woollen hat and her face was pale, tinged with blue. Her legs were shaking inside the bedding and there was a greyness to her lips, a wideness in the pupils of her eyes. As I approached she eyed me suspiciously, her expression veering between fight or flight. She wasn't out of her twenties, and though the sleeves of her jumper hid the worst of the track marks, enough capillaries had burst under her skin to tell much of her story.

I held out my hands in peace as I approached, saying, "It's okay, I'm not a copper or anything."

She chose fight. "Spare some change?" she asked. Her voice was hard and sharp. I knelt down opposite her, and opened up my bag. Her lip curled in disgust at the smell of the clothes as I pulled them out. "What the fuck you doing carrying that shit?" she demanded.

"These are the vestments of the Beggar King," I explained.

"You what?"

I gestured her to silence, and held each one up in turn. "These are the suspiciously soiled trousers of the beggar who has slept too many nights on cold, hard stone, and had nowhere to go when nature called, and lost dignity in the loss of all.

"This is the dubious shirt of third- to fourth- to fifth-hand, passing its way down into the pit of society through kindly intent and casual charity.

"This is the coat of infinite pockets, which hold not things but thoughts, memories and dreams tied away like knots in a string.

"And these are the shoes that have travelled too far. They walked too far and have been to too many places, not of speed, or distance, or time, not of maps and geography and the ordinary dirt underfoot of busy men. These . . . you wear in those places where you may only go alone." I pushed the bundle of clothes towards the beggar. "Take them. They are a blessing. Keep them well."

She took them uncertainly, closing her fingers round the thin handle of the bag, then pulling the bag in close to her. I smiled and straightened up, feeling the awkward weight of the gun in my pocket, the tightness of the bandages around my ribs. She watched me, half opened her mouth as if to say thank you, then closed it again. I wrapped my arms around my middle against the rising cold and turned to walk away, and he was there.

He stood, alone, on the other side of the street. One arm was held in a sling, and there were scratches down the side of his face. But he stood easily enough by the kerb, right arm hanging loose at his side, back straight, watching me across the traffic. People moved behind him, heading for the bus stops and the bike racks, the Underground at Chancery Lane and the restaurants of the West End. He stared at me, and I stared at him, and neither of us moved.

Templeman.

There was a sickly yellow stain to his skin, which hadn't been there before.

A crackling in the air about him as he moved, a taste on the air of damp dust and dark corners. The CCTV cameras were all turned away from him, pointing at walls or straight down at the ground.

Then he smiled, and turned, and walked away.

I followed, keeping my distance, moving between the crowd. I felt the weight of the gun and my heart beat in my throat. He stopped at a bus stop, looked up at the indicator board, sat down carefully on the little red bench designed to be impossible for sleeping on, stretching out his legs. I stopped some twenty yards back, leaning against the wall of a bank, the ATM out of order beside me. There were five people at the bus stop. Two women, Russian by their voices, great fake-fur coats dyed a deep dark red, were getting annoyed at the delay in the bus. They flapped at each other, then at the traffic, and finally turned to the others waiting for the bus and asked in broken English if it always took this long. Templeman leant across and politely explained to them that it wasn't usually this bad, and something must have happened further down the line.

"Where are you from?" he asked.

"Russia," they replied.

Ah, Russia. He'd always wanted to visit Russia; he'd heard it was an amazing place. "Whereabouts in Russia?"

"Moscow."

How beautiful it must be, and what an exciting place to live in.

It was okay. They were here for a holiday. They'd never been before. It was all right.

They must try Greenwich. The park was beautiful, the observatory was astonishing, the maritime museum was fascinating. Don't do Madame Tussaud's or any of that tourist rubbish. Go to Greenwich.

They smiled and thanked him, and with every second that passed I forced us to be still, forced us to breathe, to watch, to wait, fingers itching at our side.

Their bus came, and he boarded with them, eyes flicking back towards me as he climbed onto the bus. I let two more people file on past the driver before detaching myself from my bit of wall, and slipping on board too.

He'd gone to the top deck, sat at the very back seat.

I sat by the stairs, a pair of Chinese kids with spiky copper hair and headphones glued to their ears sitting behind me, the two Russians in front. They got off at Euston, in the grey bus station stained saturated pink by the overhead lights, as garish a gloom as the city could offer.

I watched the reflection of the passengers in the darkness of my window, and waited.

Templeman got off at Camden. He walked right by me without a word, going down through the doors between a guitarist and a goth, not even glancing my way as he passed. I got off behind him, not one person between him and me, and we thought of throats and hearts and things being crushed. Here, now? Would anyone know?

Too many people in Camden.

The Y-junction where the street divided, this way for Kentish Town, this way for Holloway, was a heaving mass of big-soled boots, black coats, painted lips and hamburger wrappers. The shops selling T-shirts honouring Bob Marley and leather jackets with iron studs were still open, even now, and the multi-storey pubs and bars heaved, windows open wide to let out the heat of crowded merriment. Coppers with fluorescent stripes on their jackets stood by the Underground station, heads turned down to talk to the radios strapped to their shoulders.

Templeman made his way to another bus stop; I stood some ten yards off, watching. A girl came up to me. Her hair was dyed blonde and pulled back eyebrow-tugging-tight across her skull. She said, "You got a fag?"

Templeman's eyes turned briefly to me; a smile lurked in the corner of his mouth.

I said, "Sorry, no; no fag."

"Come on mate, come on, you gotta have a fag."

"No, not me, sorry, don't smoke."

"Hey – you got a tenner? I really need to get a fag."

No tenner.

"Guess how old I am," she said.

"Don't know."

"Guess, go on, guess."

A bus pulled up. Templeman stood as if examining the gutter, and didn't move.

"Fourteen!" she exclaimed. "I'm fourteen years old, yeah, but all my friends say I look way older. Come on, you got a tenner right, I mean, it's not like you'd miss it or anything, guy like you. You wouldn't miss a tenner."

We looked her in the eye and she saw something in our features that made her afraid.

She moved away quickly, and was starting to cry by the time she crossed the street to the station.

A different bus came.

Smaller, a little rat-route runner. Templeman boarded and sat right at the front, by the door. He didn't look up as I passed, near enough to touch, but sat with his good hand folded in his lap. I sat two seats behind and watched the back of Templeman's head. There were barely six, seven people on this bus. With bandaged hands, I might not get a good enough aim, but I could move closer, and there'd be no chance to miss. One shot and it'd be done, blood on the windows, blood on the floor, but it would be finished.

I stayed where I was.

The bus roamed through the back streets of Camden, heading west. Two passengers got off. Then another. Four of us left on the bus, and a driver. Only three people would see it, three people would know my face, and they'd run, they'd hide, from any man who could walk up behind a stranger on a bus and pull the trigger. The police would neither know nor, once the Aldermen had done their thing, care. I could change seats, aim, fire, and be off the bus before the next set of traffic lights.

Easy.

Couldn't move.

We laboured up towards Hampstead Heath. Nearer the bottom of the hill, grey concrete estates; higher up, white Victorian terraces. Judge the quality of the home by the number of doorbells – here, houses with twelve apartments to a stairwell, while next door, just one family occupied space fit for three. The pubs had tall ceilings and served roast dinner on a Sunday. The greengrocer offered packets of polenta and salami in its window, and discount phone calls to Kenya.

Templeman got up some hundred yards before his stop, and stood by the door as the bus decelerated. It was a single stand, request stop only, no shelter above and no people waiting. The doors swished back. He got off.

I waited a beat, and followed.

Quiet streets, quiet night.

Here.

Do it here.

He turned up an alley, a patch of darkness between the houses, heading uphill towards a place where the night thickened like oil. I hesitated, felt the gun in my pocket, took a deep breath of the cold street air, and followed.

A fence on either side gave way to open grass.

A sign said: **Be Considerate – Clean Up After Your Dog**.

Underneath it, another sign warned: **Littering £100 Fine**.

The grass stretched out around us, above and below. I paused, looking up, looking down. Above was infinite sky wrapped round the crest of a bench-lined hill. Below, past the empty five-a-side football pitches lit up with floodlightss and the deserted winding paths picked out by pinpoint lights, was the city, as far as the eye could see. The red light flashing on top of Canary Wharf, the orange walls of the Houses of Parliament, the deep blue circle of the London Eye, the silver arch of St Pancras, the golden cross of St Paul's and rising spike of the Shard; it shimmered like a silent Christmas, as deep as the sky that covered it. The sight hit like a pillow fighter who forgot to pull his punch, and for a moment our hand burnt and our breath was black on the air and our shadow stretched out a pair of dragon wings.

Then someone whistled, very softly in the night.

Templeman was twenty yards ahead. He paused beneath a white lamp shining above the narrow path, and looked back at me. Then he turned again, and started to walk, up towards the top of Parliament Hill, his gait slow and steady.

I followed, eyes jerking from side to side, looking for a trap, a danger, a gun in the night.

Silence in the park.

Templeman climbed and kept on climbing, along a path that briefly vanished behind a clump of hawthorn bushes. He reappeared, looking back, waiting for me, his face open and polite. I followed painfully, the breath ragged in my chest. The magic of the city was fainter here, in all this grass and woodland, but, though faint, the distant street lights below still gave us strength, a promise of power waiting to be pulled.

And all at once he'd stopped.

On the summit of the hill stood a concrete plaque, indicating each landmark below. There was a bench nearby, where a single street lamp shone its too-white light on the narrow path and muddy grass. Templeman sat there, looking down at the city.

I went up to the bench, and sat down next to him.

And waited.

"You can't save everyone," he said at last.

Somewhere beneath us, doors slammed in the night. Taxis were hailed, buses stopped, trains flashed blue-white sparks on the tracks, foxes snarled, windows were closed, shoes were pulled off aching feet at the end of the working day, lights were switched off, music was turned down, and the city kept on turning, turning, oblivious to us.

"You can't save those who don't want to be saved," he added. "You can't save your friends. You can't save yourself."

I rolled my head a little, trying to ease the crick in the back of my neck. A few meagre stars were peeking through the clouds.

"Do you understand?" he asked. "Do you know what it is to be the Midnight Mayor?"

I eased the gun out of my pocket. His eyes went to it, with what might have been surprise, but still he didn't move.

I said, "You're not looking so good. Took something nasty, did you? Something yellow?"

"What we Aldermen do ... is irrelevant," he replied. "We are irrelevant. I am attempting to change that."

"Oscar Kramb is dead," I said, surprised to hear the words come out. "Caughey is mad, Rathnayake is cursed. Penny's fine, thanks for asking. The Aldermen have sworn allegiance, better late than never, and I've summoned a monster that is every bit as dangerous, mad and reckless as your culicidae. Every bit as stupid and pigheaded, every bit as arrogant and every bit as bad. The drug you gave me in Heron Quays ... I won't be recommending it for mass market approval any time soon. Nasty side-effects. I mean, that may just be me, it may just be what I am, and let's face it, this was always about what, not who, I am. But, basically, there's a lot of blood around, questions have been asked. You know how it is."

His eyes darted back to the gun, then away; his smile curling wider. "You can't save everyone."

"No."

"You can't save those who don't want to be saved."

"No."

"You can't save your friends."

"I . . . no. No, I can't."

"Do you understand? I did try to tell you."

"I know. I get it now. I understand. And you're right. You are right, I couldn't . . . I couldn't do it. Meera died and I couldn't . . . and people died and Nabeela . . . and I couldn't have changed it. I couldn't. All this power, all this blood, all this magic and none of it, not one thing, could have made the difference. You're right, Templeman. You are right."

"You could thank me."

"Could I?"

"I've been trying to teach you."

"I know."

"I've been trying to make you a better Midnight Mayor."

"I know."

"These lessons . . . will make you stronger. Look at you, now. You have no idea of the power of your office, no concept of what you could do, what you could be. There are things they haven't told you, that you still don't know about being Midnight Mayor . . . will you use the gun?"

I turned it over in my lap, slipped my finger into the trigger guard, thumbed off the safety catch. "Dunno," I said. "It's that or we have a major magical punch-up. But I hurt, and you hurt, and here we are, away from men and magic, and it'd be messy. I mean, I'm not saying it's out of the question. But with you on fairy dust, and me in my state, there's no way I could guarantee who'd win. But you do have to die, Templeman. There's no simple way round it. You have to die."

"Of course," he replied. "You're the Midnight Mayor."

"Which makes you my responsibility?"

"Yes. You can't save yourself."

I groaned, slipping my hand tighter round the butt of the gun, knocking the barrel against my skull as I tried to concentrate. Everything was too far, too fuzzy, even him. "Thing is," I sighed, "this whole . . . you can't save shit, shit. I mean, it sounds great, doesn't it? And you're right, I mean, you're right. You've been right about everything. I couldn't save Meera, I just couldn't; she didn't want to be saved and there's an end of it. And I couldn't make it stop, when we . . . when we did what we did, I couldn't make it stop, and then Nabeela ... you killed her, you killed her and why? Because she was there and you were there and you had a gun. I couldn't save my friend. You beat me."

We hauled ourself up, holding the gun loose at our side. He followed us with his eyes, waiting.

"But here's the thing," I continued. "In all of this, with all this shit going on, and despite truth and logic and reason, despite the bigger picture and the wider issues and the great responsibility of being Midnight Mayor, despite what must be and what can be and what should be and what can never be and despite the fact that you won – you won and you were right – despite all of this, I still think I have to try."

We raised the gun.

Our hand shook.

Levelled it at his head.

"Sorry," I breathed. "I know it's not what you were looking for."

He picked himself up from the bench, eyes locked on ours, straight past the gun. I shuffled back a pace, keeping distance between us, supporting the butt of the gun with my other hand. His eyes were liver-yellow, his skin gleaming with more than sweat, a shimmer I recognised from Meera, just before the end.

"Go on then," he murmured. "Go on."

I swallowed, took another step back, tightened my grip on the gun. He moved closer, and I retreated, backing towards the edge of the path. "Go on!" His voice rose higher, "Go on, prove it! Show me what you are, show me that you can do it, show me, prove it, show me that you can make it happen, show me, do it!" He came towards us again and we backed off, hand shaking, vision shaking.

"Do it! You call yourself the Midnight Mayor? Do it, do it, this is what has to be done, this is it, this is the greater good, this is what matters, this is it, do it!"

"Stop ..."

"What does it take? What does it take to make you do it? How many more must I kill, how much worse must things become, before you do what has to be done? What is the point of you?!"

I backed another step, slipping on the grass, eyes still focused down the length of the gun. Templeman hissed in frustration, not even interested in looking at us. He turned away, fingers flexing at his side. "Very well. If you can't do what needs to be done, even now ..."

His hand moved down to his side. We saw the shape of something beneath his jacket, something metal. His fingers closed around it; I heard the snap of the safety being released, raised my gun again, opened my mouth to shout a warning, our finger tightening around the trigger, "No, please, don't ..."

He turned, pulling up the gun from its holster in the same movement, arm outstretched, and there was a look in his face

He'd do it

He'd do it

He's going to do it

He's going to do it

Oh God

A shot in the night.

Hear it.

Not hear not with ear not hear just there and it stayed, it stayed inside us like the mind couldn't get rid of it, would never get rid of it.

I stared at my own hands, dropped the gun, staggered back.

It landed heavy on the ground, and stayed.

Templeman stood, mouth open in surprise.

The gun was still in his hand.

He raised it, slowly, awkwardly, his body lurching to one side as he overbalanced to fire. He got it to belly height, chest height, shoulder height, and there was another shot.

This one seemed quieter, though it couldn't be.

I saw the flash.

Star-like stab of yellow light in the dark behind the bench.

It briefly picked up the face of the shooter.

Templeman reeled as the bullet hit, square in his back. His legs brought him towards us, we scrambled away as he reached out, trying to hold onto us. He went, "Uh ... uh ... uh ..." lips working at the sound.

His outreaching arm pushed his weight too far forward.

He fell, landing on his palm, which gave way, knocking him onto his elbow with a grunt. There were two holes in his back, through a lung. I could see the flattened metal gleam of one of the bullets, where it had wedged against a rib.

His fingers scrambled against the ground.

"Uh . . . uh . . . you . . . "

A figure stepped into the light, gun at her side.

She wore Alderman black.

Her auburn hair was pulled back.

She had a white badge, with two red crosses, pinned to her chest.

She looked down at Templeman, who tried to turn and see.

"Uh . . . you . . . uh . . . "

"Walk away, Mr Mayor," she said.

I shook my head.

"Please, Mr Mayor," she repeated. "Please walk away."

I stared at her, and she didn't smile.

Templeman breathed out blood and foam, mixed with a sound that, if it had strength, might have been a scream. "You . . . you . . . can't . . . can't save . . . "

I looked up at Kelly, who nodded, just once, in farewell.

" . . . can't save . . . can't . . . "

I turned.

Walked away.

The first gunshot came as I rounded the path down the hill, and I flinched.

The next were easier.

Epilogue: ... But You Might As Well Try

In which things end in a way that is probably a beginning.
    There were things to be ended.
    Meetings were held.
    Agendas were noted.
    Minutes were taken.
    Reports were issued.
    At the end of the day, a memo landed on my desk. It said:

Re: The Minority Council
The special commission of the Aldermen has concluded its
investigations into the Minority Council. The full outline of our
report may be found under section 8/111BL of the special
archive. The complete version will also be filed with the bursar,
treasurer and secretary of the relevant departments. A
departmental special assembly will be held to discuss the broad
conclusions of the report, which may fall into the following
categories:
Failings
Mistakes
Lessons to be Learnt
Social Intentions
The Greater Good
The presence of the Midnight Mayor is requested.

    I considered the note, then tore it into a lot of pieces, and threw it
away.

*

There were funerals.

Nabeela's parents had outlived their daughter.

They didn't cry at first, which made things worse.

Then one of her cousins started to cry and, at the sight of it, her mother wept too, and her father held his wife's arms, and still refused to cry, and that was all we could take.

Penny laid flowers by the grave and said a few words.

They were short, and they were true, and they were right, and they were all that needed to be said.

There was a dinner engagement.

Kelly said, "The worshipful company of Magi, Maguses and . . ."

"You are kidding me."

"No, Mr Mayor. Now, I know this is a difficult concept, but this is a *tie* . . ."

"No fucking way."

"This is a *tie*, you wear it around your neck like *this* . . ."

She stepped back.

"There! That isn't so bad, is it?"

"This is a horrible moment. Just give me a second to deal with it. I can feel my life lurching in an odd and unexpected direction. This is the start of a slippery slope. First a tie, then cufflinks, then council tax and buying a mortar and pestle for the kitchen."

"I'm not quite sure I follow the derivation, or even see the problem! Now, here's your invite . . ."

"Thank you."

" . . . and please do brush your hair . . ."

"I mean it, Kelly. Thank you. You are . . . what you do . . . did . . . for what it's worth . . . thank you."

She paused.

Smiled her lighthouse smile.

"You're welcome, Mr Mayor."

There were meetings.

He said, " . . . the policy of discrimination is entirely unjustifiable!"

"The policy of discrimination . . ."

"I am willing to take this to the EU!"

"During daylight working hours?"

"You're completely misrepresenting the situation . . ."

"I'm just saying, people will talk."

"I demand my rights! According to May vs. Howell, discriminating against any one individual on the basis of their genetic predispositions is entirely unacceptable under civil law . . ."

"You really think the blood donor centre is a good place for a vampire to work?"

"Have you ever felt sick from eating too much cake and never wanted more of it?"

"Yes, but that's cake and this is kinda the life fluids of innocent victims – hell, not even innocent victims, but fine upstanding members of civil society kindly donating their blood to others . . ."

"Including vampires!"

"NHS-registered vampires . . ."

"This is the death of the liberal society . . .!"

The Worshipful Company of Magi, Maguses and Mages did, as Kelly had promised, serve canapés at their dinner.

Then fish.

Then meat.

Then salad.

Then pudding.

By the time Kelly kicked us under the table at the start of our speech, we could barely stand with the weight of our own belly.

A hundred pampered faces looked up at us.

A set of cards informed me in Kelly's stiff neat hand that today I was giving a talk on thaumaturgy in the modern age. Point one read like this:

Thaumaturgy: What's it good for?

We smiled.

I cleared my throat.

Raised my head and looked round the room.

"You will ask yourself," I said, and we were surprised at how clear we sounded, "why. What is thaumaturgy good for? We here assembled could do, if we had the will . . . marvellous things. We who feel every atom of the wind as it runs across our skin, we who bathe in streetlight, we who see the shape of the stone as it bends beneath our feet, who hear the singing in the wires and know the weight of the turning tide. We who hide beneath the city's skin, blood in its veins, beating invisible life under the surface. We could do such things, you and I. We could change . . . everything.

"You will ask yourself why. Why we do not, with the power we have. I have no simple answer. All I can do is tell you this: that to do such a thing is not to be human. If you think yourself gods, well then, here is the world, waiting to be shaped. Stand and shape it, if you dare. If you dream yourselves immortal, then take immortality. Others may stand in your way, and they may fall, and you may fail, but who will know until the moment to decide?

"But before you do this, ask yourself – what are you giving away? What will you lose, to make this wonder? Who will you become, when you are a god, no longer human? Is the victory worth the price you will pay?

"So I bring you back to my first point. Thaumaturgy: what's it good for?"

And the days trickled by.

A report came in of an explosion of imps in the rubbish dumps of Walthamstow. Whole populations of seagulls and rats had been culled and there were rumours, so they said, of tribal dances between burning tyres, and the rattling of impish song.

We nodded and smiled and did nothing.

Because, just this once, it was the right thing to do.

And a report came in of a dusthouse destroyed, and the dust itself, gone.

And tales of a creature that came from the dust and took the dust into itself, and vanished, without a trace.

Not human, and not animal.

Something silent, something new.

And I said, how interesting, I'd look into it.

Perhaps you should send me a memo.

And one day Penny said, "There's this security guy down in Guildhall who looks at me funny, and I thought at first he, like, totally fancied me because, you know, that's kinda what you'd think, isn't it?"

"Yes, Penny."

"Then he kept on looking and looking and I looked back because it was, like, whoa there, you're kinda freaking me out now and you know, I coulda sworn, as I was looking ... there was something kinda funny about the way he moved."

"What kinda funny?"

"His shadow. His shadow kept on looking even when he turned his head away."

I leant back in my chair, folding my fingers behind my head. "Penny," I said, "have I ever told you about the ways in which untrained sorcerers can manifest?"

"Um ... not really. I mean, I guessed you were kinda holding off on that, seeing as how *I* manifested by, like, you know, nearly destroying the city and shit."

"Believe it or not, that was kinda a one-off."

"Jeez, thanks for making me feel better."

"There are other ways ..."

And the days rolled by.

Until one unremarkable evening, when the sun was setting over the city and the air smelt of that chill you get before rain, we pulled on our shoes and rubbed the sunlight out of our eyes, and stood up, and went for a walk.

We walked through the city, the old city, through little alleys lined with great buildings, past the staring statues with their Rule Britannia faces and long marble spears, between the rolling mad red eyes of the watching silver dragons and down the cobbled streets that snuck between the bus routes, where only the most adventurous cabbie dared venture.

We walked across the course of old rivers sealed over long ago, under faded signs offering ha'penny cures for ancient ills, beneath clocks raised up by learned councilmen as their civic duty, past the Gothic towers of the Royal Court and round the teeming curve of Aldwych, down towards the river.

We walked through the subways beneath Waterloo, where the beggars huddled beneath changing light and white stalagmites that hung from between the ceiling cracks, and south again, past the silent black guns of the Imperial War Museum and towards that strange place where distances started to warp and the centre of the city met inner city and had a fight that left both bleeding by the one-way signs.

And as we walked, the light turned away from our shadow, and the twin crosses burnt on our hand, and the pigeons fluttered in their dens, and the rats were still beneath the city streets.

Finally we said, "Thank you for the clothes."

He fell into step beside me, as he had been beside me for a long way, though not always seen. "You're welcome," he replied. "Glad you didn't screw up too bad."

"That's my speciality," I told the Beggar King. "I screw up just bad enough for things to get moderately shit, and then by the remarkable deed of stopping them from being mega, people think I must be onto something."

"Yeah – you tell yourself that," he replied, sucking in air through his crooked teeth.

"How are your subjects?" I asked. "No more disappearances?"

"No, no more. At least – no more that end in dust. My people vanish all the time, but now . . . our evils, evils of our making . . . it is somehow better."

We walked on. I said, "Before he . . . before he died, Templeman said that there were things I don't know about being Midnight Mayor. Things I haven't worked out, haven't been told yet."

"Well, yes, obviously."

I glanced sharply at him, but the Beggar King's bearded face was unreadable.

"Anything I should be scared of?"

"Christ," he laughed. "You should be terrified!"

"That's what I figured."

We kept on walking.

Then,

"Its footsteps burn the earth."

"What?"

"Its footsteps burn the earth. The gates are down and it is coming, and its footsteps burn the earth."

"I don't know what that means."

He shrugged.

"You're the Midnight Mayor. Work it out."

We walked further.

I opened my mouth to say, hold on a second, jimbo: work it out, what kind of pretentious shit is that, what the hell is it with all these people trying to teach me lessons? Anyway I mean dammit, no one's perfect so cut me a break or . . .

. . . but when I looked he was gone.

I sighed, shoved my hands in my pockets, bent my head down against the wind, and kept on walking.

extras

www.orbitbooks.net

about the author

Kate Griffin is the name under which Carnegie Medal-nominated author Catherine Webb writes fantasy novels for adults. An acclaimed author of young adult books under her own name, Catherine's amazing debut, *Mirror Dreams*, was written when she was only 14 years old, and garnered comparisons with Terry Pratchett and Philip Pullman. She read History at the London School of Economics, and studied at RADA.

Find out more about Kate Griffin and other Orbit authors by registering for the free monthly newsletter at www.orbitbooks.net

1

It was a slow day, so I was reading a book at my desk and seeing into the future.

There were only two customers in the shop. One was a student with scraggly hair and a nervous way of glancing over his shoulder. He was standing by the herb and powder rack and had decided what to buy ten minutes ago but was still working up the nerve to ask me about it. The other customer was a kid wearing a Linkin Park T-shirt who'd picked out a crystal ball but wasn't going to bring it to the counter until the other guy had left.

The kid had come on a bicycle, and in fifteen minutes a traffic warden was going to come by and ticket him for locking his bike to the railings. After that I was going to get a call I didn't want to be disturbed for, so I set my paperback down on my desk and looked at the student. 'Anything I can help you with?'

He started and came over, glancing back at the kid and dropping his voice slightly. 'Um, hey. Do you—?'

'No. I don't sell spellbooks.'

'Not even—?'

'No.'

'Is there, um, any way I could check?'

'The spell you're thinking of isn't going to do any harm. Just try it and then go talk to the girl and see what happens.'

The student stared at me. 'You knew that just from these?'

I hadn't even been paying attention to the herbs in his hand, but that was as good an explanation as any. 'Want a bag?'

He put verbena, myrrh and incense into the bag I gave him and paid for it while still giving me an awestruck look, then left. As soon as the door swung shut, the other kid came over and asked me the price for the second biggest crystal ball, trying to sound casual. I didn't bother checking to see what he was going to use it for – about the only way you can hurt yourself with a crystal ball is by hitting yourself over the head with it, which is more than I can say for some of the things I sell. Once the kid had let himself out, hefting his paper bag, I got up, walked over and flipped the sign on the door from OPEN to CLOSED. Through the window, I saw the kid unlock his bike and ride off. About thirty seconds later a traffic warden walked by.

My shop is in a district in the north centre of London called Camden Town. There's a spot where the canal, three bridges and two railway lines all meet and tangle together in a kind of urban reef-knot, and my street is right in the middle. The bridges and the canal do a good job of fencing the area in, making it into a kind of oasis in the middle of the city. Apart from the trains, it's surprisingly quiet. I like to go up onto the roof sometimes and look around over the canal and the funny-shaped rooftops. Sometimes in the evenings and early mornings, when the traffic's muted and the light's faded, it feels almost like a gateway to another world.

The sign above my door says 'Arcana Emporium'. Underneath is a smaller sign with some of the things I sell – implements, reagents, focus items, that sort of thing. You'd think it would be easier just to say 'magic shop', but I got sick of the endless stream of people asking for breakaway hoops and marked cards. Finally I worked out a deal with a stage magic store half a mile away, and now I keep a box of their business cards on the counter to hand out to anyone who comes in asking for the latest book by David Blaine. The kids go away happy, and I get some peace and quiet.

My name is Alex Verus. It's not the name I was born with, but that's another story. I'm a mage; a diviner. Some people call mages like me oracles, or seers, or probability mages if they want to be really wordy, and that's fine too, just as long as they don't call me a 'fortune teller'. I'm not the only mage in the country, but as far as I know I'm the only one who runs a shop.

Mages like me aren't common, but we aren't as rare as you might think either. We look the same as anyone else, and if you passed one of us on the street odds are you'd never know it. Only if you were very observant would you notice something a little off, a little strange, and by the time you took another look, we'd be gone. It's another world, hidden within your own, and most of those who live in it don't like visitors.

Those of us who *do* like visitors have to advertise, and it's tricky to find a way of doing it that doesn't make you sound crazy. The majority rely on word of mouth, though younger mages use the internet. I've even heard of one guy in Chicago who advertises in the phone book under 'Wizard', though that's probably an urban legend. Me, I have my shop. Wiccans and pagans and New-Agers are common enough nowadays that people accept the idea of a magic shop, or at least they understand that the weirdos have to buy their stuff from somewhere. Of course, they take for granted that it's all a con and that the stuff in my shop is no more magical than an old pair of socks, and for the most part they're right. But the stuff in my shop that isn't magical is good camouflage for the stuff that is, like the thing sitting upstairs in a little blue lacquered cylinder that can grant any five wishes you ask. If *that* ever got out, I'd have much worse problems than the occasional snigger.

The futures had settled and the phone was going to ring in about thirty seconds. I settled down comfortably and, when the phone rang, let it go twice before picking up. 'Hey.'

'Hi, Alex,' Luna's voice said into my ear. 'Are you busy?'

'Not even a little. How's it going?'

'Can I ask a favour? I was going through a place in Clapham and found something. Can I bring it over?'

'Right now?'

'That's not a problem, is it?'

'Not really. Is there a rush?'

'No. Well . . .' Luna hesitated. 'This thing makes me a bit nervous. I'd feel better if it was with you.'

I didn't even have to think about it. Like I said, it was a slow day. 'You remember the way to the park?'

'The one near your shop?'

'I'll meet you there. Where are you?'

'Still in Clapham. I'm just about to get on my bike.'

'So one and a half hours. You can make it before sunset if you hurry.'

'I think I *am* going to hurry. I'm not sure . . .' Luna's voice trailed off, then firmed. 'Okay. See you soon.'

She broke the connection. I held the phone in my hand, looking at the display. Luna works for me on a part-time basis, finding items for me to sell, though I don't think she does it for the money. Either way, I couldn't remember her being this nervous about one. It made me wonder exactly what she was carrying.

You can think of magical talent as a pyramid. Making up the lowest and biggest layer are the normals. If magic is colours, these are the people born colour-blind: they don't know anything about magic and they don't want to, thank you very much. They've got plenty of things to deal with already, and if they *do* see anything that might shake the way they look at things, they convince themselves they didn't see it double-quick. This is maybe ninety per cent of the adult civilised world.

Next up on the pyramid are the sensitives, the ones who aren't colour-blind. Sensitives are blessed (or cursed, depending how you look at it) with a wider spectrum of vision than normals. They can feel the presence of magic, the distant power in the sun and the earth and the stars, the warmth and stability of an old family home, the lingering wisps of death and horror at a Dark ritual site. Most often they don't have the words to describe what they feel, but two sensitives can recognise each other by a kind of empathy, and it makes a powerful bond. Have you ever felt a connection to someone, as though you shared something even though you didn't know what it was? It's like that.

Above the sensitives on the magical pecking order are the adepts. These guys are only one per cent or so, but unlike sensitives they can actually channel magic in a subtle way. Often it's so subtle they don't even know they're doing it; they might be 'lucky' at cards, or very good at 'guessing' what's on another person's mind, but it's mild enough that they just think they're born lucky or perceptive. But sometimes they figure out what they're doing and start developing it, and some of these guys can get pretty impressive within their specific field.

And then there are the mages.

Luna's somewhere between sensitive and adept. It's hard even for me to know which, as she has some . . . unique characteristics that make her difficult to categorise, not to mention dangerous. But she's also one of my very few friends, and I was looking forward to seeing her. Her tone of voice had left me concerned so I looked into the future and was glad to see she was going to arrive in an hour and a half, right on time.

In the process, though, I noticed something that annoyed me: someone else was going to come through the door in a couple of minutes, despite the fact I'd just flipped my sign to say CLOSED. Camden gets a lot of tourists, and there's always the one guy who figures opening hours don't apply to him. I didn't want to walk all the way over and lock the door, so I just sat watching the street grumpily until a figure appeared outside the door and pushed it open. It was a man wearing pressed trousers and a shirt with a tie. The bell above the door rang musically as he stepped inside and raised his eyebrows. 'Hello, Alex.'

As soon as he spoke I recognised who it was. A rush of adrenaline went through me as I spread my senses out to cover the shop and the street outside. My right hand shifted down a few inches to rest on the shelf under my desk. I couldn't sense any attack but that didn't necessarily mean anything.

Lyle just stood there, looking at me. 'Well?' he said. 'Aren't you going to invite me in?'

It had been more than four years since I'd seen Lyle but he looked the same as I remembered. He was about as old as me, with a slim build, short black hair and a slight olive tint to his skin that hinted at a Mediterranean ancestor somewhere in his family tree. His clothes were expensive and he wore them with a sort of casual elegance I knew I'd never be able to match. Lyle had always known how to look good.

'Who else is here?' I said.

Lyle sighed. 'No one. Good grief, Alex, have you really gotten this paranoid?'

I checked and rechecked and confirmed what he was saying. As far as I could tell, Lyle was the only other mage nearby. Besides, as my heartbeat began to slow, I realised that if the Council was planning an attack, Lyle was the last person they'd send. Suddenly I *did* feel paranoid.

Of course, that didn't mean I was happy to see him or anything. Lyle began walking forward and I spoke sharply. 'Stay there.'

Lyle stopped and looked quizzically at me. 'So?' he said when I didn't react. He was standing in the middle of my shop in between the reagents and the shelves full of candles and bells. 'Are we going to stand and stare at each other?'

'How about you tell me why you're here?'

'I was hoping for a more comfortable place to talk.' Lyle tilted his head. 'What about upstairs?'

'No.'

'Were you about to eat?'

I pushed my chair back and rose to my feet. 'Let's go for a walk.'

Once we were outside I breathed a little easier. There's a roped-off section to one side of my shop that contains actual magic items:

focuses, residuals, and one-shots. They'd been out of sight from where Lyle had been standing, but a few more steps and he couldn't have missed them. None were powerful enough to make him think twice, but it wouldn't take him long to put two and two together and figure out that if I had that many minor items, then I ought to have some major ones too. And I'd just as soon that particular bit of information didn't get back to the Council.

It was late spring and the London weather was mild enough to make walking a pleasure rather than a chore. Camden's always busy, even when the market's closed, but the buildings and bridges here have a dampening effect on stray sounds. I led Lyle down an alley to the canalside walk, and then stopped, leaning against the balustrade. As I walked I scanned the area thoroughly, both present and future, but came up empty. As far as I could tell, Lyle was on his own.

I've known Lyle for more than ten years. He was an apprentice when we first met, awkward and eager, hurrying along in the footsteps of his Council master. Even then there was never any question but that he'd try for the Council, but we were friends, if not close. At least for a little while. Then I had my falling out with Richard Drakh.

I don't really like to think about what happened in the year after that. There are some things so horrible you never really get over them; they make a kind of burnt-out wasteland in your memory, and all you can do is try to move on. Lyle wasn't directly responsible for the things that happened to me and the others in Richard's mansion, but he had a pretty good idea of what was going on, just like the rest of the Council. At least, they *would* have had a good idea if they'd allowed themselves to think about it. Instead they avoided the subject and waited for me to do the convenient thing and vanish.

Lyle's not my friend any more.

Now he was standing next to me, brushing off the balustrade before leaning on it, making sure none of the dirt got on his jacket. The walkway ran alongside the canal, following the curve of the canal out of sight. The water was dark and broken by choppy waves. It was an overcast day, the sunlight shining only dimly through the grey cloud.